A DISTANT

Thunder

A DISTANT

Thunder

Part Two of the Jayson Wolfe Story

a novel by

Anita Stansfield

Covenant Communications, Inc.

Cover images: *Rock Concert* © 2008 Robert Kohlhuber/ istock. *Huge Lightning* © Javier Garcia/ istock.

Cover design copyrighted 2008 by Covenant Communications, Inc.

Published by Covenant Communications, Inc.
American Fork, Utah

Printed in Canada
First Printing: November 2008

15 14 13 12 11 10 09 08   10 9 8 7 6 5 4 3 2 1

ISBN 13: 978-1-59811-711-0
ISBN 10: 1-59811-711-4

To the Reader

This is part two of a three-part story. In part one, Jayson Wolfe and his older brother, Drew, are attending the same high school while their mother, Leslie, works as a waitress. The three of them are close as they work to take care of each other and avoid the boys' drunken, violent father, whom Leslie had divorced years earlier. Since money is extremely tight and Leslie's birthday is approaching, Jayson decides that he will learn one of his mother's favorite songs on the piano and have Drew play accompanying drums for the number. Nothing means more to Leslie than her sons' musical gifts, and she has sacrificed considerably to encourage them in pursuing their talents. The birthday gift is a great hit, and Jayson feels immense satisfaction in seeing his skills improve through the intense practice of a difficult number. But that night, Jayson's father shows up, drunk and demanding money. After he hits Leslie, he's surprised to face Jayson, who is much taller than the last time they met. Jayson subdues his father until the police arrive, but the entire situation reawakens Jayson's loathing for Jay Wolfe; he especially hates having been named after him.

This violent episode motivates Leslie to make a decision she's been toying with for years. Within days, she and her boys sell practically everything they own and leave Montana to find a new home in Oregon, where a friend of Leslie's has secured her a job as a waitress, along with a suitable apartment. Jayson has no problem with the arrangement, except that he has to leave his grandmother's piano behind, and the new apartment is such that he can't play the guitar without causing a problem for the neighbors. Drew playing drums would be out of the question. Jayson hates his new school, feeling that he doesn't fit in, and he struggles to focus while music plays in his head continually. He gets a crush on a girl named Elizabeth, who is in a school play and a couple of his classes. But he's sure she'd never want anything to do with someone like him. Then Jayson gets an after-school job changing oil, and eventually becomes friends with Derek, who also works there. Jayson is ecstatic to realize that Derek too has a musical gift. Everything changes for Jayson when Derek makes him welcome in his home, where there is a soundproof music room in the basement, a beautiful grand piano upstairs, and a kind, doting father, Will Greer, who is thrilled with his son's new friend. But Jayson soon learns that Elizabeth is Derek's sister, and the situation becomes complicated in spite of its advantages.

Jayson, Derek, and Drew quickly do great things with their music and get a job playing on Saturday nights in Portland, but they have to talk Elizabeth into becoming a part of the band in order to make it work. She reluctantly agrees, and Jayson finds himself growing to like her more and more, while she is completely oblivious to his romantic feelings. With the passing of time, the two families become close as Will makes up for a missing father in Jayson's life and Leslie helps compensate for Derek and Elizabeth's arrogant, workaholic mother. When Mrs. Greer announces that she's divorcing Will and leaving the family, they all take it very hard and the transition strengthens the bonds among the group of friends.

In the spring of their senior year, Jayson and Elizabeth begin dating. Jayson is certain they'll end up married someday, but Elizabeth disagrees. Jayson wants to go to Los Angeles and become a rock star; Elizabeth wants to go to college and have a secure, predictable life where she can be the kind of mother to her children that her own mother never was. She cares for Jayson, but is certain they could never make it work together.

The magical days of their youth are shattered when Derek is killed in a car accident just prior to graduation. Everyone is devastated, and the relationship between Jayson and Elizabeth becomes strained even while they rely on each other as friends in ways they never have before. When Jayson and Elizabeth both make some bad choices, the relationship has little to hold onto. Elizabeth breaks off their relationship, insisting they could never be happy together, and she tells Jayson she'll be going to school in Boston. In spite of the promise that they will always remain friends and keep in touch, Jayson feels like he's lost everything. He and Drew make the decision to do what they've always dreamed about—go to Los Angeles and find a way to make it in the music business. Jayson can only hope that by doing so he will find a way to get over losing Elizabeth *and* Derek. He's grateful for the closeness he shares with his brother, and for the constant love and support he gets from his mother. He is also grateful for Will's insistence that no matter what happens, Jayson will always be a son to him. With little more than that in his heart, he heads to Los Angeles with his brother, praying that their musical gifts are good enough to make it work.

CHAPTER 1

A week after his arrival in Los Angeles, Jayson called Will, who sounded ridiculously pleased to hear from him and was glad to know they'd found an apartment and were settling in. Jayson didn't tell him what a dump it was and that he and Drew had both already been awakened to a sense of their own naiveté. But he did tell Will that they were quickly learning how to navigate their way around the city and they had some auditions lined up.

"Have you talked to your mother?" Will asked.

"Yeah, we've called her a few times. Why? Is she all right?"

"Relatively speaking," he said. "Can I tell you something? Man to man?"

"Sure," Jayson said, grateful to feel a comfortable rapport between them in spite of all that had happened.

"I asked your mother to marry me," Will said, as if he'd mentioned that it might rain.

"And?" Jayson drawled expectantly.

"She told me no," he said, clearly expressing his heartache.

Jayson sighed. "There seems to be a lot of that going on."

"She told me that she would be going to LA before long, and I needed to stay here where I have a good career and a home."

"How very practical," Jayson said with sarcasm.

"Some home it will be with Derek and Elizabeth both gone," Will said with an equally sarcastic tone. "I think I'd rather go to LA with her than be here alone."

"But?" Jayson questioned hotly. "Apparently that's not an option."

"I thought it was an option," Will said. "But she insists that it's not; she says it's more complicated than that."

Jayson thought about that for a minute and said, "Would the complication have anything to do with me and Elizabeth?"

"I honestly don't know," Will said, "but I think that might be part of it."

"And what else would there be?" Jayson asked.

"She told me she has some pretty heavy issues with men. And who could blame her? Her father, her brothers, her husband; they all treated her unspeakably badly. She tells me she just doesn't think she has it in her to be a good wife to me. She tells me I deserve better."

Jayson made a dubious chuckle. "In my opinion, there's no woman on the planet better than my mother—except for Elizabeth. Sounds like they've been conspiring."

"It sure feels that way," Will said. "But maybe they're right; maybe it is for the best."

"Maybe," Jayson said, "but it sure doesn't feel that way." Hearing the words come out of his mouth, Jayson realized he'd actually felt very little grief over losing Elizabeth. He'd thought about her a great deal, but his emotions seemed to have become numb—except when he felt angry. But he liked it that way. Anger he could handle.

"So," Will said, "I understand Leslie has put in her notice at work, and she's going to drive herself to LA."

"That's what she tells me," Jayson said. "I'll be glad to have her here, but I think I'd like the idea of you being here with her."

"We'll just have to make good use of the phone. But I think you should let me pay the phone bill until you get a record deal."

"That could be a while," Jayson said, trying not to sound as discouraged as he felt. He'd always believed there would be a ladder to climb, but he was getting a picture of how steep and tall that ladder really was. Still, he didn't want to talk about that. "How is Elizabeth?"

"She's all right," Will said, but he didn't sound convincing. "She's keeping very busy, getting ready to go."

"Tell her hello for me," Jayson said.

"I'll do that."

"And when she gets settled out there, you let me know how I can get in touch with her, just in case she doesn't."

"I will," he said.

Jayson got off the phone and forced his thoughts away from all he'd left behind. His efforts were helped along when Drew said, "Hey, we've been invited to some party."

"We have? Who do we know that would invite us to a party?"

"Those girls we met at the movies the other night. One of them gave me her phone number."

"Really?" Jayson chuckled. "I had no idea you were such a ladies' man."

"I'm not," Drew said. "I was just trying to find you a date."

Jayson laughed. "So, let's go. There's nothing to do here."

Jayson followed Drew out to the car while his mind strayed to Elizabeth. He missed her, but he refused to mourn over her. There just wasn't any strength left inside him to grieve with. There was a whole new world just beyond his reach, just waiting for him to discover it, and with any luck it wouldn't prove to be a lonely world.

* * *

Elizabeth found settling into her life in Boston more difficult than she'd expected. She enjoyed her classes, and her roommates were tolerable, but just being away from home wasn't nearly the adventure she'd been anticipating. She missed her father but talked to him as often as possible. She missed Derek, but there was little to be done about that. And she missed Jayson far too much. She kept telling herself that she'd done the right thing, that what she'd felt in her heart had agreed with what she'd added up in her head. But now that she'd gotten some distance from the situation, it just didn't feel right.

She kept very busy with a part-time job and a heavy class schedule, and she kept expecting herself to adjust to living her life without Jayson. She'd told him that time would convince him it was right. Well, time was managing to convince *her* that it was wrong. By the middle of November, she finally asked herself the question she'd been avoiding since August. Had she made a mistake? Had she somehow allowed her emotions to distort her decision? Or had she not allowed her emotions into the decision at all? At the time, she'd felt a lack of confusion—or at least she'd convinced herself that she had. But now she felt more confused—and lonely—than she'd ever felt in her life. She longed to go home for Thanksgiving and talk about it with her father, but she knew it wouldn't be practical, and she'd be better off to wait for Christmas to have a visit home. She'd been invited to spend Thanksgiving with the family of one of her roommates who only lived an hour away, and she was actually looking forward to it. In truth, it would likely be more enjoyable than being at home with her father, where the absence of Derek—and Jayson—would be so readily evident. Her heart ached for her father, thinking of him being alone. She was relieved to hear that he'd been invited to spend the holiday with a cousin's family. He would be driving to Washington state and staying the entire weekend.

The day before she knew he would be leaving, she called home and asked, "Can I talk to you about something?"

"Sure. You know you can."

"Dad," she said, and the tears she'd been trying to hold back for days rushed forward. "I think I made a mistake."

He was silent for a long moment, and she knew he had to be well aware of what she was talking about. Still, he asked, "About what, honey?"

"I miss Jayson so much," she said. "I thought I knew what I was doing. I thought it was the right thing to do, but now . . . I can't stop thinking about him, and . . . I really think I was wrong."

"Well, then," he said, and she could hear a positive note in his voice. She could well imagine his relief, knowing how he cared about Jayson. "You need to do something about that."

"What do I do?" she muttered. "How can I face him?"

"You don't have to *face* him. He's three-thousand miles away. Just call him on the phone and tell him how you feel."

Elizabeth sniffled. "Do you really think it could be that simple?"

"All you can do is try," Will said.

"Well," she sniffled again, "I don't know that . . . I'm ready to get married yet, but . . . maybe next summer. I could probably transfer to UCLA, and . . . Oh, Dad! I miss him so much! I love him so much!"

"And I believe he loves you, too." He chuckled and added, "As a matter of fact, *I* love him too."

"I know you do, Dad. He's so amazing."

"Yes, he is." Will laughed. "So, get off the phone and call him."

Elizabeth did as he suggested, ready to pour her heart out to Jayson and beg his forgiveness, but there was no answer. She tried several more times before she left town for Thanksgiving and still got no answer. She cursed him for not having an answering machine, so she could at least leave him a message.

The people she stayed with for Thanksgiving graciously offered to let her use the phone and try to get hold of Jayson, if only long enough to tell him she wanted to talk. But still, there was no answer. She knew that Leslie had moved to Los Angeles and was living with her sons, and that she had a job similar to the one she'd left in Oregon. But even trying to call around Leslie's typical shifts, Elizabeth was still unable to get hold of anyone. She wondered if she had the right number, but her father had given it to her in a letter, and he was so meticulous with numbers.

Returning to Boston after the holiday weekend, Elizabeth called her father and double-checked the number. He told her it was right, and that he'd talked to both Jayson and Leslie a few times by calling that number. He told her to keep at it. Perhaps they'd gone somewhere for the holiday weekend.

Elizabeth quickly became busy again with work and school, but she tried to call at every possible opportunity. She began counting the days until Christmas break, longing to just be with him.

On a snowy afternoon, Elizabeth came in from classes, anxious to get to the phone and try once more. It was nearly dark, and she felt an instinctive urgency to talk to Jayson. And then the phone rang. She absently picked it up, hoping that whoever it was wouldn't take long so she could get off and try for what seemed the millionth time to call the man she loved.

"Hello, Lady," she heard Jayson say, and her heart threatened to jump out of her throat.

"Oh, it's you," she said with a little laugh. "I've tried to call you at least a hundred times and—"

"Yeah, I haven't been home much. How are you doing, anyway?"

"I'm okay," she said, then added with hesitance, "I miss you."

"I miss you too," he said, "but . . ."

"But?"

"But . . . maybe you were right."

"About what?"

"About . . . our being incompatible, our lives taking different paths; everything you said. Maybe you were right."

Elizabeth swallowed carefully, wanting to say, *And maybe I wasn't.* But the words wouldn't come to her tongue. In fact, his attitude had taken her so completely off guard that she wasn't sure what to say. She'd expected him to be missing her as much as she'd been missing him. But his tone of voice implied that he was doing rather well.

"The thing is," he said, "I've met somebody." He laughed softly.

"Well, actually . . . I met her right after I came out here, but . . . well, I didn't say anything because . . . for one thing, I've just been really busy, and . . . I didn't think it was pertinent. But now it's pertinent. That's what I called to tell you."

"What?" she asked, sinking weakly onto the couch. If he told her he was engaged, or even dating somebody steady, could she handle it? Was he just trying to make her jealous? Would he reconsider if he knew how she felt? Oh, she prayed that he would!

Jayson laughed softly, a genuinely happy laugh that she'd not heard since before Derek had been killed. "You're not going to believe it." He laughed again. "I still can't believe it."

"Just tell me," she said, wishing she hadn't sounded so terse.

"I'm married," he said, and Elizabeth couldn't respond. She couldn't even breathe. Then she had to clamp a hand over her mouth to prevent an audible sob from erupting into the phone. Her stomach tightened, and her chest began to heave painfully. She wanted to scream at him and tell him he was a fool. She wanted to tell him he'd just kicked her in the stomach and stomped on her heart. But how could she not recall telling him that she couldn't marry him? She'd told him she could *never* marry him. She'd told him that time would convince him this was for the best. Had she just expected him to wait for her and beg her to come back? She'd made a mistake; she knew that now. But it was too late. And she wanted to die. "Elizabeth?" he said, breaking the silence. "Are you there?"

Elizabeth swallowed carefully, then coughed in an effort to choke back the emotion threatening to burst out of her. Her voice still cracked when she said, "I'm here."

"Are you okay?"

"Not really, no."

"What's wrong?" he demanded, as if he'd made no connection to his announcement and her emotion.

"You're *married?*" she said, allowing a degree of anger to suppress all else she was feeling. "You're eighteen, Jayson."

"I know how old I am," he said, sounding perturbed.

"Isn't this a little . . . sudden? A little rushed?"

"I've known her for months, Lady. When it's right, it's right."

"Of course," she said and wondered how she would ever make it through another day.

"Anyway," he said, "I promised to let you know everything that happened in my life—good or bad. I didn't want you to get the news secondhand."

"That's very thoughtful of you," she said with sarcasm.

Jayson sighed loudly. "I thought you'd be happy for me. Evidently you're not."

"I'm sorry, Jayson. It's . . . a shock. Things will never be the same between us."

"Well, no . . ." he drawled as if it were obvious. "You dictated that last summer on the beach, Elizabeth. Is this not what you wanted?"

It's what I thought I wanted, she mused while hot tears seared her face. She told herself that telling him now that she'd changed her mind would do nothing but make him uncomfortable and damage what little chance they had left to maintain any kind of friendship. She convinced herself that she could deal with her emotions when she got off the phone, and at the moment, she could be a very good actress. She swallowed her hurt and coughed up some pride. "I'm sorry, Jayson. If you're happy, then I'm happy for you. It just . . . caught me by surprise."

"Okay," he said, still sounding concerned. Following a long moment of silence he added, "I *am* happy, Elizabeth."

"Good," she said, and knew it would have been polite to ask him about this woman. But she didn't want to hear it; she couldn't *bear* to hear it. She simply asked, "What's her name?"

"Debbie," he said with a lilt to his voice.

"Debbie what?"

He chuckled. "Uh . . . Debbie *Wolfe.*"

Elizabeth squeezed her eyes closed. "Of course," she muttered and felt her resolve dissipating. "Well, thanks for calling. I . . . uh . . . need to go. You'll keep in touch?"

"Of course," he said firmly. "We promised. Friends forever."

"Friends forever," she repeated and ended the call. The moment she put down the phone, a painful sob leapt out of her throat. She slid to her knees beside the couch and curled into a ball, sobbing helplessly and rocking back and forth. It just felt so wrong. So thoroughly and utterly wrong. And wasn't that what Jayson had told her that night on the beach, when he'd been crying so hard he could hardly breathe? And she had been the cause of his pain. Could she blame him for turning around and finding a life without her? No, she couldn't. But, oh how it hurt! She thought of how it had felt to have him hold her and kiss her, and how she'd been longing to see him again, to be in his arms that way. The thought of him doing the same with another woman—and sharing a bed with her—made her nauseous.

Two hours later she was still sitting on the floor, in the dark, grateful her roommates hadn't come home. She felt as if Jayson had died; but this was worse, somehow. She was startled when the phone rang. As she reached for it, she longed with everything inside of her to hear Jayson's voice calling back to tell her it was a joke, that he'd just been teasing her, trying to make her jealous. But she knew he wasn't that kind of person, and such a wish was futile.

"Hello," she said, trying to sound normal.

"Hi, honey," her father said, and the trepidation in his voice already made it clear he'd heard the news. "Have you talked to Jayson?"

"A couple of hours ago," she said, and new tears pressed themselves past her shock.

"You know, then," he said.

"Yeah," was all she could squeak out.

"He must have called me right after he called you," Will said. "I'm so sorry, honey."

"Yeah, uh . . . so am I, but . . . obviously it doesn't matter now. Please tell me you didn't say anything . . . about . . . what I said . . . about us."

"I didn't say a word," he said with sincerity.

Elizabeth struggled for composure and managed to say, "You must promise me, Dad; promise me . . . that you will never tell him. Never tell him that . . . I'd changed my mind . . . that I made a mistake. Promise me. It would be meaningless for him to know now. It would only put a strain on our friendship. Promise me."

"I promise," he said.

They talked for nearly an hour while Elizabeth cried and struggled to find some peace and understanding. Then she went to bed and cried herself to sleep.

Throughout the following days, Elizabeth suffered a grief like unto losing Derek. But this was different; so different. Only the intensity of the pain was the same. She managed to keep going, determined to follow through on her classes and meet her obligations. She had to keep living, even if she didn't feel like it. But every minute of every hour, her heart ached. And she realized that she had gained a profound empathy for the pain Jayson had endured when she had severed their relationship last summer. She'd been certain at the time that it was for the best. But now she wasn't certain about anything—except that Jayson was lost to her, and she had to find a way to make a life without him.

The flight home for Christmas was long and exhausting. The anticipation she'd been expecting to feel was completely absent. When her father met her at the airport, he lifted her chin with his finger and asked, "What's wrong with my baby?" An unexpected surge of tears rushed out, and she looked down. "Tell me," he pressed, putting his arms around her.

"It's still the same thing," she said. "I just can't seem to get over it. I made a mistake, Daddy. And now I have to live with it for the rest of my life."

"I know," he said. "I know it's hard. But . . . maybe it just wasn't meant to be. Still, you can stay close to him. He's like a son to me, you know. Surely he can be a brother to you."

Elizabeth nodded, but she found it difficult to fathom seeing Jayson Wolfe as a brother. Her feelings for him had no resemblance to what she'd felt for Derek. Still, during the holidays, her father proved to be understanding and compassionate, and they shared a good Christmas in spite of her sadness. She hardly saw her mother at all, which wasn't unusual. And they both missed Derek so much that it was an added source of grief. She couldn't believe how dramatically their lives had changed in a year.

Staying in her old room, Elizabeth looked around and saw so many things that reminded her of Jayson. But the most difficult was the music box he'd given her the previous Christmas. When she opened the drawer that activated the music box, in her mind she clearly heard the lyrics to "Somewhere," the love theme from *West Side Story,* leaving her with an eerie sensation. She abruptly closed the little drawer and went to find her father.

When Leslie called to have what was apparently a regular phone conversation with Will, Elizabeth was able to talk to her. She seemed pleased about Jayson's marriage, even though she'd obviously been as surprised as Elizabeth. Apparently they had gone to Las Vegas quite unexpectedly, and even Leslie hadn't known about it until it was done. She said that Debbie seemed like a nice girl, but Elizabeth sensed a disappointment in Leslie that neither of them seemed to want to talk about.

Leslie told her the boys both had jobs that had nothing to do with music, but they were spending a great deal of time pursuing a number of different opportunities. They'd been given the chance to do some kind of studio work that she didn't understand. It wasn't enough to make a living, but it was getting their foot in the door. She talked of how glad she was to be living near them. She was sharing an apartment with Drew, and Jayson and Debbie were living only a few blocks away. "I can wait tables anywhere," she said. "I don't want to be an intrusive mother, but they're all I have. And I want to be a part of their lives."

"I'm sure they're glad to have you there," Elizabeth said, and she was relieved when they were able to talk about something besides Jayson.

Returning to Boston for school after the new year, Elizabeth made up her mind that she just had to press forward with her life and put her grief—and the reasons for it—behind her. By keeping extremely busy, she was more easily able to do that. And that's what she'd always done. By getting involved in everything she possibly could and exhausting herself to the limit, she could avoid thinking about the things in her life that were less than favorable. Still, occasionally she couldn't help recalling that brief window in her life when everything had seemed so easy, so perfect; when performing on stage at Jayson's side had been almost as thrilling as being in his arms.

Weeks merged into months, and time slipped by. Jayson called to tell her that he and Debbie were expecting a baby. He sent Elizabeth a little package for her birthday. Carefully packed in Styrofoam was a glass ball, like a Christmas ornament, but it was half filled with white sand and several tiny shells. "Oregon sand," he had written on the card, "for all of those good times on the beach."

She couldn't help feeling uneasy over the implication. How could she not think of the inappropriate experience they'd shared on the beach? Or the night she'd told him she couldn't marry him? Was there sarcasm in his comment, or perhaps some hidden message?

For Jayson's birthday, she sent him a picture of the two of them with Drew and Derek. Her father had taken the picture. They were all laughing, and she felt it truly represented all the good times they'd shared. She had it enlarged to an eight-by-ten and put it into an expensive silver frame. On the card she wrote, "For the pie, the burgers, the all-night rehearsals, the ice cream, the trips to Portland, fires on the beach, the thrill of being on stage, and most of all the laughter. Love, your best friend, Elizabeth." She imagined him crying when he looked at the picture. After all, he had a high water table.

He called her after he'd received it and expressed deep appreciation, but he didn't mention crying over it. She asked how everyone was doing. He said his mother and Drew were doing great, and Debbie was struggling with illness related to the pregnancy, but everything was fine. He said that Drew and his mother sharing an apartment was going well, since Drew was rarely home, but he didn't like living alone. He talked about the little breaks they were getting in the music business; but they were small, and she could tell he was discouraged. She told him he couldn't give up, and he agreed, but she sensed it was harder for him than he was letting on. He talked a great deal about his mother, and Elizabeth found she preferred that over hearing about his wife.

"With the baby on the way," Jayson said, "Mom doesn't want to miss out on anything. She does a lot to help out when Debbie's not feeling well, and she is so excited about being a grandmother that she can hardly stand it." Apparently Debbie and Leslie got along rather well. He put Leslie on the phone for a few minutes, and Elizabeth was glad for the opportunity to talk to her.

Elizabeth didn't talk to Jayson again until he called her in the middle of the night, less than an hour after he had become a father. He spoke with fervor of the experience, and the intense love he felt for his new little daughter, and how beautiful she was. Elizabeth cried silent tears, alone in her apartment in Boston, thinking how it should have been *her* daughter.

"What's her name?" she asked, managing to keep the emotion out of her voice.

"Macy Elizabeth," he said, and she felt stunned. "Macy was Debbie's grandmother. And Elizabeth . . . after you."

"You're kidding."

"No," he said. "Is that a problem?"

"How does Debbie feel about naming your baby after your old girlfriend?"

"Debbie is fine with it. She likes the name."

"Does she know about me?"

"She knows everything about you," he said, then chuckled. "Well . . . *almost* everything." His voice sobered. "But she knows we were very close, and she knows that . . ." He hesitated, as if he didn't know how to say what he wanted to say.

"What?" she pressed.

"She knows that you and I still care very much for each other, and we always will. She knows you're my best friend. I figure if I'm completely honest with my wife about my relationship with you and everything we talk about, then there's no chance for any misunderstanding or problems. And she agrees. It's okay, Lady." When she didn't answer, due to a sudden surge of tears, he asked, "Are you all right?"

"No, Jayson, I'm not all right. I hate it here. I miss you. I miss Derek."

"I know," he said. "Me too."

"You too what?" she asked, giving up on her efforts to hide her emotion.

"I miss Derek. I miss you."

"You're married, Jayson."

"Yes, I'm married," he said. "And I don't know if you want to hear this or not, but I think I need to say it. I love you, Elizabeth, and I always will. My being married does not change how I feel about you, but it has put those feelings in perspective. Debbie knows how I feel about you; I've been very honest with her. That's the only way to have a decent marriage, in my opinion. I love Debbie, and I have committed myself to her for life—with all my heart and soul. And she knows that."

"All your heart except the part that loves me?" she asked.

"The part that belongs to you is different. Everything changed for me when I met Debbie. It took some time, but . . . I know this is the right path for me. And one of these days you will meet someone, and you'll know what I mean. My marriage doesn't make me care any less for you; it's just . . . different than it used to be." He sighed. "If nothing else, Derek left us with a bond that no one could ever understand. He was your brother and my best friend. I think that you and I can stay close in a way that's somewhere in between that."

"Okay," Elizabeth said, knowing that was better than not being close to him at all. She missed him. And yes, she had to admit that what she missed most was his friendship. Wanting to change the subject, she sniffled and asked, "So when are you going to send me pictures of Macy?"

"I'll mail some tomorrow," he said and went on to talk more about the baby and the experience of being present for the birth. Their conversation went on for more than an hour, and Elizabeth had to admit that in some ways she felt better. Once she got used to the idea that they were talking about his wife and his daughter, she relaxed somewhat and enjoyed the comfortable conversation that had once been so warm and familiar to her. And she could be grateful for that.

CHAPTER 2

The following day, Elizabeth wrote Jayson a long letter, which made her feel even better. Being able to write about a lot of the little things going on in her life somehow eased the ache of loneliness, knowing he would find pleasure in reading about them. She got pictures in the mail a few days later and couldn't help crying when she saw them. Jayson hadn't changed at all, except that he was a father at the age of nineteen. The baby was beautiful—and so was Debbie. Elizabeth had a good cry over seeing them together, then she put a picture of Jayson with his little daughter into a frame and put it on her dresser.

He called when he got the letter and thanked her, saying it had been really nice to hear from her. He admitted that he wasn't so good at letters, but he'd try his hand at it once in a while. Elizabeth wrote him another letter and sent it, along with a baby gift for Macy. A thank-you card written by Debbie came a couple of weeks later. Not only did she thank Elizabeth for the gift, but for being such a good friend and support to Jayson.

Elizabeth started getting pictures of Macy in the mail about once a month, and Jayson usually included a little note. But he chose to keep her up on all the details of his life through a lengthy phone call once or twice a month. When Macy was four months old, Jayson called to tell her with a great deal of excitement that he and Drew would be touring with some new band. They were just hired musicians, playing what they were told to play, and the band wasn't well-known. They would be opening for some other band that was supposed to be pretty hot, but Elizabeth had never heard of them. Still, Jayson and Drew were getting paid to play music, and they were both thrilled.

When Elizabeth knew that Jayson was on the road, she didn't bother writing to him. She just hoped he would call once in a while. It was seven weeks into the tour before he finally did. Once their greetings were exchanged, he said, "Guess what?"

"What?"

"I don't know why I didn't think of this before; just dumb, I guess. I hope it's not too late to do something about it."

"What?" she laughed.

"We're performing in Boston tomorrow night," he said, and Elizabeth sucked in her breath. She wanted to see him so badly it hurt, but knowing he was married made her wonder if that was a good idea. He added, "I know there are still some seats available. It would mean a lot to us if you'd come, and then we could all go out after or something."

"We?"

"Drew and I."

Elizabeth understood the implication. He was married, and it wasn't appropriate for him to be alone with her. And in truth, the idea of having Drew along made her more comfortable; she probably would have declined, otherwise. "I'd love to," she said. "I've got some things I'll have to rearrange, so I can't promise. But I'll do my best. I'd really like to see the show."

"And after?"

"I would love to see you. Call me back tomorrow."

He called early the next morning to tell her that the band would be on the bus immediately after the show in order to get to the next city. She felt intensely disappointed until he said, "But we'll be in Boston in a few hours. How about an early dinner before the show? Can you do that?"

Elizabeth knew she'd have to miss a class, but it would be worth it. "I'll make it work," she said.

He asked her to pick a place since she was familiar with Boston. She looked up the exact address of a little Italian restaurant she loved and gave it to him. They agreed to meet there at four o'clock, and Elizabeth spent the rest of the day with butterflies in her stomach. She got to the restaurant a few minutes early, liking this time of day when she found it practically empty. She waited on a bench just inside the door once she'd told the hostess she'd wait for her friends before getting a table. Through the window she saw a cab pull up. Her heart quickened, and she heard herself chuckle to see Drew get out. She was even glad to see *him,* although they had rarely ever had anything to actually say to each other personally. He blocked the view while it was evident that Jayson was paying for the cab. Then it drove away, and Jayson came into view as they walked toward the door.

"Oh, help," she muttered under her breath and wrapped an arm around her quivering stomach. She wanted to throw herself into his arms and had to remember that he was a married man. *A father.*

When he came through the door and their eyes met, she felt uncertain and hesitant, not quite knowing how to act. He laughed and moved toward her. Wrapping his arms around her, he lifted her feet off the ground, making her laugh as well; she was feeling better already. When he eased back, she looked into his face. "Oh, it's good to see you," she said.

"And you," he said. "You're as beautiful as ever."

"And you haven't changed a bit," she said, even though he had. He *did* look older. No, she decided, more mature. Although she couldn't quite pinpoint how.

She eased reluctantly away and turned to Drew, hugging him tightly as well. "It's good to see you too," she said.

He laughed and kissed her cheek. "And you," he said. "I think you should be on stage with us, personally."

"Oh, no," she said. "I don't think I could handle the touring."

The hostess seated them at a booth, and Jayson eased onto the seat next to her and across from Drew. Once they had ordered, they quickly settled into a conversation that felt natural and comfortable—until they all became silent at once, and Elizabeth knew they were all thinking the same thing. It was Drew who said, "It just doesn't seem right without him. If I knew he was home in Oregon or something, I wouldn't feel like crying."

"Yeah, I know what you mean," Elizabeth said. She turned to look at Jayson, expecting him to show some tears. But there was no sign of emotion beyond a solemn expression.

Elizabeth thoroughly enjoyed their lengthy visit over a meal that she barely touched. She felt disconcerted by the wedding ring on Jayson's finger, but she had to admit she was growing accustomed to the idea. She asked him how he could bear being away from his wife and baby for so long, and he told her that he'd flown home a couple of times when the buses and trucks had a long trek with a few days between shows. And Debbie had flown with the baby once to meet him in Florida. Elizabeth concluded that they seemed to be handling the temporary separation rather well.

It was hard for all of them to say good-bye when Jayson and Drew admitted that they had to go. She was therefore relieved when Drew said, "Hey, once we do the preshow, we're just sitting around for a couple of hours. Why don't you meet us somewhere and we can visit a little longer."

"Oh, I'd love to," she admitted, and since she was familiar with the hall where they were playing, she told them a good place to meet.

Elizabeth didn't mind going to the concert on her own. That way she didn't have to talk to anybody, and she didn't have to explain her occasional tears and her reasons for keeping a tissue handy. The place was huge, but her seat wasn't too bad since it had been a single and therefore still available. She was still some distance from the stage, but she had a little pair of binoculars in her purse that she'd gotten years earlier. She'd used them for ballets and operas, and even a couple of rock concerts. But she'd never imagined looking through them and seeing someone on stage that she knew, someone that she wondered how she was ever going to live without.

When they first came out on stage, Elizabeth's stomach was smitten with a fresh swarm of butterflies. To see them this way was incredible! But as the show progressed, she couldn't help thinking that it just didn't seem right for Jayson to be in the background, playing someone else's music. He did beautifully and put forth a great deal of energy and personality, but she thought that he should have been front and center. Trying not to be biased, she still couldn't help feeling that Jayson's music was so much better than what they were playing. At one point he did an amazing guitar solo that got a great deal of applause, and Drew did the same on the drums. When the band members were introduced by name, they were applauded again. Nevertheless, it just didn't seem right. Elizabeth reminded herself that this was just one step toward bigger and better things.

She was grateful to be able to see them again afterward, but all too soon they were needing to leave on the bus that would take them to their next stop—and Jayson didn't know for sure where that was. She said good-bye to Drew and hugged him tightly before he got onto the bus, then she was facing Jayson.

"It was so good to see you," she said, determined not to cry.

"And you," he said, pulling her into his arms. It was a brotherly kind of embrace. But that was the way it needed to be. Looking into her eyes, he added, "You take care of yourself . . . and be happy now. You hear me?"

"And you," she said. "Call or write whenever you can."

"And you," he echoed. "You never call *me.*"

"I promised to call you if anything special happened. Nothing special has happened. It's just the same old thing."

"I need to go," he said and kissed her cheek. "Thank you . . . and be good."

"You too," she said and watched him get onto the bus.

She walked to her car, crying just a little, and she didn't actually talk to him again until he called her in Oregon to wish her a merry

Christmas while she was home for the holidays. They had exchanged some cards and letters, but she'd not heard his voice since the night he'd been in Boston. They talked for an hour and caught up, although he had a great deal to tell her about his work, his wife, his baby. And she had nothing to tell him except that she'd done one more play and she was chalking up credits toward a degree. Will insisted on talking to him, and they talked for nearly forty-five minutes. He handed the phone back to Elizabeth when he was done, and they talked another half an hour. She didn't talk to him again until an evening three months later when she called his apartment from Boston.

"Hi," she said when he answered.

"Who is this?" he teased. "This can't be Elizabeth Greer. She never calls *me*. She thinks she's too good for me or something. Snobbish debutante that she is."

"Very funny," she said, trying to sound angry, then she laughed.

"What's up?" he asked. "It's good to hear your voice and . . . Whoa! Whoa. Just a minute." She heard a clunk as if the phone had dropped, then some noise in the distance—and then a baby's cry. "Sorry," he said into the phone. "I forgot to hook the baby gate and Macy was eating the cat food."

"You have a cat?"

"We do," he said. "Her name is Fender."

"You named your cat after your guitar?" She laughed.

"I did," he said. "And you're the only person besides Drew that I didn't have to explain that to. I should send you a prize."

"Just send me a graduation present."

"Really?" he said, sounding genuinely pleased.

"Really," she said. "I'll have my associate degree next week. Dad's coming out. Mom's too busy, of course."

"Of course. Is she still with the same guy?"

"I think so, but I don't know. Honestly, I don't care. Anyway, I just wanted to let you know that I did it; I got this far anyway."

"Well, I'm proud of you," he said. "I wish I could be there. But I *will* send you a present."

"I was just kidding," she said. "A card would be fine. Write something sentimental in it."

"I'll see what I can do," he said, and they talked for quite a while. Debbie was at work, and he was left in charge. While he didn't come right out and say it, she got the impression that Debbie was making more money than he was at the moment, and he was doing laundry and changing diapers more than playing music. She felt certain it was good for him, but still she knew he must be struggling.

A few weeks later, Elizabeth met Robert. She was still living in Boston, mostly to finish up a musical at a community theater. And she saw him at the library. They both put a stack of books onto the checkout counter at the same time, and turned to look at each other. He was shorter than Jayson, and more muscular, with dark curly hair and a face that looked like an innocent little boy. They started chatting while the librarian was on the phone, and when they were finished at the counter, he walked her to her car. Before they'd parted he'd asked her out to dinner. It was the first date she'd been on since Jayson where she didn't feel completely bored or disgusted. She'd certainly tried to distract herself with dating, but until now it had been fruitless. One date with Robert led to three, and then she was seeing him at every possible opportunity. She felt truly happy for the first time since she'd lost Derek—and then Jayson. And five weeks after their first date, they were engaged.

She called her father to tell him the news and was pleased with his enthusiasm. Then she called Jayson, even before she called her mother or any of her girlfriends. A woman answered and took her momentarily off guard. It was the first time she'd actually heard Debbie's voice.

"Hi, is Jayson there?" Elizabeth asked.

"He's not," Debbie said. "May I take a message?"

"Uh . . . yes. This is Elizabeth Greer. His friend from—"

"Oh, I know who you are," she said, sounding perfectly delighted. "He's told me so much about you. I do hope we can meet one of these days."

"That would be great," Elizabeth said.

"Well, Jayson is meeting with a guy who is supposedly pretty good with a number of instruments. Jayson told me this guy would be perfect to do all the fill-in stuff. He does a little bit of guitar, keyboards, even some sax. He says if this works out the way he's hoping, he might actually have the right connections to put a real band together."

"Really?" Elizabeth said. "Does that mean he's got a bass player?"

"He does, actually. A guy named Rudy Morris. They hooked up a few months ago, and Jayson says he's the only bass player he's jammed with since Derek that he's felt any real connection to. Apparently they do well together, although I haven't actually had the chance to hear them yet."

"That sounds great," Elizabeth said, feeling saddened as always at the reminder of Derek's absence.

"Oh, you're Derek's sister," Debbie said as if she'd sensed her mood.

"That's right."

"I'm so sorry for your loss. Jayson talks about Derek all the time. In many ways, I think they were closer than he and Drew."

"Yes, I think they were."

"Although Drew is great," Debbie said. "They have so much fun together."

"They always did," Elizabeth said, wanting to get off the phone. Debbie was genuine and warm, which was better than having her cool and guarded—which she could have been, knowing that Elizabeth was Jayson's old flame. Still, she didn't necessarily feel comfortable with the conversation, even if she couldn't pinpoint why.

"Jayson will be so glad you called," she went on. "He's always a little more cheerful after he's talked to you."

Elizabeth read between the lines and took a chance on making it sound as if she knew more than she did. "So, I understand he's been having a rough time."

"Yes, he certainly has," Debbie said, sounding genuinely concerned. "You would think with his talent, and even the reviews he got in Oregon, he could get somebody's attention—but it just isn't happening. I think it's a lot harder for him than he lets on. Sometimes I think he'd just like to break down and cry, but you know Jayson. He's like a rock, and it's hard to know how he's feeling. But somehow he just stays steady and keeps going."

Elizabeth absorbed what she was hearing. Beyond her heartache in hearing of Jayson's struggles, there was something terribly incongruent here. Never would she have described Jayson as a person who was difficult to read emotionally. He'd inherited his mother's high water table, and beyond that, she felt certain that with his artistic personality, he was likely more emotional and sensitive than the average person. Had something changed? Testing the theory a little further, Elizabeth said, "With the way Leslie cries so easily, you would think at least one of her sons would have inherited that high water table."

"You'd think," Debbie said with a little laugh. "Leslie certainly *does* cry easily, but I've never seen Jayson—or Drew for that matter— ever shed a single tear."

Elizabeth was too stunned to respond. Jayson was married to this woman; they had brought a child into the world. She'd heard that many men—even tough ones—would cry when they'd been present for the birth of a child. She felt deeply concerned for Jayson, but she didn't know how to pinpoint the problem, and she didn't feel it was appropriate to discuss her concerns with Debbie— or anyone else for that matter.

"Oh, hold on," Debbie said, and she could hear talking in the distance. Debbie then said into the phone, "Leslie just got here. She took Macy for a walk. Would you like to talk to her?"

"Oh, that would be great, thank you," Elizabeth said, relieved to end the conversation.

"I'll tell Jayson you called as soon as he gets back."

"Thank you," Elizabeth said again. "Tell him it doesn't matter how late he calls. I'll be up."

"I'll do that," Debbie said, then Elizabeth was relieved to hear Leslie on the phone. She told her the news, but made her promise not to say a word until she had a chance to tell Jayson herself.

Leslie talked a great deal about Macy, and the child was obviously her pride and joy. And she was thrilled to know that Elizabeth would soon be married. Elizabeth hung up the phone feeling a little disoriented, as if she were existing in some kind of altered state. She felt as if Leslie should be her own mother-in-law, and a grandmother to *her* children. But it wasn't going to happen, and she felt certain that with time she would eventually come to feel peace over the matter. She loved Robert and felt certain that their life together would be a good one. Surely nothing else mattered.

* * *

Jayson got home just in time to spend a short while with Macy before she went to bed. He gave her a bath and read her some stories before he kissed her and tucked her into her crib. There was little in life that gave him as much joy as his daughter did, and he felt truly grateful.

Once Macy was down, he found Debbie on the couch, looking exhausted. She always looked exhausted these days. She worked hard, and he knew it. She kept their little apartment in order, took good care of Macy, and put in long hours working for a catering company. He longed for it to be different, and he knew that all it would take was the right break to completely change all of that. He just wondered how long it would be until the right break stopped eluding him. Still, he did his best to focus on the present and be grateful for all they *did* have. He plopped down on the couch beside her and took her hand.

"Hey there, babe," he said. "You look tired."

"Oh, I am," she admitted, but she said it with a smile.

"I wish you didn't have to work so hard," he said. "It won't always be this way, you know."

"Yes, I know," she said and put her arms around him, nestling her head on his shoulder. "But it's okay, Jayson. I have everything I need right here." She tightened her arms for emphasis.

"You got that right," he said, returning her embrace. He pressed a kiss into her hair. "Tell me about your day."

"First, you tell me how it went with this guy."

"Not well, I'm afraid," he said, trying not to sound as disappointed as he felt. There was simply a missing ingredient, and until he could put together the right band with the right chemistry, he knew he'd never get anywhere in this business. He couldn't help thinking how Elizabeth could well be the missing ingredient, but he knew better than to think that he could talk her into coming to Los Angeles to join his band.

He told Debbie just a little of how badly the meeting had gone. "It'll happen," she said. "We just have to be patient."

"Yes," he agreed, feeling terribly impatient. He scrutinized their surroundings, hating the fact that he'd moved down the ladder from the dumpy apartment he'd lived in as a teenager while his mother had waited tables. This place was tiny and in much need of repair. The neighborhood was questionable to put it mildly, and it wasn't uncommon to have the police in the area at least once a day. But the place was clean, and they were together. He just hoped they didn't have to live like this much longer.

"Oh," Debbie said, "your friend Elizabeth called. She said to have you call her—no matter how late."

"Okay," he said. "Did she say why?"

"No."

"I hope it's good news and not bad news."

"You don't think she'd call just to chat?"

"No," he said. "I mean . . . we always end up chatting, but that's not why she'd call."

"Maybe you'd better call her."

Jayson tightened his arms around Debbie and eased her closer. "Later," he said. "First tell me about your day."

Debbie started to talk, telling him all the funny little things that Macy had done, and how they had gone grocery shopping with Leslie. By the time she had said all she wanted to say, she was getting sleepy.

"You'd better get some sleep," he said.

"Oh," she said through a yawn, "I forgot to ask if you're hungry. I can heat up some—"

"I'm fine," he said. "Drew bought pizza. I'll save whatever you fixed for lunch tomorrow."

He picked her up and carried her to the bed. "Oh, that's nice," she said as he set her down and kissed her, "but I need to brush my teeth." She yawned again. "You go call Elizabeth and I'll see you in the morning."

He kissed her once more and peeked in to see that Macy was sleeping soundly. He kissed her little head then went to the kitchen and dialed Elizabeth's number. It occurred to him as it began to ring that it was after midnight in Boston. Just hearing her say hello seemed to soothe something in him.

"Hi," he said. "Deb told me you called."

"I did."

"Sorry it's so late."

"No problem," she said.

"What's up?" he asked.

"I'm getting married," she said.

Jayson was so taken off guard he didn't know how to respond. He thought of how he'd felt when he'd called to tell her of his own marriage. Now he had some idea why she'd not sounded pleased. Through a long moment of silence he reminded himself that he was happily married and this was what he'd wanted for Elizabeth. But he couldn't deny feeling a little disconcerted.

Following a long pause, he spoke in a toneless voice. "Wow. That's great."

"That was not convincing, Jayson."

"What do you want me to say?"

"I thought you'd be happy for me."

"I am," he insisted.

"But?"

"But nothing. I'm happy for you."

"You don't sound happy," she said.

Jayson checked himself and forced the proper frame of mind. In a softer voice he said, "I'm sorry, Lady. I really am happy for you. It just . . . took me by surprise."

"Not nearly as much as *your* getting married took *me* by surprise, I can assure you," she said, wishing it hadn't sounded so brusque.

"I'm sure you're right," he said gently. "So . . . tell me about this . . . knight in shining armor. Does he get straight As?"

"Yes, actually," she said. "We'll be staying in Boston for another year. By then he'll be a CPA."

"Ooh, like dear old dad," Jayson said.

"Yes, that's true."

"Once he gets his degree, we'll decide where we want to settle down. He's just . . . a really great guy, Jayson."

"Well, he should be. You deserve the best." He said it with a subtle tone of self-recrimination, but she couldn't bring herself to call him on it. "What's his name?" he asked.

"Robert; and no, he doesn't go by Bob."

"That's a relief," Jayson chuckled. "Robert what?"

"Robert Aragon."

"Wow. Elizabeth Aragon. That's a mouthful."

"You just keep calling me Lady, okay?"

"Okay," he said. "I wish you every happiness . . . Lady. You deserve to be happy."

"Thank you. So do you."

"Oh, I am," he said.

"That's good, then."

They talked for only a few more minutes, and Elizabeth was relieved to get off the phone. She hadn't felt this much tension in their conversation since he'd told her about his own marriage. Then she realized she'd forgotten to ask if his meeting with the potential musician had gone well. She figured if it had, he would have said something.

Throughout the course of preparing for her wedding, Elizabeth often found herself questioning what she was doing. She couldn't deny that her experience with Jayson had left her doubting her own ability to make a big decision correctly. She had firmly believed that letting Jayson go was the right thing to do, but she'd later come to regret that decision. And now she firmly believed that marrying Robert was the right thing to do. But did she even have the ability to read her instincts correctly? She discussed her feelings with her father over the phone.

"Do you love him?" Will asked.

"Yes," she admitted readily, even though she couldn't deny that what she felt for Robert was nothing like what she'd once felt for Jayson. They were very different men; she knew that. And it was okay. Still, she did love Robert.

"Is there anything about his character or behavior that concerns you?" Will asked.

"No," she said easily. "And we've talked everything through very carefully, just as you've taught me to do. We've talked about finances, our roles in the home, and our views on child rearing and politics and religion and . . . well, everything. We're extremely compatible. Our goals are practically identical as far as what's really important and how we want to raise our family."

"You can't get much better than that," Will said. "If he's a good man and you love him, then surely this can't be a bad thing."

"But . . . things go wrong. There's no way of knowing what the future might bring."

"That's exactly right, honey. There's no way of knowing, so you just have to make the best decision you can on the best informa-tion you have. And if you can feel good about that, then you go for it and give this marriage all you've got. That's the best you can do."

Elizabeth thought long and hard about that, and she decided that there was no reason on earth why she shouldn't marry Robert and expect to be happy. In analyzing her feelings, she had to admit that she felt a little concern over his apparent lack of passion. He was perfectly proper with his affection for her; in fact he'd never attempted more than a gentlemanly kiss, and that was the way she wanted it. Still, there seemed to be something lacking in his kiss, something she couldn't quite define. She convinced herself that once they were married and properly sharing an intimate relationship, surely such problems would solve themselves. There was no denying her attraction to him, and his to her. And she came to greatly anticipate being married.

The wedding ended up being exactly as she'd always wanted. It wasn't elaborate or overwhelming, but it was very nice. She loved Robert's family, and they clearly loved her. The day was beautiful, practically perfect. Her only real disappointment was that Jayson didn't come. She'd imagined him coming with his wife and baby and wondered how it would feel to face him while they each stood beside their spouses. But he didn't come, and she wondered why. She knew the travel could be a problem, but she also knew that her father had called him and offered to pay their way, and he'd politely declined.

Elizabeth merged easily into married life. She enjoyed using her homemaking skills in their little apartment. Her part-time job was pleasant, and Robert treated her like a queen. They were both thrilled when she became pregnant right away, and it was pleasing to discover that she was one of those women who didn't become terribly ill with pregnancy. She often felt tired and had to be careful with her eating habits or she would experience some minor nausea. Other than that, she felt relatively well, and the very idea of being a mother made her happier than she'd perhaps ever been.

A month before Bradley was born, Robert got his degree. When Bradley was six weeks old, they relocated to Phoenix, Arizona, where Robert was taken on by a reputable accounting firm. They rented an apartment while a fine house was being built, and when Bradley was starting to walk, they moved into their new home. As they settled comfortably into a nice neighborhood and Elizabeth made some friends, her contentment deepened. When Bradley was two, she heard an advertisement for auditions for a play in a community theater. She talked to Robert about it, and he enthusiastically encouraged her. She got the lead in *The Sound of Music,* and Robert graciously kept everything under control while she went to time-consuming rehearsals, then several nights of performances. She thoroughly enjoyed the experience and made a few friends through the theater, and she became involved in the next play they were doing. But Jayson Wolfe still remained her closest friend. They talked on the phone at least twice a month and continued to exchange cards and letters—and gifts for Christmas and birthdays—even though they were usually simple and inexpensive.

Through her contact with Jayson, she knew he found great joy in his daughter, although she wondered why there had never been another baby. She came right out and asked once. He simply said, "There won't be any more." Then he changed the subject. His marriage seemed to be good, and she knew his ties with Drew and his mother were good. While his personal life appeared to be going well, she knew that his frustration on behalf of his music was beyond his ability to express. He told her stories of politics in the industry that left her mouth hanging open. His discouragement became so keen that on three different occasions she had to talk for hours—literally—to convince him to keep going. When nothing else worked, she could always get him with, "And what would Derek say if you gave up now?"

Robert was as supportive of her friendship with Jayson as he was with everything else she became involved in. He didn't like to cook the way her father did, but he was more than happy to heat up whatever she might have prepared earlier, and he was very good at keeping the house in order and seeing that everything remained under control while she did whatever she felt inclined to do. She quickly discovered that he wasn't terribly fond of going to movies or plays, although he always attended her opening night and gave her flowers to celebrate her fine performance. When Elizabeth wasn't involved in a play, she often found girlfriends who were willing to go to movies and plays, concerts and ballets, while Robert stayed home and kept everything running smoothly—always greeting her with a smile and a kiss when she came through the door.

When Bradley turned three, her desire for another baby was finally fulfilled. Trevin joined the family with little trouble, and Elizabeth was thrilled to have two fine sons—brothers, like Jayson and Drew. When she called Jayson to tell him the good news, she was thrilled to hear that he also had good news.

"I found the missing ingredient," he said as if he'd uncovered buried treasure.

"Really? Tell me about it."

"Okay, well first allow me to point out several things that you already know, but humor me."

"I'm listening," she said.

"Well, you know how important it is to find someone that I can just . . . connect with, musically as well as personally."

"Yes, I know."

"And you know how important it is that they have exceptional skill; mediocrity isn't going to cut it if we're really going to get somewhere."

"Yes, I know," she said again.

"Also, I need to have someone who can accept me as the principal songwriter here. I'm not trying to get all the glory. I want this to be a band, a team of equals. But I can't deny this gift in my head . . . in my heart. Input is good; I like that. But I can't work with somebody who doesn't understand and accept the way I am. I couldn't work with someone who had the same intensity going on in his head."

"Somebody like that needs to form their own band."

"Exactly."

"So, I take it this guy's okay with that."

"He's thrilled with it. He says he gets a little idea here and there, but he's never been much of a songwriter. And he's okay with *not* being the front man."

"Good so far."

"And of course, you know that it's important to me that drugs and drinking stay out of the picture. And I'm not going to have any garbage in the music—or on stage."

"Of course," she said.

"Now, this is the part that's really bugged me all these years, but it's a sad fact that to really get their attention in this industry, the band's got to look good. They keep telling me that pictures sell records and concert tickets. So . . . as much as I've hated it, we've been looking for someone who is . . ."

"Pleasing to the female eye," she said when he hesitated.

"Yeah, I guess that's what I mean," he said with chagrin.

"Which was never a problem for you, I might add."

"Oh, well, thank you," he said facetiously. "Maybe you could write up a testimonial that could help me get a record deal."

"I'd be happy to," she said with a little laugh. "Go on."

"Okay, well . . . this guy walks into the audition. He's about my height, got black hair that's like . . . long . . . well, not as long as mine, but it's sort of curly, and he doesn't tie it back. He wears these little glasses and looks like a cross between an art professor and a model for one of those romance novels you see in the grocery store."

"Never read one, but I can't help noticing the pictures," she said, and he laughed.

"Okay, well . . . so I'm thinking: but can he play?" Jayson laughed. "Boy can he play! He's good with the guitar *and* the keyboards, and he's great with the idea of the two of us going back and forth, depending on the number. Or there are songs where we'd both need to do guitar, or both keyboards, or—"

"I know how it works, Jayse."

"Yes, of course you do. He also plays a pretty mean sax. He admits that his voice isn't real great, but it's good enough for basic backing vocals. We did a test recording of our voices together and it was sweet." He laughed again.

Elizabeth laughed with him. "That's wonderful. So he's in."

"He's in. And Rudy's still sticking with us, even though we've all been scattered doing what we can to make it. Drew even hit it off with this guy. They were actually *talking*."

"Whoa. Drew talking? This is serious. So now what?"

"Well, putting together enough material for an album won't be a problem. We just have to get the attention of the right person in the right place at the right time."

"It'll happen," Elizabeth said firmly. "And I have a feeling it's getting close."

"I hope so," he said. "I knew it would be hard; I knew it would take some time, but honestly, it's making me crazy."

"Oh, no," she said, "you were crazy a long time ago. I mean . . . you hung around with Derek."

"Yes, I did," he said proudly.

"So, what's this guy's name?"

"Barry Hadley," he said.

"That's got a nice rock star ring to it."

"Yes, I think it might."

"So, your band has its missing ingredient, but does it have a name?"

"Yes, it does actually. It was Drew's idea. Rudy and Barry really like it; they think it has class."

"And what do you think?"

"I'm okay with it."

"Don't leave me in suspense. What is it?"

"First of all, I want to tell you that it has significance; it has deep meaning for me. So, when I tell you the name, I want you to tell me the first thing that comes to your mind. I want to know if you get it."

"Okay," she drawled impatiently. "I'm waiting."

He chuckled. "Too bad Drew isn't here for a drum roll."

"Just say it!" she insisted, and he laughed.

"Okay . . . Here goes. *Gray Wolf.*"

Elizabeth was startled by how those two simple words seemed to leap into her heart. She was momentarily stunned into silence as she absorbed them fully into herself.

"So . . . do you get it?"

"Yes, I get it," she said with a solemnity to her voice that made him certain she had, even before she added, "It's an indirect tribute to Derek. You always said the world was gray without him, that the color was gone."

"Yes!" Jayson said and laughed. "I knew you would get it! That's exactly it. Drew was playing around with the wolf thing and he said he was thinking of Derek, and how he's kind of the honorary member of the band, and he remembered me saying that very thing. That's it."

"It's perfect," she said. *"Gray Wolf.* Wow, one day soon it will be all over the radio."

"You keep telling me that, Lady."

"Oh, I will," she said. "And I want your first autographed CD."

"You got it. You've earned it."

"I'll look forward to it," she said, and they both laughed.

CHAPTER 3

Elizabeth put two-year-old Trevin into his high chair and set a little bowl of pasta in front of him. While she looked through the mail Bradley had just brought in, Trevin quickly spread the marinara sauce all over his chubby little face. She let out a pleasant gasp to see a familiar-looking envelope. This was the kind of envelope Jayson always used to send pictures. Inside was a little note that read, *Macy's birthday party. She's nine. Can you believe it? Hope all is well with you and your family. Sending a hug, Jayson.* Elizabeth read the note three times before she even looked at the pictures. Nine years old. It was difficult to believe. And how long since she had even seen Jayson? She honestly couldn't remember. She appreciated him sending a hug, but she couldn't help wishing they might share a real one. She missed him. She set the note aside and looked through the pictures, smiling several times. Macy was a beautiful little girl with her father's brown hair, but she'd obviously gotten the natural curl from her mother. Still, the older she got, the more she looked like Jayson.

She finally had to put the pictures down and rescue Trevin when he grew tired of his lunch and started throwing food on to the floor. She washed him up and set him free, then she dug into cleaning the high chair and the floor beneath it. She was rinsing out the rag when the phone rang.

"Hello, Mrs. Aragon," Jayson said.

"Hello, Mr. Wolfe," she replied. "Funny you should call. I was just looking at the pictures you sent. They're adorable, as always."

"Of course," he said. "I just got the ones you sent a few days ago of Bradley's first day of first grade. That's pretty exciting."

"Yes, it is."

"And do you have warm cookies for him when he comes home from school?"

"Occasionally," she said, not wanting to admit that she felt a bite in the question, even though she knew he'd not intended there to be.

"Are you baking cookies now?"

"No, it's Saturday."

"Oh, so it is. Did you bake cookies yesterday?"

"Yes, actually, I did. I considered sending you some, but they wouldn't have been warm by the time they got there. And I know you like them warm."

"Yes, I do," he said, and she realized he sounded in a fairly good mood. "I was going to call you yesterday, but it was a pretty crazy day. While you were baking cookies, I got a new pen."

"A new pen?" she echoed. "Is this supposed to mean something to me?"

"No, but it will when I explain it."

"Okay. I'm waiting."

"After I signed the papers, they let me keep the pen."

"What papers?" she asked. "Did you buy a house?"

"No, not yet. I will be doing that soon, however."

"What papers, Jayson?" she asked, wondering if this was what she hoped it would be.

"The contract," he said, then he laughed as if he couldn't hold it inside any longer.

"Are you saying what I think you're saying?" she asked and laughed as well.

"I am," he drawled.

"Just tell me!"

"*Big* record deal," he said, and she squealed into the phone, provoking more laughter. "*Big* money. *Big* marketing plans. *Big* world tour in the making." Elizabeth squealed again, and he added, "I did it, Lady. This is it."

She laughed, then made him tell her every detail of the auditions and challenges that had led up to this point. Now the red carpet had been rolled out, and *Gray Wolf* was officially born.

"I bet your mother is wearing a permanent grin."

"She is, actually," Jayson said.

"Have you told my dad yet?"

"Do you honestly think I would call *anybody* before I called you? I will call him as soon as we get off."

They talked for a while longer, but for the remainder of the day, Elizabeth felt as if she were floating right along with Jayson. Derek would be so thrilled! He'd done it; he'd really done it. And she felt such joy on his behalf. But lying in bed that night, she was surprised to have her joy melt into a poignant sorrow. Her distance from the situation felt wrong, somehow. She reminded herself that she was living the life she'd always dreamed about, and Jayson was doing the same. They had both gotten exactly what they'd wanted. Then why did she feel so discontented? Elizabeth couldn't bring herself to answer that question without allowing a heartache to surface—one that she wasn't prepared to face. So she swallowed her minor reasons for claiming any unhappiness at all and reminded herself to stop being so selfish and instead be grateful for what she had. She thought of Leslie Wolfe, whose husband had frequently beaten her senseless. She thought of her father, once living under the same roof with a bitter, selfish wife. Ten thousand people in this world would give their right arm to have Elizabeth's marriage problems. Still, there was a problem, and she knew it. She just didn't know what to do about it.

* * *

A few days later Jayson called again, saying, "I only have a minute, but I need a really big favor."

"Okay."

"Do you still have those red shoes? You did promise you'd never get rid of them."

"I have them," she said.

"Can you send me one?"

She laughed. "What on earth for?"

"I just . . . need it."

"Just one?"

"That's right. It's kind of . . . a surprise. Please!"

"Okay, fine. I'll send it."

"Send it as fast as you can get it here. I'll reimburse you for the postage."

"It's not a problem. I'll send it."

"Thank you. I love you. I gotta go."

Elizabeth mailed off one of her red shoes that afternoon, then she didn't hear from Jayson again for many weeks. The couple of times she tried to call him, Debbie answered, saying that he was in recording sessions and meetings night and day. Elizabeth lost track of time and became involved in other things, and then it happened. She got into the car on a Saturday morning and turned the key, but before she got the car in gear she was hearing Jayson's voice on the radio, singing familiar lyrics with a sound that was only vaguely familiar. *Time will stalk you like a predator, yeah, never giving you a chance. Just when you think that you've got it beat, time will knock you off your feet, feet, feet.* And then the chorus, beginning with a strong drum sequence that Elizabeth knew so well. *And I'm feeling like something's in the wind. Something's coming for my soul. And I'm feeling like something's in the wind. Something that I can't control.*

Elizabeth gasped for breath. She laughed. She cried. She sat in her car in the driveway and listened to the remainder of the song. She expected it to merge into another song, but the DJ spoke over the final bar with excitement in his voice. "That was the title track from a brand new band, *Gray Wolf,* from the about-to-be-released album, *Predator.* Hot stuff this is. The single is already burning up the request lines." An advertisement began, and Elizabeth turned off the radio. For several minutes she just sat there and cried. She cried for the joy of this moment, for the triumph of what it meant to Jayson and Drew and all who loved them. She cried for the sorrow of Derek's death and the reality that he was not alive to participate in this dream—but he was still a part of it. And she cried for the ongoing poignancy she felt in relation to her own place in the picture.

She finally composed herself and embarked on her errands. By scanning stations in the car she heard part of the song twice more during the hour or more that she actually spent in the car between her stops. She couldn't believe it! It was incredible.

Returning home she excitedly told Robert the news. He smiled and told her it was certainly exciting, but he obviously didn't share her enthusiasm. So she called her father and told him, and he *did* share her excitement. That afternoon when the mail came, there was a small overnight package from Jayson. She tore it open with trembling hands, and the CD appeared.

"Wow," she said to an empty room, then she laughed. The front had a photo of the band; a very artistic shot in gray tones, and they were all dressed in black, standing barefoot on a beach. Besides the photo, the front simply said: *Gray Wolf. Predator.*

She didn't even think about the absence of shrink-wrap on the case until she opened it and saw that the CD itself was simply gray, with minimal information printed on it. And written there in black marker, in Jayson's hand, it read, "*To Elizabeth, my inspiration, my motivation. With love, Jayson Wolfe.*" Again she cried with a mixture of emotions, then she pulled out the little booklet inside the case. There she found familiarity in the lyrics of every single song. She was touched to note that where credit for the writing of the songs was noted, some of them listed Derek Greer as one of the contributors. On the last page each of the four band members had separately listed acknowledgments. Under Drew's name it read, *I want to thank my mother, my little taller brother, and the Greer family.* It then went on with some names that Elizabeth didn't recognize. Under Jayson's name it read, *First and foremost, my mother, who raised us to believe in dreams and to honor the gift of music. And to my wife, Debbie, and my daughter, Macy, for your love and patience. To William Greer for taking me in and making me his son. And to Derek Greer, for being the truest of friends.* He then listed a number of other people, and at the very end it simply said, *And to Elizabeth, for everything.* With tears in her eyes it took Elizabeth another minute to realize that at the bottom of the page it read, *This album is dedicated to the memory of Derek Greer.*

Looking on the back, she was surprised to read in fine print, *A Red Shoes Production.* And there beside that was a tiny little logo, a simple replica of the shoe she had sent to Jayson. She laughed, then she cried, then she laughed again. Then she asked Robert if he'd look after the kids. He eagerly agreed, and she went to her bedroom where she put the CD into the stereo, put on her headphones, and laid back on the bed, crying steadily while she listened to fifty-four minutes and seventeen seconds of *Gray Wolf.* She could feel her brother's spirit in the music, and she admired what *good* music it was when the industry was so full of things that were questionable, even vulgar and crude. She listened to the CD again, while memories mingled with the present, leaving her with a deep inner peace that she could never explain. She felt a poignancy too, but mostly peace.

Over the next couple of days, she tried to call Jayson several times but found no one home. On Monday she put a card in the mail that read: *Congratulations! And thank you for the CD. It's perfect! No one (except maybe your mother) could be more happy and proud than I am. Call me some time. Don't let fame make you a stranger. With love, Elizabeth.*

Less than a week later, he *did* call, making a comical fuss about her insinuation that fame would diminish their friendship. She knew it wasn't fame he wanted, except in the way that it represented the number of people listening to his music. They talked for nearly three hours, and she thoroughly enjoyed hearing all the details of his getting to this point, things he'd not taken the time to tell her before. His voice was filled with happiness as he told her how he'd sent autographed copies of his CD to all of his neighbors in Montana who had been patient with the noise he and Drew had made. He told her of the great promotional things underway and of the preparations they were making for a world tour. The first single was already on the top forty in the United States and in several countries in Europe. Just hearing him say something like that made her laugh with perfect delight, and he laughed with her. They needed no words to share the joy of this huge milestone. Seeing the reality of a lifelong dream was deeply gratifying, to put it mildly.

During the following months, Elizabeth developed a habit of perusing certain magazines that followed the entertainment industry. She kept a meticulous scrapbook of every piece or picture she could find. The single, "Predator," hit number one in several countries, and the album became platinum in almost record time. Two more singles buzzed the radio waves, and both hit the top ten; Elizabeth was hearing Jayson sing to her nearly every time she got in the car and turned on the radio. She saw many magazine articles with great headlines, but one of her favorites was the bold declaration: *The Rock World Gets a Touch of Class.*

In spite of all the attention, Elizabeth was still surprised to stop in her tracks in a bookstore one afternoon when she came face-to-face with Jayson Wolfe—on the cover of *Rolling Stone Magazine.* The other band members were in the picture, but Jayson was definitely in the foreground, with the greatest emphasis on him. He was wearing the long, black leather coat she'd given him in high school. She reached out to touch it as if it might self-destruct before she could actually convince herself that it was real. The headline read: *Wolf on the Prowl.* She bought three copies and went home and called her father. They had talked regularly, marveling at the evidence of success that wasn't a surprise to either of them. But

Will nearly flipped out with excitement when she said, "Have you seen the cover of *Rolling Stone* recently?" He got right off and went to buy it, then they talked later for more than an hour.

Jayson regularly called both Will and Elizabeth, keeping them posted on his career from a different perspective. When the tour was actually underway, the publicity hype magnified immensely. Elizabeth could hardly keep up with the scrapbook when dozens of pieces became hundreds. She just clipped and filed them and listened to the music over and over, deeply grateful for the privilege she had of knowing the man behind the music. In fact, she felt a deep gratification in knowing things about Jayson Wolfe that the general public was apparently baffled over. The teen magazines especially were constantly dissecting the lives of the members of *Gray Wolf,* with lists of their birthdays, their favorite colors, and other such pertinent information. And several times Elizabeth had read speculations over what Jayson Wolfe had on that chain he wore around his neck, tucked beneath his shirt. One issue for speculation that crossed from the teen magazines into the adult articles was the fact that Jayson Wolfe always wore black. Not just *something* black, or *mostly* black; he never appeared on stage or in any photo shoots without being dressed *entirely* in black. Other members of the band appeared in a variety of wearing apparel. Jayson certainly had variety, but it was always black. Elizabeth knew the answer. Even though it had never been discussed between them, she knew. The first time they had all appeared on stage together, all dressed in black except for her own red accessories, Derek had commented, *"It looks like we're all going to a funeral."* Jayson had worn the very same clothes when he'd played at Derek's funeral, and now he wore black as a constant reminder of the part Derek had played in his life and in his music.

Elizabeth said to her father over the phone, "Do you know why he wears black?"

"Oh, yes," he said firmly. "I know why."

"But we're not telling, are we."

"Never," he said with a little laugh. "It will always be our little secret."

"Do you talk to Leslie much?"

"Every week," he said. "She's doing well. The boys actually bought her a condo and a new car."

"Wow, that's great," Elizabeth said, not surprised. "So, is Drew still living with her?"

"No, he got his own condo, which is less than a mile from Jayson's new home, as I understand it. They both live fairly close to Leslie. She's quit waiting tables; she's working part-time at a care center for elderly people, and she's loving it. She said the boys have paid for everything, she has no debt, and she only has to work enough to pay the utilities and meet her own needs. I can tell she's very happy. And of course, she's so proud of her boys. She helps look out for Macy quite a bit with all the craziness Jayson and Debbie are involved in. But they all seem happy."

"That's great," Elizabeth said, unwilling to admit the little pang she felt deep inside. If she admitted to it, she might never be able to keep going.

Elizabeth pressed forward in her practically perfect life. Robert was supportive and sensitive and helpful. He was the best father she'd ever seen, in close running with her own father. He provided their every need and want, and supported her in all that she did. She kept busy with her community theater commitments, and her hobby had become a distant following of the career of *Gray Wolf*. There were some photos of Jayson that she felt hard-pressed not to frame and hang on the wall. One was so compelling that she finally did, putting it next to some pictures she had of their high-school days with Derek and Drew. In this photo he was dressed in black jeans, a black silky shirt, and a black tuxedo jacket. The black shoes he wore looked like circa 1900, lacing up the front and going high on the ankles. He had his ankles crossed and was hugging his knees, looking pleasantly thoughtful as he gazed directly into the camera, sitting on top of a shiny, black grand piano. The picture had been printed in *GQ Magazine,* along with an in-depth personal interview with Jayson Wolfe. The printed interview was similar to the one he did on a television talk show in the middle of their tour, where he was the featured guest and the full hour was focused on him. Elizabeth was grateful for the way Leslie always called to forewarn her of such things, since she rarely watched television otherwise.

Jayson spoke candidly about his alcoholic father and the violence that had once been in his home. He told the interviewer that he was willing to share such things with the hope that kids out there with musical gifts, growing up in difficult circumstances, could recognize their own potential. He told the story of learning "Funeral for a Friend" for his mother's birthday, and then having to sell the piano to move. He told of his friendship with Derek Greer, and of Derek's tragic death, and playing that song at the funeral. When the interviewer asked when the world might get to hear that rendition, he coolly said, "I don't play that song in public."

"But you do in private?"

"Sometimes," he said. "I now have a beautiful piano in my home, and once in a while I just have to sit down and play that song. It's the song that grounds me; it reminds me of where I've come from and keeps me focused. I can't explain why it has that effect on me; it just does."

"It represents something from your youth and your connection to Derek?"

"It certainly does, but it's more than that. That was the song that helped me conquer the piano, so to speak. Still, there's more. Something more personal; difficult to explain."

Elizabeth videotaped the interview and watched it several times, often crying for no apparent reason. When she talked to Jayson about the interview and what he'd said about that song, he made a point of telling her, "The more personal part is related to you."

"How is that?" she asked, taken by surprise.

"Well, it was my playing that song that got your attention."

"So it did," she said, and there was a tense period of silence, as if both their thoughts had been drawn to a time when what they had shared had been deeply romantic.

Jayson broke the silence by saying, "And as long as we're being personal, I need to tell you something that's tempting to say publicly, but I would prefer keeping it close to my heart."

"What's that?" she asked, fighting a surge of emotion.

"I never would have made it without you, Lady. When I think of how you talked me into moving forward after Derek died, and all those times through the years when I was ready to give up . . . well, there are a lot of people that have supported me and believed in me—your dad and my mother among them. But you were the one who truly understood my heart, Elizabeth. It was you that kept me going."

"It was a pleasure," she said, her voice quavering.

"I should give you a royalty or something," he said lightly.

"Just send me a letter once in a while," she said. "Phone calls are great, but sometimes it's nice to have something written that I can go back and read."

"I'll see what I can do," he said.

The next time Elizabeth saw Jayson on TV, he was publicly announcing the foundation of the *Derek Greer Musical Scholarship Fund*. Elizabeth cried as she listened to his explanation of how a certain percentage of his profits would go into this fund, and for as long as it lasted, scholarships would be awarded to a number of different universities with good music programs. The most important qualifications for the scholarships would be a passion for music that would be determined through applications and personal interviews, and the student would have to come from a low-income background.

When the interview was over, Elizabeth called her father. "Did you hear that?"

"I did. It's a good thing Leslie keeps us posted."

They talked in awe—and with emotion—about the amazing journey they had been able to share with Jayson, if only from a distance. They were both equally grateful for the way he had kept his promises to them—and to Derek. And they both agreed that it was a privilege to know the real Jayson Wolfe.

As reviews and articles continued to splatter the press, Elizabeth wasn't surprised to see the focus concentrating on Jayson. While the band was critically acclaimed and their unified abilities and teamwork highly commended, the big talk was Jayson Wolfe being the brain *and* the brawn of *Gray Wolf.* Reviewers marveled at his voice, his songwriting, his skill with both piano and guitar, and his stage presence. It was often said that many talented musicians didn't have the ability to connect with an audience and perform the way Jayson Wolfe did.

Elizabeth had grown accustomed to frequently hearing *Gray Wolf* on the radio, and she was certainly aware that Jayson was in the midst of a slow-moving tour. But she was struck with a breathless sensation when she heard a DJ follow one of the band's songs with the announcement that they would be performing in Phoenix and tickets were now on sale. She ordered two tickets that very day, surprised at how quickly the good seats had sold—though she figured she shouldn't have been. She wasn't surprised when Robert declined her request for him to attend with her. He said rock concerts were just too loud, but then he'd always declined ballets, movies, and plays— unless she was in them, and then he only went once.

Elizabeth tried to consider who she might invite to go with her. She was acquainted with many women and occasionally had lunch or went shopping with any number of them. But no one knew about her passion for music—specifically *Gray Wolf.* She mentioned the concert casually to a few women who lived in her neighborhood, but they obviously had no interest in such a thing. They liked the music and were aware of it, but concerts just weren't their thing.

Three days after she bought the tickets, Elizabeth was at a play rehearsal and got talking with a college-aged girl named Diana, who was also in the cast. They had gone out to lunch a couple of times, and Elizabeth liked Diana. She had a passion for many of the same things that Elizabeth did, and subsequently they had been to a couple of movies together, and even a ballet. But Elizabeth didn't know if she would be the rock-concert type. She seemed a little too highbrow for such things, although she was quite worldly—which was one of their vast differences. But in the context of their relationship, it was easy to overlook.

Attempting to get a feel for her preferences, Elizabeth said to her during their break, "So, do you like the band *Gray Wolf?*"

"Oh, my gosh," Diana said. "It's only my favorite these days. They are so amazing!"

Elizabeth smiled. She'd found the right person. "Guess what? I have tickets."

"Tickets? They're coming . . . *here?*" She squealed, and everyone in the room looked at her, then she quieted her voice. "Here?" she repeated.

"Yes, indeed. I have tickets; they're not the best seats, but I didn't hear about it until a few days ago and—"

"I didn't even know they were coming. Oh, my gosh."

"So, you'll go with me?"

"Go with you?" Diana laughed. "My dear Queen Elizabeth," she said in a dramatic British accent, "I shall kiss your feet if you take me with you. How much was the ticket?"

Elizabeth chuckled. "Don't worry about it. It's on me. You can buy me dinner before the show."

"Done!" Diana said. "Do you like steak and lobster? What's the most expensive thing I can feed you? Oh, my gosh!"

"I like steak and lobster, but anything would be fine."

Elizabeth left out her personal affiliations with the better half of *Gray Wolf.* She didn't want Diana making a big deal out of it, or trying to push for privileges or something that could end up being an embarrassment. She just wanted to go to the show, experience the wonder, and leave it at that. She suspected that Diana would appreciate her scrapbook and video collection, but she decided to save that for another time.

Elizabeth knew better than to try to get hold of Jayson while he was on tour, so she was pleasantly surprised when he called her three days before the Phoenix show.

"Guess what?" he said right off. "I'm going to be in Phoenix."

"I know. I already have tickets."

"Really?" He laughed. "How clever of you. By tickets being plural, I assume Robert's going with you."

"Actually no. He's a stay-at-home kind of guy—but that makes getting a babysitter easy. I'm taking a friend; someone I'm doing a play with. Her name is Diana."

"Okay. Well, maybe you and Diana would prefer front-row seats."

Elizabeth laughed. "Diana would probably go gaga. As for me, I've seen you up close before."

Jayson laughed as well, and she thought how good it felt to hear his voice, to hear him laugh. "Well, sell your tickets; give them away. Whatever. I want to see your face on the front row."

"And why is that?" she asked lightly.

"I always imagine your face in the audience. It will be nice to actually see it."

"How did you get these tickets if they're all sold out?"

"They keep some back for press and such; I pulled a few strings." Before she could think of a response, he added, "I gotta go. Just get there a little early. The tickets will be at the will-call office under your name."

"Thank you," she said. "But don't expect me to wave."

He laughed again. "No, we should probably be a little bit discreet."

"Probably," she said and ended the call.

During the next few days, Elizabeth frequently scolded herself for getting butterflies every time she thought about seeing Jayson perform. She felt sure she wasn't alone. Every other female with a ticket was probably feeling the same way. She was able to sell her tickets to one of the sound technicians at the community theater, and when she told Diana about the front-row seats, she *did* go gaga.

"How did you pull that off?" she asked, barely able to breathe.

"I have a friend with connections," she said and left it at that.

Elizabeth's anticipation was difficult to contain as the day approached. Going to the will-call office with Diana at her side, she had a momentary panic, wondering what she'd do if something had gone wrong. Fouled communication could really mess up her evening. But when she told the woman her name, she was handed an envelope. While Diana was distracted, Elizabeth peeked inside and not only found two tickets, but two backstage passes. She took a sharp breath, and Diana asked, "Something wrong?"

"No," she said, "it's just . . . front-row seats. Pretty exciting. Let's go in."

Inside the concert hall, she was amazed at the size of the place and the realization that the show was sold out. She wondered how many similar venues he had played in, and how many more there would be. She felt impatient when she realized another band would be doing the preshow. She realized that *Gray Wolf* had never gone through the stage of opening for another band, and she now recalled Jayson telling her that they had somebody in the right place that had caught the vision of *Gray Wolf* so completely that he'd helped catapult them straight to the top. Not without a price paid for years before that, Elizabeth thought.

When the preshow was over, she felt impatient once again while the stage was changed. Her heart quickened as members of the stage crew set up and adjusted a microphone that she knew would be used by Jayson. Butterflies erupted inside of her when three different guitars were put into stands, and she knew they were his. When the lights finally went down, the roar of audience anticipation was deafening. It became even louder when the flicker of little flashlights made it evident the band members were moving into place. Then out of the darkness a familiar voice boomed,

"Hello, Phoenix!" And the crowd went wild—including Diana. Elizabeth was just quietly taking it all in while her insides felt like a popcorn popper. The applause and cheering were barely softening when the familiar strains of a hit single broke the air, and the noise of the crowd rose again. The lights came up in a brilliant flash, full of color and movement, clearly illuminating *Gray Wolf.*

Elizabeth felt herself caught up in an experience that was something like a dream as she absorbed the reality before her. Jayson's presence onstage—and even Drew's—was so deeply familiar to her. But the grandeur of the entire performance was breathtaking. She enjoyed becoming familiar with Barry and Rudy. She'd heard a great deal about them from Jayson and had read about them and seen many pictures. But this was different. Drew was amazing, as she'd expected. It was still difficult for her to believe that this mega drummer, whose hands and feet often moved in a blur, was a quiet, easygoing reader of science fiction.

Overall, the music was incredible. And she couldn't help feeling the good spirit about the show. No swearing, no sexual innuendos; just good, quality, clean music. And the audience was obviously very impressed. There were repeated standing ovations from those who weren't on their feet the entire time. The applause and cheering was often more deafening than the music. While every aspect of the show was amazing, Elizabeth's main focus was on Jayson. She was amazed at his energy. He ran, he jumped, he danced. He sang powerful belting notes as if they took no effort whatsoever. He played his instruments while he sang and moved at the same time, doing it all as if it took no more effort than breathing. In a word, he was astounding! Not that she'd expected anything less, but witnessing it firsthand took her breath away over and over. How long had it been since she'd seen him at all? She couldn't even remember for certain. She only knew that just being in the same room with him filled a need within her. He was her best friend and as good as her brother. Anything more than that was in the past and irrelevant. But few could fully understand what his friendship meant to her, along with the connections to their past with the music he was performing—even if the room had more than twenty-thousand other people in it. Looking around at the awestruck audience, she had to admit that it was about time the world got to share in the magical gifts of Jayson Wolfe.

When the initial energy of the first few numbers had settled a little, Elizabeth felt him discreetly scanning the front row with his eyes and smiling when he saw her. She appreciated his discretion, but it was still a secret thrill to have him look her way several times with a subtle smile.

Following a brief intermission, Jayson sat on a stool, wearing black jeans and T-shirt, and those black lace-up shoes Elizabeth loved. He was minus the black jacket he'd worn during the first half of the show.

Settling a black acoustic guitar onto his thigh, he said into the microphone, "We're back." The crowd cheered. He looked toward Barry and Rudy, who were standing close together, ready to play, and said, "They missed us, guys." The two made dramatic bows and performed some humorous antics while the audience went wild. Drew did a comical drum roll. Jayson laughed into the microphone.

When the crowd settled he said, "This is a new song." More applause, which made him laugh again. "I wrote it not long ago, on the back of a cocktail napkin while sitting in an airport, missing a dear friend." He started to pick out a melody and added in a melodic voice, "This song is for Elizabeth." Diana nudged her with an elbow and chuckled, but she obviously had no clue that it really *was* for her. While her heart quickened and her stomach quivered, that dreamlike sensation deepened as he closed his eyes and crooned a beautiful string of lyrics about friendship and caring and understanding. Then he hit incredibly high notes as he sang the chorus, *"My lady true, my lady true, a heart of gold and eyes of blue. The world may spin with the noise and din of grief we cannot fathom. But through and through, my lady true keeps my heart and soul in rhythm."*

Elizabeth tried in vain to hold back the tears. He only glanced discreetly toward her a couple of times, and she felt embarrassed when he looked her way just as she was wiping tears from her cheeks. A moment later Diana whispered, "Why are you crying?"

"It's a beautiful song," she said.

The remainder of the show continued to build a momentum that made it evident Jayson and his band mates had the audience eating out of their hands. At one point he introduced the other members of the band, showing a great deal of respect and admiration for them. Barry and Rudy each got a great deal of applause and responded with some silly antics. Then Jayson said, "And the guy on the drums is my little brother." A loud drum beat seemed to protest that and he added, "I'm sorry, my older brother." He then said some genuinely respectful things about him and finished with aplomb, "Ladies and gentleman, on the drums, Drew Wolfe." The crowd went wild. "And I'm Jayson," he added quickly, as if he were insignificant, and the crowd's laughter merged into the next song.

When the show ended, and the encore was done, the lights went up and Elizabeth felt a letdown that she knew was shared by everyone in the room. But she had the pleasure of knowing that Jayson Wolfe would probably be calling her on the phone in a few days. Then she remembered . . . how could she have forgotten? Backstage passes in her purse.

"Come on," she said to Diana, taking her by the arm.

"Where are we going?" she asked in a panic.

"Just . . . follow me and pretend you know what you're doing."

"Okay," Diana said as if she liked the sense of adventure.

Elizabeth considered the most obvious direction to go. She noticed a couple of security guards near a door that led in the direction of the stage. She approached them with a smile and showed them the passes.

"Go right on in, ladies," one of them said, pushing the door open for them.

As they slipped through, Diana said in astonishment, "Just who is this friend of yours with connections?"

"It would seem you're going to find out," Elizabeth said and laughed.

CHAPTER 4

Elizabeth felt so excited to see Jayson she feared she might make a fool of herself. She caught her breath when she realized that the band was actually standing on the stage, just behind a curtain that separated the area where they had been performing. She could hear the crew taking down the equipment, and she could hear talking and laughter. They peeked around a small partition, and Diana gasped quietly. All four members of the band were chatting with a few people; probably children of the execs who owned the building, Elizabeth thought. Jayson looked so incredibly familiar, albeit his hair was moussed a little more than normal. She watched Jayson signing an autograph for a young man, and she wasn't surprised by his genuine and sincere manner as he signed several more autographs and talked comfortably with these fans. He was visibly humble and kind, just as he'd always been.

When the little crowd was moving away, he turned absently toward them, then did a double-take and smiled.

"Oh, my gosh," Diana squealed in a whisper near Elizabeth's ear. "He's coming over here."

"Yes, he is," Elizabeth said and smiled at Jayson.

"Well hello, Mrs. Aragon," he said, and Diana gasped.

"He knows you," she sputtered. "You . . . know him."

"It would seem so," Jayson said, taking both of Elizabeth's hands and kissing her cheek. "How are you?" he asked.

"I'm well. And you?"

"I'm great," he laughed. "And who might this be? Your friend, Diana, I assume."

"That's right," Elizabeth said, then laughed at Diana's expression as Jayson took her hand.

"It's a pleasure to meet you, Diana. I hope you enjoyed the show. Did you have a good view?"

"Oh, yes," she said. "On both counts."

Elizabeth watched as Jayson asked Diana if she would like to meet the rest of the band. Drew was still busy talking with someone else some distance away, but Jayson graciously introduced Elizabeth and Diana to Barry and Rudy. They were kind and both told Elizabeth they'd heard a lot about her. Within a minute, Barry was flirting with Diana while she looked as if she'd gone to heaven. Elizabeth found Jayson facing her, his eyes delving into hers, while she felt transported to a higher sphere herself. To remind him—if not herself—of the situation, she said, "How's Debbie?"

"She's well," he said. "I talk to her at least twice a day, and I'm flying home for two days to surprise her."

"Good. And Macy?"

"She's beautiful," he said with a little chuckle. "She likes my music better than anyone."

Elizabeth glanced toward Diana and muttered lightly, "That must be quite a bit."

"How's Robert?" he asked. "And the children?"

"They're all fine," she said, then smiled. "It's good to see you."

"It's good to see *you.*"

"The show was incredible, Jayson. *You* were incredible. But then, you always were. I knew you could do it."

He sighed. "Yes, you did."

"And the song was beautiful."

"I wrote it for you," he said.

"Now, why would you do something like that?" she asked.

"I do not attempt to explain why or how I can write a song. I only know that I was thinking of you when it came to me. You're my best friend, Lady."

Elizabeth sighed and couldn't help admitting, "And you are mine."

"Is that why you were crying?" he asked, and she looked away, unable to come up with an answer.

Their eyes met for a long, poignant moment before he said, "Do you want to get something to eat?"

"You dare go out in public after—"

"No," he laughed, "but we've got this ridiculously huge hotel suite, and the room service isn't bad. We actually get to enjoy a room for a night occasionally before we're back on the bus. I'm sure the boys would love to join us," he added, looking to where they were entertaining Diana.

Once she was certain he intended it to be a group gathering, she said eagerly, "It sounds great. How do we get out of here?"

"We have it all worked out; however . . . I think we'd do well to kill a little time and let the crowds thin." He peeked around the curtain and said, "Maybe I should play a song for you. The piano's still here."

"I think that you should," she said with a little laugh. "The drums are still there too," she observed.

"Hey, Drew," Jayson called. "I need to play a song for this sweet little lady."

"Elizabeth!" Drew said when he saw her. He hugged her tightly while Diana watched in amazement.

They talked for a minute, then Jayson said to his brother, "Can you do 'Harmony' with me?"

"Sure," Drew said and walked out onto the stage, lightly telling the crew that they just needed to use the drums and the piano for about three minutes.

Jayson sat at the piano, motioning for Elizabeth to sit beside him. She was amazed at the view of the auditorium from this perspective, and noted that there was only a handful of people remaining. She was surprised when Jayson said to her, "Now you do the backing vocals, just the way we used to."

"I don't know if I can even remember," she said. Glancing around discreetly, she could see that Rudy was gone, but Diana was hovering close by, seemingly in a state of awe, and Barry was apparently lingering close to Diana.

"Sure you can," Jayson said and nodded toward Drew. Then they began together with perfect synchronization. Jayson sang the familiar lyrics that took her back in time. After the first verse, he lifted his brows comically, and she laughed. He readjusted himself on the bench and went on. During the chorus she managed a few oohs and aahs, with some laughter in between when she did it far from perfectly. He went on with the second verse, while the lyrics of the entire song suddenly came flooding back to her, invoking feelings of joy and sadness, irony and poignancy all at once.

Before he had finished, she was crying. He was about to ask why when a handful of people remaining in the audience cheered and whistled. Elizabeth discreetly wiped away her tears. Jayson and Drew both did a dramatic bow, then Jayson ushered Elizabeth off the stage, saying to the crew, "Thanks, guys."

Behind the curtain he said to Drew, "Thanks, Bro. It's been a while."

"Still sounds good," Drew said.

Rudy opened a door and hollered, "The van's leaving in three."

"What?" Elizabeth said lightly. "No limo?"

"The limo left a long time ago," Drew said. "It's a decoy, actually. But don't tell anybody."

"Your secret is safe with me," Elizabeth said.

"Me too," Diana added firmly.

"So," Jayson said to Elizabeth, "you ladies going to come back to the hotel with us and get something to eat?"

Diana looked at Elizabeth with something close to petty

begging in her eyes. "Sure," Elizabeth said. "Unless Diana has to get back home to wash her hair or something."

"Oh no, my hair's clean," Diana said, and Barry laughed.

They all moved toward the outside door where the van was parked. Jayson took Elizabeth's arm and urged her back a little as he asked quietly, "Why were you crying?"

"I'm not sure," she said quite honestly. "When I figure it out I'll let you know."

As they all squeezed into a van with dark windows, Elizabeth noticed that the driver and the guy sitting in the other front seat looked more like security than anything else. Her suspicion was confirmed when she heard them talking and it was evident they were trying to avoid a significant crowd of fans that had gathered at the hotel where the bus was parked—except that it was parked at a different hotel than where the band was staying.

The van was crowded, and Elizabeth found herself squished between Drew and Jayson, with Jayson's arm on the seat behind her. "Just like old times," she said. Jayson and Drew both chuckled.

"Like . . . what old times?" Diana asked, her voice lightly scolding. "You've been holding out on me, girlfriend."

Elizabeth chuckled and said, "Old times . . . hmm. I don't remember. You know, it's been so long, I don't think I can recall any old times."

"Drew will remember," Jayson said.

"Oh, I remember," Drew said with drama. "I remember how you stole my pie. I didn't want to share pie, but the peer pressure was horrible." He pretended to cry, and Jayson laughed.

"I remember something about red shoes," Jayson said, smirking at Elizabeth.

"Oh, I remember the beach," Drew said. "It's coming back to me. Oh, we had some good times on the beach."

Elizabeth couldn't resist meeting Jayson's eyes. She read there the poignancy of her own memories just before he turned away and said, "Oh, yes. I remember the beach."

"And there were those stupid hats Derek wore," Drew said.

"That was so embarrassing," Elizabeth said. Jayson just chuckled.

Arriving at the hotel, they were let out at a service entrance in the back, and two members of hotel security met them, guiding them up the staircase, apparently to avoid the elevators. "So this is how you stay in such good shape," Elizabeth said after four flights. "I'm older than you, you know."

"You're older than Jayson," Drew said. "But I'm older than both of you. I'm old."

Once they were settled into the large suite, and dinner had been ordered, Drew relaxed with a book. Rudy went into one of the bedrooms to call his wife. Barry urged Diana to a sofa where they sat to talk. Jayson made a couple of calls, one to his wife and one to his mother, then Elizabeth called Robert so he wouldn't worry. Then she sat down near Jayson where they could talk without anyone close enough to overhear.

"You know," she said, "I could almost hear Derek singing right along with you."

"You'd be amazed how much I hear that," he said. "Or maybe you wouldn't. Not a performance goes by when I don't think of him and wonder why he isn't up there with me; Rudy's a great bass player—but he's not Derek. Derek could practically read my mind."

"Yes, I know," she said, wondering if her strong connection to Jayson was mostly due to their mutual love of Derek.

Jayson glanced to the other end of the huge room where Diana and Barry were sitting. "I think Barry likes your friend," Jayson said. "He'll probably try to get her to spend the night with him." He looked alarmed and asked, "She won't, will she?"

Elizabeth glanced over her shoulder. "I don't think so, but . . . I really don't know her that well. She is pretty gaga over you guys." She laughed softly. "I bet she'd take a kiss and brag about it for the rest of her life." She thought more deeply on what Jayson had said and added, "So, I take it that you and Barry don't have a lot in common in your personal lives."

"I'm afraid not. But who am I to dictate his morals? Thankfully, I know better. I have a beautiful wife waiting for me at home." His voice sobered. "I love her and she loves me. I have no desire to do anything to mess that up." He glanced at her and added, "And I have equal incentive not to do anything to mess up *your* life."

"Not that I would be concerned. I know how very disciplined you can be on that count," she said. An awkward silence followed until she added, "How wise you are. Your morals certainly make you a man among men, and especially a man among rock stars."

He chuckled again. "I have to admit it makes me peculiar among many of my peers."

"That's what I like about you," she said.

Jayson looked into her eyes and wondered why such a statement would make him feel sad. He was a man on top of the world. He had a beautiful wife who loved him—and he loved her. He had an incredible daughter. And he had the career he had always dreamed of. But just seeing Elizabeth had stirred something in him that he had trouble acknowledging. He'd been content in his relationship with Debbie since the day he'd met her, in spite of certain challenges. He'd given her his whole heart and soul, holding nothing back. His friendship with Elizabeth had neither strained nor detracted from his marriage. He knew it beyond any doubt. But at the moment, he saw a formless yearning in her eyes that made him wish things were different. The thought hadn't once crossed his mind for years. So why now? Watching her closely as they talked of trivial things, he couldn't deny that the way she looked at him was stirring memories that he'd be better off forgetting. But why? He had every reason to believe her own marriage was ideal. He'd heard nothing but ravings of Robert's fine qualities and what a good husband and father he was. And she wouldn't lie to him. Would she? He decided that the state of Elizabeth's marriage had no bearing on his own feelings, and he needed to remember where his commitment lay. He had no business allowing his mind to wander, and he forced it back where it belonged, focusing on the incredible friendship he shared with this woman.

Elizabeth thoroughly enjoyed dinner with the band and Diana. She liked seeing the interaction between Drew and Jayson and these men they'd become very close to. And she appreciated getting this glimpse into his life. They visited long after the meal was over, then Elizabeth looked at her watch and realized it was nearly two in the morning.

"Nice watch," Jayson said, and she smiled at him.

"Thank you. It's a lot like yours, I noticed. I've seen yours in many pictures, you know. Magazines, newspapers. That watch I gave you is all over the place."

Jayson laughed softly. "If you'd bought a cheaper one, it would have given out before now."

"Touché," she said, holding up her own wrist.

Jayson called for a cab and told the guys he was riding with Elizabeth and her friend back to their car. Then Barry told Jayson that he'd call a cab for Diana later. Elizabeth noted the smile on Diana's face, and the implication settled in. She wanted to yell at her friend and tell her she was being an idiot, but Diana said, "Don't worry about me. I'll see you at practice."

Jayson and Elizabeth went down the stairs and to the service entrance without the presence of any security. Elizabeth said, "So, Barry's a real ladies' man."

"I'm afraid he is," Jayson said with obvious chagrin.

"So, that means what I think it means—with Diana staying behind."

"Probably," he said. "You'll have to ask Diana tomorrow."

"If I don't slap her first," Elizabeth said, feeling angry and embarrassed, and wondering if she'd been unwise to invite Diana along.

"It's her choice, Lady. No point letting it get to you."

Elizabeth took a deep breath. "No, you're right." She didn't want to waste her last few minutes with Jayson preoccupied by her anger with Diana.

Just riding in the cab with Jayson fed something in Elizabeth that felt starved—no, *deprived,* she corrected. She felt herself fading, shriveling up inside. It took all her willpower not to spill her heart to him. She wanted to cry in his arms and beg him to hold her, the way he used to hold her. But he was happily married. And in spite of the challenges she faced in her own marriage, Robert was a good man, and he did not deserve betrayal and deceit—even in her heart. She scolded herself for her straying thoughts and focused on reality. She told herself that whatever temptation she might face, it was her resistance to it that mattered. And she refused to even entertain a thought that would jeopardize the good things in her life—or Jayson's.

"Tell Debbie hi for me." She laughed softly. "Sounds pretty silly when I've never actually met her face-to-face."

"I haven't met Robert either."

"Maybe we ought to make that happen someday. We could all go out to dinner, or something."

"Sounds fun," he said, but his tone implied that he didn't think it would be. And she silently agreed.

"Will you see your mother on your quick trip home?" she asked.

"I will."

"Give her a hug for me. I miss her."

"She misses you too. How's your dad?"

"He's good; but then, it hasn't been that long since you've talked to him. He loves your phone calls."

"So do I," Jayson said.

"When will you be flying out?"

"Tomorrow morning," he said. "Then I'll be catching up with the band in . . ." He chuckled. "You know what? I don't have any idea where I'm going. Somebody else arranges all that stuff. I just go where I'm told."

"But you love it," she said.

"I love most of it," he admitted. "No job is perfect. But I admit, for me, this one's close." His voice turned solemn. "Sometimes I just . . . fear that . . ."

"What?" she urged when he hesitated.

"That it's too good to be true; that it won't last."

"Well," she said, "I think we both know that rock stardom is not necessarily something you retire from when you're sixty-five."

"Not usually," Jayson said. "I just hope that . . . I can ease out gracefully and not . . . drop like a rock."

"Or fall like a star?" she said lightly, but he didn't seem amused.

Elizabeth guided the cab driver to where her car was parked. It wasn't difficult to find since it was practically the only car left in the huge parking lot. Jayson got out of the cab with her, and they both stood in silence for a long moment before he laughed tensely and said, "It was so good to see you, Lady."

"And you," she said, smiling up at him.

"I'll call you in a few days."

"I'll look forward to it," she said. "The show was incredible, Jayson. It's everything I knew it could be."

He smiled humbly and glanced down. "I never would have made it without you. It was tempting, you know, to pull you up on the stage with me and announce, 'This is the woman who deserves your deepest praise. You wouldn't be enjoying this moment if not for her.'"

"I'm glad you didn't do that," Elizabeth said.

"I was relatively certain you wouldn't appreciate it."

"I should go," she said, and he nodded. "Thanks for dinner . . . and the tickets, and . . . everything."

"A pleasure." He bent to lightly kiss her cheek, and Elizabeth wanted to hold the moment forever.

He waited until she got into the car and drove away before he got back into the cab. She cried on the way home, filled with a combination of joy and sorrow. But she was deeply grateful for the experience of this day and equally grateful to come home to a man who loved her and took good care of her and her children. She was truly blessed.

* * *

Jayson was grateful the flight from Phoenix to Los Angeles was brief. He took a cab to his home, anticipating seeing Debbie for the first time in three weeks; before that, it had been nearly a month. Macy would be in school for a few more hours, and with any luck Debbie wouldn't be out running errands or something. If he found her home alone they would be able to spend some much-needed time together before school let out.

He opened the door with a key, since they always kept it locked, whether they were home or not. He could hear loud music playing from upstairs and set his bag down in the entry hall. He glanced into the room that housed his piano and couldn't resist just touching it before he hurried up the stairs, taking them three at a time. He found the bedroom door ajar and pushed it open, feeling a warm anticipation as he saw her from behind, sitting on the edge of the bed, brushing through her hair. The joyful quickening of his heart turned to a painful thudding before his mind fully accepted the evidence before eyes. Debbie was dressed in lingerie—a lacy black thing he'd given her for Christmas, a nightgown that no woman would ever wear to sleep in, or to lounge around the house in during the middle of the day. The bed was a mess when it should have been neatly made by this hour. And there were clothes on the floor—a man's clothes. And they certainly weren't his.

He was grateful for the loud music that gave him a minute to digest what he was seeing. The shock and horror he felt was reminiscent of some of the worst moments of his life. He kept telling himself that this kind of thing only happened in movies—not to him. Not like this. A part of him wanted to believe that it wasn't what it seemed, that he shouldn't jump to conclusions. But what else could it possibly mean?

Knowing he had to face her and get it over with, he moved stealthily toward the stereo and flipped it off. Debbie gasped and stood as she turned. Her startled expression quickly filled with blatant horror and guilt. *It was true,* he concluded. He needed no more evidence than the guilt in her eyes. In the absence of the music, another clue struck him. The shower was running. *His* shower.

A starkly unfamiliar sensation burned behind his eyes. *Tears.* Painful, searing tears. He'd not cried tears since he'd come to Los Angeles. How many years had it been? He forced the tears back and efficiently replaced them with anger. Anger he could handle. Then he realized there was nothing he could say, nothing he could hear her say, that would make any difference, so he hurried toward the door.

"Where are you going?" Debbie asked frantically.

"I'm leaving before I kill him—or you." He started down the stairs, and she followed him, hesitating on the landing.

"Wait, Jayson . . . we need to talk. Just . . . give me twenty minutes and I'll get rid of him." She blurted, "He's got a photo shoot, and he'll be leaving."

Jayson stopped and turned. "A photo shoot?" he echoed, knowing that could only mean one thing. He moved back up the steps. "So it got to you, didn't it. The fame and glamour were just too addictive for you, weren't they? I saw the way you were thriving on them, but I told myself it was nothing to worry about. You'd adjust. Well, it looks like you've adjusted, all right. Who is he?"

She moved directly in front of him, as if to block his way. He heard the shower turn off and glanced toward the bedroom. Her expression and body language were terribly transparent. She knew that he would recognize whoever it was, and she didn't want him to know.

"Who is he?" Jayson repeated. She said nothing, and against his better judgment he went back into the bedroom just in time to see a muscular young man with a towel tied around his waist come out of the bathroom. Jayson couldn't remember his name, but when their eyes met, he certainly recognized the face. He was some punk rocker who was so covered with tattoos and body piercing that Jayson was overcome with nausea. This kid was probably ten years younger than Jayson and wouldn't know real music if it slapped him in the face. But he was making millions shouting profanity into a microphone—and he was sleeping with Jayson Wolfe's wife.

"Hey man," the kid said, "I was just . . ."

He stopped when Jayson belted him squarely in the jaw, saying firmly, "Put *that* in your photo shoot. It'll look great on your next album cover."

Jayson hurried out of the bedroom and found Debbie in the hall. "Jayson," she said.

"What are you?" he shouted. "Some overgrown groupie? Sleeping with one rock star wasn't enough so you had to find another one? How long has it been going on? Tell me! And don't lie to me!"

"It's just been . . . the last couple of weeks," she said tearfully.

"How many have you slept with?" he demanded. "Tell me! If I have any reason at all to expect that I might end up with AIDS or something, you'd better come clean now."

"It's not like that," she said. "It just happened . . . since you left last . . . and . . . he's the only one, and . . . we were . . . careful about that . . . anyway."

"Oh, you were careful," he muttered, horrified to realize what she meant.

Her apparent regretfulness merged quickly into something cruel and haughty as she said, "I don't know what you expect when you leave me alone for weeks at a time."

"I expect you to remain faithful to me, the way I've remained faithful to you, even though I've had women of all ages throwing themselves at me, willing to do anything at the drop of a hat."

"And you expect me to believe you've never given in to that?"

"Yes, I expect you to believe it because it's true. I had everything I needed right here at home. Or at least I thought I did. It seems I was wrong."

Jayson took a long look at his wife while an unfathomable anger filled his every nerve, perhaps to instinctively insulate and protect the inevitable pain. He turned around and hurried down the stairs, realizing that his greatest fear in that moment was that he would turn into his father and actually hit her as well as her boyfriend. He grabbed his bag near the door and went out through the garage where he got into his SUV and drove away. The shock kept him from falling apart while he wondered where he would go, what he would do, how he would cope. He drove to Drew's condo, knowing that his brother had told him he was welcome there any time. Jayson had a key, just as Drew did to his home, in case they ever needed to help each other with something. For a moment, he considered going to his mother's place. But he couldn't. She would be torn apart by this. She loved Debbie. It was such a nightmare. No, he couldn't tell his mother until he'd at least had a chance to accept it himself and get a grip.

Once inside the condo, he locked the door and immediately sank to the floor. He couldn't believe it. He just couldn't believe it.

* * *

At breakfast, Robert asked Elizabeth how the concert had been the previous evening. She told him it was wonderful, but with his barely polite interest she felt no motivation to share details. Throughout the day she vacillated between drastic moods. At moments she felt a floating euphoria as she recalled how amazing the experience had been seeing Jayson perform that way, how he'd made his dreams come true. At other moments she felt a deep sadness that was difficult to define. She reasoned that she simply missed seeing Jayson; as close as they were as friends, it was ridiculous how rarely they saw each other. It had been years. And it would probably be many more years. She also reasoned that seeing him was poignant in the respect of the memories it stirred, especially related to Derek. And every time she thought of Derek, she couldn't help wondering how it might have been if he had lived to reach his eighteenth birthday.

Elizabeth called her father and shared the experience with him. His enthusiasm was refreshing, and as always, she enjoyed their visit. He actually had tickets to take a date to see the same show that was coming to Oregon in a few weeks. Once their call ended, Elizabeth dreaded going to play practice, knowing Diana would be there. She wasn't sure how to handle her feelings regarding what she suspected had happened last night.

Diana was late for rehearsal, and Elizabeth didn't have a chance to talk to her until they had a break, but she noticed that Diana looked terribly happy, or perhaps pleased with herself. During a break, Elizabeth reminded herself not to jump to conclusions or be judgmental.

"So, did you have a good time last night?" Elizabeth asked her.

"Oh, it was incredible. I can't thank you enough."

"Glad you could make it," Elizabeth said.

"I can't believe how you held out on me. I mean . . . Jayson Wolfe? Did you see the way he looked at you? And that song . . . for Elizabeth. That was you, wasn't it."

"So he tells me," Elizabeth said. "But . . . can we keep this between us? I really don't want to have anybody else knowing that—"

"Oh, I understand," she said. "Your secret's safe with me, so long as my secret's safe with you."

Elizabeth thought about that for a few seconds and said, "I don't think my secret is the same as your secret."

Diana chuckled. "Oh, come on. He is obviously in love with you."

"Jayson and I are just friends."

"Just friends?"

"Okay. Best friends."

Diana laughed. "You've got to tell me how you got to be best friends with Jayson Wolfe. I mean . . . it's obvious there's some history there, but . . . best friends?"

"He was my brother's best friend, actually. My brother was killed and . . . Jayson and I just . . . became close." She didn't mention that it wasn't necessarily in that order, or how close they'd actually been.

"Your brother? Is that the guy the CD is dedicated to, that helped write some of the songs?"

"That's him," she said. If only to divert the conversation from herself, she asked, "So what time did you get home?"

"About seven this morning; after the bus left."

"You really spent the night with him," Elizabeth said, trying not to sound as disgusted as she felt.

"I really did," Diana said.

"You will probably never see him again."

"Not necessarily."

"Don't you think he says those things to every girl in every city?"

Diana looked only slightly dejected. "Well, at least I was the girl in *this* city."

"And he won't remember your name in a week. Doesn't that bother you?"

"A little, maybe, but hey—"

"I don't want to hear about it," Elizabeth said, relieved when their break was over.

When she got back from play practice, Robert was finishing up the dishes. He greeted her with a kiss on the cheek and asked her how it went. She told him, then he said, "Oh, Jayson called. He didn't sound very good. Said he wasn't feeling well. He's at his brother's condo. The number's by the phone."

"Thank you," she said, feeling concerned. Not feeling well? He'd never been sick a day in his life. His brother's condo? Why would he be there when his own home was a mile away?

Robert said he'd help the kids with their homework and see that they got to bed so she could talk to Jayson. She thanked him and went into the study to make the call.

"Jayson?" she said right after he'd said hello.

"Oh, thank heaven it's you," he muttered.

"What's happened?" she demanded.

"Oh, I can't believe it," he said, and she could tell he was crying. "I just . . . can't believe it."

"What? Just tell me."

"Debbie . . . uh . . ."

"Is she all right? Please don't tell me she's dead or—"

"No," he said, "that would be easier."

"Oh, help," Elizabeth murmured under her breath.

She could feel it coming even before Jayson said, "There was . . . another man . . . there . . . when I came home."

"Oh, Jayson. I'm so sorry," she said, her chest tightening. "Do you want me to come out there? Is there anything I can do to—"

"No," he said, "just talk to me. Tell me what to do. Tell me how to get through this."

Elizabeth felt sick as she listened to the stark evidence of his heartache. She had witnessed his grief in the past, and it was easy to imagine how he might look now. She thought of the experience she'd shared with him twenty-four hours earlier. He'd been charged with energy and full of life, wooing thousands with his music. Now he was broken, his heart bleeding. And she was too far away to put her arms around him and tell him everything would be all right. But then, she concluded, maybe that was best.

CHAPTER 5

Jayson struggled to tell Elizabeth everything that had happened when he'd come home earlier. He then told her how Debbie had found him at Drew's place, insisting that they talk. For a moment he had hoped that she would regret what she'd done, that she'd beg his forgiveness, that they could put their family back together. But it had quickly become evident that her attitude had no regret—perhaps only in being caught. He really believed she was telling the truth about it not happening prior to his last time away. Elizabeth pointed out that his timely trip home may have been a huge blessing in making him aware of it before she'd become more involved. He'd looked forward to sharing a bed with his wife and had no idea that she might have been sleeping with somebody else. The very idea made him so sick he was hard-pressed to keep from throwing up. He simply hoped that Debbie had been telling him the truth, that there hadn't been others.

"So now what?" she asked gently.

"I don't know," he said, pressing a hand through his hair. "I can't even . . . think. She's blaming me for this, Elizabeth. She told me I was neglectful . . . that I had hurt her."

"How?" she demanded, unable to comprehend such a thing.

"I don't know. When I asked for an example she couldn't give me one. I've thought about it until my head hurts. I know I wasn't a perfect husband. We had our challenges, but . . . I always tried to be sensitive to her needs. I know that having me on the road wasn't easy, but . . . she had help with Macy. She has friends and family. I called her at least twice a day. I came home every chance I could. What else could I have done? Am I just rationalizing here?"

"Obviously I wasn't there, but . . . I know you, Jayson. I know you better than anyone. I was never married to you, but it's difficult for me to imagine your being neglectful and hurtful. At any rate, even if there was a problem, being unfaithful is not the course a person takes when they want to make a marriage better. She made the choice to do that. Even if you *had* been neglectful, she's accountable for her decision. Not you."

Jayson appreciated her insight and validation. He only wished it could take away the pain. He'd felt anger and sorrow when Derek had been killed—and when Elizabeth had told him she couldn't marry him. But never had he known such betrayal.

Suddenly exhausted and overwhelmed, he thanked Elizabeth for being there and ended the call. He took something to help him sleep and was awakened the next morning by the phone ringing. He didn't answer, certain it would be someone trying to call Drew. But it rang and rang until he knew it was Debbie trying to get hold of him.

"What?" he answered tersely, thinking if it wasn't her, he could tell anybody else that they had the wrong number.

"Jayson, we need to talk."

"About what?" he asked.

"We need to work this out."

"What's your definition of working it out, Deb? If I felt like you regretted what you'd done, that you wanted my forgiveness, I might be able to consider eventually learning to trust you again. But the impression I got from you yesterday was that you weren't terribly sorry. So . . . what am I supposed to think?"

"Jayson," she said in a tone that implied he was being difficult, "I really thought that you were just . . . well, doing the same thing."

He made a scoffing noise. "What in the name of heaven ever gave you the remotest idea that I ever have been, or would be, unfaithful to you?"

"Well . . . it's just the way this world works. You know that. I couldn't fathom that any man in your position would ever be able to resist such opportunities."

"If that's what you think, then it's evident you never really knew me. And I obviously never really knew you."

"Okay, so . . . we live and learn. But can't we just . . . go on and . . . we can be married, we can be Macy's parents and . . . we can each live our own lives."

Jayson gave a bitter chuckle to avoid screaming as he digested what she was saying. "What horrific cult have you become involved with while I've been gone, Mrs. Wolfe? I don't care who does it and what the norm is in this business. I will not live in a marriage that is a farce, and I will not tolerate my wife sleeping in other beds. If that's the way you're going to live, then we will live divorced."

"You can't mean it!"

"You can't be that surprised. You can keep the house, and I will pay reasonable child support for the time Macy is with you, according to the state's guidelines. But I will not support your newly developed spending habits while you make yourself a tramp."

"I can't believe you're talking to me this way; I can't believe what I'm hearing."

"Well, I have trouble believing that I came home yesterday to find what I found. I can't even find words to describe how I feel. You're pathetic. You know what? I don't want to talk to you. I'll have my attorney call you. Tell Macy I'll be by to pick her up after school. I want to see her before I fly out tomorrow."

"Fine," she snarled and hung up the phone.

"Oh, Macy," Jayson said under his breath and threw the phone at the wall. She would be the casualty in all of this, and the thought made him curl up in bed and cry like a baby. A few hours later he made up his mind that he would never be able to cope if he kept on like this. He hadn't cried for ten years, and now he couldn't stop. He told himself he had to be strong. He had several concerts left to perform. He had to get onstage and smile and enthrall his ticket holders. He had to be a good father to Macy as far as it was possible. He had to go on. Consciously he tucked the pain safely away, and locked the tears away with it. Then he called his attorney.

Following a lengthy call with him, he went to visit his mother to tell her what had happened. He wasn't surprised by her anger and her tears, but he was deeply grateful for her unquestioning love and support of him. She promised to keep seeing Macy regularly while he was gone, just as she'd been doing. She didn't figure it would be a problem. Debbie seemed to have so much to keep her busy these days, and she was eager to let Macy stay with her grandmother.

"Better that she's here than exposed to . . . oh!" He groaned. "I still can't believe it. The whole thing is just so . . . hideous."

"Yes, it is," Leslie said gently, "but great people rise up out of the dust of adversity, Jayson." He looked up and met her glistening eyes. He'd never forget the last time he'd heard her say that. It was the day she'd told him they had to sell the piano. "You *are* great, Jayson," she said. "You were great long before you met Debbie, or got a record deal, and no matter what happens, you will always be great."

"Oh, Mom," he said, hugging her tightly. "What would I ever do without you?"

She hugged him back, then told him to go and get Macy, and she would bake some cookies. He pulled up in front of the house and honked, and his daughter came running out to the car. He got out to meet her and picked her up, twirling her around. "Oh, you get more beautiful all the time," he said.

"Everybody says I look like you," she said.

"Well, you're beautiful anyway," he said, and she laughed.

In the car she said, "Mom told me you're staying at Uncle Drew's house."

"That's right," he said, wondering what else Debbie had told her.

"How come?" she asked, and Jayson felt angry with Debbie for putting their family into a situation where he had to say things that should never have to be said to a child. He reminded himself that he had survived much worse in his own childhood. Still, he hated it.

Part of him wished that Debbie had told her, but then he wasn't sure he would like Debbie's slant on the problem. He attempted to find the simplest, most honest answer to the question, and he said it directly. "I'm kind of upset about some things your mom's done, baby." She looked concerned, and he added, "I want you to know that no matter what happens, I'm always your dad, I'm always there for you, and the problems between me and your mother have nothing to do with you."

"Okay," she said with a confused crease in her brow. He felt sick at the thought of having to leave town tomorrow in the midst of such a horrible crisis. He prayed that Macy could be protected from the worst of it, and he was grateful for his mother's presence and her relationship with Macy.

They arrived at his mother's place and helped her finish baking cookies, then they ate some while they were warm, washing them down with milk. Jayson sank his teeth into one and for some reason thought of Elizabeth's determination to make warm cookies for her children. He wondered how it might have been if . . . no, he couldn't think of that.

Jayson, Macy, and Leslie played Monopoly and Life, then they worked together to cook spaghetti and make a green salad. After dinner was eaten and cleaned up, Jayson sat close beside his daughter on the couch and asked her to tell him everything she'd been doing while he'd been away. She talked about school and her friends, and it was evident she set a high priority on her nail-polish collection. She still loved to play with Barbies and Legos, and she wanted an American Girl doll for Christmas, which was still a long ways off. He was just wondering if he ought to take her home when the phone rang. His mother answered it, and he could hear her talking quietly in the kitchen. When she was finished, she came into the room and said, "Macy, honey. Would you run upstairs and get that photo album we were looking at a few days ago?"

"Sure," Macy said and hurried up the stairs.

Once she was gone, Leslie said quietly, "That was Debbie. She told me she's leaving town in a couple of hours and she wondered if Macy could stay here. Of course I told her it was all right. She said she'd bring her things over, and I have a key if I need anything else."

Jayson sighed. "Well, I'd rather have her here than over there. I just hope that doesn't complicate your life or—"

"Are you kidding?" She laughed softly. "Macy is the light of my life, especially with my sons gone all the time."

Jayson smiled. "What about your job?"

"My job is flexible. I usually work during school hours, but she can even go with me. Those elderly people love to have her read to them."

"Oh, you're amazing," Jayson said, hugging her tightly. "With you around, we might actually get through this."

Macy brought the photo album back, and Leslie said with excitement, "Guess what? Your mother called and you get to stay with me while she goes out of town." Macy seemed pleased, and it was evident to Jayson that his daughter had become more comfortable with her grandmother than with her own mother.

Jayson didn't see Debbie when she brought Macy's things by. Looking through her backpack he realized she had some homework, so he helped her with it, then tucked her into bed, saying he would call her every day, just as he'd been doing.

When Macy was asleep, Jayson hugged his mother and thanked her for everything before he left to sleep at Drew's and leave for the airport early in the morning. Before going to Drew's place, he went to his own home. Reassured that Debbie was gone, he hurried to pack up the things that really mattered to him. He found an old set of luggage and some boxes, and he loaded everything he could fit into the SUV. He wasn't going to trust anything he really cared about to be left in the same house with Debbie while they negotiated a divorce. He said good-bye to his piano and promised to send for it as soon as possible, then he drove to Drew's place and put most of his stuff into the guest room where he'd slept the previous night. Some of it he left in the garage, and a few things were still in the SUV, since it would be parked in the garage next to Drew's car until he came home again.

Even though it was late, Jayson called Will in Oregon. He was still awake, reading as he often was. He told Will what had happened, and was grateful beyond words for his fatherly support and advice and the way he could offer the perfect balance of understanding and compassion.

Jayson didn't want to take something to help him sleep, fearing he might miss his flight. He slept very little that night, but managed to get some sleep on the plane. His manager, Blake, met him getting off the plane. As they walked through the airport together, Blake said, "Oh, we got some free publicity."

"Really?" Jayson said, and Blake slapped a rolled magazine into Jayson's hand. *A tabloid.* He felt sick even before he unrolled it. Had that jerk, whatever his name was, reported the bedroom incident to one of these sleazy papers for some sensationalism? If so, he could feel a legal suit in the air. He unrolled the magazine and was startled to realize the front page story was about him. But it wasn't about Debbie's affair. The headline read: *Who is Elizabeth?* Jayson actually laughed. It only took him a moment to figure that Debbie would get a lot of mileage out of this, but he actually found the timing rather humorous. In the cab he read the article and kept laughing. Someone had taken note of his dedicating a song to Elizabeth, and that her name was in the acknowledgments on the CD. But since there was no last name, she was suddenly a great mystery. And there was actually a photo from some press party he'd attended months earlier. He was standing beside a woman that he didn't even know, and the photo claimed that this dark-haired woman who looked tawdry and cheap was some secret involvement of his.

"Well, that was entertaining," Jayson said, handing the magazine back to Blake. "At what point can I sue them?"

"When you stop laughing," he said. "But then, if you just threaten to sue them, they'll write a retraction and grovel, and we might get some mileage out of it."

"Great. I'll let you know when I quit laughing, and I'll let *you* threaten them."

"That's my job," Blake said. "So, how's the family?"

"My mother and daughter are great. My wife has pretty much destroyed my every expectation of love and marriage, and she's shattered my heart, but—"

"You're serious," Blake said, looking at him over the top of his sunglasses.

"Yes, I'm serious. I'm getting a divorce, but don't tell the tabloids that just yet."

"You okay?" Blake asked.

Jayson looked out the window. "The show must go on. I'm fine."

* * *

Jayson didn't see Drew until they were in the artist's lounge that evening, waiting for the show to begin.

"Hey, little brother," he said, sitting on the couch beside him. "How did the trip go?"

"I stayed at your place," Jayson said. "In fact I moved some of my stuff to your place and my car's in your garage."

"Okay," Drew drawled. "Trouble in paradise?"

"We're getting a divorce," Jayson said, amazed at his own lack of emotion.

"Whoa. Whoa. A few days ago I heard you talking to her on the phone, and it was all, 'I love you, honey. I miss you, honey.' So, what's the deal?"

Jayson sighed loudly. "Apparently she wasn't missing me as much as I missed her."

Drew's astonished expression gained an edge of impatience. "And?" he pressed, motioning with his hand for Jayson to get to the point.

"I walked into the bedroom and she was . . . uh . . . well, everything looked . . . and some guy was in the shower."

"No!" Drew gasped and put a hand over the center of his chest as if he actually felt pain. "I can't believe it."

"Well, we should start a fan club on that one. And here's the clincher. Remember when we were at that charity thing a couple of months ago, and there was that punk band that was so disgusting?"

"I remember. Guys like that are hard to forget."

"Remember the lead singer? The guy with all the tattoos and the hardware?"

"Yeah?" Drew said, looking a little nauseous, as if he could guess what was coming.

"Well, that's him. That's who walked out of my bathroom."

"Oh, I'm gonna puke!" Drew said. "He looks like a teenager. An *idiot* teenager. He's what? Twenty-two at most?"

"Probably. And he's the idiot who is sleeping with my wife."

"I can't believe it," Drew said again.

"Yeah, well . . . neither can I, but . . . I've got to get a grip and stay focused. When the tour's over I'll get a place of my own and—"

"Why?" Drew asked. "We lived together in a tiny bedroom as teenagers and survived. I'm sure we can manage. The place is huge, and even when we're not on tour I don't spend that much time there. Just move in for the time being."

Jayson had to admit he liked that idea. "Okay, well . . . that's better than being on my own."

"Yes, it is," Drew said. "If we really get sick of each other, you can stay with Mom, but I don't think it'll be a problem. Her place is huge, too."

"I should pay you some rent or something."

"No, you shouldn't," Drew said with a little laugh. "It's paid for, Jayson. I have more money in the bank than I will ever know how to spend. I'm set for life. And I never would have made it without you plowing your way through like a freight train. You're my hero, Jayse. Let me do this."

"Fine, but . . . you can stop with the hero thing. That's ridiculous."

"Just plan on moving in, okay?"

"Okay, but . . . I need my piano. Are you okay with—"

"Yes," Drew said. "I know you better than to think that you would come without a piano. You can put it in that front room that presently has absolutely no furniture. It's not a problem."

"Thanks, Drew. What would I do without you?"

"We're family," Drew said and gave Jayson a firm embrace that almost tempted him to cry. But he couldn't cry. He had to perform in a matter of minutes.

Later that evening when the show was over, Jayson asked the crew to leave the piano in place long enough for him to get something out of his system. When the hall was completely empty and most of the crew was elsewhere, Jayson sat at the piano and played "Funeral for a Friend." He played it with a passionate anger that didn't begin to be released through the music—but it helped. He finished the song and looked up to see a few stagehands standing nearby. He was grateful when they didn't applaud. "That was amazing, Jayse," one of them said.

"Thanks guys," he said, walking away. "You can load the piano now."

Jayson called Elizabeth before they got onto the bus to head out, even though it was late. It had occurred to him just before the show started that the tabloid story that had given him a good chuckle might cause grief for her. He told her about it and apologized for any trouble it might cause. She laughed with him over it and took it all lightly. She asked how he was doing, and he had to admit that while he was keeping it together, he was struggling. They talked for just a short while before he had to go, but he promised to keep in touch.

A few days later, another story appeared in the tabloid. And when Jayson read it, he wasn't laughing. Apparently someone had figured out who Elizabeth was—and they were right on. There were even a couple of the promo photos from the days of *A Pack of Wolves,* one with Elizabeth sitting on his lap. What really made him angry were the photos taken last week in Phoenix that showed the two of them going into the hotel together; the other four people who had gone in the door with them had been cropped out of the picture.

"You want me to threaten the tabloid?" Blake said, alerting Jayson to his presence. "You're not laughing."

"No, I'm not laughing. But there's a problem with this story."

"What's that?"

"Everything it says is actually true. There're some nasty implications, but it doesn't actually come out and say anything false."

"I hate it when that happens," Blake said, as if he would have dearly loved to give the tabloid some grief.

At the first opportunity, Jayson phoned Elizabeth and once again apologized for the story in the tabloid. "It's okay," she said. "Nobody I know reads those things anyway."

"You never know," Jayson said. "I just don't want it to cause any problems with Robert."

"It's okay, Jayson. He knows that I'll always tell him the truth."

"How incredible that would be!"

"What?"

"To know that your wife would always tell you the truth."

Elizabeth wished there was something she could say to console him, to help him through this. The truth was that the breakdown of his marriage had urged her own marital problems closer to the surface. And she was struggling too. But she didn't want to talk about it; she didn't even want to think about it.

Later that day she picked up a copy of the tabloid. When Robert got home they had a good laugh over it, but when she got to play practice it became evident that she *did* know someone who read tabloids. Diana. Why wasn't she surprised?

"You've been holding out on me," she said with laughter. "You were in a band with Drew and Jayson Wolfe in high school?"

"That's right," Elizabeth said. "But I'd appreciate your keeping that to yourself."

"It's in the tabloids!"

"Just keep it there, okay?"

"Well . . . why aren't you on stage with him now?"

"That's a good question," Elizabeth said. "Although . . . I was just kind of a . . . filler. It's evident where the real talent lies."

Elizabeth couldn't shake Diana's question from her mind. She really didn't want to be on stage with Jayson. But there were things she *did* want, and she wondered what had gone wrong, and why she had been such a fool.

* * *

Jayson wasn't surprised to find out that Debbie Wolfe had seen the tabloids. And she was all over the story. It quickly became evident that while he might be able to prove that she was guilty of infidelity, he couldn't necessarily prove that he *wasn't* guilty of it. He reasoned that he didn't want an ugly court battle that would end up getting smeared all over the papers, with Macy being the biggest victim of the fallout. It was only money, he concluded, and he had plenty of it, and the ability to make a lot more. He discussed with his attorney the few stipulations that mattered to him and then left it in his hands while he finished his tour.

With only a few concerts left on the schedule, Blake told Jayson, "I got a phone message for you. You need to call Elizabeth. Is that 'tabloid Elizabeth'?"

"It is," Jayson said, "but if you tell anybody, I'll sue you." He smirked when he said it and went to find a phone, wondering what might be wrong.

"Hi," she said, not sounding upset. "I just wanted to let you know that my grandfather died last night. My father's father."

"I thought your father's parents both died a long time ago," Jayson said, feeling confused.

"They did. This is actually his stepfather."

"Oh," Jayson said, "I don't think I've heard much—if anything—about him."

"Well, they weren't close, even though he had a significant hand in raising my father. They kept in touch some, but . . . see, after Dad's mother died, he remarried and kind of made himself a part of his *other* family."

"I see."

"Anyway, Dad's having a rough time over it. I guess it brings up issues and grief."

"I can understand that."

"I just thought you should know. That's all."

"Thank you."

"Dad's flying to Kansas for the funeral, and I'm going to meet him there. I barely remember this guy, but I feel like I should be there for my father. I didn't want you to call and be told we were at a family funeral and have you think we'd left you out."

"No, we couldn't have that," he said lightly. "Well, if I don't talk to him before the funeral, give him my love."

"I will."

"And give *you* my love, too."

She hesitated. "I'll do that."

Two days later, Elizabeth was standing close to her father, who was hovering near the open casket where his stepfather lay. She was tired of talking to people she didn't know, and hating the memories that any funeral stirred for her. She did a double-take when she saw a man in a long black coat come through the door, wearing dark glasses. While she was thinking that from a distance he reminded her of Jayson, she realized that it *was* Jayson.

"Dad," she whispered just as she saw him turn in their direction, "Jayson is here."

"Where?" Will said with a thrill in his voice that made Elizabeth's heart quicken. Jayson removed his dark glasses, and his eyes connected to Elizabeth's across the room, then Will's. And he smiled. They all crossed the room, and Will took Jayson into his arms with a great deal of fervor and a rush of tears. "Oh, it's so good to see you!"

"It's good to see you, too," Jayson said and hugged him again.

He then hugged Elizabeth, who said, "I thought you were on tour."

"I am," he said. "I have to leave for the airport in an hour. I'm sorry I can't stay for the funeral. I just had to be here, if only long enough to hug both of you." He smiled at Will and added, "You'd do the same for me."

Will hugged Jayson again, as if he just couldn't get enough of him. Jayson laughed and said, "I should come to funerals more often."

Will took Jayson by the arm and introduced him to some of his cousins and a couple of siblings whom Jayson had never heard anything about. Will told each person with pride, "This is my unofficial son, Jayson."

Most people he met were likely too old to care about the rock music scene, but there were a couple of people who said, "You look familiar."

Jayson just smiled and said, "I just have one of those faces that looks like somebody famous." This made Will laugh.

The three of them sat together in a secluded area of the funeral home for what little time was left before he had to go. Jayson sat between Will and Elizabeth, holding their hands in his. They walked him out to the cab when he had to go, and they both shared lengthy embraces with him before he got in and it drove away.

"He's a good man," Will said, putting his arm around Elizabeth.

"Yes, he is," Elizabeth agreed and forced her mind to the good man she had waiting for her at home.

* * *

Nearly the last stop of the tour was the city in Montana closest to where Jayson and Drew had grown up. This had been done on purpose, and Jayson knew that a lot of hype was going on in the papers and on local television about their roots being in this area. He found it humorous to recall how he'd basically been a joke at school and that he'd never had close friends here. He wondered what his classmates were thinking now as they read the paper. The show went well, and Jayson enjoyed every minute, well aware that this was nearly the last time they would be doing this particular concert. He was grateful to be staying at a hotel that night, knowing that the bus would start out early to get the band to the next gig.

The band was gathered in one of their suites eating a late dinner when the phone rang. Rudy was closest and got up to answer it. He listened for a moment, then held up the phone, saying, "Hotel security. He wants to talk to one of the Wolfe brothers."

Jayson stood up to take the phone, facetiously saying to Drew, "Why do I always have to be in charge and deal with the garbage?"

"You're so good at it, Mr. Front Man," Drew said lightly. "You're my hero."

"Give me a break," Jayson said, then into the phone, "This is Jayson Wolfe."

A voice on the other end of the phone said, "There's a guy in the lobby who says he's your father." Jayson's heart dropped like lead, and he felt sick to his stomach. Even with all of his awareness of being this near their hometown, thoughts about his father hadn't even crossed his mind.

"Is this guy giving you grief?" Jayson asked. He turned to meet Drew's eyes, seeing concern and confusion there.

"No, not really. He just insists that he needs to see you and your brother. His ID says, 'Jay Wolfe.' What do you want us to do?"

"Hold on," Jayson said and put his hand over the receiver. He said to Drew, "Our father is in the lobby."

Drew made a disgusted noise. "Well, I don't want to see him. He wants money; you can bet on it. You do what you want."

Jayson sighed and measured his feelings carefully. He didn't want to see him either, but he felt sure his conscience would never let him rest if he didn't at least make an attempt. Into the phone he said, "Is there someplace in the hotel . . . a meeting room or something . . . where I could talk to him?"

"Yeah, we can do that," the officer said, "but we've still got fans combing the place. Why don't I come up and get you."

"Thanks. I appreciate that."

"I'll be right up."

Jayson hung up the phone and sat down to put on his shoes.

"You're really going to talk to him," Drew said.

"I really am."

"Well, don't give him any money. He'll just drink it."

"You don't have to tell me that," Jayson said. To make a point he demonstrated how his pockets were empty. "See, no cash, no wallet; not even a quarter."

"Good plan," Drew said.

The officer knocked at the door, and Jayson left with him. As they walked together down two flights of stairs in order to avoid the elevators, the officer said, "I take it this guy is your father, then."

"Well, my father's name is Jay Wolfe, and he lives in this area, so I have to assume. Was he sober?"

"Hard to tell."

"Yeah, that's my father. I'd appreciate it if you'd stay real close. The last time I saw him, I needed stitches. But then . . . he did too."

The officer chuckled. "I'm not worried about this guy. It's those crazy girls you gotta worry about. I'm amazed at what lengths some of them will go just to try to get to you guys."

Jayson snorted a laugh. "Crazy is right. They don't seem to realize we're all just a bunch of idiots."

They stopped at a door marked as a meeting room. The officer opened it, saying, "I'll be right outside the door."

"Thank you," Jayson said and stepped into the room.

Coming face-to-face with Jay Wolfe, Jayson felt so much anger that it took all his willpower to remain calm. He looked more like he should be Jayson's grandfather with the way he had aged. Jayson folded his arms over his chest and muttered a barely polite, "Hello."

"It really is you," Jay said.

"It really is," Jayson replied. "I was just thinking the same about you."

"So where's your brother?"

"He didn't want to see you. Can't say that I blame him."

Jay ignored this and asked, "How's your mother?"

"She's great," Jayson said. "Did you just want to reminisce, or what?"

"I don't blame you for being angry with me, boy. But I was pretty surprised to see your pictures in the paper that way. Apparently you've made it pretty big for yourselves."

"We're doing well at the moment," he said.

"I was thinking you might be willing to help out your old dad. Now that you're rolling in the dough, you shouldn't miss a little here and there."

Jayson let out a disgusted chuckle. "You're so predictable, old man. But what makes you think I would give you a dime when I know you'll just go out and drink it away and end up a little further down the gutter?"

Jay began to argue, using a string of profanity that made Jayson's skin crawl. He just opened the door and said to the officer in a quiet voice, "Can you get a manager down here without leaving?"

"Sure," he said and pulled the radio off his belt.

Jay overheard and said, "So, you're gonna have me kicked out, boy? Is that it? You gonna throw your money around and prove how powerful you are?"

He went on with a lot of babbling that Jayson ignored. He was relieved when the night manager arrived quickly and asked Jayson, "What can I do for you, Mr. Wolfe?"

"This man is my father," Jayson said, noting the mild surprise in the man's eyes. "I want you to give him a room for three nights, and whatever he orders to eat on room service. No liquor. Put it on my bill. If he causes any trouble, kick him out."

"We'll take care of everything," the manager said. "Is there anything else?"

"Yes, but we'll talk about that elsewhere." Jayson turned to his father and added, "I wish I could say it has been a pleasure. I'll talk to you in the morning before I leave."

He hurried from the room with the manager and the officer at his sides. While they walked back to Jayson's room, he asked some questions, and the manager eagerly agreed to help him. Jayson thanked them both, then went back to the suite to find that Rudy and Barry had gone to bed. Drew was reading, waiting for him.

"Did you kill him?"

"No, but I was tempted."

"Did he ask for money?" Drew asked.

"He did."

Drew made a scoffing noise. "He's so predictable."

"That's what I told him."

"What else did you tell him?"

"I got him a room and some meals and specified no liquor."

"Ah, the Good Samaritan," Drew said.

"I think the Good Samaritan had a better attitude," Jayson said. "It was more for my own conscience than anything." He sat down and told Drew what he intended to do, then he got on the phone to make some arrangements.

It was still dark when the bus pulled out the following morning, but Jayson wasn't on it. As soon as business hours began, he made several phone calls according to the hotel manager's suggestions. Then, with a different security officer, he went to his father's room and knocked until his father finally answered the door. Jayson entered the room with the officer and closed the door. "Here's the deal, old man." He handed him a business card. "On this side is my manager's number. I don't give out my personal number to people who might harass me. If you have a need that doesn't have anything to do with booze, you can get hold of me through him. He will be given strict instructions not to put you through to me unless you are sober." He turned the card over. "Here is the name and number of a woman who works at a local rehab facility. They can help you sober up and make a decent life. They will send me the bill, and I will gladly pay it. When you have successfully completed this program, I would love to hear from you, and I'll send you pictures of my daughter. If you're really behaving your-self, I'll take you out to dinner and you can meet her." Jayson looked at his father hard, noting his bewildered expression. "Are you sober enough to remember this conversation?"

"Not drunk enough to forget it," Jay said with an edge to his voice that tempted Jayson to tell him to rot in purgatory. Instead, he just left the room, and the officer followed him, closing the door.

"Good move," the officer said, "if I may say so."

Jayson sighed. "He'll never do it. But at least I know I tried."

Jayson took a cab to the airport, a little disconcerted with having to take a hired security officer with him, who escorted him to the door of the plane. Another officer was waiting when he arrived at his destination, and he escorted him to the hotel where he would meet the band when they arrived later. Alone in his hotel room, Jayson contemplated the encounter with his father—and the memories it had stirred up. He worked very hard to talk himself out of the anger. When he finally had it out of his system, he called Elizabeth, and they had a long talk. Oh, how he missed her! He called his home to talk to Macy, and he listened to all the little things going on in her young life. He missed his daughter as well, but they had great plans together in less than a week when the tour was officially over.

Then he called his mother.

"Guess who I saw?"

"Who?" she asked with anticipation.

"No, don't get excited. Just guess."

"I don't know."

"I was in Montana."

"Oh," she said with chagrin.

"That's right. I saw my father."

"I'm sorry," she said.

He told her what had happened, and what he'd done. She said she was proud of him, but they both agreed Jay would never do it. They had a long talk about all that was going on in both their lives, then he hesitantly said good night. He missed her too, and he was so grateful that she had made a life for herself beyond Jay Wolfe. Then, with too much time on his hands, trapped in a hotel room that would protect him from overzealous fans who were anticipating a performance the following evening, he called

Elizabeth back. He appreciated the insight she could give him regarding his feelings for his father.

Eating dinner alone in his room, he contemplated these three women in his life—his mother, his daughter, and Elizabeth. He loved them all in such different ways. They were all amazing, all beautiful. And he missed them. And yes, he missed Debbie too. But he wasn't going to think about that.

CHAPTER 6

Jayson felt a mixture of emotions to see the tour end, but mostly he felt relieved. It had been great, but he was exhausted, and certain aspects of his life had fallen apart since the tour had begun. He quickly settled in with Drew and spent a great deal of time with Macy and his mother. Drew had enough empty rooms that Jayson had Macy help him decorate and furnish one of them for herself. This gave her a place that was her own when she stayed with her father. They talked about the divorce, as they had a number of times. He felt she was as well adjusted as a girl of ten years could be with such a thing, but still he worried for her.

Jayson quickly felt comfortable living with Drew. His brother didn't date much, but he did have groups of friends that he hung out with, and he was rarely home. It was a good arrangement, but once the piano had been moved, Jayson felt better. As long as he could play the piano, he believed he could survive almost anything. Not as he played it on stage, but when he could just play whatever he felt and do it with all of the anger and fear and passion that he felt bottled up inside.

The divorce went through quickly, and he hardly had to see Debbie at all throughout the proceedings. Jayson willingly gave her the house and a reasonable settlement, and his attorney had told him that her attorney had advised her to take the money and run while the running was good. Thankfully she did. And Jayson was grateful to have official joint custody of Macy. She was the joy of his life, and he spent every minute with her that he could. And when he couldn't, his mother helped cover for him, giving Macy all the love and appropriate guidance she was capable of giving. While Jayson certainly would have preferred not being a divorced man, he had to admit that, all things considered, his life was good. He only prayed that it would last.

* * *

Elizabeth was baking cookies with her boys when the phone rang. She wiped her hands on a towel and answered it.

"Hi," Jayson said brightly.

"Hi," she replied in the same tone. "Guess what I'm doing."

"Baking cookies," he said.

"You win! You're right."

"Of course," he said. "I know you. What do I win?"

"The chance to talk to me on the phone," she said. "I'm famous, you know. I've been in the tabloids."

"So you have," he said with a chuckle.

"So, what's up?"

"I bought my mom a TV."

"I thought you did that a long time ago; you didn't want her to miss any of that promo stuff you were doing."

"Well, that's true. But I bought her a bigger one."

"Okay," she said with a little laugh, wondering if there was a point to this.

"Do *you* have a TV?"

"I do," she said.

"Is it a big one?"

"It's adequate. I don't watch much TV."

"But you watch TV when I'm on it, don't you?"

"Usually," she said. "What are you getting at?"

"Well, maybe you should consider getting a bigger one. Like I told Mom, you want to be able to see it really well."

"Jayson?" she drawled and laughed. "Just tell me!"

"We're performing on the Grammy Awards," he said, and she let out a delighted squeal.

"But here's the best part," he said.

"There's something better?"

"We're nominated for three awards," he said, and she squealed again while the boys observed her with pleasant intrigue.

"That's incredible!"

"Yes, it is," he said. "I don't even care if we win. Just getting this far is . . . well, this is what I've always dreamed of, always imagined."

"Derek would be proud."

"Yes, he would," Jayson said. "And being there just won't be the same without him; I often imagined him performing on TV with one of those stupid hats."

"And he would have done it," Elizabeth said.

A familiar silence descended between them. It happened every time they talked about Derek. It was if they both felt the same sadness but didn't know how to express it. They'd become accustomed to being without him, but neither of them had ever stopped missing him.

The night of the Grammy Awards, Elizabeth forewarned Robert that she would be glued to the television. He agreed to keep the children happy so she could enjoy the performance. He hovered near her occasionally, apparently curious but not terribly so. Elizabeth was glad she had a videotape running through the entire thing when a few different times the camera scanned the audience and she clearly saw Jayson sitting with Drew and Macy. He'd told her that he'd invited his mother to come, but she preferred to watch it at home. The reality made her too nervous. Elizabeth was in agreement with Leslie.

When it came time for their performance, Elizabeth felt the same excitement she'd felt when she'd seen them live. She wasn't surprised to see Jayson wearing a tuxedo, but he wore it with a black shirt so that he was wearing all black—of course. Before the song began, Jayson said into the microphone, "Hi, Mom," and Drew did a little drumroll in the background, as if to echo it. Elizabeth laughed and wished she could be with Leslie, holding her hand.

Elizabeth held her breath when the first award they were nominated for was announced. The woman announcing the award leaned into the microphone, saying, "And the winner is . . . *Gray Wolf.*"

Elizabeth squealed and jumped up and down, which brought Robert and the boys on the run to investigate. "They won!" Elizabeth said, and her family sat down to see Jayson and Drew and the others come to the stage to accept their individual trophies. Barry, Rudy, and Drew each said a few words, expressing thanks to many of the behind-the-scenes people they worked with. Jayson was last, saying, "I think they've all pretty much covered it. I would like to add that there are three women in my life who have had a great impact on me. My mother, Leslie; my daughter, Macy; and my very best friend, Elizabeth." He held up the trophy. "This is for you. I love you all."

While Elizabeth was wiping tears, she couldn't help wondering if Debbie was watching this. Did she know she had severed herself from that list, a list that should have had *four* women on it? Did she realize that the love and support she'd once given Jayson had been wiped away with her betrayal? Did she care?

Of the other two awards *Gray Wolf* had been nominated for, they received one. And Elizabeth felt a deep peace on Jayson's behalf. Derek *would* be proud. The minute the show was over, she did a three-way call to Leslie and Will, and they relived the joy through a long conversation that included a great deal of reminiscing. They had all shared the journey with Jayson and Drew, a journey laden with much heartache and grief. It seemed right that they should share in the joy.

* * *

Jayson stood in front of the glass-door cabinet he'd purchased soon after moving in with Drew. In it he had put some photos in frames that represented the people who were dear to him. He'd also put in Derek's hat that Will had given him the summer he'd graduated. And he'd put Elizabeth's red shoe in there as well, hoping she'd never ask for it back. And now there were two Grammy Awards. He stood for a long while just gazing at them, pondering the path he'd taken to get them and all that they represented. He reminded himself that while he had achieved an incredible goal, it was just a step in a journey, and he had to keep moving forward. There were songs to write and record and a daughter to raise.

He enjoyed his relationship with his daughter and was pleased with the amount of time he was able to spend with her between his working hours. More and more it seemed that Debbie had too much life to live to be too mindful of her daughter. The situation suited Jayson fine, since he'd rather have her in his own care or with his mother. But it reminded him a bit too much of Elizabeth's youth and her relationship with her mother. It wasn't a good image. But he looked to Will's example of being the best father he could possibly be, hoping he could be equal to the task of making up for the lack of mothering she was getting. One thing Macy had that Elizabeth hadn't had was the presence of a grandmother in her everyday life. For that, too, Jayson was grateful.

Jayson enjoyed creating a new album, taken at a slow and steady pace. The work was gratifying and went smoothly for the most part. In spite of Barry's overzealous attention to women and Rudy's occasionally getting drunk, they managed to press forward.

On a rainy morning Jayson was just sitting down to breakfast when the phone rang. Macy answered it, then handed the phone to him, saying, "It's Blake."

"Hi, Blake. What's up?" he asked, buttering his toast.

"I just got a call from a hospital in Montana," he said, and Jayson stopped buttering. He set down the knife. "Apparently they found my card in your father's wallet. He died about an hour ago."

Jayson was surprised to feel sorrow, and equally surprised by the tears that came with it. He'd not cried since he'd found out another man had been sleeping with his wife. He pressed a hand over his eyes and felt Macy put her hand over his arm.

"Jayse? You there?" Blake asked.

"Yeah," he said. "Uh . . . thanks for the call."

"I guess they need somebody to approve arrangements or something."

"Okay, uh . . . do you have . . . the information?"

"Yeah. You got a pen?"

"Just a second," Jayson said and stood to open a kitchen drawer where he found pen and paper. He scribbled down the name and number of the hospital and the person he needed to talk to. When he had it down, he said, "Thanks, Blake. I guess I'm flying to Montana. I'll call you when I get back."

"Montana?" Macy asked when he hung up the phone.

"Uh . . . yeah. My father just died."

"Oh," she said.

"Did you want to come with me?" he asked.

"Not really. I can stay at Megan's."

"You can stay at Grandma's, and if she says it's all right, you can spend some time with Megan."

"Okay, Dad," she said with a loud sigh.

"I'm sorry, baby. I guess we'll have to wait on that roller-coaster adventure you've got cooked up. I'll make it up to you."

"I know," she said. "Why are you crying? I thought you hated your father."

"I don't know," Jayson said. "Just the fact that he's my father, I guess. And maybe . . . I feel sad about the pathetic waste his life was."

Macy didn't seem to understand, but then, he didn't understand, either. When Drew got out of bed a short while later, Jayson gave him the news. He showed little response, but Jayson felt grateful that he was willing to go to Montana with him. He called his mother to tell her Macy would be coming over because he and Drew were leaving the state.

"Where are you going?" she asked.

"To bury our father," he said, and she made no response. He filled in the silence by telling her what little he knew.

"You really don't have to go, you know," she said. "We could make arrangements over the phone to—"

"It's okay, Mom. I think we need to go."

"You're a good man, Jayson; and your brother, too."

"Whatever good we have in us came from you," Jayson said.

"I don't know about that, but . . . I am glad you're going. I did love him, you know. But living with such horrors quickly squelches any tender feelings."

"I know," Jayson said. "You just think about the good times and enjoy Macy's company. We'll be back tomorrow."

On the plane, Jayson and Drew talked about their childhood and the impact of their father in a way they never had before. They rented a car and went straight to a mortuary that Jayson had called from Los Angeles. They made arrangements for a suitable burial, and they were present when the casket was lowered into the ground. They ordered a simple headstone, then wandered the area a bit, reminiscing and both agreeing that they were grateful to have moved to Oregon when they had. Jayson's thoughts naturally went to Elizabeth. He missed her so much! He knew he could call her any time, and he would. But deep inside he ached to be with her, if only to hold her hand and talk with her face-to-face. He couldn't deny that he missed her far more than he missed Debbie, but he didn't want to think about the reasons. She was happily married, and he needed to remember his place. While he'd been married to Debbie and their relationship had been good, he'd never once longed for Elizabeth inappropriately. He'd given his whole heart to Debbie and to making a good marriage. He knew that, and he felt at peace with it. But now with Debbie gone, his thoughts strayed far too often to Elizabeth.

Late that evening he called her and talked through his feelings about his father's death. She had a way of putting such things into perspective, and he felt deeply grateful for her insight and friendship. He got off the phone and went to the piano, grateful that Macy was well-accustomed to sleeping through his spurts of song writing, as long as he didn't play too loudly. And Drew was still out. Before Jayson went to bed, he had a well-formed chorus that he sang several times before giving up for the night.

And every now and then I had to stop and wonder . . . how it might have been . . . if she had loved me, the way I loved her, the way it should have been.

Ironically, the following day the band was laying down tracks for a song that he'd also written for Elizabeth—even if no one else knew it.

You are my light that shines through darkness. You are the peace that calms my storm. You are safety in the face of danger, a friend within a crowd of strangers. You are the flame that keeps me warm, safe from harm, in your arms . . . forever.

* * *

Jayson was toying with the piano, realizing he felt incredibly bored—and lonely. Rudy and Barry were each out of the country, taking lengthy vacations with family. Drew was doing the same with some good friends. Macy was in Europe with her mother—and her mother's boyfriend. And Leslie was on a cruise with a couple of her lifelong girlfriends.

When the phone rang and it was Will, Jayson felt certain he'd been inspired to make the call. They talked for a long while about many things. He'd recently returned from staying a week with Elizabeth and her family, and he'd had a wonderful time. It was evident he had a great deal of respect for Robert, and he thoroughly enjoyed his grandsons. Elizabeth's happiness was readily apparent, and Jayson felt grateful on her behalf.

Will talked about the rehearsals Elizabeth had been doing for *The King and I* at the community theater where she'd become extremely involved with nearly every production they did. She had the part of Anna, and Will had been disappointed in needing to leave and get back to his job before it opened. A couple of hours after Jayson had ended his call with Will, he called him back.

"Hey, do you think it would be possible for me to just . . . go see that play?"

"I don't know why not," Will said. "She'd be thrilled!"

"Okay, but . . . I don't want to cause any problems. I'd like to surprise her with some flowers or something, but . . . do you think Robert would be okay with that?"

"I think Robert could stand to be a little more jealous," Will said, and Jayson wanted to question him on that. But Will went on to say, "I think it's a marvelous idea."

With Will's help, Jayson was able to order a ticket for the play over the phone with his credit card, and he quickly made arrangements for the trip. Seeing that he wasn't in any hurry, he made the decision to drive from Los Angeles to Phoenix, rather than dealing with airports and a rental car. He actually enjoyed the drive while he listened to music that brought back his youth—mostly Elton John. Arriving in Phoenix, he realized that his time was brief before the play began. Rather than checking into a hotel, he just grabbed a quick bite to eat, hoping the clothes he had on would be suitable. He stopped and bought a ridiculously large bouquet of flowers. He chose a variety of colorful blooms, avoiding roses for the sake of skirting around any possible romantic implications.

He arrived at the theater to find that most of the audience was already seated. By asking a few questions, he got the flowers into the right person's hands, a kind woman who agreed to see that they would be presented as Elizabeth would be taking her bows immediately following the performance. Taking his seat, he realized this was an extremely small theater, housing probably fewer than two hundred people. And since it was theater in the round, every person had an excellent view of the stage.

When the show began and she came on stage, memories of Jayson's youth washed over him. He was sixteen again, watching *West Side Story*, falling helplessly in love with that face and that voice, knowing absolutely nothing about her. Well, now he knew everything about her, and the years had not diminished the way he felt. But the situation was still the same. He felt like that boy in high school again with a helpless, hopeless crush, admiring her from a distance. *I can't touch but I can see.* As the lyrics came to his mind, he had to smile to himself to realize that the whole world knew that song. And like much of what he'd written, it had been inspired by Elizabeth.

Jayson felt a secret thrill to see her perform. She was so incredible on stage! Her costumes were elaborate gowns with full hoop skirts that only enhanced her natural beauty. Her voice was breathtaking, and the intensity of her acting left him in awe.

At the end of the performance, he felt a perfect delight to see her surprise at being given flowers on stage. She quickly subdued her visible intrigue and cradled them in her arm while she took her bows. Jayson glanced at his watch. The anticipation of being with her was sweet, and he relished it, counting the minutes.

* * *

The moment Elizabeth was out of view of the audience, she plucked the little card from the center of the huge bouquet in her arms, wondering who on earth would do such a thing. Robert always gave her roses on opening night, but that had happened last week. This wasn't his style at all. She was thinking that possibly her father had ordered them, but her heart quickened as she read, *Incredible as always, my Lady. Jayson.* And it was written in his hand! She looked around, almost expecting him to appear. When he didn't, she hurried to change her clothes, wondering if he'd simply planned this ahead and had mailed the card to the florist. Coming out of the dressing room, she again found herself looking for him. Walking out to the parking lot, she wondered if she was supposed to assume that he was somewhere around or not. She was so busy looking for him that she was startled to glance up and see him leaning against her car.

"Your father told me it was a green Tahoe with Mickey Mouse hanging from the rearview mirror."

"Did he now?" she said with a laugh and wrapped her arms around him, holding the flowers in one hand. He laughed and lifted her briefly off the ground with his embrace. "Oh, it's good to see you," she said, stepping back. "Thank you for the flowers. They're beautiful."

"Were you surprised?"

"Oh, yes," she said.

"I was going to get roses, but I thought that might not sit well with your husband. I wouldn't want him getting suspicious or anything—especially since you and I both know there's nothing to be suspicious about."

Elizabeth looked down. "Oh, he wouldn't be suspicious."

"And why is that?" he asked, reminded of what Will had said.

"He's just not the suspicious type," she said with a smile.

"Your performance was astounding," he said with conviction.

"Thank you," she said. "I don't draw the crowds that you do, but . . . it gives me something to do."

"With two children, you need something to do?"

"I need something to do beyond the drudgery of dishes and laundry." She chuckled softly. "Don't get me wrong. I have a great life, and I have a great family. I just . . ."

"Need more?" he guessed.

"Yes, I suppose I do," she said, looking down in a way that made him wonder why something about that made her uncomfortable. But they were standing in a parking lot, and he didn't want to get into it.

"Hey," he said, "you want to get something to eat or a drink or something?"

"I'm actually hungry," she said. "I usually don't eat much before a performance, then I have to heat up leftovers when I get home."

"So . . . let's go get some dinner."

"Okay," she said. "I just need to find a phone and call Robert."

He handed her the new cell phone he had clipped to his belt. "Oh, thank you," she said.

"I need to give you that number, so you can call me whenever."

"That would be nice," she said and handed the flowers to Jayson along with her car keys. He took the hint to unlock the car and put the flowers in the backseat while she dialed home.

"Hi," she said brightly. "How's everything?" He listened to her side of the conversation with breaks in between while she was listening. "Good. How was Bradley's game? Oh, that's great. Did you get that video? Hey, listen, my friend Jayson came in from LA to see the play and surprise me. Oh, really. Wow. Okay. Well . . . he wants to get some dinner. Are you okay with that? Well, yeah, that's true. We do get talking. I'll probably be late. Would you like to join us? I'd really like you to." Long pause. "I'd love for you to get to know him. Okay, well . . . kiss the kids for me. I'll see you in the morning, then. Love you too."

"In the morning?" Jayson asked after she'd ended the call.

"He'll be asleep when I get home," she said. "He told me to have a good time and not to hurry."

"He's okay with that? Really?"

"Yes, Jayson, he's okay with it. Actually, he knew you would be here. Dad let him in on the surprise."

"Really?" Jayson said. "Good thing we didn't want to keep it a secret. He's really okay with this?"

"Yes, he really is. Is there a reason he shouldn't be?"

"Well, I have no inappropriate intentions," he said, mildly facetious. They both knew he never would. "But . . . if I were him

I think I'd be wanting to join you and your old boyfriend for dinner."

"He doesn't see you as my old boyfriend. He sees you as you are—my oldest and dearest friend."

With mock astonishment he said, "You don't have any friends older than me?"

She laughed. "Yes, but I don't have any friends that I've known longer than you."

"Clarify yourself, Lady."

"So . . . do you have a car?"

"Yes, but I like yours better. Besides, you know your way around."

Jayson opened her door for her, then walked around and got in on the passenger side.

"So, what are you in the mood for?" she asked.

"Anything," he said. "Just so it's not *fast* food."

"Okay, well . . . how about a really good steak? Shrimp maybe."

"Sounds divine."

She turned the key in the ignition, and the Elton John CD she'd been listening to blared loudly. Elizabeth turned it down; they both laughed and she said, "I listen to this CD almost as much as I listen to *Gray Wolf.*"

"You have good taste," he said and began to sing along.

"You're buying, right?" she said, pulling out onto the road. "You are rich and famous enough to take me out for a really great steak dinner, right?"

"For you, I think I could manage."

Elizabeth had a perfectly marvelous time sharing a lengthy meal with Jayson. They talked and laughed and reminisced. And as always when they were together, Derek came up, and a brief silence fell between them. When Elizabeth shed a few tears, Jayson reached across the table and took her hand. She became preoccupied by the feel of his hand in hers and had to remind herself that she was a married woman. She became distracted when she looked up at him and noticed something highly unusual. "How come I'm crying and you're not?"

"Is that a crime?" he asked with a chuckle.

"No, but . . . highly unusual."

"Not really," he said.

"It used to be highly unusual," she said, recalling now what Debbie had once said, that she'd never seen him shed a tear.

"I guess I grew out of it."

She wanted to ask exactly when that had happened, when she'd last seen him crying not so many months before he'd married Debbie. Instead she asked, "You don't cry any more?"

"I cried the day I found Debbie cheating on me," he said. "I cried when my father died; why, I don't know."

"That's not so hard to figure," Elizabeth said, and the conversation moved that direction. But Elizabeth couldn't help wondering what had changed inside of him—and if she had something to do with it.

When the restaurant was closing and they were still sitting there, he asked, "Would you like to take a walk or something?"

Elizabeth smiled. "I'd love to."

They drove first to a park where a path wound around a pond and through some trees. They walked for a long while, never running out of things to say to each other. Elizabeth finally stopped and leaned up against a tree where she could see Jayson in the glow of a nearby streetlight. For several minutes she just watched him while he talked, telling her of Macy's comical antics. His love for his daughter made him practically glow, and she marveled at how thoroughly pleasant it was to be with him.

Elizabeth looked into his eyes and reminded herself that she was a married woman with no business feeling this way about him. She told herself that she was just caught up in childish memories, that what she felt for Jayson was trite and insignificant. But in her heart she knew the truth. Robert was a good man, and she loved him. She respected him; she was committed to him. But she couldn't remember the last time he'd even touched her, let alone kissed her or held her close. And even when he had it had been so inadequate. She felt utterly starved for something that she tried desperately not to think about.

While Jayson rambled with some silly story about Drew, she realized how close he was standing to her, and she took a sharp breath. Even the smell of him stirred her memories. Had he always used the same aftershave? Or was there simply a vague, masculine aroma that was distinctly him? Either way, she felt intoxicated. Without realizing what she was doing, she took hold of his upper arms if only to remain steady on her feet.

"Is something wrong?" he asked.

"I just felt . . . a little dizzy," she said, not wanting to let go of him, but stepping back.

"You're not pregnant, are you?" he asked lightly.

"No," she said severely, "I'm not pregnant."

"Then what's wrong?" he asked gently, moving closer to her.

Elizabeth looked up at him, and she could hardly breathe. She closed her eyes if only so she wouldn't be able to see him, then she realized that only intensified his distinctive aroma and the sound of his breathing. She heard him whisper, "Elizabeth. What's wrong?"

"I . . . don't know," she said. "I guess I've just . . . missed you . . . more than I realized."

"I've missed you too," he said with a tenderness that intensified her memories of all they had shared. She opened her eyes and looked up at him, startled at how close together their faces were. She felt suddenly as if she had been in a desert without water to drink for so long that she had lost all sensibility in the face of her thirst. With no thought or premeditation, she lifted her lips toward his, as if to replenish her parched spirit.

When Jayson realized she was about to kiss him, he was so stunned that he almost stopped breathing. His brief temptation to allow her to do it was quickly squelched by a split-second barrage of memories of all the suffering they had endured the last time they had crossed inappropriate boundaries. Now everything was different. And this was wrong—even more wrong than when they'd been teenagers and had gotten carried away. She was married. *Married.* He felt a deep conviction in respecting her marriage vows; he knew what it felt like to be cheated on. But oh, how he loved her! Since he'd come to terms with his divorce, he'd missed her so much! He wondered for a moment if he had it in him to follow the path where a kiss might lead. The part of him that had been deeply hurt and betrayed by his cheating wife felt certain that he could easily take anything Elizabeth was willing to give. But the flip side of that was his absolute knowledge that if he took something that didn't belong to him, there would be the devil to pay. And he simply wasn't up to any more such payments. He stepped back abruptly, while placing his hands firmly on her shoulders, saying, "Whoa. Whoa. What is this?" He looked at her stunned expression and wondered why she looked like a starving child who was being denied a crust of bread.

Elizabeth felt a tangible pain from his sudden distance. Taking a moment to consciously accept what had just happened, she felt suddenly mortified and a little sick to her stomach. "Oh," she said and took a step back, briefly putting a hand over her lips as if to assure herself that they had almost betrayed her. "I'm so sorry. I don't know what I was thinking."

"Obviously you *weren't* thinking," he said. She made no response. If only to make a point, he added, "So . . . now what? Should we get a room or something?"

"No!" she said and forced a laugh as if to convince them both that he was teasing.

Evidently he saw through her when he said, "And what if I am serious?"

"You could never do it," she said just as intensely.

Jayson wanted to believe she was right, but he felt compelled to bring home the point of how serious this could be if he weren't a man determined to be moral. "Are you willing to bet on it? How do you know my idealistic values didn't diminish significantly when I found out another man had been sleeping in *my* bed with *my* wife?"

"But you're better than that," she said.

"Don't be so sure."

"What are you saying, Jayson? That you've become promiscuous? Have you been hanging out with groupies?"

He looked insulted. "No, I have not! That's not what I'm saying, at all. There was only Debbie . . . and you."

Elizabeth wanted to remind him that what they'd shared together had never reached the point of what they had each experienced in their marriages. But even that wasn't quite true—at least for her. As memories she had struggled to block out all of these years suddenly meshed with the reality of her life that she'd been fighting to ignore, a painful knot gathered in the center of her chest, making it difficult to breathe. An equally intense pain pounded between her eyes, making her dizzy. Why now? Why like this? Was this the reason she'd worked so hard all these years to keep the feelings at bay? Had she known instinctively that looking at them would be too painful? But why did her emotions have to choose now to jump out and make themselves known? She tried to tell herself to get a grip and wait until she was alone, but it was too late. Her reasons for almost kissing Jayson had triggered it all, and there would be no holding it back now.

Jayson felt tangibly afraid as he watched Elizabeth gasp for breath and stagger as if she might pass out. When she sank to her knees, he broke her fall, kneeling to face her, holding her hands while her gasping turned to sobs. She groaned intermittently as if the pain she felt was unbearable. She wrapped her arms around her middle and curled herself around them, doubling over until her head nearly touched the ground. Jayson sat beside her and put his arm around her, attempting to offer some comfort with soothing words. But his fear only deepened as her emotions became more volatile. He was grateful for the late hour, and to see that they were completely alone. He wondered what was going on inside of her to create such havoc with her emotions. He thought of the times in his life when he had faced such intense emotional pain, and the causes of that pain were by far the worst things that had happened in his life. To this day, those experiences stood out prominently in his mind. Derek's death. Elizabeth's rejection. Debbie's betrayal. But *what* was going on in Elizabeth's life that could even come close to such events? And why would it make her behave so rashly? Was there a connection, or was she simply out of her mind with grief? Either way, he was determined to get to the bottom of it.

CHAPTER 7

For more than an hour Jayson just stayed close to Elizabeth and held her while she wept and sobbed and groaned with pain. She finally became quiet beyond an occasional sniffle, with her head against his chest. He lifted her chin with his finger and looked into her tear-swollen eyes. "What's going on, Elizabeth?" he asked gently, but she turned away.

"I don't want to talk about it," she insisted.

"Is that why whatever it is just exploded all over the place? Because you haven't wanted to talk about it? How long have you not been talking about it?" he asked. She whimpered and hung her head. Again he lifted her chin with his finger and made her face him. "Why don't you want to tell me?" he asked. "You think it's too personal? Is it something feminine? You think you'll embarrass me? You should know we're past that, Lady."

Elizabeth struggled to come up with an honest answer. "If you were happily married, it might be easier to talk to you about . . . the truth of . . . my own marriage."

Jayson took a sharp breath at the implication. But he was quick to say, "Are you thinking that I might take advantage of you if I knew there was a problem? Did you think I might try to lure you away from him?"

"No," she said gently, "but I feared that if you knew the truth, it would add to your own heartache."

Jayson looked down abruptly. She had him there. But he still didn't know what the problem was, and this conversation had come too far to let it drop now. He looked back up at her, saying firmly, "Just tell me what's wrong, Elizabeth. I've been given every impression that you are *happily* married. But a happy woman does not carry around the emotion you just experienced. And for the record, I'm not going to take advantage of you, and I'm not going to let anything happen between us that shouldn't. I never could, Lady. Never! But I'm not leaving until you tell me what's wrong. You might as well just get it over with."

Still she hesitated, and Jayson couldn't help thinking of his mother's experience in marriage. Sitting beside her, he quickly said, "He didn't hurt you, did he? Because if he ever hit you or—"

"No, he's never hurt me, Jayson." Elizabeth looked down and sighed deeply. "I guess you're right that . . . I shouldn't be worried about embarrassing you. Maybe I'm worried about embarrassing myself, or . . . maybe I just don't want to admit aloud that the problem exists." She sighed again. "Robert is a wonderful man, Jayson. He's responsible. He has integrity. He works hard. He's a perfect father; you should see him with those boys. He has the perfect balance of love and discipline with them. He cleans. He does grocery shopping. He doesn't cook, but he's great at heating up leftovers and making sure the kitchen is clean. He helps the kids with homework. He helps with the laundry. He's kind, thoughtful, supportive, and—"

"I get the idea, Elizabeth. Get to the but."

"What?"

"I know there's a 'but' in this oratory; just get to it. We've established that Robert is an incredible man. *But . . .*"

He motioned with his hand for her to continue. Elizabeth struggled to form the words. As close as she and Jayson were—and had been—they had talked about sensitive issues before. But that had been a long time ago. In spite of her father's very frank example of discussing such things, she found it difficult to think of discussing them with her own children when the time came. And discussing them now with Jayson certainly wasn't going to be easy. She reminded herself that they were both mature adults. The issue at hand was talked about lightly and crudely in the world they lived in, so much so that perhaps she hesitated talking about it at all for fear of feeling that she might fall into that category. Then it occurred to her that if she had been willing to talk about it frankly a long time ago, perhaps it wouldn't have gotten so bad.

"I'm waiting," Jayson said, but he said it tenderly.

Elizabeth took a deep breath. "Uh . . . what happened between us . . . on the beach . . ."

She hesitated, and Jayson felt confused. Was she trying to tell him that because of what happened she wasn't comfortable talking to him? Or was there something else? Not wanting to jump to conclusions, he kept quiet and motioned for her to continue.

"What happened between us, Jayson, I just took for granted that . . . such things would be a part of marriage. But . . . for me, it's never happened since."

Jayson's eyes narrowed, and his brow furrowed with confusion. "You're a mother, Elizabeth. You have two children," he said as if she didn't know.

"Obviously what it takes to create a child has happened, Jayson. But that's it. And what happened between you and me did not go that far. That's the point, Jayson. What I have experienced in my marriage is completely technical. It has been solely for the purpose of creating children. There has been nothing that I would describe as intimacy. *Nothing.* He doesn't kiss me or hold me or touch me. There is a complete absence of affection in my marriage, Jayson. There. That's the truth." She blew out a quavering breath and squeezed her eyes closed. "I said it."

Jayson was stunned. He couldn't believe it. He'd been exposed to many people who were so completely preoccupied with sex that they would do anything to get it. It had simply never occurred to him that someone might *not* want it. He took a long, hard look at

Elizabeth and could only think how he'd give almost anything to share every aspect of his life with her. She was so incredible, so beautiful. How could a man in his right mind not want to kiss her and hold her?

Elizabeth watched Jayson, waiting for a reaction. She was surprised to see clearly, even in the dim glow of a nearby street-light, a candid admiration come into his eyes. There were no words needed for her to feel completely beautiful and lovable. And she had spent so much time doubting herself in both respects that she could never tell him what his silent validation meant to her. He clinched it when he simply asked, "Is he crazy?"

Elizabeth couldn't hold back a hefty spurt of new tears. "No, he's not crazy."

"Then what? Is he gay? Has he got a porn problem? Was he abused? What? What logical explanation is there for a man to live with *this,*" he motioned toward her with his hand, "and not be affected?"

"I don't know, Jayson. But I'm absolutely certain that he is not gay, he was not abused, and he does not have a porn problem."

"Well, okay. That's somewhat of a relief. If he was gay or into porn I would have to steal you away from him. I'm glad to know you haven't been inadvertently subjected to such horrors." He hesitated and added, "Are you sure?"

"I'm sure," she said firmly. "I started trying to figure this problem out years ago, Jayson. I have studied such things extensively. I have learned the signs. I can assure you that's not the case."

"Have you talked to him about this?"

"A little; but it's hard to talk about."

"And what does he say?"

"He just . . . doesn't like it."

"It," he said. "You mean sex. Why is it so hard to say?"

"I don't know. But it is."

"Because you've been living with a man who doesn't like it? Is that why it's hard to talk about?"

"Maybe."

"Well, I'll tell you something, Lady, if we don't learn to talk about *it* we're going to lose our children to *it*. You would be stunned to know the questions Macy has asked me—things that have come up at school."

"She's not even in junior high."

"No. She attends a relatively decent school in Los Angeles. And she has come home with questions about things that I would be shocked to hear Drew bring up."

"Oh, good heavens," Elizabeth said and briefly put a hand over her mouth.

"What we heard in school was much more mild, and it didn't start coming up until we were almost adults," he said. "But things have changed. The point is, if we don't talk to our kids about that stuff appropriately, then they will get the crude, distorted version from their peers. We try to protect our kids from bad movies and books and television, but do we realize what they're assaulted with everywhere they turn when their parents aren't around? We can do our best to protect them, but burying our heads in the sand isn't going to do that. Ignorance is not bliss. We have to teach them how to handle it, not to hide from it. If they don't know how to make good choices now and handle what's out there, they'll never be able to cope with such things when they are adults. Macy's attempts to talk to her mother have been answered with things like," and he raised his voice to mimic Debbie, "'Oh, don't say such things; that's so disgusting.' So what does that teach her? Sex is disgusting, but she's going to want it anyway, so how does that make her feel about herself? Debbie doesn't want to talk about sex; she just wants to sleep around. The point is that these kids are not growing up in the same world we did, and it hasn't been all that long since we were growing up in this world." He cleared his throat and said more softly, "Okay, I'm stepping down off my soapbox now. I know that doesn't have anything to do with what you just told me—except that there's obviously a problem in your marriage, and it's not going to get solved if you don't learn to talk about it. I assume if he doesn't like sex, he doesn't like to talk about sex either. Most people don't talk about it; they just do it."

They were both silent for a couple of minutes. Jayson attempted to fully absorb and accept what she had told him. He couldn't help his incredulity when he said, "He doesn't *kiss* you?"

"No, he doesn't."

"But . . . you had to kiss to get married, right? Didn't he kiss you when you were dating, engaged?"

"Yes, he kissed me when we got married. It was one of those quick, lips-barely-touching sort of things. It's the way I would kiss my father. And that's how he kissed me when we were dating. I naively assumed that he was just being a gentleman and that once we were married, he would lighten up. We talked about everything, Jayson. I was very clear on communicating my beliefs and expectations on every matter I could think of—except that one. I just assumed that people got married and had a good sexual relationship."

"So, I take it the honeymoon wasn't what you'd expected." He said it almost lightly, but she put her head down and sobbed. The disappointment and rejection she'd felt as a new bride still hurt deeply. "Talk to me," he urged gently.

"It was just . . . well, I have to admit that after what had happened between me and you, my expectations were . . . well, let's just say my expectations were not even remotely met. It completely lacked any . . . intimacy . . . or love." She sighed and wrapped her arms around her knees. "It happened twice on our honeymoon. Fortunately a pregnancy resulted. If I was a woman who had a difficult time getting pregnant, we'd be sunk. It didn't happen again until Bradley was three."

"Not once?"

"Not once. He admits that he's not a touchy person. He admits that he doesn't like it, and that his stand is not necessarily normal. He believes that sex is for the purpose of bringing children into this world, and for that reason he's willing to do it."

"And what do you think?" Jayson asked.

New tears fell. "I don't know what to think."

"Well, I'm no expert, but I can tell you what my mother taught me."

"Okay," she said, turning to look at him.

"Do you believe that God created us as human beings?" he asked.

Elizabeth had never thought about that too deeply, but she instinctively believed that was true. "Well, yes."

"Then why do you suppose He created us—men and women—to feel such pleasure?" While she was thinking about that, he said, "He created us with a need to love and be loved. And when that need is kept within marriage, it's sacred and beautiful. It is not only for the creation of children, Elizabeth, but for the expression of love between a man and a woman who are committed to each other."

"That makes sense," she said.

"My mother went through an immense amount of counseling for sexual abuse," Jayson said. "She worked very hard not only to heal, but to know what was true and healthy in regard to such things, if only so she could teach her children and break the negative cycles."

"She's an incredible woman," Elizabeth said.

"Yes, she is."

"And she succeeded, you know. She has incredible children."

"I don't know about that, but . . . I do know that the situation you're in is not normal or healthy. Robert acknowledges that it's not normal, but does he realize how it's affecting his wife? If you have normal needs, and he's not meeting them, how can a marriage survive that way? You're starving and desperate, and if you don't do something about it, you're going to end up doing something you'll regret."

Elizabeth took a good, long look at Jayson and felt the irony of the situation envelope her. While she had struggled, year after year, with the blatant lack of affection in her marriage, she had been unable to keep Jayson out of her thoughts. Even when she'd consciously fought them, they had held her bondage in the far recesses of her mind. And now she could see how those thoughts and feelings had set her up for near disaster. She was immeasurably grateful for his discipline and firm resolve. But all she could think to say was, "You mean like . . . throwing myself into your arms and . . . making an utter fool of myself."

"I wasn't looking at it exactly like that, but . . . obviously that's not the way to solve the problem. You need to go home and work this out with your husband." His voice saddened but held conviction as he added, "I can't be the other man in your life, Elizabeth. As tempting as it is, I can't do to Robert what somebody else did to me. There is no marriage problem big enough to justify betrayal. If there's something wrong, it needs to be addressed."

"And what if it's not fixable, Jayson?"

"Then you've either got to live with it or get a divorce. If you get a divorce, you've got to do it for the right reasons, and with careful consideration for the children." He looked down. "That's my opinion. You need to do what you feel is best."

Elizabeth let that sink in for a couple of minutes, then said, "So, you don't think there's something wrong with me?"

He made a scoffing noise. "Wrong with you? What would be wrong with you?"

"I don't know. I just . . . I can logically add it up in my head, Jayson. I can think it through and accept that this is his problem, not mine. This is about him, not me. But emotionally, I struggle with . . ." Emotion overtook her again. "Maybe I'm not . . . pretty enough, or—"

"Oh, give me a break," he interrupted, almost sounding angry. "You are the most beautiful woman I have ever known in my life."

She turned to look at him. "You really mean that."

"I really mean that," he said firmly. "And I bet if you ask Robert, he'll tell you the same thing."

"Not necessarily. He's very kind, but I can't hear him saying something like that."

"Well, I'm sure he's thinking it," Jayson said, and Elizabeth could only appreciate his efforts to make her feel better.

A minute later she said, "So, you think I should talk to Robert, very straight and up front about how difficult this is for me."

"Yes, I do. And in my opinion, if he really loves you, he'll be willing to compromise to some degree. If the problem is as bad as you tell me, I think he could use some counseling. If he's willing to do that, then you've got something to work with."

"And if he's not?" she asked. "How can I leave a man who is otherwise such a fine husband and father?"

"That's a decision you have to make, Elizabeth. Like I said, you've either got to get help and live with it or get a divorce. I think any decent marriage counselor would tell you that sex is a vital part of a good relationship; you can't pull that thread out without having the tapestry unravel. It's my opinion that if he disregards your needs once he knows what they are, then the problem is more than just sex." He paused and added cautiously, "Under the circumstances, some counseling probably wouldn't hurt you either." He then attempted to lighten the mood by saying, "You *are* a passionate woman." For clarification he added, "You always were, you know. You were passionate about everything you did. You were passionate about acting and singing and music and . . . life. Just . . . everything."

Elizabeth sighed and knew he was right. And she was married to a man who was passionate about nothing. She felt compelled to admit, even though it was difficult, "I got just what I wanted, you know."

"What's that?"

"I wanted a life that was stable, secure, predictable. Well, it's certainly that. I got exactly what I wanted."

Jayson couldn't think too deeply about the ramifications beneath that statement. "Is that so bad?" he asked. When she didn't answer, he added, "It wouldn't be if it weren't for this one problem. You did nothing to warrant this, Elizabeth. It's just life. What did my mother do to deserve marrying some alcoholic imbecile who beat her? You just have to do everything in your power to make it right and break the bad cycles."

Elizabeth looked at him firmly and asked, "What do you want me to do, Jayson?"

"I already told you. I think you should—"

"No. I know what you think I should do. I need to know what you *want* me to do."

Jayson swallowed carefully and said, "I want you to go home and work it out. I want you and Robert to be happily married and have three more babies and raise these kids the way your dad raised you."

Elizabeth tightened her gaze on him and said, "I think that's the first time you've ever lied to me."

He looked away abruptly and said, "I didn't lie to you."

"Okay, well . . . it's not the whole truth, then. I understand what it's like to do your best to be noble and to say what you know is the best thing. Maybe it's irrelevant, Jayson. I know what I have to do. I know what's the right thing to do, and I know you would never do anything to hurt me. But . . . I just need to know . . . if you could have it any way you wanted . . . what would you have me do?"

Jayson erupted to his feet, actually frightened by the way his heart reacted to that question. She'd hit a nail right on the head. There was a part of him that knew neither of them could ever be truly happy by leaving divorce and destruction in their wake—the way Debbie had done. But there was a base, human part of him that knew the answer to that question. Still, he felt hesitant to say it, even though something inside of him knew she needed to hear it. If she'd spent her entire marriage feeling unloved and unwanted, maybe she just needed to know the truth.

"What do you want?" she asked again. "Is it so difficult to tell me?"

"Maybe," he said and turned to face her. She remained sitting on the ground while he stuffed his hands into the pockets of his jeans and looked down at her. "First I have to say that I really meant what I said. I want you to go home and work it out, because I want you to be happy. And putting your marriage commitment first is the most likely way to ensure your happiness. In my opinion, that's just the order of the universe. Now, with that said, I'll tell you what I want, Elizabeth." He lowered his voice to an intense whisper. "I want to tell you that he's had his chance and he blew it. I want to go belt him in the face for neglecting you and leaving you alone and hurting. If I were your husband I would make you feel more loved, more beautiful, more adored than you could possibly imagine."

Jayson watched the tears fall down her face.

Elizabeth sighed deeply and said, "You already have made me feel more . . ." her voice broke, "loved, and more beautiful, and more adored than I had ever imagined possible. And this feeling isn't temporary, Jayson. It's real and I'll never forget it, because you *didn't* resort to doing something wrong to prove those things to me. I know you love me enough to do what's right, and what's best." She stood up and looked into his eyes. "My father once told me that when a person is willing to sacrifice their own wants for another person's happiness, that was the measure of true love." She put a hand to one side of his face. "Thank you, Jayson. Now, I think I need to get home. My husband will be worried about me if he wakes up and finds me gone."

Jayson sighed and felt a deep peace insulate his frustrations. He turned and followed her back to the car, where he opened the door for her. Then he walked around and got into the passenger side. When she started the car, she gasped to see that it was nearly two in the morning.

"Where are you staying?" she asked, pulling out onto the road.

"I haven't got a room yet, but I'll manage."

"I'm sure you could manage, but why don't you just come home with me. There's a nice sleeper sofa in the basement. It's private; there's a bathroom down there that nobody uses. That's where my dad sleeps when he stays." She smiled. "I'll cook breakfast for you."

"Will Robert be there?" he asked, not willing to subject himself to any further temptation. "I assume he has to leave for work a lot earlier than I will be waking up."

"Tomorrow's Saturday," she said. "He'll be there."

"Good, I'd like to meet him. You talked me into it."

Elizabeth smiled and took his hand. "I love you, Jayson. You're the best friend a girl could ever ask for."

"I love you too, Lady," he said, pressing her hand to his lips. "And the feeling is mutual."

Elizabeth drove back to the theater where Jayson got into his car and followed her to the home where she lived. It was larger than average and seemed nice from what he could tell in the dark. He watched her car disappear into the garage. He parked in the driveway and went to the front door, which she opened. She led him down the stairs to the basement, and for a moment his memories of being in the home of her youth and going to the music room were so strong he could taste them. She made certain he had everything he needed, then she pressed a kiss to his cheek, saying, "Thank you . . . for everything."

"Thank *you*," he said.

"Sleep as late as you want . . . although I can't make guarantees about the noise level upstairs."

"Don't worry about it," he said. "I'll see you in the morning."

Elizabeth went upstairs and quietly got ready for bed. She slipped beneath the covers and silently recounted the events of the evening. For the first time in years she felt hope and a determination to make her marriage better. And there was something strangely comforting about knowing that Jayson Wolfe was safely beneath the same roof. Oh, how she loved him! He truly *was* the best friend a girl could ever ask for.

She woke to daylight and found Robert sitting on the edge of the bed, pulling on his shoes.

"Good morning," she said.

"Good morning." He smiled and pressed a kiss to her cheek. "Did you have a good time last night?"

"I did, actually," she said. "Where are you going?"

"I promised Bradley some batting practice," he said.

"Okay," she said. "I'll cook some breakfast." As he moved toward the door, she hurried to add, "Oh, Jayson's here. He slept in the basement."

"Oh," Robert said with a tone of pleasant surprise. "I'll finally get to meet him. Let us know when breakfast is ready. I think Trevin is still asleep."

Elizabeth got up and dressed quickly in her household uniform of jeans and a button-up shirt that she'd stolen from Robert. She didn't know why she liked to wear his shirts; she just did. She barely put a brush to her hair and went to the kitchen to find Trevin standing in front of the open refrigerator, yawning.

"Hey there, buddy," she said. "How are you?"

"Fine," he said through another yawn. She sat down and pulled him onto her lap and talked with him for several minutes before he declared that he was hungry. She fixed him a piece of toast and told him to get dressed and then he could have pancakes and bacon. She watched him scurry away and felt deeply grateful for the life she'd been blessed to live. And equally grateful that she wasn't having to face a guilty conscience for doing something stupid the previous night. She had Jayson to thank for that.

* * *

Jayson was surprised at how quickly and deeply he slept, in spite of the mixture of emotions consuming him. He woke to the sound of little feet running over the floor above him. He was reminded of Macy and wondered if she was having a good time perusing museums with her mother.

Jayson got up and made the bed he'd slept in before he took a quick shower and went upstairs. The smell of bacon teased him as he opened the door at the top of the stairs and was struck with a great amount of sunlight. Closing the door quietly behind him, he took in his surroundings in daylight. Looking in one direction he could see the front door and a staircase that rose from the entry hall. He could also see into a room where one side of a grand piano was visible. Of course she would have a piano, he thought, feeling a sudden urge to play it, but he figured he'd do well to resist. Looking in the other direction, he could see a dining area with a beautiful oak table; the flowers he'd given her last night were in a vase in the center of it, and beyond it glass doors revealed a spacious backyard. And there were windows everywhere, filling the house with sunlight. It just felt like Elizabeth.

Jayson took a few steps and paused to look at several framed photographs artistically arranged on the wall in the hallway. Among them he wasn't surprised to find a few from their high school days, with him and Drew and Derek in them. He *was* surprised to see one of himself that he knew had been in a magazine. He thought she was a little crazy for putting such a thing on the wall, but he felt somehow comforted to see evidence that she was mindful of him.

Hearing noises from the kitchen, he felt sure he'd find her there. He was about to move in that direction when a young boy with curly blond hair came running down the stairs, decked out with a plastic Viking helmet and shield and wielding a plastic sword. He ran past Jayson, apparently oblivious to anything but his quest, yelling at the top of his lungs.

Jayson chuckled, then heard Elizabeth speak to be heard above the child. "Okay, that's good. If you're going to be that loud, take it outside."

Jayson watched him go out through the sliding glass door, leaving it wide open. He moved toward it to close it, but Elizabeth got there first. She slid the door closed then hesitated, apparently watching something outside. Her feet were bare, and she wore faded jeans and a dark green shirt that looked like it belonged to her husband. It hung past her hips, and the sleeves were rolled up nearly to her elbows.

"Good morning," he said, startling her. "Sorry," he said when she gave him a scolding glare. "I guess my entrance got lost in the din of the mighty warrior."

Elizabeth laughed softly. "I figured if you weren't awake already, you would be by now."

"I was awake," he said.

"How did you sleep?"

"Very well," he said, moving beside her to see what she might be looking at.

"How did *you* sleep?" he asked.

"Fine . . . all things considered."

Jayson focused on the view outside the window and felt something swell inside of him. He recognized Robert and the boys from many photographs. Robert was pitching a baseball to Bradley, who was trying futilely to hit it with a bat. Robert went down on one knee next to the boy and gently showed him how to adjust his swing, then he moved across the lawn and pitched again. The boy hit the ball, and Robert cheered and applauded. Bradley's joy was evident, even though he missed the next time. Trevin was running around the lawn, oblivious to his father and brother, sometimes running between them. For several minutes Jayson just watched the scene, noting that Elizabeth was doing the same. Robert finally ran after Trevin, provoking loud laughter from the child as he squealed and ran faster. His father caught up with him and tickled him, only to have Bradley jump on his back, and then he was managing to wrestle and tickle them both while they all laughed. Elizabeth let out a spontaneous laugh, and Jayson said, "Wow. I used to have dreams like that."

"Like what?"

"Playing baseball in a beautiful backyard with my father and my brother. I hated baseball. But if my dad had been willing to play with me, I would have played just about anything."

Elizabeth turned to look at him. "I'm sorry."

"For what?" he asked, looking at her as well.

"That you grew up without a good father."

"You grew up without a good mother. We managed." He looked out the window and added, "But it's nice to see our children have what we didn't have."

"Yes, it is," she said and turned her attention back to the kitchen. "I'll have some breakfast ready in a few minutes."

"Don't worry about it," he said. "Can I help?"

"No, thanks." She smiled toward him. "Just make yourself comfortable."

Jayson sat on a barstool and watched Elizabeth moving efficiently around a beautiful kitchen decorated with sunflowers. She hummed as she worked, and he couldn't help wishing . . . No, he couldn't go there, he told himself. He needed to accept life as it was.

The door opened, and the boys ran in. Robert followed them, calling out, "Get yourselves washed up for breakfast."

Robert closed the door, then his eyes focused on Jayson. For a split second, Jayson wondered if he might feel some kind of skepticism or concern from this man. In truth, he had no idea of the dynamics of their marriage and how his friendship with Elizabeth fit in. But Robert offered a genuine smile; even the look in his eyes was genuine as he eagerly reached out a hand, saying, "You must be Jayson."

Jayson stood and accepted the handshake. "Guilty," he said, smiling. "And you are obviously Robert," he added. "It's so good to finally meet you."

"And you," Robert said. "I've heard so much about you, and yes, it was all good."

Jayson wanted to say the same, but after what he'd heard last night, he had some reservations. Instead he said, "You have a beautiful home . . . and a couple of fine sons."

"Yes." Robert laughed softly. "They're great kids. They give me lots of exercise." He moved to the kitchen sink to wash up, saying, "Make yourself at home, Jayson." While he was drying his hands, he said to Elizabeth, "Oh, Diana called last night. She said she would be dropping by on her way to work this morning to return that stuff she borrowed."

Elizabeth gave Jayson a cautious glance and said, "Her timing's impeccable. Do you think she had ESP about there being a rock star in the neighborhood?"

Robert chuckled. "Probably. Maybe Jayson would prefer to hide when she comes."

"On the contrary," he said, "I wouldn't want to miss the fun."

Robert leaned his forearms over the bar and said to Jayson, "So, do you have fun with the fame thing? I imagine it would get tedious."

"Both," Jayson said, surprised at how comfortable he felt talking to this guy. "I never really sought after fame; I just wanted lots of people to love my music. But one goes with the other. It's nice to be recognized sometimes and to know that people have enjoyed or appreciated what I've done. At other times it can be hard. It all depends on the people. Most are very gracious and appropriate. Some can be a real pain."

"Like Diana," Elizabeth said, flipping pancakes.

"No, Diana was perfectly gracious," Jayson said.

"You mean they come more gaga than Diana?"

"You have no idea," Jayson said with a comical scowl that made Robert chuckle.

"Well, you have no idea how Diana has become a fanatic *Gray Wolf* groupie. Of course, Barry is her idol of worship."

"Of course," Jayson said.

"Oh, but tell him about the tattoo," Robert said while he was getting dishes out of the cupboard.

"Oh, not a tattoo!" Jayson said. "What? A wolf, right?"

"No, that would have been tasteful," Elizabeth said. "If I believed in tattoos, that is. Barry signed his name on her upper back with a black marker; she came home and had it tattooed."

"Oh, I'm going to be sick," Jayson said. "That is pathetic. Does she realize he wouldn't remember her three days later? Does she have any idea that he finds a girl in every city?"

"He really does that?" Robert asked, appalled.

"He really does," Jayson said. "He's a fantastic musician, so I try to overlook his personal habits. It's none of my business, but it still makes me sick."

"Yeah, that's pretty sad," Robert said, setting the table.

"Can I help?" Jayson asked.

"No, you're fine," Robert said, but Elizabeth slid a pitcher of orange juice and a big spoon across the counter toward him.

"Stir that," she ordered, "until the concentrate thaws and it's mixed well."

"Yes, ma'am," he said, and Robert chuckled.

The boys ran into the kitchen very noisily, and Jayson was reminded of himself and Drew as children. They both stopped when they realized somebody strange was sitting there. It was Bradley who said, "Hey, you're that guy my mom's always watching on TV."

Jayson saw Elizabeth smile. Again he heard Robert chuckle. Jayson just smiled and said, "I have been on TV a few times, but just between you and me, I think your mom needs a new hobby."

"Do you play the guitar?" Trevin asked with a sparkle of intrigue in his eyes.

"I do," Jayson said. "Do you?"

With chagrin, the boy said, "Mom said I can't have a guitar until I learn to play the piano and the violin first."

Jayson suppressed a smile and said, "Your mother is very wise. You'll be able to play the guitar much better if you learn those things first."

"I will?" he asked with excitement.

"Yes, you will," Jayson said.

"I've told him that a dozen times," Elizabeth said, "but he doesn't believe me."

"He hasn't seen his mother on TV," Robert pointed out.

"So, do we have budding musicians in the family?" Jayson asked.

"Maybe," Elizabeth said.

"Oh, they get it from their mother," Robert said with enthusiasm. "She's taught them herself."

Jayson comically glared at Elizabeth and said, "You've been keeping secrets from me."

"Oh, by the way, Jayson, I'm teaching my children how to play music, although they have had lessons elsewhere, as well."

"Do I get a sample while I'm here?" he asked.

Robert interjected, "I was wondering the same about *you.*"

"What?" Jayson asked.

"Whether we get a sample while you're here. I'd really love to hear you play something. But only if you're comfortable with that."

"Oh, he'll play," Elizabeth said. "If he wants anything to eat, he'll play."

"I could go to McDonald's, you know," Jayson said.

"My breakfast is much better." She tossed a smile toward him.

"Okay, I'll play," Jayson said. "You talked me into it."

CHAPTER 8

Jayson thoroughly enjoyed breakfast with the Aragon family. Observing the interaction among them, he could easily see what Elizabeth had meant when she'd told him what a good man Robert was. In fact, he practically glowed with goodness. And it was so genuine. Growing up with an alcoholic father, and surviving in the music industry, Jayson had learned to read false diplomacy in people. And this guy was as sincere as he was kind and full of love for his wife and children. He hoped deep inside that the problem between them could be solved—or at least a reasonable compromise found. It would be a crime to break up such a beautiful family.

During the meal, Robert asked if Jayson was in any hurry to leave. He admitted that he wasn't, but he didn't want to intrude on any plans they might have.

"Oh, we'd love to have you stick around," Robert said. "The boys have been begging me to barbecue some hamburgers. I'm not much of a cook, but I can do a pretty decent burger on the grill. And I was thinking of taking the boys to a game this evening. Why don't you come along and just stay until tomorrow?"

Jayson caught an encouraging glance from Elizabeth and said, "Well, I certainly don't have anything to hurry home to. That sounds nice. Thank you."

Jayson insisted on helping wash the dishes. He was washing the pancake griddle when the doorbell rang and Robert went to answer it. Jayson could hear him say, "She's in the kitchen."

Elizabeth added softly, "Here goes."

She just kept loading the dishwasher, and he worked on rinsing the suds off of the griddle as he added, "Oh, you love having a rock star washing your dishes."

"Yes, I do actually," she said. "But we don't need the world to know about it."

Diana came into the kitchen, saying, "I'm sorry I kept this stuff so long. I finally got some cleaning done and . . ." She plopped an armful of clothes and videotapes onto the counter, then froze. She said to Elizabeth, as if she didn't know, "Jayson Wolfe is in your kitchen."

Elizabeth glanced toward Jayson as if she'd not noticed and said, "So he is. Washing dishes, apparently. Don't go calling the tabloids."

Jayson sniggered and glanced over his shoulder. "Hello, Diana."

"Hello, Jayson," she said as he turned to lean against the counter while he dried the griddle with a clean towel. "How's Barry?"

"I'm glad to say that I have no idea. We have been working together far too much and driving each other crazy. We are now both on vacation on separate continents."

Diana gave a little laugh and added, "When you see him, tell him hello for me."

"I'll do that," he said, not bothering to add that he knew Barry's response would be a baffled, *Who?*

"Well, I've got to get going," Diana said as if she sorely regretted it. Jayson just smiled and waved at her as Elizabeth ushered her from the room.

She came back a minute later and said, "You do look good with a dishtowel in your hand."

He lifted his brows comically, then twisted the towel and tried to flip her with it. She laughed and dodged it, but he chased her until he managed to get her at least twice. "You're cruel, Jayson Wolfe."

"Yes, I know. Just ask my ex-wife."

Jayson found he enjoyed Saturday with Elizabeth's family far too much. It reminded him of the days in his youth that he'd spent with her and Derek and their father. It was home in a way he'd never known. While Robert manned the grill, Jayson helped Elizabeth put together a green salad and a pasta salad, and they sat in the yard at a little picnic table and ate. Then they played croquet, made brownies, and jumped on the trampoline.

"Macy would love this," Jayson said to Elizabeth while he was methodically jumping up and down in his bare feet as she sat in a lawn chair nearby.

"You should come again and bring her. We've got plenty of room."

"I just might do that," he said, and she smiled.

That evening they all went to a baseball game. Jayson was no more fond of sports than Elizabeth, but it was a joy to see the boys thoroughly enjoying themselves, and Jayson appreciated the interaction between them and their father. Beyond Will, he'd never been exposed to an example of a good father. He found he was actually learning something.

On Sunday morning, Robert begged Jayson to play something for them. "I'd really love to hear the song you did at Derek's funeral. I know it's personal for you, but we are practically family, right?"

"Of course," Jayson said and was surprised to have Elizabeth give him a thumbs-up. "I'd be happy to do it," he said. "But only if I get to hear a song from these boys."

They all gathered in the front room around the piano, and Jayson insisted that the boys go first. Elizabeth accompanied them on the piano while they played two different violin duets that Jayson figured sounded pretty good for kids that age. Robert and Jayson both applauded and cheered ridiculously loudly. Each of the boys did a short piano piece and received even more applause.

When Jayson sat at the piano, he said lightly, "This is just a little something I put together for my mother's birthday."

"Oh stop trying to be humble and just play it," Elizabeth said, making Robert laugh.

Jayson adjusted himself on the bench and began to play. Elizabeth quickly became lost in memories so intense that she couldn't hold back tears. Robert handed her a tissue and held her hand. She was well aware of Robert's astonishment as the song progressed. And how could Elizabeth ever forget her own wonder the first time she'd seen Jayson play this way? He was amazing, pure and simple.

Looking back and forth between Robert and Jayson, she decided she'd almost become accustomed to being with them both at the same time. The time Jayson had spent with them had held a certain surreal quality, although she wasn't terribly surprised at how well the two men got along. She felt certain that it was good for Jayson to see this perspective of her life—especially after what they had talked about Friday evening. And it was good for her to have him in her home.

Jayson humbly brushed off Robert's compliments about his talent, and he let Elizabeth talk him into playing "Harmony," as well as a few songs he'd written that actually worked solo on the piano. But he finally had to give it up and be on his way.

Driving home was far more difficult for Jayson than he'd antic-ipated. Home to what? Of course, everything would be better when Macy returned. But in the meantime, he just felt alone and lonely. He'd only been home an hour when he called Elizabeth to thank her for the wonderful visit. She thanked him for his sound advice and promised to be doing something about it soon. When he ended that call, he dialed Will's number. They talked for a long while, and when he admitted to his present struggle, Will said, "I struggle with that every day. Why don't you hop a plane and come and stay with me for a while?"

Jayson wondered why he hadn't thought of that. Will didn't even have to talk him into it. He was on a plane to Oregon the next day, and had a marvelous time, even though Will had to be at work during the days. By the time Jayson returned to Los Angeles, both Macy and his mother had returned home, and he felt more relaxed and at peace when he didn't have to be alone. The band was soon back at work, preparing for the release of a second album, but with plenty of time to do it. Months slipped by while he found life fairly pleasant. Elizabeth had let him know that she'd had some heartfelt conversations with her husband concerning the problems in their marriage. He had agreed to get some professional help, and she felt better just knowing that Robert cared enough to do something about it. She wished she had been willing to speak more forthrightly about the issue a long time ago, and the self-respect to admit that there was a problem. Whenever the subject came up, he told her he was proud of her and wished her the best. And when Elizabeth called to tell him she was expecting a baby, Jayson shared in her joy.

On two different occasions Jayson took Macy for a visit to Phoenix. She seemed to enjoy her time in Elizabeth's home, and their two families actually meshed rather well. He shouldn't have been surprised seeing as how his family and Elizabeth's had practically been one many years earlier. On the second visit, Leslie went with them. Elizabeth, Leslie, and Macy went shopping together and to a chick flick while Robert, Jayson, and the boys went to a game. Jayson especially liked the way Trevin had warmed up to him. The child often sat on his lap and asked him questions about music that were far beyond what would be expected from a boy his age.

The release of *Gray Wolf's* second album was every bit the success they had been hoping for, and a concert tour was soon underway. Elizabeth found this one an entirely new adventure for her, since most of the music had been written in the years since she and Jayson had been dating. The first single to hit the radio waves was upbeat, and it was great dance music, even though the lyrics had a poignancy that touched her deeply. She loved the song, and she loved to hear Jayson sing it, especially from the car stereo.

The second hit single was titled, "Weird," and she knew it well. The third was another poignant experience, and Elizabeth wouldn't even allow herself to consider whether it had been written about her. Instead she just enjoyed the music, certain his source of inspiration was simply something abstract and hypothetical. *Regret wets my eyes and stings a trail to my heart, where dusty caverns cling . . . to wondering how it might have been . . . if I had only seen . . . the power to be found in one decision. With such precision, I chose wrong. Now the nights are long . . . and the days are weighted down with thoughts of you.*

This time when *Gray Wolf* came to Phoenix, Robert went to the concert with Elizabeth, and they took the boys along. The family went backstage afterward, and then they all went out for a late dinner. More and more, it truly felt as if she and Jayson were brother and sister. It felt natural and right, and a great blessing to all of them.

About the time the tour ended, Jayson found out through Will that Robert had been laid off at the accounting firm where he'd worked for years. He was applying for jobs all over the country, and they had the house on the market. When he talked to Elizabeth, she was positive and cheerful about it, but months later, Robert still hadn't found a job, and the situation was becoming desperate. The unemployment had run out about the same time that Elizabeth gave birth to a healthy baby girl with no medical insurance to cover the costs. Jayson wanted to help, but something kept him from offering. He didn't want to cross any lines that Elizabeth wouldn't want him to cross. He knew that Will had helped them some, but in spite of doing fairly well, he'd done all he could without putting himself in a difficult situation. And then an idea occurred to Jayson, and he called Blake to have him check into it. He was appalled to realize that something so significant had been overlooked, but then he wondered if it was a blessing in disguise that it hadn't come up until now. He just hoped that Elizabeth would see it that way.

* * *

Elizabeth forced herself to gain her composure when the phone rang.

"Hi, honey," her father said, and the tears quickly came again. With him there was no need for pretenses. They talked for a few minutes about the situation, and then Will said, "I just got something interesting in the mail."

"What's that?" she asked, glad for a distraction.

"I've got a letter from the accountant who handles all the finances for *Gray Wolf.*" Elizabeth's attention was immediately piqued. "There is a copy of a page from the original record contract, dated more than four years ago, and a letter explaining that a stipulation had been put in right from the start, but it had been overlooked. He apologizes for the oversight and has enclosed a check."

"A check? What for?"

"The portion of royalties for Derek's contribution in writing some of the music."

Elizabeth gasped and realized that she felt angry. "I'd wager this is some backdoor attempt from Jayson to rescue me from—"

"It's not, honey. I've got the page from the contract. It was there from the beginning. And even if it *were* Jayson attempting to help you, is that so wrong? He's practically family. He's got millions. So lose your pride, girl. And thank God for a miracle. I'll have the funds transferred to your name and send it to you this afternoon."

"All of it?" she asked.

"Yes, all of it," he said firmly. "I don't need it. I have everything I want or need. I just wish I had more to help you. Now I have it." He gave a little laugh. "You're not going to believe it," he said. "Honey, there's enough here to pay off all of your debts and get the mortgage current, and you could live off the rest for a year."

Elizabeth gasped again but couldn't speak. Will said with emotion in his voice, "I guess all that putting up with the music in the basement paid off, eh?"

"I didn't get the impression you were ever putting up with anything," she said, equally emotional. "I got the impression you loved every minute of it."

"Yes, I did," he said, "but I never dreamed that Jayson's dream would bring such blessings into our lives. I wonder sometimes how losing Derek would have been without Jayson. He's remained true to his word, honey. He's been a son to me and a brother to you, and he's kept Derek alive through the music. He's one-in-a-million."

"So he is," Elizabeth said.

When she got off the phone, she sat down and cried—but for different reasons than she'd been crying earlier. Three days later when the check arrived in the mail, she cried again. She couldn't believe it. When Robert came home from another difficult day of job hunting, she showed him the check, and he cried as well. For Robert, tears were few and far between, but his relief and gratitude were deeply touching.

That evening, Elizabeth called Jayson. After he said hello, she muttered with mock anger, "You know, I really wanted to call and tell you to mind your business. I really thought you were just desperate to find some ploy to make me a charity case and rescue me. And don't tell me you have no idea what I'm talking about." He said nothing, and she hurried on. "I wanted to tell you where to get off, but I'm so thoroughly grateful that I can only say thank you. I don't know what we would have done. The next step was for me to go back to work, but—"

"But who would bake the cookies?" he asked.

Elizabeth gave an emotional laugh. "Cookies or not, I could never make enough to get us out of the hole we've gotten into. So . . . thank you, Jayson."

"I don't know why you're thanking *me*. It's not my money. It's Derek's, and he would want you to have it. If you're going to thank anybody, thank God. Funny how it occurred to me that maybe nothing had ever been done about that."

"Yes, that is funny, isn't it."

A month later, Robert got a job with an excellent, well-reputed firm in a city half an hour south of Salt Lake City, Utah. The firm was willing to pay all of their moving costs, and they paid for Robert and Elizabeth to make a trip to the area to find a home. Following an exhausting search, they found what Elizabeth felt was absolutely perfect. And Robert agreed. The night after they returned to Phoenix, Elizabeth called Jayson with the news.

"How's the baby?" he asked right off.

"She's perfect," Elizabeth said. "I'm not getting much sleep, but she's doing great." She hurried to add, "Guess what?"

"Robert got a job," he guessed.

"Yes!" she said exuberantly. "And in many ways it will be better than the last one. And guess what else?"

"You're moving!" he said with exaggerated enlightenment.

"Well . . . duh! But we already bought a house, since this one finally sold last week. Can you believe the timing?"

"It's a miracle," he concluded firmly.

"So, guess where I'm moving."

"Alaska," he said, and she laughed. "New York."

"No! It's in the western United States."

"Nevada," he said.

"No, but you're getting close."

"Utah."

"That's it."

"Utah?"

"That's right. We'll be living less than an hour from Salt Lake City."

"Ahh!" he said with exaggerated fear. "You'll be overrun by Mormons!"

"Not necessarily," she said with a little laugh. "We already met several of our new neighbors. They were very kind, very normal people. And the house is beautiful. It's Victorian style, with a wraparound porch. And the backyard slopes down to a wooded area that's just dreamy."

"It sounds wonderful," Jayson said, feeling genuinely happy for her. She called him a few weeks later to tell him the move was complete, even though it could take her months to get all of the boxes unpacked. She gave him her new address and phone number, and a few days later he sent her a housewarming gift, a little porcelain statue of a woman with a violin.

With the passing of weeks, Elizabeth let Jayson know that she had settled well into her new neighborhood, and she had quickly made friends. Life seemed to be going relatively well for both her and Jayson; their children were growing, and they had each found a certain contentment in their lives. And then Jayson turned around and wondered what he'd been thinking. He felt a sick foreboding that he was looking at the first steps of a downward spiral when he learned that Rudy had been arrested for possession of cocaine, and he'd been stoned at the time of the arrest. The band was actually together with the record company executives when Jayson heard the news of Rudy's arrest, and of his being bailed out of jail by his wife. Jayson felt so thoroughly angry and betrayed that he grabbed Rudy by the collar and slammed him against the wall, snarling in his face. "You promised me no drugs when we went into this." He slammed him again. "You *promised* me!"

Rudy only looked down and apparently had nothing to say. Drew calmly removed Jayson's hands from Rudy's shirt and urged him away. Jayson was appalled later to read of Rudy's drug problem in a tabloid, and the story included a report of Jayson's outburst upon hearing the news.

Rudy's time in rehab only temporarily solved the problem. While Jayson was futilely searching for a new bass player, Barry was diagnosed with AIDS. Jayson felt equally furious with Barry, but he couldn't bring himself to let that anger show. Barry's life would now be a living nightmare, and Jayson's getting angry wouldn't change that. Barry quickly became unable to work at all, and what little hope Jayson had had that Rudy would come around soon dwindled when the drug problem persisted. A record company executive retired about this same time, and *Gray Wolf* was put into the hands of someone who simply didn't feel the passion for the band that had been there previously. The drug abuse and AIDS got all over the tabloids, and the bad publicity left the band quickly disintegrating. Jayson knew in his heart that *Gray Wolf* was his brainchild and he could find other musicians and make it work, even though there had been a certain chemistry among the band that wouldn't be easy to replace. He quickly discovered, however, that even if he found the right musicians in a big hurry, the record company simply wasn't going to back him any longer.

The final blow for Jayson came when Drew handed him an entertainment newspaper, and on the front page was the headline: *Gray Wolf Dies Painful Death*. The picture was of him, dressed completely in black, as he usually was when a camera was around. And the heading beneath the picture was a sarcastic comment about Jayson Wolfe mourning the loss of his establishment. The entire article used metaphors of death and funerals, and once he'd read it, he threw it at the wall and cursed, while Drew just sat close by, staring at the wall, saying nothing. He went to the piano and played "Funeral for a Friend," and then he cried while Drew sat beside him with a hand on his shoulder. But he wasn't easily consoled. He quickly bottled up the tears and put the pain in a place where he couldn't feel it. But he felt so angry. He felt like his right arm had been cut off—just as he'd felt when Derek had been killed, when Elizabeth had left him, when Debbie had cheated on him. It *was* like a death, and he felt so blasted angry! But at least anger was something he could handle.

He talked to Elizabeth nearly every day, and he wondered how he could ever survive without her. She told him that he didn't need record sales and a concert tour to validate his worth as a musician. Whether he could technically claim rock-star status or not, he would always be a musician. And he had a huge amount of money and many awards as byproducts of his success. She said that a day might come when he'd be grateful to not have the pressure of making records and touring the world. She told him that his years of success were only a phase of his journey through life, and that he needed to press forward and enjoy the path that his music might lead him down now. He appreciated her insight and encouragement. He knew in his heart that she was right, but still he grieved deeply.

Jayson was feeling the need to sit down with his brother and discuss where they might go from here when Drew came to him and said, "There's something I need to tell you."

"Okay," Jayson drawled skeptically, wondering why Drew was visibly nervous.

"I've got a job with a new band," he said, and Jayson sucked in his breath. "I auditioned for it last week, and I didn't say anything because I really didn't think it would work out, but . . . they like me, and I actually like them. I think it's a good thing. And before you say anything, I want to make it absolutely clear that this has nothing to do with me and you. You're my hero, Jayson. You always have been. You always will be. We'll always be brothers; we'll always be friends. But . . . like the Bible says, there is a time and season to every purpose. And I just think it's time that you and I take different paths for a while. Maybe one day down the road we'll be able to do something together again. But for now, this is what's right for me. I hope you can understand."

Jayson swallowed carefully. "Of course I understand," he said. "If you feel good about it, then it must be right."

They talked for a while longer, and Jayson managed to hold himself together until after Drew had left for a rehearsal. Then he had a brief meltdown. He and Drew had done *everything* together musically since the cradle. How could he go on without his brother? He just had to; there was no other possibility. When he had calmed down he phoned Elizabeth. Her astonishment over the news was somewhat validating, but it tempted his emotions to the surface, and he had to work especially hard to put them away.

With the passing of time Jayson struggled some with boredom, but he found a few odd jobs in the studio and was grateful to know that his expertise was respected and appreciated by many in the industry. He wrote a few songs here and there and actually had one recorded by another popular artist. It guaranteed some royalties and afforded Jayson a certain amount of gratification when it hit the top ten, but he would have preferred to perform the song himself. He found that music was his saving grace, however. As long as he could daily get his hands on the piano or the guitar—or both—he could find grounding and some level of peace.

Leslie kept Jayson busy with some projects around the house, even though he wasn't necessarily good at much of what she asked him to do. Drew was on tour with his new band when Leslie told Jayson she needed to talk to him. When she started to cry before she got a word out, he had a pretty good idea that whatever it was, he wouldn't like it. Still, he never would have dreamed that she could deliver such a harsh blow with three little words.

"I have cancer," she said, and he actually felt dizzy. While he struggled to come up with protests and questions that might have answers that would soothe him, she went on to say, "I found a lump in my breast a couple of months ago." Jayson put a hand over his mouth to keep himself from screaming. "I got an appointment for a mammogram; it was long overdue. They found a significant growth. A biopsy was done last week. I didn't say anything because I was hoping it would be nothing and I wouldn't even have to tell you." She took a deep breath and said, "I will be having a mastectomy the day after tomorrow."

Jayson watched his mother through some kind of haze while he felt himself regress nearly thirty years. He was a child again, frightened and hurting, and he needed his mother. She was there to wrap her arms around him while he cried, but he felt like he should be comforting her. He wished he could be stronger for *her.* But the very idea of *anything* being wrong with his mother seemed utterly unbearable.

Throughout the next several days, Jayson talked himself into believing that the surgery would solve the problem, that she would yet live a long and full life. When the results of the surgery revealed that the cancer had traveled into far too many of the lymph nodes, he talked himself into believing that chemotherapy would solve the problem. It would be difficult and miserable, but they would get through it, and she would grow to be an old woman. But holding his mother's hand through a visit with her oncologist left him little to believe in. This man had been treating cancer for more than thirty years. The best they could hope for was a lengthy remission if the chemotherapy was effective. He stated gently, but with no room for misconception, that Leslie Wolfe would die of cancer—he didn't know when, but he knew that she would. He asked how aggressively Leslie wanted to fight the cancer, and she replied emphatically that she would fight with everything she had, to live every day she possibly could with her family. He told her he would make arrangements to begin the chemotherapy the following day.

Jayson drove his mother home from the appointment in a state of shock. She seemed to be feeling the same way when she said nothing, didn't make a sound. He thought of all he would be willing to give up if it could spare his mother's life. He would give away every dollar he had, his piano, his guitars, even this gift inside of him that was the only truly steady thing in his life. He would give it all away if he just didn't have to give up his sweet mother.

He walked with her into the condo he and Drew had bought for her. She loved this place; she called it her palace. She set down her purse and said, "How long until your brother's tour is over?"

"Two or three months, I think. Why?"

"I don't want you to say anything to him when he calls. He has to be there. I want him to enjoy it. When he comes home, we'll tell him."

Jayson tried to imagine how he would feel to be on tour and find out later that such a thing was taking place. He tried to talk her into letting him tell Drew the truth, but she wouldn't bend.

"I know you'll talk to Elizabeth," she said. "I also need you to call William. We promised each other that we would always share our struggles. I have to keep that promise." She sighed loudly. "In fact, you should call him first. Call him now."

Jayson knew Will would be at work, but then, his mother would know that too. He was almost disappointed when Will's assistant said that he wasn't in any meetings or on the phone and she could put the call straight through.

"Hey, kid. What's up?" he asked.

"Uh . . . there's something I need to tell you," Jayson said, unable to disguise his mood.

"What's happened?" Will demanded, his voice panicked.

"There's no easy way to say it, Will. My mother has cancer." He heard Will take a sharp breath. "She's starting chemo tomorrow. The best we can hope for is . . . remission."

"No!" Will said in a voice that was hoarse and broken. There was complete silence between them for a few minutes before Will asked, "How is she taking it?"

"Not very well at the moment, but give her a couple of days, and she will be full of courage and determination. You know my mother."

"Yes, Jayson, I do." Jayson recognized the underlying heartache in Will's voice. He knew this man loved his mother, and if he'd had his way, they would have been married all these years, instead of keeping in touch by phone from different states. "Tell her I'm coming to see her," Will added.

"No," Jayson said, "I'm not going to tell her. If I tell her, she'll protest, and she'll make me call you back and talk you out of it. She doesn't want you to see her when she's anything less than at her best."

"Are you saying I shouldn't come?"

"I'm saying we shouldn't tell her. I'm saying you should just come."

Jayson ended his call with Will and immediately dialed Elizabeth. "You were right," he said.

"About what?"

"You said someday I might be grateful to not have the pressure of making records and world tours. Well, I'm grateful. But I'm not happy about it."

"What's happened?" she asked, so much like her father.

"My mother has cancer," he said, and Elizabeth started to cry. He told her everything he knew, wishing he could cry himself, but the tears just wouldn't come. He appreciated Elizabeth's perfect understanding and compassion, in spite of how hard it was to talk about. But it was most difficult to tell Macy. Leslie had been more of a mother to her than her own mother had ever been. She was understandably upset, but he realized she had her grandmother's strength and courage when she set her mind to enjoying every minute they had together.

The chemotherapy quickly proved to be hard on Leslie. Not only did she lose her hair, but she became terribly ill and weak. Jayson pretty much moved in with his mother, willing to do anything in his power to keep her comfortable and be with her all that he could. Macy was also there a great deal more than usual. She would sit on the bed with her grandmother and read aloud to her, or just hold her hand and talk. Macy also helped pick out a wig and some hats and scarves to make Leslie more comfortable around others.

Will showed up at the front door with no warning less than a week after he'd first learned of the cancer. Leslie cried when she saw him, and it quickly became evident she was grateful for his company. Jayson often found them snuggling on the couch, watching movies together or just talking quietly. He stayed for ten days, then had to return to work. A week after he left, Elizabeth came. She'd made arrangements for a daytime sitter for little Addison—or Addie, as they called her. And Robert would see that everything was taken care of when he was at home after work. She spent two full weeks with Leslie, while Jayson did his best to stay in the background and let the women enjoy their time together.

However, he learned a great deal about bedside manner and how to handle delicate situations by observing Elizabeth with his mother. She was incredible, and he loved her for that.

Leslie clearly enjoyed Elizabeth's company. A couple of times when Leslie was having a good day, Elizabeth took her out. Jayson used the time while Elizabeth was with his mother to tie up some loose ends with some musical projects, and put everything in order so that he could devote his full attention to caring for his mother if the need arose. It was difficult to see Elizabeth leave, and a few days after she left, Leslie said to Jayson, "I have a favor to ask you."

"Anything," he said eagerly.

"It could be a lot of work, but it would give us something to do besides sit here and stare at each other. I've given it a lot of thought, and it's what I want."

"What, Mother?"

"I would like you to help me go through all of my things and pare everything down, so that what I have is only what's really of value, and organized."

"It's all pretty organized anyway, but I can do that."

"Good," she said. "When that's done, do you think it would be all right if I were to stay in one of the extra rooms at your place—with you and your brother? And Macy?"

Jayson was a little surprised, but said, "I'm sure that would be fine. There's plenty of room. Why?"

"Well, whether I live five months or five years, I think I would really like us to be under one roof. I think it would be easier for you if you're going to be taking care of me, as you seem so determined to do. But that's not the biggest reason I want to be there."

"What is the biggest reason, Mom?"

She smiled and took his hand. "I don't have a piano. I need you to play for me, Jayson. Nothing could help me through this better than your music."

Jayson felt deeply comforted by her request. It certainly would simplify their lives to live under one roof. And if music would help her more than anything, then he felt capable of helping her—instead of feeling helpless and useless.

During the next few weeks, Jayson and Macy both helped Leslie go through her home and pack it up. Beyond her clothing and personal things, she kept little that wasn't sentimental. Everything else was boxed up and given to charity. Jayson put her bed into one of the two empty bedrooms in the condo he shared with Drew. Macy helped make the room feminine and comfortable and supervised the buying of a few new things to give it some flavor. Jayson put his mother's condo up for sale and was relieved when it sold quickly. Once she was comfortably settled in, Jayson began filling his time at the piano or with the guitar. Leslie would make requests and curl up on the couch and listen, often with her eyes closed, but usually with a smile on her face. Sometimes she wanted the same song over and over, but Jayson was willing to play just about anything for her. There were a few things she asked if he could learn how to play; old songs that had meaning for her. He learned to play them, and she would always zealously tell him that no gift meant more to her than when he gave her the gift of a song.

By the time Drew came home from his tour, Leslie had survived several chemo treatments and was doing a little better. He was stunned with the news, but glad to have his mother under his roof. He stayed around quite a bit, and it almost seemed like old times, except that Macy was there much of the time. But she was a light to all of them. Drew loved her dearly, and they were close in their own way. The four of them often played board games or had video parties.

When the standard chemo treatments were finally completed, Leslie gradually regained her strength, and a number of different tests and screenings revealed no further sign of cancer. Drew and Jayson conspired to do some traveling that they'd always dreamed about in their youth but could never afford, and once they were able to afford it, they'd been too busy. Drew's band was enjoying a post-tour hiatus, and he had some time to kill. They took their mother on a cruise and had a marvelous time. Then Jayson took Macy out of school, and they all went to Disney World, staying a couple of weeks in Florida.

They'd only been back from their second vacation a couple of days when Blake called very early one morning to tell Jayson and Drew that Rudy had died of an overdose. They all attended the funeral, since Leslie and Macy had both gotten to know him and his family very well. The very idea of attending *any* funeral was difficult for Jayson, and he prayed that it would be years before they had to face this with his mother. But the reasons for Rudy's death made him sick to his stomach. Seeing the heartache of his wife and children was pathetic, because Rudy's death was such a waste. Even Derek getting killed in an accident had been easier to take than the senselessness of Rudy's death.

Jayson wasn't surprised to see the story hit the press. He hadn't taken the time to call Elizabeth and tell her, but she called him, having read it in the paper.

"There was a picture of you," she said, "all dressed in black with your arm around the grieving widow."

"Is nothing sacred?" he snarled.

"Apparently not," she said. Then she added tenderly, "I'm so sorry, Jayson. I know you haven't been close to Rudy since he got into the drugs, but . . . it's got to be hard."

"Yes, it's hard," he admitted, but he couldn't say much more for fear of tapping into that place somewhere inside of him where the losses of his life were kept neatly locked away.

Some weeks following Rudy's death, Jayson heard a horrible noise coming from Macy's room and went to investigate. He opened the door to find her playing something on her stereo that sounded like noise to him—and he had made a fortune playing what Elizabeth would jokingly call screaming guitars. The noise didn't bother him so much as the three vulgar words and the sexual inference he heard in the thirty seconds he stood there before he flipped it off.

"What are you doing?" she snapped in a tone of voice he'd *never* heard her use before.

"That kind of music is not acceptable, baby."

"What do you expect me to listen to? Your stuff all day?"

"I don't care what you listen to as long as it is free of bad language and garbage. I thought that rule had been made clear a long time ago."

She then called him old-fashioned and stormed out of the house to go to her friend Megan's house. He found his mother in the kitchen and said, "My daughter just called me old-fashioned."

Leslie sniggered and stole a glance at him. "That's exactly the term I would think of," she said with sarcasm. "She'll get over it."

As the weeks passed, Jayson grew steadily more concerned. Macy *wasn't* getting over it; she was getting steadily worse. Almost literally overnight she had become a stranger to him. She started spending more time at her mother's house, and he didn't have to be a rocket scientist to figure out why. Debbie hardly paid any attention to when or where Macy was coming or going. She could listen to anything she wanted to, and liquor was all over the house. Jayson attempted to discuss the situation with Debbie, but she told him to lighten up and let Macy be a typical teenager. She called him overprotective and told him he had too much time on his hands.

Jayson was grateful to have his mother to talk to, but she admitted that her sons had given her little grief in their teen years, and she had no experience with that. She did believe that firm boundaries and consequences could often save children from their own stupidity, but Jayson found it impossible to enforce either when she was in his care less and less. When she did spend time with him, he noticed behavior that deeply troubled him. He made a point to have some very frank conversations with her—reiterations of many things he'd taught her and retaught her since she was nine or ten. He talked plainly about the inevitable heartache of drugs and drinking, smoking and sex. She responded to each point of advice with a snide, "I know all that, Dad." But he felt instinctively terrified with her attitude that seemed to say that she felt indestructible, as if the rules just applied to other people and not her. He wondered where his sweet little girl had gone, and Leslie had to remind him regularly that sometimes kids just make bad choices no matter what a parent does or doesn't do. She told him he could only do the best he could do, but that didn't make it easy. Instinctively he felt like he was losing her, and he didn't know what to do about it.

Jayson's concerns deepened dramatically when Macy showed up for one of her visits with her hair cut short and gelled straight up and dyed a ridiculous purplish color. On her next visit, she had three new holes in each ear. She started wearing gobs of hideous makeup, clothes that were as immodest as they were ugly, and he had absolutely no doubt that she was smoking and drinking. He laid awake at nights trying to figure how he could reach her. He took her away with him on a vacation, just the two of them. He felt like they'd made some progress, but she was only home a matter of hours before she was back to her snide, cynical ways. He wondered about the source of this apparent anger and self-destruction. Had he failed somewhere? Was there something he'd overlooked? And just when he'd believed it could get no worse, she became inseparable from some hideous, sixteen-year-old kid who claimed to be her boyfriend. And Jayson found condoms in her purse the same day he saw the tattoo on her shoulder. He argued with her and pleaded with her, all the while feeling sick and frantic. His fifteen-year-old daughter was having casual sex with some idiot she hardly knew, and she had admitted it outright.

After Macy had stormed out of the house, Jayson called Elizabeth and poured his heart out to her—not for the first time—about the helplessness and fear he felt on behalf of his daughter. She listened, and she shared some insights she'd heard from some of the mothers in her neighborhood, but deep inside Jayson knew he'd done everything he could do. And he feared Macy would be lost to him forever.

CHAPTER 9

Jayson answered the phone in the middle of breakfast and heard Debbie frantically say, "Oh, Jayson! She didn't come home last night."

"What?" he screeched. "When did you figure this out?"

"When I got up this morning," she said as if it were obvious.

Jayson snarled, "You can't stay up long enough to make sure your daughter comes home? She should have been in by eleven."

Debbie began a tirade, defending her exhaustion, but Jayson interrupted her. "Where did she say she was going?"

"She didn't."

"Did you ask her?"

"She's a big girl, Jayson."

"She's fifteen years old! Her mother ought to know where she's going."

"If you're going to lecture me, then—"

"I'm going to find our daughter," he said and hung up the phone. He told his mother what the problem was and hurried to the garage. Once he was in the car, he called the police and told them what little he knew. He went to Debbie's house and walked inside the second she opened the door.

"What are you doing?" she demanded, following him up the stairs.

"She's got to have phone numbers of her friends somewhere; something, anything to give us a clue. Debbie followed him into

Macy's room, crying dramatically. He found everything such a mess that it was difficult to know where to begin. He turned full circle, and a piece of paper taped to the mirror caught his attention. He stepped forward and took it down, feeling something inside of him shatter into thousands of irreparable pieces.

"What does it say?" Debbie demanded.

Jayson allowed his anger to muffle all else that tempted him to crumble here and now. In a terse voice he read, "'Dear Mom, I hate it here. I can't take it any more. I'm leaving town with Cory. I don't know if I'll be back. Love, Macy. P.S. Tell Dad I love him.'"

Jayson tossed the note to the floor and glared at his ex-wife. "What happened?" he demanded.

"I don't know what you're talking about. You can't blame me for this."

"What happened?" he repeated. "Something must have happened to push her over the edge, and I want to know what it was—not that it will make any difference now."

"She was being a little snot, like she always is these days. I told her I'd had enough, and if she didn't start behaving like a human being I was going to lock her out of the house."

Jayson squeezed his eyes closed with sudden anguish. He shook his head as he tried to imagine how Macy must have perceived such a statement. He wanted to scream at Debbie. He wanted to throw something and break it. But most of all he want to wilt onto the floor and cry like a baby, and he wasn't about to do that in front of Debbie. He rushed from the room and out to the car. He gasped for breath once he was inside with the door closed, and he told himself he needed to get home before this volcanic eruption occurred. He passed the police as he drove away, but he didn't care. Debbie could give them the news. There was nothing they could do about one more runaway, and he knew it.

He pulled the car into the garage and watched the door lower in the rearview mirror, then he pressed his head to the steering wheel and felt the unspeakable agony come from somewhere inside of him, threatening to eat him alive. He had no idea how long he sat there before he turned to see his mother opening the car door. "She's gone," he said in response to her unvoiced question. "She's run away with that . . . creep she's been sleeping with."

Leslie wrapped her arms around him and let him cry. Eventually the tears subsided into shock, and Jayson did his best to put the emotion in a place where he could cope with it. But the sorrow of losing Macy didn't relent as easily as other losses in his life. Leslie had to call Will and Elizabeth; he couldn't even make himself say it out loud. He kept telling himself that Macy would quickly realize she couldn't handle the world, and she would come home. He kept his cell phone fully charged and within his reach every minute of every day, knowing she had the number memorized and that she would call that number if she needed him. He couldn't sleep; he barely ate. His mind became filled with horrid images of what she could be subjected to out there.

A week after Macy left, Leslie insisted on taking Jayson to see a doctor. He was so plagued with insomnia that he felt nearly dead. He was losing weight. He had constant stomach pain and headaches. The doctor prescribed something to help him sleep, along with an antianxiety medication. He was finally able to sleep, and he was able to stay calm—as long as he took the drugs. But an hour didn't go by when he didn't feel sick at the realization that his baby, his only child, was out there somewhere, likely starving and cold. And he had to wonder if he would ever see her again.

When Macy had been gone nine months, Leslie's routine cancer screening showed a problem in three different places. They all turned out to be cancerous. Leslie insisted on more chemotherapy, not willing to give up without a fight. While Jayson watched his mother's health deteriorate from the treatments, he kept praying that she would live to see Macy come home. When his daughter had been gone a little more than a year, tests showed that the cancer was out of control and the chemo wasn't doing any good. The treatments were stopped, and Leslie's bedroom became laden with medical equipment. Hospice nurses were in and out of the home at regular intervals, while Jayson stayed near his mother and wondered how he could go on living without her. He found himself alone with her a great deal, since Drew was heavily involved with recording sessions. Leslie mostly slept due to the heavy pain medications. When she was awake, she wanted Jayson to play for her. He often carried her back and forth from her bed to the couch so she could listen to him play the piano. Or he'd sit in a recliner in her bedroom with the acoustic guitar on his lap that Will had given him for graduation. She told him over and over that nothing in life had given her joy like his music.

When they were told it was only a matter of days, a week at the most, Jayson called Will and Elizabeth. He'd been reluctant to tell them how bad it had become, and when he was faced with telling them the present reality, they were both understandably upset. And they were both at the front door the following morning. Through torturous days and nights of bedside vigil and a morbid anticipation, Jayson wondered how he ever would have coped without Will and Elizabeth. Drew came and went, seeming almost grateful that he had work commitments that made it impossible for him to be with his mother for very long at a time. Jayson knew he loved her, and he would do anything for her, but he and his brother had always responded differently to emotional situations. While Jayson wanted to be with his mother every possible moment, Drew seemed to put more of a priority on remembering her the way she used to be before this unspeakable evil had taken over her body, eating it alive from the inside.

As the end drew near, Jayson stopped playing music for his mother. She was mostly unconscious, and on the rare moments when she came around enough to be aware, she was either too drugged or in too much pain to care. Jayson, Will, and Elizabeth took turns sitting with her and trying to get some rest. Jayson found it impossible to sleep without taking something to help him, and he feared sleeping too deeply and missing any opportunity to be with Leslie. So he chose not to sleep. In the middle of the night he became sick of just lying there, staring at the ceiling. He went downstairs, where he'd left his guitar, certain that toying with it would ease his anxiety. He was startled to find Elizabeth in the common room at the bottom of the stairs, leaning against the piano, looking at the cabinet where his awards were kept. Among them were Derek's hat—and her red shoe.

Their eyes met as he moved off the last step. "I was hoping you'd never ask for it back," he said. "It looks good there, don't you think?"

"I suppose it's a matter of taste," she said. "It's an interesting contrast to the hat with the propeller."

"You wore red shoes; he wore a hat with a propeller. It *was* an interesting contrast."

"So it was," she said then glanced up the stairs. "Dad's with her, but I couldn't sleep. Last I checked she hadn't made a peep for hours."

Jayson could only say, "I couldn't sleep either." He picked up his guitar and sat on the couch, but he just held it.

"Did I ever tell you why I wore red shoes?" she asked, remaining on her feet.

"Was there a reason? I just thought it was because you looked so good in them."

"Oh, there was a reason," she said. "It was something one of my drama teachers once said. It really stuck with me."

Following a minute of silence he asked, "Well, are you going to tell me, or did you just want me to know there was a reason and then leave me hanging with anxiety for the rest of my life?"

"Sorry," she said. "I think the exhaustion is slowing my brain waves."

"Yeah, I know what you mean."

"We were doing *The Wizard of Oz* at the time."

"Ah, ruby slippers," he said.

"Yes, ruby slippers. But the teacher was talking to the class about the different gifts and talents that each person is given. He likened them to ruby slippers. He said there had been many times when his obsession with drama had been more like a curse in his life than a blessing, but in the long run, it had brought him a great deal of joy, and it was the very thing that gave his life some of its greatest meaning."

"Okay, I can relate to that," Jayson said. In fact, he was relating very deeply.

"He talked about Shakespeare and Beethoven . . . and Mozart. And many other great artistic people, and he said that in looking at their lives it was easy for him to imagine that they had each been given a pair of ruby slippers. Dorothy didn't want the ruby slippers, but they were given to her anyway. And eventually they were the very thing that took her home." She raised her voice to mimic the good witch of the north, who had said in the movie, "'There they are, and there they'll stay.' Or something like that."

"Wow," Jayson said, struck by her analogy in a way that was difficult to define. Then a thought occurred to him. "You know that Elton John album we're always listening to; the one with all those songs we borrowed?"

"Goodbye Yellow Brick Road?" she said, then gasped.

"That's the one. In the drawing of him on the cover, he's wearing red, shiny shoes."

"So he is," she said, recalling it well, although she'd never made the connection.

"Maybe I need some red shoes," Jayson said.

Elizabeth turned to look at him. "I think black is more your color."

"Yeah," he said with sarcasm, "the color of mourning; that's me. Is there anyone in my life that hasn't either died or left me?"

"I'm still here," Elizabeth said firmly.

He met her eyes and wanted to shout at her and tell her that she was in his life, but not the way he wanted her to be. Instead he simply said, "For which I am grateful."

"I'll see if Dad needs a break," she said and went up the stairs.

Ten minutes later Will came down the stairs and plopped onto the couch beside Jayson. "I don't think I can sleep," he said.

"Must be a plague," Jayson muttered and dramatically strummed his guitar for emphasis.

They sat together in silence broken only by Jayson's sporadic picking at the strings. Will finally said, "I know it's not a good idea to live with regret. I mean . . . you can't change the past. But," his voiced cracked with emotion and he hung his head, "how I wish she would have married me!"

Jayson stopped picking. Will wiped tears from his face and went on. "I love her, Jayson."

"Wouldn't it be harder to let her go now if she was your wife?"

"I don't know," he said. "But at least we would have had the memories of having spent some real life together. We've stayed close. Her friendship has meant a great deal to me, but . . . it could have been so much more."

Jayson knew exactly how he felt. Rather than commenting, he began to play a complex strain and softly sang the verse of a song that had once been on the top ten. *Regret wets my eyes and stings a trail to my heart, where dusty caverns cling . . . to wondering how it might have been . . . if I had only seen . . . the power to be found in one decision. With such precision, I chose wrong. Now the nights are long . . . and the days are weighted down with thoughts of you.*

"Oh, thank you very much," Will said with sarcasm. "That cheered me up."

"I didn't think either of us really wanted to cheer up," he said. "I thought we were singing the blues."

"So we are," Will admitted.

Jayson had to ask, "Do you think her reasons for not wanting to get married were mostly due to the abuse when she was a kid?"

"I think so," Will said. "You know as well as I do that in most ways she had healed remarkably well. But the scars were deep. I think she put all of her focus and energy into being a good mother; she just didn't think she could be a good wife, too. I believe she could have. I've wondered if she was simply afraid of letting me down, or of having our relationship tainted if problems came up." He sighed loudly and went on to talk about the grave issues that had troubled Leslie from an abusive childhood and an abusive marriage. Jayson's grief deepened as he pondered the horrors his mother had survived. But she had survived them with grace and dignity, and she *had* been a good mother; the best, in fact. And how could he not be grateful for that?

With the first light of day, one of the hospice nurses came to check on Leslie, then she told them that it was getting close. She likely wouldn't last through the day. Drew said good-bye to his mother while she was unconscious, and then he left the house. In spite of mutual exhaustion, Will, Elizabeth, and Jayson stayed beside her. Jayson longed for it to be over, for her to be freed from this horror, but he also longed for it to never end. While he'd done his best to prepare for the inevitable, he felt completely unprepared for this final separation.

When Leslie finally took her last breath, she was cradled in Jayson's arms while he sat in the center of her bed, weeping into her hair. He cried helplessly, feeling completely lost and alone, reluctant to let her go. Elizabeth finally managed to urge him away from the body, and Will stayed with him in another bedroom while the mortuary came and took his mother away. Then he took two sleeping pills and slept for fourteen hours. When he finally came around, the reality of planning a funeral had to be faced—although there wasn't much planning to do. Leslie had made it clear what she wanted. And she wanted the same music that had been at Derek's funeral. Jayson felt reluctant, but he was willing to honor his mother's wishes.

While planning the funeral and seeing it through, Jayson's emotions receded into an almost debilitating shock. He felt robotic, going through necessary motions, unable to feel anything at all or grasp the reality. He played "Funeral for a Friend" with intensity and passion, just the way she would have wanted him to.

Then he stood beside Elizabeth, and together they sang "Amazing Grace." He tried to find the comfort from the lyrics that he knew should be there. But he couldn't.

Will and Elizabeth stayed a couple of days beyond the funeral, but they had lives to get back to. The problem was that Jayson had no life left at all. He had no career, no daughter or mother who needed him. His brother was busy with a flourishing career, and Elizabeth had her family. Will encouraged Jayson to come to Oregon with him, to not be alone. Jayson insisted he would be fine, that he just needed some time to adjust.

For days after they left, Jayson mostly slept. He took whatever he had to in order to remain unconscious and oblivious to the emptiness. He finally put himself together only so he could get to a doctor's appointment and get more of the prescription for anxiety he'd been taking since Macy had left home. The doctor also started him on an antidepressant, assuring him that it would help get him through this difficult time.

Jayson forced himself to some kind of schedule. He slept long hours, but he made himself get up in the morning, get dressed, and eat something half decent. His only incentive was some abstract hope that his mother was somehow aware of him, and she'd be disgusted by his self-neglect. And he held onto the hope that any minute Macy might call and need him. He had to keep his life together, if only for her.

Three weeks after the funeral, Jayson and Drew were informed that Barry had died of AIDS. Jayson managed to get a grip enough to make a showing at the funeral, but he felt deeply sick over this loss, the same way he'd felt about Rudy. It was a senseless waste. He felt angry to think of these two men who had made choices that had cut their lives short. And his sweet mother, who would have chosen to live a long life, had been snatched away so cruelly.

After the funeral, Drew went to the studio and Jayson went home to a torturous silence. The anger inside of him swelled while his thoughts tumbled senselessly. He sat in front of the piano, feeling so wracked with pain he could hardly move. He'd not been able to shed a tear since his initial response to his mother's death. Everything felt tightly bottled up inside of him, as if he might explode. He toyed with the ebony and ivory of the piano, while the losses filed through his mind. Derek. Elizabeth. Debbie. Rudy. Macy. Barry. His mother. And he just felt so angry.

With no warning, the anger rushed out of him. He stood from the bench and kicked it over as he crossed the room and instinctively reached for the only object in the room capable of creating any serious damage. The fire poker. With no thought or precision he groaned and smashed the poker down on the keys. For more than an hour he mercilessly took out his pain and anger on his most beloved possession. Then he tossed the poker on the floor, sank to his knees and sobbed. With the anger worn off—or at least worn out—he sat on the floor, looked at the horror of what he'd done, and felt sick to his stomach. He felt a sudden need to leave, to get some space, to find some distance between his surroundings and the reality of his foolishness. He left Drew a note on what was left of the piano and packed a bag.

Driving up the coast toward Oregon, he felt some formless tie pulling him there, as if a huge rubber band had kept his heart attached there all these years, and it was suddenly snapping him back. He stopped at an obscure motel in northern California when he couldn't drive any longer, and with the help of a few pills, he slept soundly.

* * *

Elizabeth finally got Addie to sleep and felt exhausted. But her need to just absorb the peace was more compelling. She found Robert in the study and impulsively said, "I know it's late, but I don't want to go to bed. I want to revel in the quiet of all the children sleeping. I want to watch a movie that makes me cry, and eat crackers and smoked oysters and drink red Kool-Aid and fall asleep on the couch." She took his hand and said, "Come sit with me. Let's watch a movie together and—"

"It sounds delightful," he said with a smirk that implied he was being sarcastic. "But I'm really tired. I'm afraid you'll have to enjoy the movie on your own."

Elizabeth reminded herself to be grateful for all they shared that was good, and not to feel irritated over something that didn't matter a bit in the vast scheme of raising a family and sharing life.

"Okay," she said, kissing his cheek. "Sleep well, then."

She went to the basement with her crackers and oysters and Kool-Aid and made herself comfortable with the remote control. She was in the habit of watching movies alone, and once she became absorbed in the story, she forgot all about Robert sleeping upstairs. She was surprised to hear the phone ring. Glancing at the clock, she saw it was nearly midnight. Checking the caller ID, she expected to hear Jayson when she answered. Instead it was Drew. She couldn't recall his ever phoning her before.

"What's wrong?" she demanded.

"Well, I'm assuming he's all right. The note he left does sound reasonable, but . . ."

"But?" she pressed.

"It looks like he spent a couple of hours beating the heck out of the piano with a fire poker."

Elizabeth gasped, then put a hand over her mouth. The image made her ill. Trying to imagine what kind of pain would drive him to do such a thing put her stomach in knots.

"What does the note say?" she asked.

"Well, let me read it to you," he said and cleared his throat elaborately. *Sorry about the mess. I'll clean it up when I get back. I'm driving to Oregon. I have a sudden urge to stand on the beach. See you in a few days. Love, your little brother.* He finished, then said, "I just thought you should know. Maybe you could call his cell phone or something and check on him."

"Thank you, Drew," she said. And the moment she hung up, she *did* call Jayson's cell phone. He answered, sounding groggy, and mumbled something about being in a motel room somewhere. She let him go back to sleep, assured that he was alive and well—relatively speaking. First thing the next morning, she called her father. Will figured it was a long shot that he'd actually see Jayson at the beach, but he was going to give it a try.

* * *

Jayson found himself alone on a familiar stretch of beach, stunned by how it all looked the same. *Twenty years.* He couldn't believe it. Twenty years had passed since he'd first come to this place. Those years had been filled with unbelievable highs, and unspeakable lows, and now he had hit the bottom. He'd been a musical icon, a rock star in the truest sense. But he'd dropped like a rock, and fallen like a star. And he could do nothing but pray that he could find some reason—any reason—to keep living.

His cell phone rang, and his heart quickened as it always did with the hope that it might be Macy. But it was his agent. The opportunity she presented to him of playing guitar with a band touring Europe had its appeal, but it also had a certain irony that didn't sit well with him. On his way back to the car it started to rain. He turned his face upward and let it bathe over him, wishing it could wash away the pain.

Moving on toward the car, he froze for a moment when he realized Will was leaning against it. "What are you doing here?" Jayson demanded.

"What are *you* doing here?" Will countered. "You come to Oregon and don't even stop to pay a visit?"

"I haven't left Oregon yet," Jayson said.

They stared at each other a long moment before Will opened his arms and Jayson moved with no hesitation into his fatherly embrace. Following a long, firm hug, Jayson drew back and asked, "How did you know I was here?"

"Well, there was a definite string of gossip. Drew found your note and a hunk of firewood that used to be a piano." Jayson looked down. "He called Elizabeth, who called me. Your note did say you wanted to stand on the beach. I took a chance."

"Well, I'm glad you did," Jayson said. "I think I needed a hug."

"I suspected that maybe you would."

When the rain worsened, they got into their separate vehicles and met less than an hour later at Will's house. Jayson felt deeply comforted just to sit in Will's kitchen while he cooked pasta and they ate together. When the rain let up, Jayson asked if they could go to Derek's grave. Again Jayson was struck with the passing of time as he gazed at the dates below Derek's name. Life was moving on and leaving him stranded, somehow.

Jayson spent the night at Will's house and left early, needing to be home by evening in order to be able to work in the morning. At least he had some purpose for going home. That in itself was a blessing.

He walked into a dark, silent house and flipped on the light, deeply dreading having to face the destruction he'd inflicted in his rage. He took a sharp breath to see instead a brand-new piano, with a note left in exactly the same place he'd left the note for Drew on the old one. He couldn't help smiling as he read: *If you break this one, you're grounded, and it's coming out of your allowance. Love, your big brother.*

Jayson called Drew's cell phone and found him at the home of one of his band members. "Thanks, Bro," he said.

"A pleasure actually, little brother," Drew said. "Although I had to do some hefty politicking to get those people to have that one delivered and the old one removed before you got home."

"Well, I'm grateful."

"It's okay. I can afford it. Besides you're my hero. You're the greatest brother on the planet."

"I think it's the other way around," Jayson said.

"You okay?" Drew asked.

"Yes, actually, I think I am. I spent some time with Will. And I have a job; I start in the morning." He filled Drew in on the details, and they talked a few more minutes before Jayson ended the call and sat in front of the piano. He moved his fingers over the keys and found it perfectly tuned. Closing his eyes, he played random bits and pieces of many things, including Mozart and Elton John—and some classics from *Gray Wolf*. He knew that as long as he could play music, he could survive.

* * *

Elizabeth was busy in the kitchen while Robert and Bradley were finishing up their packing for a river trip the Scouts were taking. She smiled to hear their comfortable banter and the laughter between them. She stopped what she was doing and closed her eyes, struck with a sudden, inexplicable peace. With the changes that had occurred in her life, such peaceful moments had become common. She felt deeply grateful and in awe of the opportunity she'd had to become a part of a community that had exposed her to the greatest thing that had ever happened to her. Embracing a new religion had never been on her list of things to do in life, but now she wondered how she had ever coped without it.

Many times she had been tempted to share what she'd found with Jayson, believing deep inside that it could go far in assuaging his grief and putting his struggles into perspective. But she'd felt constrained, as if the time wasn't right, or he simply wasn't ready. And maybe he never would be. She had to accept that this might be one more aspect of their lives where they would follow separate paths. She'd not talked to Jayson for a while, but Drew had assured her that he would keep track of him and let her know if there was a problem. It seemed Jayson needed some time and space in order to deal with his mother's death. Elizabeth kept a prayer in her heart for him and tried to stay focused on her family. She couldn't deny being troubled that Robert had chosen not to have any involvement with the Church, especially when it meant more to her than anything ever had. As with everything she did, he was supportive and encouraging, but he preferred to stay at home while she went to church. The children had embraced the gospel eagerly, and were actively involved. Even Addie, as young as she was, loved going to church and being involved with everything they did.

The one aspect where Robert had become involved was the Scouting program. The Boy Scouts of America was directly integrated into the Church's program for young men, and Robert had volunteered to help out on many outings, if only to be with Bradley. And now they were preparing for a river trip that Bradley had looked forward to for weeks. Amidst their preparations she was struck with a conscious gratitude for the peacefulness of her home and the love Robert had for her and their children. It was as if the Spirit had urged her to take notice of how greatly she was blessed, and to etch this moment into her memory. She recounted all of the evidence she had that Robert was a good husband and father—a truly good man. And Bradley was so much like his father; instinctively good and kind. He was a unique young man, and she looked forward to the great things he might accomplish throughout his life. His enthusiasm for the gospel, even at such a young age, made her certain he would make a fine missionary one day. She tuned in more closely to the common, comfortable sounds of her husband and son going over last-minute checklists to see if they had all they needed, and the serenity inside of her deepened. It was as if her heart overflowed with a tangible love for both of them, and again she thought how thoroughly blessed she was. Her life was rich and full, and she was grateful.

"I think we're ready," Robert said, coming into the kitchen. Elizabeth turned toward him, startled from her comfortable nostalgia. "What's wrong?" he asked when he saw her face. Only then did she realize there were tears on her cheeks.

"Nothing," she said, laughing softly as she wiped them away. "I was just struck with how blessed I am."

Robert took her shoulders into her hands. "We certainly are," he said and kissed her brow. "Will you be all right without us?" he asked, looking into her eyes.

"Of course," she said. Seeing Trevin hovering in the doorway, she added with a smile, "Trevin will take very good care of us."

"I'm certain he will," Robert said, smiling at his second son. He turned back to Elizabeth, and something in his eyes bordered on an intensity that wasn't common for him. "I love you, Elizabeth," he said. "I couldn't ask for a better wife." Soberly noting his sincerity, she had to wonder if he'd somehow been struck with the same feelings that she had been having.

"I love you too," she said, fighting back the threat of more tears, "and the feeling is mutual." He kissed her with a touch of passion, then embraced her tightly. She felt reluctant to let him go for reasons she couldn't discern. He kissed her once more, then turned toward Bradley, who was looking impatient.

"Give your mother a hug," Robert said. "It's time we were going."

Bradley hugged Elizabeth, looking a little sheepish as he usually did with such sharing of affection. He gave her one of his winning smiles as she said, "You be careful now. I love you."

"Yeah, me too," he said with a little shrug and followed his father out the door.

Impulsively, Elizabeth stepped outside and watched them get into the SUV, thinking how she would miss them. She reminded herself they would be back in less than a week. They both grinned and waved as they drove away, and Elizabeth returned to her work in the kitchen. She quickly became busy and didn't give their farewells another thought—until three days later when the bishop and one of his counselors showed up on her front porch. She pulled the door open to see them standing together, their expressions grave.

"Hello, Elizabeth," the bishop said, and her heart quickened. He always called her Sister Aragon.

"Hello," she said, motioning them inside. "Is something wrong?" she added, closing the door.

They both looked at her but seemed hesitant to speak, as if they were each waiting for the other to say something. Elizabeth felt something change inside of her. Her memories of saying good-bye to Robert and Bradley came back to her with clarity, while something inside of her recognized now that some kind of preparation had been taking place. It was as if her spirit had subconsciously known she would never see them again, even though she could have never recognized such a premonition on a conscious level. The breadth of a second seemed eternal as her spirit absorbed all she had felt then—and what she knew now, even before the bishop said in a quavering voice, "There's been an accident, Elizabeth."

Hearing the words pressed a fearful reality into her conscious mind, mingled obscurely with the night Derek had been killed. "What . . . kind of accident?" she asked, feeling herself tremble from the inside out.

The bishop cleared his throat. "We don't know . . . exactly what happened, but . . . Robert's being life-flighted to the medical center in Provo; his condition is critical."

"And Bradley?" she asked, moving unsteadily onto the couch.

The bishop sat close beside her, and Brother Babcock sat across the room; both remained on the edge of their seats. "Bradley didn't make it," the bishop said.

Elizabeth felt her chest tighten for want of air, then she gasped. Her gasp turned to a moan, and her moan to a sob. She found herself crying against the bishop's shoulder, while Brother Babcock moved to sit on the other side of her, holding her hand. Somewhere in the midst of her attempting to accept what was happening, the Primary president showed up and was there to help the bishop tell the children what had happened. When she offered to stay with the children while Elizabeth went to the hospital, a new reality struck her. The shock over Bradley's death had momentarily distracted her from the fact that Robert was in critical condition.

The bishop and Brother Babcock took her to the hospital, while she cried tears from a source so painful that she couldn't even fathom ever being free of such pain. She heard the bishop talking on his cell phone and knew he was getting more information concerning what had happened. When he got off the phone, he gently explained what the Scout leaders could only call a freak accident. No one could say for certain how Bradley had ended up in the water without his life jacket, because he wasn't a careless boy, nor was he a show-off. But when the current sucked him under, Robert went in after him without a moment's hesitation. Elizabeth squeezed her eyes closed; that was just like Robert—a hero to the last. No, not the last, she told herself. He was still alive; he would make it through this. Surely God would not take her son *and* her husband.

When there seemed nothing more to say, Brother Babcock asked her, "Is there anyone you should call? Family? Could we help you with—"

"Oh!" she said frantically, reaching into her purse for her own cell phone. She pushed the first number on her memory dial and impatiently waited for it to connect. When it didn't even ring, but went straight to voice mail, she knew the phone was turned off. Just hearing Jayson's recorded voice gave her some degree of comfort. "Hi there. If you know who you're talking to, leave a message." Hearing the beep on the other end, she roused herself to say what she needed to say. "Uh . . . Jayson . . . I need you." Her voice broke with emotion, and she took a moment to sustain it. "I'm sorry, I . . . I'm on my way to the hospital." She recalled from visiting ward members there that the use of cell phones might not be allowed in certain areas of the hospital. She quickly added, "I might not have my phone on there, so . . . I'll just try to call you back. If you get this message, try to stay near your phone and . . . I'll talk to you soon." She hung up, then stared at the phone as if it were a lifeline.

"Is Jayson your brother?" the bishop asked gently, startling her to the fact that she wasn't alone.

"Uh . . . no, but . . . as good as. He . . . uh . . . he was my brother's best friend in high school; practically a part of the family. When my brother was killed, he just kind of . . ." She noticed the two men exchanging a concerned glance, as if to silently assess that this wasn't the first time her life had been touched by tragic death. *Tragic death?* No! Her mind screamed silently. Forcing her thoughts elsewhere, she went to the next number on her memory dial and was relieved to hear her father answer, until she was struck with what she needed to tell him. The words bubbled out with so many tears that he could hardly understand her. But he spoke gently to her, assuring her he'd be on the next plane to Salt Lake City. She reluctantly ended the call as they pulled into the emergency parking area. Brother Babcock was driving and let her and the bishop out at the door. Once inside they were told to wait. The wait dragged on, and every twenty minutes Elizabeth stepped outside to turn on her phone and see if she had any messages. The fourth time she tried, she read the words: one missed call. The number was Jayson's cell phone. She didn't bother listening to the voice message he'd left. Instead she just called him back, her fingers trembling. She heard only part of one ring before his voice said frantically, "What happened?"

The undeniable evidence of his genuine concern felt, in itself, like a balm to Elizabeth. He cared, and she knew it. The emotion that had hovered in her throat burst out with the words, "Oh, Jayson. Bradley is dead."

"No," he muttered, his voice raspy. "No, Elizabeth, no."

She cried while she sensed that he was too stunned to know what else to say. A voice of perfect compassion finally asked, "How, Elizabeth? Tell me what happened."

Elizabeth forced some composure into her voice. "It was . . . they were . . . river rafting. He drowned."

"Oh, help," Jayson muttered. He realized he was shaking while he couldn't help being drawn back to the night that Derek had been killed. Then, just as now, the grief they shared created a bond beyond any description—even with the miles between them. While his time spent with Elizabeth's sons had been minimal, the very fact that this tragic death had happened to one of *her* sons made him feel as if he'd lost his own child. He thought of his sweet Macy. The only thing that had given him any comfort at all was the belief that she was all right, that she would one day come home to him. How could he cope if he couldn't see her again?

Realizing he needed to say something, Jayson forced his voice past the knot in his throat. Still, all he could think to say was, "Oh, Elizabeth, I'm so sorry."

"Robert tried to save him," she added, knowing there was more she needed to say.

As if he sensed the sorrow behind her words, he asked in a cautious voice, "And how is Robert?"

Elizabeth's emotion bubbled out again. Jayson's heart tightened so hard and so fast he could hardly breathe. Would she tell him the worst? He knew well enough what it was like to have your spouse torn from the center of your life. When she couldn't speak, he pressed gently, "Oh, Lady, don't tell me that he—"

"He's in a coma," she finally managed to say, and he took a sharp breath. "They tell me the prognosis isn't very good, but . . ." she sobbed quietly, "I can't lose them both, Jayson. I can't. Would God take my son *and* my husband? Would He do that to me?"

Jayson wanted to tell her that He wouldn't. But he knew better than to second-guess God Almighty. He wanted to tell her not to give up hope, but even now he sensed the hopelessness of the situation. He simply said, "I don't know, Elizabeth. But whatever happens, you will get through it. You're amazing; you're strong, and you're—"

"I'm not strong," she said. "I'm falling apart. I'm—"

"As you should be. You've got every right to be falling apart." He sighed and added what he knew had to be said; she would be wondering. "I only wish I could be there to help hold you up."

Elizabeth felt her heart drop. Deep inside she'd hoped that he would be on the next flight, just as her father had promised he would be. He was her best friend, and she needed him—perhaps more than she ever had since they'd lost Derek. She knew that he would be there if he could. She swallowed carefully, determined not to whine. "Where are you, anyway?"

"Europe."

"Europe?" she echoed, wishing her voice hadn't betrayed the added despair she felt at the thought. She needed him, and the distance between them felt daunting. But it couldn't be helped. She would have thought that she might have learned to live without Jayson Wolfe a long time ago. But apparently that wasn't possible.

CHAPTER 10

Forcing a more steady tone, Elizabeth asked into the phone, "What are you doing in Europe?"

"I'm touring with *Bandanna.* Their lead guitarist broke his arm, so I'm filling in. I've known some of these guys for years."

"Aren't they a country band?"

"Yes," he drawled, and she couldn't hold back a skeptical snort.

"But . . . you're a rocker, through and through."

"Thank you for pointing that out." His voice made it evident this was hard for him. But he added with a courage and determination that was typical. "They're a fantastic band—and good guys. It keeps me off the streets."

"Still," she said, glad to be distracted from her own grief, "it must be tough for you. You're used to being center stage."

"Yes . . . I am. But it's not as bad as you might think. There's less pressure, and they're treating me well."

"That's good then."

Following several seconds of silence, he said, "I won't be able to make it to the funeral; I wish I could, but . . . I just . . . can't."

Funeral? Her mind echoed the word silently. He was talking about her son. She hadn't even considered what would happen next. She'd only been able to feel the reality that she had lost her son, her husband was comatose, and she needed Jayson. Robert's parents were struggling with some serious health problems and were grief-stricken at being unable to be there with her and their son. She knew her father was coming; he was strong and insightful, and he would help her get through. But no one understood her the way Jayson did. Hearing the silence grow too long, she cleared her throat and murmured, "I understand."

"My heart is with you, Lady."

"That means more to me than you could possibly know."

"I know your heart is with me in my struggles—and I know what that means to *me.*"

Silence settled again, and he could hear her sniffling. "Will you be all right?"

"I don't know how I'll ever be all right again. I mean . . . I'm sure I'll cope; I have no choice. I've survived losing Derek—and your mother, but . . ." she sobbed, "my baby is gone. Oh, Jayson, he was such a good boy; so talented and amazing."

Jayson felt his insides tighten even more. He said in a broken voice, "Like his mother."

Elizabeth ignored his compliment. "And if I lose Robert . . . no, I can't. I just can't."

"Everything will be all right, Elizabeth," he said gently. "Somehow, it will be all right."

"All right is relative," she snapped. "I might be all right living without my husband and my son, but it isn't how I want to live." She sobbed again. "He's such a good man, Jayson. We've come so far. How can I lose him? What will I do?"

Jayson wiped a hand over his face, feeling as if the helplessness and grief would tear him in half. "I can't answer that, Lady. And I can't tell you that I know how you feel, because I don't, but—"

"Or do you?" she countered. "You've lost a spouse and a child."

"It was different," he said, wishing it hadn't sounded so defensive. "I have every reason to believe Macy will come back. I don't consider her lost; well . . . only temporarily."

"And Debbie?" she asked, and he wished he could hear her name without feeling angry.

"To be quite frank, Elizabeth, I have wished a thousand times that Debbie would have died. If she had left this world against her will, leaving me with the knowledge that her love for me was true, I think I could almost cope."

"Does that mean you're not coping?"

"No!" he snapped. "I'm not coping!" He forced a calmer voice and added, "Forgive me. My intention was not to minimize your pain. I'm truly sorry for your loss, and I will be praying that Robert makes it through. I just want you to realize that . . . there are things worse than death. At least you know that he loves you."

Elizabeth recalled her last words with her husband and the peace she had felt. She had to admit that was true. "Yes," she said quietly, "I know he loves me, and . . . I'm sorry for your loss as well, Jayson."

"I know you are. You've always understood; you were always there for me. I wish I could be there for you now. I wish I could be on my way to the airport right now."

"Knowing you wish it soothes my heart," she admitted. "Will you call me tomorrow?"

"I'll call you every day," he promised. "Or you call me . . . any time . . . if you need to talk or cry or scream. The only time my phone will be off is during the shows, and we don't have one the next couple of days. We just finished up in Germany, and we're on our way to Belgium."

"Wow," she said. "Take some pictures and send them to me."

"I might do that," he said, sounding more like himself.

Ending their phone call felt like one of the hardest things Elizabeth had ever had to do. Going back into the hospital was almost as hard. The bishop met her with the news that the doctors had done all they could do for Robert and he'd been taken to the intensive care unit, where she would be able to see him in a short while. They had told the bishop that Robert would be on a ventilator and he wouldn't look very good. Even with the warning, Elizabeth had a hard time accepting how bad he looked, and she didn't even want to count all the things that were hooked up to him. Still, seeing Robert wasn't nearly so difficult as having to make a positive identification of Bradley's body. The whole thing was a nightmare, and she couldn't imagine how she would ever survive it.

The following days went by in a blur while her father remained at her side and people rallied around, bringing in meals, looking out for the children, and helping see that the funeral was arranged and carried out. Before Bradley's body was laid to rest, Elizabeth was surprised to find that she felt an undeniable peace. It had been his time to go; she knew it beyond any doubt. What had seemed like a freakish occurrence to those who had witnessed it had in fact been carefully orchestrated by the Lord to take Bradley home at a pre-appointed time. If only she could feel the same peace concerning Robert. Everything inside of her refused to accept that it was *his* time to go. Once the funeral was over, she spent every possible minute at Robert's side, holding his hand, talking to him as if she could talk him into living. She was told over and over that even if he survived, he would not be the man she had known. But she just couldn't let him go.

Jayson called every day as promised, sometimes more. Elizabeth got used to the time he would try to call and managed to be where she could use her phone for a lengthy conversation. She would tell him all that had happened in the hours since they'd talked. He would offer compassion and insight, and always she felt his genuine love and concern for her. It was ten days after the accident when he said in a typically gentle voice, "Elizabeth . . . maybe you just need to let him go."

"Let him go?" she countered hotly. "I can't just . . . let him go. If he doesn't survive, I'll . . . I'll . . ."

"You'll what?" he retorted. "You'll spend the rest of your life holding his hand while he's kept on life support? Forgive me if I'm being brash and insensitive, Elizabeth. But maybe someone needs to say it, and maybe I'm the only one who cares enough to see the big picture here. What are your options? Maybe, just maybe, he's holding on because you won't let go. You told me you know in your heart it was Bradley's time to go. Well, maybe it's Robert's time too, and you're just too scared to ask God *that* question, because you don't want the answer."

Jayson held his breath while only silence answered him. Almost fearing the call had been disconnected, he finally asked more softly, "Are you with me?"

"I'm here," she said with an edge.

"And you're angry."

"Yes, actually, I am. I'm doing everything in my power to keep up hope here, in a hopeless situation. If I can't get the support I need from you, who will I get it from?"

"Forgive me, Lady. I just said what I felt needed to be said. Sometimes a true friend is the one who has enough courage to be honest—because it's what you need to hear. That's just it; the situation is hopeless. If he comes around, then you can slap my face next time you see me, but if this is just the end being dragged on miserably, then—"

"I have to go," she said abruptly. "I'll talk to you later."

Jayson heard the call end and looked at his phone as if it might tell him that her reason for hanging up had been legitimate. But he knew better. She was angry with him. He cursed under his breath and wondered if he was wrong. And even if he was right, perhaps he could have been more tactful.

He dialed her number again, not surprised when it went straight to her voice mail. But that was fine. He knew she'd listen to the message, likely long before she'd talk to him again. He gently spoke into the phone. "Forgive me, Lady. If you feel you need to keep hoping, then keep hoping. My prayers are with you—and with Robert. I'll talk to you later."

Before Elizabeth returned to ICU, she turned her phone back on and wasn't surprised to find a message there. She cried when she listened to it, then she turned the phone off and hurried inside, knowing that she couldn't give up hope; she just couldn't! But three hours later, after staring at Robert's lifeless form, Jayson's words began to haunt her. She prayed with all her heart and soul that Robert would wake up, that he would be a husband to her again. But just like when she'd first entered this room to sit beside him, her mind swirled in confusion and turmoil. Was it possible that she'd really been praying for the wrong thing? Had she needlessly prolonged Robert's life because she'd been praying so hard for him to stay? Was she missing the most important point in what was happening here? Anguish engulfed her as she honestly probed her heart for the answers. Jayson's gentle words coursed through her mind. *There are things worse than death.*

Elizabeth felt more afraid than she ever had in her life as she bowed her head and forced her mind to fervent prayer. She asked for peace and understanding; she asked for it over and over. After praying for nearly an hour, she finally managed to mutter the words, *Thy will be done.*

Once she knew the inevitable, she eased carefully onto the bed beside Robert, gently placing her head on his shoulder. She hoped that he knew how much she loved him and how thoroughly blessed she was to have had such a good man in her life.

Robert died later that night. Elizabeth sat for a long while, holding his lifeless hand in hers. But now there were no noises from the ventilator and monitors; only a calm silence. And while she felt a distinct emptiness at the reality that she was now a widow, she also felt an undeniable peace. Robert was free from his struggle to survive, and she was free from her quandary. As difficult as it was to let him go, she felt a deep relief to know that it was over. No more worrying or wondering. She went home and held Trevin and Addie close to her while they cried together. She marveled at their simple faith and the way they inspired her to keep going. And she had to admit that it felt good to be at home with them, and to be able to put her focus into moving on, instead of holding on.

The following day, funeral arrangements were made, and again

Elizabeth marveled at the rallying support of her neighborhood and ward members. This time, Robert's parents were able to fly in from back east and were loving and supportive as they shared her grief. She only wished that Jayson could be there. Still, she dreaded talking to him for reasons that were difficult to admit. She was alone in her bedroom with the cell phone in her hand when it rang, right on time.

"Are you still angry with me?" he asked right after she said hello.

"No, of course not," she said. "I think I was only angry because I knew deep down that you were right, but I didn't want to look at it."

"Are you looking at it now?" he asked, feeling immense relief.

"Oh, yes. To make a long story short, I prayed very hard and very long for understanding. I told God that I would accept His will."

Jayson felt a little stunned. He knew she believed in God, but he'd never heard her speak of prayer and having a relationship with Him in such a way. He wanted to ask what had changed, but stuck to the point by saying, "That's a pretty brave thing to do."

"That's debatable," she said. "Brave or not, it was apparently the *right* thing to do."

"Why is that?"

"Robert died last night," she said, and Jayson squeezed his eyes closed abruptly.

"I'm so sorry," he said, and she could tell that he meant it.

"Yes, well . . . so am I, but . . . as my very dearest friend recently told me, there are things worse than death."

Jayson sighed again. "Yes, but . . . it's still hard."

Recalling how it hadn't been that long since they'd both watched his mother die, Elizabeth's tears began to flow, tears she'd hardly been able to shed since the reality of Robert's death had left her in a numb kind of shock. "Yes, it's hard," she admitted with emotion. "But I know it was right. I can see now that . . . well, you were right, Jayse. My prayers were being answered. I was praying with everything inside of me that he would hold on, that he wouldn't be taken from me. But you were right. I needed to let go. I just want to say that . . . I'm sorry for my anger. And I'm . . ." her emotion deepened, "I'm grateful that you care enough about me and . . . know me well enough to see what I couldn't see, and that you had the courage to say it. I couldn't ask for a truer friend."

"The feeling is mutual, Elizabeth. And I just said what I felt should be said. I'm only sorry I can't be there with you."

"Maybe it's just as well," she said, laughing softly through her tears.

"Why is that?"

"It might be difficult to explain to everyone in my neighborhood why I'm sobbing in the arms of a handsome rock star at my husband's funeral. They might get the wrong idea. Maybe some of them were reading the tabloids a few years back."

"Not likely." He chuckled briefly. "But it's *former* rock star. Apparently you haven't kept up on the gossip."

"Still handsome," she said.

"I don't know. You haven't seen me for a while. I think life is starting to show in my face."

"I don't care, Jayson." Emotion rose in her voice again. "I would be so lost without you."

Jayson swallowed carefully, hoping she couldn't sense the path of his thoughts. He ached for her loss, and his grief was genuine. But how could he not feel some measure of hope in knowing that this woman he loved was now free? Guilt immediately came with the thought, and he reminded himself that she would need time. Even given that, how could he be sure that she would be any more interested in marrying him now than she had been when they were eighteen? At least then he'd had his whole life before him; now his life was a mess. Their friendship was deep and true. But that wasn't necessarily enough to build a good marriage. He thought of Robert; in spite of certain challenges, he was a man with many fine qualities. Thinking of himself in comparison, wandering the world with a guitar, he felt, quite frankly, like a loser. And Elizabeth deserved better than that. She deserved the best.

When the silence grew long, he finally said, "It's the other way around, Lady."

During the following days, Elizabeth spoke with Jayson every day. He helped get her through the funeral and the initial shock of adjusting to life with two less family members. The calls became less frequent when her father took her and the children on a lengthy vacation. He'd been staying with her off and on since the initial accident, as much as he could manage and still remain employed. Two months after Bradley's death, Elizabeth told Will that she didn't know how she could ever manage without him. She even considered moving with the kids to Oregon, but she was hesitant to uproot them from positive situations with friends, school, and church. They'd already had too many big changes in their young lives. Will solved the problem when he proposed to Elizabeth that he retire early and just move in with her. They carefully analyzed their combined financial situation with the money they each had in savings, his accumulated retirement benefits, and Robert's life insurance. If Will could sell his home for a reasonable price, they could both be completely debt free, including the home that Elizabeth was living in, and he could still make some good investments that would see him through the remainder of his life. If he could do some freelance tax work, they would be able to get by just fine. Elizabeth was thrilled with the idea, and felt certain it was an answer to prayers. Her father seemed even happier about it than she did, and she realized he'd been alone for many years. His greatest joy was his family, and even though they were few in number, they all got along well, and it would be a good arrangement.

God's hand in the situation became increasingly evident when Will's house sold quickly, even though he didn't get out of it quite what he'd hoped. He settled in with little trouble, since he'd been staying with Elizabeth's family off and on for the last few months. He had a couple of rooms to himself in the basement where he had everything he needed. Elizabeth was grateful to have a man around the house for a number of reasons, but mostly for her children to have a father figure in the absence of their own father. They all benefitted from his love of cooking as much as his sound wisdom, but most of all, Elizabeth was simply grateful to have her father to lean on. His shoulder was frequently used to absorb her tears. She felt certain she never could have coped with the deep losses in her life if not for his continual love and support.

Their contact with Jayson diminished somewhat with the drama mostly behind them. Elizabeth felt concerned for him, but she knew she was so preoccupied with her own challenges that it was difficult to feel in tune with his emotions. Jayson was pleased to know that Will was now living with her, although he shared her sentiment in thinking of the good times they'd enjoyed in the home that had been sold. Now it belonged to someone else. Their music room would probably soon be a home theater. Elizabeth commented lightly, "I wonder what the new owners of the house would think to know that the roots of *Gray Wolf* were germinated in that basement."

"I think we'll just keep that to ourselves," he said.

While Elizabeth struggled to come to terms with the deaths of her husband and son, she found too much time on her hands and too much to think about. So naturally, she was pleased when a woman who lived on her street called with an offer for her to get away for a few days. Paula was someone that Elizabeth had gotten to know right after her move to Utah. She was an amazing woman, involved in many things and raising a large family. They had gone to lunch a few times and were well acquainted. While Elizabeth wouldn't say they were terribly close by any means, they were certainly friends and comfortable with each other. And now Paula had a convention she needed to attend in Denver related to some product that she sold as one of the many sidelights in her life. The friend that had been planning to go with her had unexpectedly needed a minor surgery and wouldn't be able to go. The plane ticket was nonrefundable, and the hotel room would cost the same for two as it would for one. Paula simply didn't want to go alone. She said that Elizabeth would be welcome to attend the workshops and seminars, many of which covered a wide range of positive aspects of managing life. Or Elizabeth would be welcome to just hang out at the hotel and relax and get some distance from the drudgery of trying to cope. Elizabeth jumped at the chance, and with her father in the home and well accustomed to their routine, leaving the children in his care was not a problem. Arrangements were quickly made, and Elizabeth felt certain this opportunity was just one more piece of evidence that God was with her in her struggles.

* * *

When Jayson finally felt recovered from the tour, he felt a need to make up for his absence in Elizabeth's life during the loss of her husband and son. He also had a desire to see Will. It was convenient to have them now in the same location, and he wondered how they would feel about him paying a visit. Beyond Drew, they were the only family he had. And Drew was never around.

He phoned Elizabeth's home and was pleased to hear Will answer the phone. With the comfortable relationship they shared, it wasn't difficult to express what he was feeling. Will said he would love to see Jayson, but Elizabeth was out of town for a few days.

"I know she would really love to have a good visit with you," Will said.

"Do you know where she's staying?" Jayson asked.

"I do, actually. Hold on. I'll get the number." A minute later Will returned to the phone and gave Jayson the name and phone number for a hotel in Denver where Elizabeth would be for the next three nights.

"Thank you," Jayson said, then felt he should add, "I really wish I could have been there for the funeral . . . funerals; both of them."

"We wish you could have been here too. But we know how the music business can be."

"Yes, well . . ." Jayson cleared his throat. "So . . . how is Elizabeth?"

"She's coming along," Will said. "You know her. Somehow she always manages to keep going."

"Yes, I know."

They talked for a few more minutes while Jayson felt a nearly tangible need to never break the connection. Will had always been a father figure to him. And Jayson felt like the orphan he was. He so wanted a parent to lean on and be with. He quickly picked up the phone to dial the hotel in Denver, then he examined his feelings and called his travel agent instead.

The following morning, Jayson parked his rental car at the hotel where Elizabeth was staying, and took his one bag inside. Once he'd checked into the room he'd reserved the previous day, he found the registration table for the conference she was attending.

"Excuse me," he said to the woman seated there. "I'm—"

"Did you want to register for the remainder of the conference?" she asked with a big smile.

"No, actually, thank you. What I need is to find a friend of mine who is attending the conference, and—"

"Well, everyone is gathered in the main ballroom at the moment where the keynote address of the day is being given." She pointed down the hall. "In about twenty minutes it should be over, and everyone will go to separate workshops. Everybody will have to come out of those doors eventually."

"Thank you," he said, feeling his heart quicken. "Thank you very much."

Jayson paced the hall for a few minutes, then he carefully opened the door at the back of the room. He peeked inside and was able to slip into the room without being noticed. Standing behind a crowd of a couple of hundred people, he leaned against the wall and searched for familiar blonde hair. He reminded himself that she could have changed the way she wore it since he last saw her. He found one possibility, but when this woman turned and stretched, it wasn't Elizabeth. He found another possibility with a second blonde woman, although her hair was straight and hung to the shoulder. Elizabeth had always worn it longer and curly. He watched this woman for several minutes before she finally turned to whisper something to the woman next to her. Jayson's heart quickened further. *It was her.* And just seeing her made him feel better than he'd felt in weeks, maybe months. He'd last seen her when she'd come for his mother's funeral, which seemed an eternity ago.

When the meeting ended, Jayson was the first one out the door. He leaned against a wall not far from the ballroom door where he could clearly see those who exited. He was beginning to think she'd never come out when he saw her. The emotion he felt made him wonder if he'd truly come to offer belated condolences for her losses, or if it was he who needed comfort.

Elizabeth stepped into the corridor, listening to something that Paula was telling her. They stopped as Paula opened her program to see which direction she needed to go for the next session. While Elizabeth waited, she absently looked around, then did a double-take, certain her eyes were deceiving her. Her mouth went dry, and her heart beat painfully hard as she found Jayson Wolfe staring back at her. She wondered what he was doing here, and how he had found her. But she was so completely glad to see him that it didn't matter. He offered a subtle smile, and she returned it, feeling momentarily frozen. Then she held up a finger to indicate that he just needed to give her a minute. He nodded.

Without drawing attention to her true intent, Elizabeth said to Paula, "Listen, I think I'm going to just walk around, maybe go to the room and rest."

"You sure?" Paula said.

"Yes, thanks. Don't worry about me. I'll catch up with you later."

"Okay," Paula said. "Send me a text message if you need anything."

"I'll do that, thanks," Elizabeth said, and Paula hurried down the hall.

Elizabeth took a deep breath and moved toward Jayson, completely unprepared for the raw emotion that gathered in her chest. She moved effortlessly into his arms and felt something tangibly warm and sustaining engulf her with the reality of his embrace.

Jayson was so preoccupied with how good it felt to be with her that it took him a minute to realize she was crying against the front of his shoulder. He felt her tremble and took her shoulders into his hands, forcing her to look at him. "What's wrong?" he asked quietly, but she only shook her head. He put his arm around her and guided her in the opposite direction from the crowd. He kept going until they were alone in an elevator. "Now, what's wrong?" he asked gently, wiping at her tears with his fingers.

She gave an embarrassed chuckle. "I'm just so glad to see you."

Jayson laughed softly. "Well, the feeling is mutual, but . . . I don't think that warrants so many tears."

Elizabeth sniffled and dug into her purse for a tissue. "I don't know. It's as if . . . I'm so completely comfortable with you, and I know you care, and you genuinely want to share my burdens and . . . so everything I hold inside most of the time just comes . . . rushing out when I'm with you." She laughed softly and wiped at fresh tears. "I'm sorry about that."

"Don't be sorry. I think that's one of the greatest compliments I've ever received."

"Better than winning a Grammy?"

"Even better than that," he said conclusively.

"What are you doing here?" she asked, gaining control of her emotions.

"The tour is officially over. I wanted to see you. Your father told me where you were. I was going to call, but . . . I just figured I'd take a chance. I don't want to mess up your plans or anything, but . . ."

"I don't have any plans except to keep Paula from being in Denver alone. They've got a pretty tight schedule of stuff I have no desire to go to. I think if I'm in the room with her at night and show for breakfast and dinner, she'll be happy."

Jayson smiled and reached out to touch her hair. "It's straight," he said.

"So it is," she muttered. "I just got tired of the same old thing. Don't you like it?"

"You look beautiful as always," he said. "But I think I liked it better curly."

"You were just used to it that way," she said, and he smiled again as the elevator doors opened.

"Where are we going?" she asked.

"I have a room," he said, taking her hand. "I was hoping we could talk to our hearts' content." He stopped at the door and put his plastic key card into the door slot. "Unless you'd be more comfortable someplace else or—"

"No, this is fine," she said, reminding herself that she wasn't a married woman any more. The thought sent a jolt of pain to her heart, but it was just as quickly calmed simply by being in Jayson's presence. What was it about him that always produced this effect? They held hands and talked through all of the details of the losses in her life that she'd not shared with him during their long-distance conversations. She cried, and he offered his compassion. They talked about his mother's death and how he was still struggling to come to terms with not having her in his life. A part of her longed to share with him what she'd learned about life after death through embracing the gospel, but instinctively she knew this wasn't the right time.

They had lunch brought to the room and talked on through the afternoon. Jayson drank in Elizabeth's presence like a barren desert soaking in rain. He felt so thoroughly comfortable and captivated that he wondered why they weren't married, living in the same house, raising the same children. Knowing she was free made it difficult for him to keep such thoughts to himself, but he knew she loved her husband deeply, and he would not dictate the length of time it might take her to recover from his death. Even then, he wasn't certain he could ever approach her with his deepest feelings. The very idea of hearing her tell him, once again, that she didn't—and could never—love him that way, was simply more than he could bear. He didn't want to mar their comfortable relationship by trying to put something romantic into it. So, he kept his feelings to himself and simply basked in her presence, grateful to observe that being with him meant a great deal to her. That in itself gave him great peace.

Jayson noticed she was wearing the necklace he gave her in high school: a gold chain with a treble clef dangling on it. He'd seen her wear it a couple of times through the years, but then, he'd seen her so little. But now there was something else on the chain. He finally had to reach over and take it into his fingers to figure out what it was.

"The treble clef you gave me," she said.

"I can see that but . . . oh," he said as he realized it was the little gold angel his mother had given her for graduation. His father had given it to his mother the day he'd been born. "I just couldn't tell what it was," he said, hesitant to let go of the little charm.

"It's taken on new meaning," she said. "Your mother is truly an angel now. I'm often comforted to think of her looking out for us."

"That's a nice thought," he said and finally let go, putting some distance between them as the conversation took a different path.

A while later, Elizabeth glanced at the clock and couldn't believe that it was past six. The time had flown. She was just about to ask if he was getting hungry again when her cell phone rang. She answered it and heard Paula say, "Hi, where are you?"

Elizabeth gave a nervous chuckle and reminded herself that she wasn't doing anything wrong. The habit of feeling married was still strong. "The most amazing thing happened," she said.

Jayson watched Elizabeth while she talked to her friend. He hoped beyond hope that he would be able to spend every possible minute with her, but he didn't want to be to pushy or presumptuous. He heard her say, "Well, I ran into an old friend, and . . ."

Jayson feigned astonishment and whispered, "Old? *Old?*"

Elizabeth laughed softly and added, "I mean . . . a longtime friend." She paused to listen, then said, "No, it's not really a coincidence. He called my father, who told him where I was. Didn't I ever tell you about my friend, Jayson? Well, I should have. No, it's not romantic," she added, and Jayson wanted to cross the room and kiss her, if only to make her feel like a hypocrite. He wanted to say, *It should be romantic.* But he just listened to her as she went on. "He's more like part of the family. He was my brother's best friend in high school, and . . ."

"And yours," Jayson whispered.

She smiled and turned her back to him. "Anyway, well . . . no, I haven't mentioned my brother because he was . . . killed in high school, and . . . I can tell you about that some other time. Anyway, Jayson couldn't be there for the funerals. He just got back in the country and he wanted to see me, so he flew out here, and . . . oh, no problem. We can still do everything we talked about. I just think I'll bow out of the workshops and stuff and visit with him while you're busy. Are you okay with that?" She was silent a couple of minutes, then said, "Are you sure? Okay, well . . . we'll meet you in the lobby in about ten minutes, then. Jayson will buy." She turned back to look at him, giving him a crooked smile. "I don't need to ask him. He'll buy. Won't you, Jayson?"

"I'd love to," he said loudly.

She ended the call and said, "She'd love to meet you, so we're all going out to dinner."

"How lovely," he said with a grin. "Are you sure she's okay with this?"

"She didn't want to be alone out here. She wasn't necessarily needing one-on-one time with me, and she didn't really expect me to go to all those workshops anyway. She's totally fine with it."

"Good," he said. "I will try to be my most charming self."

"That shouldn't be too hard," she said with a little laugh.

"Is something funny?"

"No," she said, "it's just so good to see you."

"And you," he said.

In the lobby, Elizabeth introduced the two of them by simply saying, "Paula, this is Jayson. Jayson, this is Paula." They shook hands and exchanged small talk, then they decided to just eat at the restaurant in the hotel rather than going out. The meal was relatively good, and the conversation comfortable until Paula casually asked Jayson, "So, what do you do?"

Elizabeth could see that he felt uncomfortable with the question, and she wondered why. Even when he'd had to deal with crazed fans, he'd never been hesitant to admit what he did. He met her eyes as if he expected her to rescue him, so she did. But she wasn't certain he necessarily approved of her tactic when she said, "He's a professional musician. He just got back from touring Europe with *Bandanna*."

"Really?" Paula was obviously impressed. "You're actually in that band?"

"Not officially. I was just filling in for their regular guitarist who broke his arm."

"That sounds awfully exciting."

"It's a job," Jayson said. "Actually, it gets old after a while."

"I suppose that's understandable," Paula said, and Jayson seemed to relax. "So, I assume you started very young with the guitar."

"I did, yes," he admitted, "although I started with the piano first. I wanted a guitar, and my brother, Drew, wanted a drum set. Our mother told us she would help us get them if we each first learned the piano enough to play a Mozart piece by reading music, and a song by Elton John that she thoroughly loved. We both did it, and she kept her part of the bargain. Drew never touched the piano again, but I've maintained a deep love for it. Although, I think I'm more adept with the guitar."

"Don't let him fool you," Elizabeth said. "He's marvelous on the piano. He can play a number of Elton John's best pieces with ease."

"Really?" Paula said. "I'd like to hear that."

Jayson gave Elizabeth a comical scowl. "Well, perhaps you should hear Elizabeth play."

"Play what?" Paula looked pleasantly astonished.

"Violin, flute, piano," Jayson said like a proud parent. "And she has a marvelous voice."

"Really?" Paula said again with a little laugh.

"Really," Jayson said. "In fact, our friendship began when we—"

"Okay, that's good," Elizabeth said. "Mind you, there's a great deal I can tell her about you that she hasn't heard yet; things you prefer to keep quiet about."

Jayson laughed. "At the moment, I think that might be worth it. It's been a long time since I've been able to tell somebody the truth about you." He turned to Paula. "You see, she was once playing rock and roll in a band called *A Pack of Wolves,* and she was belting her voice into the microphone on stage; she was the hottest act in west Oregon. And she wore these great red high-heeled shoes and—"

"Enough," Elizabeth said, but she laughed as she said it.

"Is he serious?" Paula asked dubiously.

"I'm afraid he is," Elizabeth said.

"So, what happened to *A Pack of Wolves?*" Paula asked.

"Well," Elizabeth looked down after she and Jayson shared a sobering glance. "My brother, Derek, who was the bass player, was killed in a car accident. Jayson and his brother went to LA to get into the music industry. I went to college back east. But as you can see, we've stayed very close. Jayson's always been my best friend."

"That's quite a story," Paula said. She looked directly at Jayson and asked, "So, have you worked with any other bands I might know? I'm pretty hip when it comes to music; I like all kinds of music, if you must know."

"Yes, actually," Elizabeth said smugly, and Jayson gave her a comical glare, knowing she was getting even. "Are you familiar with *Gray Wolf?*"

"Are you kidding?" she asked with a laugh. "They're incredible. You toured with *Gray Wolf?*" Her question made it evident she was one of those people who listened to music but didn't pay much attention to the pictures on the CD inserts or what was going on in the entertainment news.

"Yeah, I did," Jayson said. To Elizabeth he added, "Let's leave it at that."

"Oh, no." Elizabeth chuckled, then turned to Paula. *"He* is *Gray Wolf."* Elizabeth leaned back in her chair, taking great pleasure in Jayson's sheepish expression and Paula's astonished one. "Paula Merkley, meet Jayson Wolfe."

"No!" Paula said with a little laugh. "You're kidding."

"I'm quite serious," Elizabeth said.

"Prove it," she said, leaning across the table.

Jayson leaned toward her and sang quietly, "Time will stalk you like a predator." It had been years since he'd performed that song, but he still hit every note with precision.

Paula laughed. "That's incredible! I *love* that song." She laughed again. "Well, it's a pleasure to meet you, Jayson Wolfe."

The remainder of the evening was equally enjoyable, and Jayson was pleased to see that this woman didn't treat him any differently now that she knew who he was.

Jayson walked the women to their room, while Paula talked about her plans for the following day. She actually had an early business breakfast, a workshop luncheon, and an awards banquet in the evening. She told Elizabeth she would be welcome to join her, but it was evident that if Elizabeth spent the entire day with

Jayson, Paula would never miss her. He told Paula good night at the door, and she went inside, leaving Elizabeth alone in the hall with Jayson.

"What a wonderful day," she said, smiling at him.

"Indeed," he said. "Are you up to another wonderful day tomorrow?"

"I was hoping you'd ask," she said.

"Okay, well . . . I have a car, so . . . let's start with breakfast and then we can just . . . see what Denver has to offer. I've played this city a few times, but I didn't see much."

"I'll look forward to it," she said and kissed his cheek.

"Is eight too early?" he asked.

"Oh, no," she said. "I wouldn't want to waste a day like tomorrow by sleeping in."

He smiled. "I'll see you in the morning, then."

He kissed her cheek, and she went into her room to find Paula sitting on one of the beds, smirking. "Wow," she said. "Jayson Wolfe is your best friend."

"He is," Elizabeth said, tossing her purse onto a little table and taking off her shoes.

"He seems like a pretty amazing guy. Now that you're a widow, do you think it could ever become something romantic?"

Elizabeth didn't want to tell her that it once had been *extremely* romantic between her and Jayson. "I don't know," Elizabeth admitted with mixed feelings. "It hasn't been nearly long enough for me to even . . . think that way. But . . . our lives are so different. I just don't know if it's possible. He's not a member of the Church, for one thing. I struggled with that gap between me and Robert; I don't know that I want to do that again."

"That's understandable, but . . ." Paula laughed, "he sure is adorable."

"Yes, he certainly is adorable," Elizabeth said. "And he's a good man." *One of the best,* her mind added silently.

CHAPTER 11

Elizabeth could hardly sleep that night, preoccupied as she was with the changes in her life and how Jayson Wolfe fit into them. She knew how she felt about him—and she was relatively certain how he felt about her. Their friendship had proven to be strong and true; it had stood the test of time. But that didn't necessarily mean they had what it took to make a good marriage. Whether or not that was a possibility, she felt far from ready to even be considering such things. She needed time, and hopefully with that, all else would eventually come into focus.

In spite of her lack of sleep, the day she spent with Jayson felt like a slice of heaven. He held her hand as they talked endlessly and explored the city. Their time together was reminiscent of their high school days, but the struggles of life they'd endured, and the maturity they had gained, added a richness to their comfortable companionship. She was grateful that he made no romantic inferences, subtle or otherwise. She hoped he understood that it could be a good, long while before she could cross that bridge. And whether or not she would be able to cross it with him remained to be seen.

By evening they had returned to his hotel room, both exhausted and tired of being on their feet. Elizabeth insisted on soaking her tired feet in the bathtub. She rolled up her jeans and removed her shoes and stockings to sit on the edge of the tub and put her feet in the water. Jayson did the same and sat beside her, laughing as he said, "It's not exactly the beach, but in Denver one must make do." They sat there talking until the water became uncomfortably cool. While Elizabeth was stepping out onto the bath mat, Jayson reached down and flipped water on her. "Oops," he said, "I must have slipped."

"Yeah, right," she said with mock anger and leaned over to send a healthy splash in his direction just as he stepped out of the water. He laughed and turned to grab her before she could run. He tickled her just a little, and she squealed with laughter, attempting to squirm out of his grasp.

The next thing he knew she was in his arms, her hands against his shoulders, looking into his eyes. And the laughter stopped. He debated whether or not to kiss her. Oh, how he wanted to! But he wondered if it was too much, too soon. Reading an unmistakable desire in her eyes, the decision became easy, and he pressed his lips to hers. Her response was immediate and undeniable, and he allowed his kiss to gain fervor. Then, in an instant, she went from soft to resistant. He let go abruptly and stepped back as if he'd been burned. He was stunned to see as much shock and self-recrimination in her face as there had been the time she'd *almost* kissed him—when she had been a married woman.

"I'm sorry," she muttered. "I just . . . I'm not ready for that."

Jayson could accept that, but a question screamed through his head that he knew he needed an answer to. "Okay," he said, "but . . . does that mean you're not ready for that *at all,* or you're not interested in *that* with me?"

"At all!" she said firmly, almost angrily.

"So . . . is there a *maybe someday* in this situation, or should I just . . . accept now that it will never be a possibility between us?"

"I don't know, Jayson," she said. "I'm still struggling with the grief of losing my husband. How can I possibly answer such a question?"

"I didn't ask you to marry me," he said. "Did you notice the words *maybe* and *possibility* in that sentence?"

"Well, the answer is still the same. I don't know."

Jayson sighed and deeply wished this conversation was not triggering so much emotion for him. It seemed that every fear and hurt in his life was somehow linked together, and he doubted he could feel one of them without tempting others to the surface. And he wasn't going to have a meltdown here in front of her, especially over *this*. He swallowed carefully and willed the emotion to recede. "Okay," he said in a voice that was more calm. "You must forgive my being so presumptuous. I really thought you wanted me to kiss you; your eyes told me you wanted me to kiss you." Her eyes turned guiltily downward, and he added, "You almost kissed me when you were married. Forgive me for assuming that your being single would make it all right to kiss you."

Elizabeth wanted to be angry over his statement. She wanted to interpret his saying it to be edged with an anger that would justify her being defensive. But the truth was that he'd said it with complete sincerity, and everything he'd said was true. Without looking at him, she said, "I don't question the mixed messages I may have given you—now and in the past. I won't deny that I still find you . . . attractive." She met his eyes and could vividly see *his* attraction for *her*. Her stomach quivered in response, but she spoke with a steady voice. "But that's not enough to potentially substantiate a lifelong relationship."

"We've already had a relationship for more than half our lives, Elizabeth. I think we've proven that we're capable of making it last a lifetime."

"What we share is wonderful, Jayson; it's priceless to me. But it is not necessarily indicative of being able to live under the same roof and to deal with all the challenges of life."

At the risk of making her defensive, he had to say, "If you think we are not capable of that, Elizabeth, you're either a fool or you're blind."

"Maybe I'm both," she said curtly. Looking into his eyes, Elizabeth was assaulted with the memory of her anguish in having let Jayson go, and then losing him to Debbie once she'd realized she'd made a mistake. She knew she needed some time, but she wasn't willing to make the same mistake twice. She said more gently, "And maybe when I get past losing my husband and son, I will be able to see clearly enough to avoid messing up my life by being a fool."

Jayson wasn't certain what she meant by that, but the implication he heard rang loud and clear. Did she fear that involving him in her life any more than he already was would mess up her life? He reminded himself not to jump to conclusions and cause himself grief over unclarified assumptions. He was trying to find a way to ask when she touched his face and said tenderly, "I need some time, Jayson. There have been some changes in my life that we haven't even talked about; things you're not aware of; things that could make a big difference in the long run."

"What things?" he demanded, appalled at the very idea that she'd make changes in her life without telling him, although he couldn't possibly imagine what she might be talking about.

"I don't want to get into it right now. I promise I'll tell you everything when the time is right. It's nothing to be concerned about. I just . . . need some time to adjust. And I don't want tension between us over this. I need you."

"I need you, too," he admitted. "And there's no reason there should be tension between us. We've come too far for that. We just need to be completely honest with each other."

"Of course," she said. "You won't run off and marry someone else while I'm trying to get a grip, will you?"

With sarcasm he said, "I'll be sure to call and ask your permission before I marry anybody else."

Elizabeth wondered if that was meant to be a gibe. She wanted to yell at him and tell him if he'd done that the last time, their lives might have been dramatically different. But that was something better left unsaid, and she was too tired to analyze this situation any further.

"Are you going to buy me dinner?" she asked. "Or should I go raid the vending machines and go back to my room and wait for Paula?"

"Which would you prefer?" he asked.

"I'd prefer to be with you, of course."

"Then I would love to buy you dinner, but you'd better put some shoes on."

When they were both ready to go, he took her hand and held it as they walked to the car. She was relieved to see that their difficult conversation hadn't left unwanted strain between them. They went to a very nice seafood restaurant and reminisced over the wonderful seafood they'd eaten together in Oregon.

"What do you miss most about being there?" Elizabeth asked. "Other than the seafood?"

"Truthfully, I don't find myself consciously missing the seafood." He became more serious. "And you know the answer to that question."

"Okay," she said, "besides Derek, what do you miss the most?"

Jayson thought for a long moment and asked, "Do I have to answer that in fifty words or less?"

"Take as many words as you want. I'm not in any hurry."

Jayson sighed. "I miss the naiveté of youth. I miss making music in the basement and eating your father's cooking, with nothing more to worry about than how much time I could spend just playing my music and being with the people I loved." He sighed again. "I miss eating pie at the diner where my mother worked, and sitting around the fire on the beach with you and Drew and . . . Derek. And yes, I miss Derek. I miss him every day."

Elizabeth couldn't hide the fact that she was a little choked up when she said, "I echo that . . . all of it. And I miss the rain."

"Yes, I miss the rain, too. I especially miss the sound of the rain."

"Living in Phoenix was torture in that regard, after growing up in Oregon. It rains more in Utah than it did in Arizona, but . . . it's still not Oregon."

Following longs moments of quiet, Jayson said, "The Oregon rain wouldn't mean much now without all of the other things that aren't there any more. And rain is . . . just rain . . . and no matter where I go, it's always raining in my heart."

Elizabeth took in his words and the stark sadness beneath them. Briefly considering the losses in his life, she was hard-pressed not to burst into tears on his behalf. But if she started crying for him, she'd never quit . . . because she had her own losses that were still too raw. Attempting to lighten the mood, she said, "You're talking like a songwriter again."

He made no response beyond a subtle brittleness in his eyes. She hadn't intended to prick something painful, but apparently she had. Deciding it was best to just change the subject, she simply said, "Yes, I think it's raining in my heart, too." And then she started telling him about the antics of her children, which always made both of them laugh.

While they shared a chocolate dessert that they were both too full to eat much of, Elizabeth said, "So, tell me how you're doing without your mother. I mean really."

She saw something harsh pass briefly through his eyes. "I don't know if you want to hear the 'really' answer."

"I do, or I wouldn't have asked."

Jayson sighed and set down his fork. "I never imagined that anything could be so hard." Elizabeth reached across the table and took his hand. "Throughout my life there have been two unfailing constants—my music and my mother. I mean . . . you've been there for me a great deal, and quite honestly, you're in close running. But . . . she's my mother. The sacrifices she made on my behalf are innumerable. And through every loss, everything I've struggled through, she was beside me, behind me, all around me. Having her gone just leaves a big, black hole that I don't think anything could ever fill. Now, the only thing that keeps me grounded at all is the music. I shudder to think what I would do without *that.*"

"So, how are you coping?" she asked. "The music is wonderful, but . . . you've got to have more to your life than that. Surely there is a way to find some deeper meaning."

"I'm doubtful," he said, not wanting to admit that if he believed they might one day be able to share their lives completely, he could certainly find meaning to his life. But at the moment, such a possibility felt as out of reach as the moon. "I even tried going to church, but that didn't work."

"Why not?" she asked cautiously.

"All I got at church was guilt and the fear of God. They claim to have all the answers, but so much of it doesn't make sense. You know what I mean?"

"Yeah, I know what you mean."

"It's like they just expect you to take what they say completely on faith, and this guy at the pulpit gives me no reason to put any faith in him. If I'm going to put my faith anywhere, it will be in God. I don't need to go to church to do that."

"I hear what you're saying," she said. "I think every human being is entitled to a personal relationship with God. I think we're all entitled to get our own answers."

"Exactly," he said. "But then . . . I don't seem to get the right answers. I have more questions than answers."

Elizabeth felt highly tempted to tell him what she knew, to bear testimony to him of the truth she had found and how it had changed her life. But she felt compelled to hold her tongue. The time wasn't right, and she knew it; he wasn't ready. She settled for planting a seed for him to think about by saying, "Maybe you just went to the wrong church."

He gave a scoffing laugh. "They're probably all the same."

"Maybe; maybe not. It wouldn't hurt to keep an open mind. You just never know when you might find what you're looking for."

He changed the subject then, and she was relieved. But in her heart she prayed that a day would come when he could be open enough to accept what she longed to tell him.

It was late when they returned to the hotel, and Elizabeth knew it was time to say good-bye. She and Paula would be leaving for the airport very early. They stood outside the door of her room and had nothing to say. She shared a lengthy gaze with him and wondered how to say that she did deeply hope that they could yet share every aspect of their lives. She neither wanted him to get his hopes up futilely, nor to let him slip away as she had once before. Unable to find the words to express her hopes on his behalf, she impulsively took a step toward him and lifted her lips to his, hoping he wouldn't think she was a hypocrite.

While Jayson had been prepared for a hug, he was surprised to have her kiss him. Her lips met his with a meek reticence that well exemplified the friendship they shared, but there was a lengthy tenderness to her kiss that implied something more. She put her hand to the back of his neck as if to keep him from withdrawing—as if he'd want to. She drew back enough to look into his eyes and set her other hand against his face. "Don't give up on me, Jayson. I do love you."

"I know," he said, adding silently, *But not enough.* "I love you too," he said and resisted the urge to take her into his arms and kiss her the way he wanted to.

"You'll call me soon?"

"Now that I'm back in the country with nothing to do, I'll be calling you often, I'm sure."

"I'll look forward to it." She smiled and added, "You should come and stay with us for a while. Dad would love to see you."

Jayson had mixed feelings on that and could only say, "Thanks. I'd love to see him too. I'll keep that option open."

Jayson returned home to find a letter from his agent, letting him know that she was making some changes and she would no longer be able to represent him. The letter was very diplomatic and made it sound like it had nothing to do with the lack of money he was likely to make for her, but he couldn't help feeling that was the biggest reason. He told himself it didn't matter and did his best to accept life as it was, but that was easier said than done.

* * *

Elizabeth felt a definite letdown upon returning home. She'd enjoyed her time away, especially her time with Jayson. Coming back to the reality of all that was missing in her life, she felt discouraged. And she had her father under the same roof, and children who needed her. She couldn't even imagine how Jayson was coping at all. Not certain what to do about it, she kept a prayer in her heart for him, specifically asking God to help her know what she might do to help him. They talked on the phone every few days, and he seemed to be doing all right. But there was a lack of happiness in him that concerned her deeply.

An opportunity arose for her to take on some part-time work that she could do at home, typing legal transcripts on the computer. They could probably manage without the money, although they'd had a few tight moments. But she felt some incentive to have something to do to occupy her time and her mind. Her father helped with the children and in the kitchen enough that she simply had too much time on her hands. She talked to Jayson about it, and he offered to give her any amount of money she might need; he had plenty in the bank. She assured him that if a need arose she wouldn't be too proud to ask, but she mostly just needed to fill her time. As with everything she did, he was completely supportive.

Three and a half weeks after her trip to Denver, the phone rang just after Trevin had left for school. Elizabeth glanced at the caller ID, surprised to see the name of a hospital she'd never heard of, with a number that was obviously out of state. She'd barely said hello when she heard Jayson's voice, "Oh, thank heaven you're home. I only have a few minutes."

"What's wrong?" she demanded, hearing a clear indication in his voice that he was upset. "You're calling from a hospital?"

"That's right," he said. "I . . . had a little . . . accident."

"What kind of accident?" she countered, her voice rising.

"It was stupid; just stupid. I couldn't sleep and was going down the stairs in the night—well, early this morning, and I slipped. I don't know how I slipped; I just slipped. And no, I wasn't drunk."

"I wouldn't have expected you to be."

"Well, at least four medical personnel have asked me if I was," he said, his irritation evident.

"So, what happened?"

His voice broke as he told her, "It's my hand, Lady." Elizabeth sucked in her breath and held it. For him, nothing could be worse than this. "I landed on my left hand," he said, his voice more steady. "It's swollen and discolored and it hurts like . . ." He didn't finish, and she knew he'd resisted cursing. "They're taking me into surgery in a few minutes to—"

"Is it broken?"

"Apparently not; although they said it might have been better if it had been. I don't know what the deal is, but it's . . . ligaments, tendons. It's a mess." Emotion came into his voice again. "They said it will be weeks before I can use it at all, and months of physical therapy before it will be close to normal, and they said that . . . it may never be the same."

Elizabeth heard emotion in her own voice as she said, "It just has to be the same, Jayson. It has to be. We won't stand for anything less. If I have to come out there and personally learn the physical therapy and do it myself, it will be the same. Are you hearing me?"

Jayson couldn't answer. He had his right hand pressed over his mouth to avoid sobbing into the phone. She could never know what hearing those words meant to him. Only Elizabeth would know what this meant to him, and she was the only person in his life who could come up with enough faith and determination to make him believe he could get through this. The very idea of not being able to play the piano or the guitar for months seemed more than he could bear, but to never be able to play the same again was simply unthinkable.

"Jayson?"

"I'm here," he managed to say. "You keep telling me that, okay?"

"I will; every day if I have to. Do you want me to come out now? I can be on the next plane, Jayson. Just say the word and—"

"I appreciate the offer; I really do, but . . . no, I don't want you to come."

"Why not?" she asked, trying not to feel deflated.

"Because . . . just because. I can't explain it. I just . . . need your support from a distance on this one. There's not much you can do here, and . . . your family needs you; you have work to do. I'd feel too guilty if you came."

"Now that's the stupidest thing I ever—"

"Hold on, your majesty. If I really needed some help, I would ask. But actually Drew is here. He's between jobs. He's here with me, and he's going to be with me until I can manage on my own."

Elizabeth took a deep breath. "Okay, but . . . tell him I said he'd better take really good care of you, or I'll give him a piece of my mind."

Jayson laughed softly. "I'll tell him." Silence settled for a moment before he added, "Thank you, Lady. I don't know what I'd do without you."

"The feeling is mutual. You'll be in my prayers. Please call me as soon as you can, or have Drew call and tell me how the surgery went."

"I will; I promise."

Elizabeth got off the phone and had a good cry until her father caught her at it.

"What's wrong?" he demanded.

"Jayson just called and—"

"What's happened?" he asked, his tone going from concern to panic.

Elizabeth explained the situation, and they discussed how difficult this was going to be for Jayson. She was surprised when Will said, "He should come and stay with us. We can make certain he does the therapy, and that he doesn't get depressed. Drew may be around to help him get through the surgery and recovery, but it's the long haul that's going to get him."

"I'm sure you're right," Elizabeth said. While there were aspects of having Jayson stay with them that unnerved her, she had to admit that it felt right. "Well, when he's coherent, you can invite him. I think he'd take it better coming from you."

"Fine, I will," he said. "In the meantime, I'm going to order some flowers or something."

"Flowers?"

"Okay, a plant."

"He hates plants. He says they always die."

"So, flowers are supposed to die. I'll send flowers."

"Fine, Dad," Elizabeth said. "You send flowers."

* * *

When Jayson finally became coherent enough to be fully aware of his surroundings, he found his hand throbbing and Drew sitting nearby, reading a science fiction novel. "That stuff'll fry your brain," Jayson said, and Drew looked up.

"Hey," he chuckled, "you're still alive."

"Too bad," Jayson said and closed his eyes.

"Are you in pain?"

"Yes," he said.

"I'll tell the nurse," he said and stood up. "Oh, by the way, you got flowers. They were delivered about an hour ago."

Jayson watched Drew leave the room, then he turned his head in the other direction and focused on a huge bouquet of various, brightly colored blooms. He couldn't recall ever getting flowers before. When Drew came back, Jayson asked him, "Who are they from? Is there a card?"

"There is," Drew said and plucked it from a plastic stick poking up out of the flowers. "Although, I would think you could guess.

There are only a minimal number of people out there who love you—beyond me, of course, and I'm here, so why would I send you flowers?"

"Good point. Just read it."

"It says, *We love you, and everything's going to be all right. Dad and Elizabeth.* Isn't that sweet? Of course, I should point out, this is from your *real* dad."

"The only one that matters," Jayson said and closed his eyes, feeling tears leak out of their corners.

"But look at this," Drew said, and Jayson turned back toward him, grateful he'd apparently not noticed his emotion. He comically pointed out four little plastic musical instruments dispersed throughout the bouquet. A guitar, a piano, a violin, and a harp.

"A harp?" Jayson actually chuckled. "If that's supposed to have some angelic implication, I think they goofed."

The doctor came in before any pain medication arrived, and Jayson was told that the surgery had gone well and everything should heal fine with time.

"Does that mean it will heal completely?" Jayson asked.

"That's difficult to say," the doctor answered. "Therapy can make a big difference, but there are always variables. Only time will tell."

Drew said firmly, "This is not a man who needs his left hand to drive the car and tie his shoes, Doctor."

The doctor had been well aware before he'd gone into the surgery that he was working on the hand of a great musician, and Jayson knew he was considered the best hand surgeon in the state; Drew had practically thrown a fit, demanding that only the best would do. Now the doctor turned to Jayson and said with compassion, "I gave you the very best I have to give. With diligent therapy, there is no reason you shouldn't be able to have full use of your hand. But it will take time, and it will take commitment on your part to retrain and strengthen all the parts of your hand." Jayson just nodded. At the moment, he couldn't imagine feeling committed to anything.

A minute after the doctor left, a nurse came in and gave Jayson some pills for the pain. Before they took effect, he said to Drew, "Will you call Elizabeth? Let her know what's going on. Tell her I'll call her when I get home in a couple of days."

"I'll tell her," Drew said. "You just get some rest. I'm going to stick around. If I'm not here when you wake up, I won't be far."

"Thank you," Jayson said and closed his eyes, letting the medication lure him into oblivion.

When Jayson came home from the hospital, Drew helped him get settled with everything he needed within his reach. He was astonished by the ongoing pain in his hand, and how his other hand felt useless and empty when the discouragement lured him to play music that he couldn't play. He actually went to the piano a few hours after their arrival home and attempted picking out something with his right hand, but his hands were trained to work together. He simply couldn't make music with one hand. So he took a pain pill and went to bed.

When he came around that evening, Drew said, "I've got something for you to eat. You'd better keep up your strength. Elizabeth called once and Will called twice. You should call them before you drug yourself again."

"Fine. Hand me the phone," Jayson said, and a moment later he realized that having only one hand to hold the cordless phone and dial it was a definite challenge.

"Here," Drew said and rescued him. Jayson repeated the number aloud from memory, and Drew handed him the phone when it began to ring. He told Elizabeth he was doing better than he really was, then she put her father on the phone. Will emphatically told Jayson that when he was able to travel he should come and stay with them. Will even offered to drive to Los Angeles and get him so he could bring as much stuff as he wanted. Jayson told Will he appreciated the offer, and he'd keep an open mind, but for the time being, he just needed to be home. He could hardly explain to Will his reasons for being hesitant to live under the same roof with Elizabeth, when he didn't fully understand them himself. Romantic feelings for her aside, there were things about himself that he simply didn't want Will or Elizabeth to know about until he could get a handle on his life. And living in the same house would make it impossible to keep such things to himself. He just needed some time.

Over the next seven months, Will offered at least once a week to come and get Jayson so that he could stay with them. Jayson insisted that he was fine, and managed to convince both Will and Elizabeth that he was. But in his heart he knew he *wasn't* fine. He kept telling himself that he could fix the problem, that with enough willpower he could get a handle on this and no one would have to know how messed up his life really was. But the problem only became worse instead of better.

Jayson's hand showed gradual improvement. The initial pain of the surgery had receded into a deeper pain that only occurred when he tried to use it. Eventually he'd been able to do simple things with it, but anything that required any twisting or pressure sent him into orbit. He'd usually curse aloud and sit on the floor with his head between his knees until he could breathe normally again, and he quickly learned not to do *anything* with that hand that didn't absolutely have to be done. The physical therapy had been horrid—since these people seemed to take pleasure in doing the very things with his hand that hurt the most. They kept telling him, "No pain, no gain," until he finally told *them* that the next person who said that to him was going to need to do therapy on his right hand after he belted them in the face. He eventually reached a point where he was taught the exercises he needed to do every day, multiple times a day. But he felt no incentive to do them. He'd almost gotten used to not playing music, and with no apparent reason to go on living at all, he certainly couldn't find a reason to endure any unnecessary pain.

Jayson felt a certain relief when he came to the decision to end his own life. He reached this decision through careful thought and precision as he'd assessed the possible repercussions of his absence in this world. He could only think of three people who would be hurt by his choice; three people who would miss him. But he could easily see that while they would experience some temporary grief, they would be better off in the long run when he wasn't a burden to them. He considered the possibility of Macy coming home, but nearly two years had passed with no word from her at all. Deep inside he felt certain she was dead. How could she go two years and never once call her father? He imagined her as some Jane Doe with a toe tag in some hospital morgue, then buried in a grave with a number.

Considering ways to end his misery, Jayson firmly decided that pills would be the least painful and would take the least amount of courage. He knew he'd need a lot of them, since his body had become desensitized to so many different prescriptions that he'd completely lost track of how many pills a day were going down his throat.

During a week when Drew was out of town, in the middle of a sleepless night, Jayson found every pill in the house and laid them all out on the kitchen table. He counted them twice; he rearranged them three or four times. He looked at them long and hard while a voice in his head seemed to scream that this was the answer to his every problem. Still, in spite of his calculated preparations and his desire to be free of his pain, he felt a deep sadness at the thought of leaving this world. He thought of better times in his life and wished it could be that way again. The tiniest part of him didn't want to do it, but the pain was speaking louder, beckoning him to an oblivion that was eternal. In a last-ditch effort to be certain there was no other choice, he heard himself saying aloud, "Okay, God, I can't think of one reason to keep on living. If you've got a reason, you'd better be letting me know. Otherwise, this is it."

He rearranged the pills again. He wandered the house, making certain everything was in order. He even took out the garbage and made sure there was no food in the fridge that would spoil. He knew the lady that came in twice a week to clean would be there tomorrow afternoon, and she would discover the body so that Drew wouldn't have to. He imagined the story in the tabloids. *Has-been rock star overdoses on prescription drugs, a ruined man.* He filled a large glass of water and sat again at the table. He glanced at the clock. Three-forty A.M. And then the phone rang.

* * *

Elizabeth came awake abruptly out of a sound sleep, expecting to find one of her children in the room. She was certain that she'd been nudged. She turned on the light to make certain she was alone. Walking into the bathroom she convinced herself that she must have been having some kind of vivid dream. As she was walking out of the bathroom, a thought came clearly into her head. *Call Jayson.* She stopped in the hall and tried to convince herself that it was the middle of the night and surely he would not appreciate being startled out of a deep sleep. The thought came more clearly. *Call Jayson. Do it now.*

"Fine," she said aloud and went to the phone. Her fingers were trembling as she dialed the memorized number. What could be so imperative that she would be awakened from a deep sleep and given such an undeniable prompting? She counted the rings: fifteen, twenty.

Jayson stared at the phone in astonishment, disbelieving that anyone would call at this hour. He let it ring and convinced himself that it had to be a wrong number. When it rang and rang he finally stood up and looked at the caller ID. A startled sob leapt out of his throat, then another and another until he sat on the floor, sobbing so hard he could hardly breathe, let alone pick up the phone.

Elizabeth finally hung up, feeling a panic that was difficult to define but undeniable nevertheless. She dialed the number again, praying in her mind while she counted the rings. Ten, eleven, twelve. She heard it pick up and held her breath.

"Okay, I'm here," Jayson said in a voice so strained with emotion that her heart quickened painfully.

"What's wrong?" she demanded.

"How do you know something's wrong?" he asked and sniffled loudly.

"I know you well enough to know you've been crying," she insisted. He just sniffled again, and she asked, "What's going on, Jayson?"

"I'm sitting in the middle of the kitchen floor, bawling like a baby."

"Why?" she asked gently.

"Why did you call me in the middle of the night?" he demanded, almost sounding angry.

Elizabeth wasn't certain how to explain. She prayed silently for guidance and felt she should say, "Would you believe me if I said that God told me to?" She heard him sob, then she heard only silence as if he'd put a hand over his mouth. She went on to say, "I woke up out of a deep sleep as if I'd been nudged, and the words came to my mind that I needed to call you." She hesitated. "Why did I need to call you, Jayson? You come clean with me, boy, or I will get in my car right now and drive down there and slap your face. Are you hearing me?"

"Maybe you should anyway," he said, so emotional she could barely understand him.

"Should what?"

"Slap my face."

"Why, Jayson? What's going on?"

"I . . . I told God that . . . if there was a reason . . . for me to . . . live . . ." She gasped, then put her hand over the receiver to keep him from hearing her reaction as the reality began to settle in. "I told him . . . He needed to let me know . . . or . . . or . . ."

"Or what?" she demanded, now crying herself. "What are you doing, Jayson? What's going on?"

"Forgive me, Elizabeth," he said. "I just . . . didn't think I could go on. I just . . ."

"What?" Her voice was so filled with emotion that Jayson felt strangely comforted. She *would* miss him if he were gone. And he was stunned at such undeniable evidence that God *had* heard his prayers. That alone made him believe he could get through another day. His growing hope was interrupted by Elizabeth practically shouting through the phone. "Are you saying what I think you're saying? What if I hadn't called, Jayson? Would Drew be calling me in a few days to tell me you were gone? Is that what you're trying to tell me?" She waited for him to answer, but he didn't.

"Tell me!" she shouted, and Jayson knew she was *really* upset. He couldn't recall *ever* hearing her use that tone of voice.

Jayson swallowed carefully and drew courage. He realized he was shaking as the fear took hold of him. He'd come so close to really doing away with himself. "Yes," he croaked, "that's what I'm trying to tell you."

Elizabeth felt something hard take hold of her heart, reminding her of the moment she'd been told that Bradley was dead, that Robert was dead. But this was *different*. While she felt immeasurably grateful for the prompting that had apparently saved Jayson's life, the reality of what he'd just admitted to made her want to scream and throw something. As it was, all she could do was cry.

Jayson heard Elizabeth crying so hard that she couldn't talk. He wanted to tell her that the evidence of her love for him meant more than words could say. He wanted to tell her that he was truly sorry for what he'd almost done, for even considering it. But all he could do was cry with her.

Elizabeth was startled to see her father come into the room, tying a robe around his waist. "What's wrong?" he demanded.

"It's Jayson," she said, knowing he could hear her through the phone.

"Is he all right?"

"He's alive," Elizabeth said and handed the phone to Will. "You talk to him for a minute. I can't." Elizabeth went into the bathroom, forcing herself to calm down and think clearly.

Jayson held his breath, realizing Will was on the phone. If he could have predicted this moment, he never could have even contemplated suicide. Losing Will's respect was likely more painful than losing the use of his hand.

"Jayson?" he said, his voice filled with concern.

"Yeah, it's me," he said, more calm but with a hoarse voice.

"What's happened, son? Talk to me."

"I don't know what to say," Jayson muttered. "I know I was being stupid, but . . . I just felt so helpless."

"Don't beat around the bush, Jayson. Just spit it out."

"I was going to take some pills; too many pills."

Jayson expected astonishment, anger, a well-deserved lecture, but William Greer said in a voice etched with perfect love and acceptance, "Why don't you tell me what would make you want to do such a thing when there are people who love you?"

It was difficult for Jayson to say, "I don't know. Everything just felt so . . . hopeless." But once he got some momentum, he talked to Will for over an hour, and together they concluded that now he *did* have hope, and he had to keep going. Will made him promise that he would come and stay with them. And while a part of Jayson didn't want Will—and especially Elizabeth—to see what a mess he was, he reminded himself that they had both just heard stark evidence of that. If he'd gone to stay with them months ago, perhaps it never would have gotten this bad.

Elizabeth mostly paced the floor while her father talked to Jayson. She heard him talking Jayson into coming to stay with them and felt relieved when it became evident Jayson had agreed. Will promised to arrange the flight, and three times he asked Jayson if he would promise to be on it. He finally said good night, then handed the phone to Elizabeth. "He wants to talk to you," Will said. "You know where to find me if you need me."

He got up and left the room. Elizabeth swallowed hard and said into the phone, "Hello."

"Hello."

"Are you all right?" she asked.

"I'm much better now, thank you. Thank you for calling. It sounds trite, but . . ." His voice cracked. "I'm grateful."

"Yes, so am I."

"Are *you* all right?" he asked.

"I'm more calm now, but still shaking if you must know."

"I'm sorry, Lady; truly I am."

"It's going to take some time for me to accept that."

"What?"

"Your apology on that count. I'm still . . . having a hard time with this. I'm not . . . blaming you for feeling desperate, Jayson. But I wonder . . . how it got that bad when . . . you know we're here. We've talked every few days. What was all this 'I'm fine' garbage? Were you lying to us, then? Obviously you're not fine. And contemplating suicide doesn't happen overnight."

Jayson sighed loudly. "I didn't see it as lying to you," he admitted. "It was more . . . trying to be brave. I thought I could handle it on my own. Obviously I was wrong."

"So, it's pride that nearly killed you tonight. Is that what you're telling me?"

"It would seem so," he said.

She became emotional and murmured, "I'm not trying to be hard on you, Jayson. I just . . . you're my best friend."

"And you are mine," he admitted readily.

"I've already lost too many people in my life. Don't think for a moment that I could ever cope with losing you—especially like this. If that makes me selfish, so be it. I'm having trouble feeling sorry for you right now because I'm too busy feeling sorry for myself. Okay?"

"Okay," he said. "If it's any consolation, it's nice to be feeling sorry for you instead of myself for a change. Somehow I convinced myself that you wouldn't really miss me."

"Well, somebody's been lying to you!" she shouted. Then she calmed down and added, "Sorry. I'm just a little . . . vehement about your staying alive."

"That's nice to know."

"I'm going to bed now, Jayson. I'm getting up in an hour or so to get Trevin up for school, and then I'm going to call you, and you'd darn well better answer the phone."

"I promise," he said. "If I go anywhere, I'll have my cell phone with me." He added with emotion, "You never know when Macy might call and need her father."

"You never know," she echoed.

CHAPTER 12

Jayson packed some clothes and personal belongings into two pieces of luggage, and he put his acoustic guitar into a hard-sided case. He knew he couldn't play it, but having it close still afforded him some degree of comfort. He wandered through the house, feeling no regret about leaving anything behind except for the piano. But he couldn't play it anyway. Impulsively he took Derek's silly hat and Elizabeth's red shoe from inside the glass cabinet, but he left the Grammy trophies there. He took a few pictures in frames that he'd had sitting around and tucked them carefully between his clothes. On a hunch he grabbed a few copies of each of his CDs and tucked them into the bag he would carry onto the plane. His manager had suggested years ago that it never hurt to carry them. He hadn't done it for a few years, but for some reason he felt compelled to now. He left a note for Drew on the piano that simply said: *I've gone to stay with Will and Elizabeth. I don't know when I'll be back. Little Brother.*

Jayson began to feel on edge waiting for the cab. He told himself he could get through the next hour without taking a pill, but his anxiety became too intense and he had to take it anyway. It was raining when the cab arrived, and he hurried to get his guitar and luggage into the trunk. He became preoccupied with the rain drizzling down the car windows during the drive to the airport. He had a feeling it would be a good long time before he saw California rain again. It wouldn't take Will or Elizabeth long to figure out the obvious, and then heaven only knew what might happen. A part of him knew their knowing the truth was inevitable; he knew at some level that he needed their help, that he couldn't break this on his own. But another part of him felt determined to do it on his own, to find a way to get himself out of this mess he'd gotten himself into. Either way, his recent brush with self-inflicted death had left him terrified to be alone, and he wouldn't be returning to his home until he knew he could be there and cope with the reality of his life without becoming suicidal.

At the airport, he gave the cab driver a healthy tip and carried his luggage inside. He was waiting in line to check his luggage and get his boarding pass, his guitar at his feet, when the woman behind him in line touched his arm and said, "I'm sorry to bother you, but . . . I just have to ask . . . are you Jayson Wolfe?"

He turned to look at her fully. She was about his age, with eyes that looked as if they'd witnessed a holocaust. *Like his mother.* Her smile was kind and timid. "I used to be," he said lightly, and she let out a meek little laugh.

"I thought so," she said. "I have a poster of you in my office, so I am pretty familiar with what you look like. Even with those dark glasses you're wearing, you're definitely you. I didn't want to invade your privacy or anything, but . . . I just couldn't pass up the chance to tell you something . . . if I may."

"Sure, why not?" he said. "We could be in this line for another week or so."

She laughed again as if she appreciated his sense of humor. "I've thought about writing you a letter, but you must get hundreds, and . . ."

"Not many these days," he said.

"Well . . . maybe this is better, if you don't mind."

Something about her made him far more intrigued than irritated. Of course, he'd not been approached by a fan in a long time. Such encounters had lost the threat to his privacy that they had once been. "I don't mind," he said. "But you didn't tell me your name."

"Karen," she said.

"It's nice to meet you, Karen," he said, shaking her hand.

She looked pleasantly surprised by the gesture as she went on. "Well . . . I just wanted to tell you about my son. His name is Jason too, only it's spelled differently than yours. He was always one of those kids who needed music. Right from the womb he was just happier with music playing. We got him a guitar when he was pretty young. It was what he wanted more than anything. He doesn't think he'll ever do anything great with it, but it brings him a lot of pleasure—and me; I enjoy hearing him play."

Something quivered inside of Jayson as he was vividly reminded of his mother—again. He felt the need to comment, "There's no better audience for a boy than a mother who believes in him."

Her eyes sparkled from the comment, and she said, "He was really getting into music when 'Predator' came out. And we both just loved it. Your music was always a common bond for us. As he got older, he had some struggles, but we always agreed on one thing—and that was your music. We could drive in the car together and listen to it, and it would settle any differences between us. But the thing I really wanted to tell you was that . . . well, about a year ago, Jason's best friend killed himself."

Jayson gasped, and Karen got a little teary. "I can't even begin to tell you how hard that's been—for both of us. This kid was almost like one of my own. And he was a good kid, with so much potential. It's truly tragic. But . . . anyway, the thing is . . . Jason's actually doing pretty well now, all things considered, and he's told me a hundred times that it was listening to your music that got him through. I read an interview you did in a magazine, where you talked about your best friend getting killed in high school. I think some of those songs let Jason know that he wasn't the only one who'd ever lost somebody like that, and if you could get through it, he could too. Anyway. I just wanted you to know that."

She motioned with her hand to indicate that the line was moving without them. They each picked up their luggage and moved forward, then set it down again. Jayson turned to look at this sweet woman and felt tempted to tell her the full depth of what her story meant to him. He wanted to tell her he'd nearly taken his own life not so many hours ago. He wanted to tell her that he'd completely lost perspective on the impact he'd had on the world. He was just thinking she couldn't have possibly said anything to touch him any more than what she'd said, when she added, "I hope you'll always keep making music. I know the band had some tragic things happen, but I know you'll find a way to keep sharing your gift with the world."

"That's a nice thought," he said, certain it would never happen, but it was still nice to hear. "I guess we never know what the future might bring."

"We never know," she said brightly.

"Well, thank you for sharing your story with me, Karen. I think I needed to hear that today."

She smiled as if she were pleased by the idea. When it became evident the line still had a long ways to go, she said, "I assume you're not going on vacation if you're taking a guitar." She glanced at the case.

He sighed. "I'm going to stay with some friends for a while. The guitar's kind of my security blanket." For the sake of making conversation he asked, "And where are you going, Karen, all by yourself?"

"A friend of mine has cancer," she said. "I'm going to spend some time with her and help her out."

Jayson took a deep breath; this conversation just kept getting more eerie. He was surprised to hear himself admit, "I lost my mother to cancer last year."

"Oh, I'm so sorry," she said. "She couldn't have been very old."

"No, she wasn't," he said. "Is your friend going to be all right?"

"We hope so. We're just trying to make the best of it."

Jayson felt helpless, wishing he could do something for Karen, her friend, her son. And then it occurred to him . . . music. He bent over and unzipped a side pocket on his bag, while he asked, "So which CD was your favorite?"

"Oh, they were both great, but . . . I think I liked the second one better. Although Jason leaned a little more toward the first. I don't know. It's a toss-up."

They moved their luggage again as the line made some headway. "Well, here," he said putting one each of his two CDs into her hands. She gasped and looked startled. "Would you like me to sign them for you?"

"Oh . . . that would begreat," she said, seeming a little dumbstruck.

"Surely the copies you have are getting worn out."

"Terribly, if you must know."

Jayson tore the cello-wrap off the first CD and stuffed it into one of his jacket pockets, then he reached into the other pocket in search of a pen. He found a guitar pick and stuck it between his teeth. Then he found the pen and pulled out the printed insert, where he wrote, *To Jason. From one musician to another. If you keep going, I'll keep going. Jayson Wolfe.*

Karen watched him write it, and she let out a delighted laugh. "Oh, he will love it!" she said with excitement. "I think you'll make his day; maybe his month. You've certainly made my day."

"I think it's the other way around," Jayson said and unwrapped the second CD as he asked Karen how to spell her name. On the insert he wrote, *To Karen, for making my day, and for raising a fine son. Jayson Wolfe.* "Now," he said, handing that one to Karen, "which one do you think your friend would like?"

"Oh, you're being way too generous," she insisted.

"I have boxes of these I need to get rid of," he said, and she laughed softly. "Which one?"

"The second one," she said. "I think that will help get her through."

Karen spelled her friend's name, and in the CD insert he wrote, *To Simone, a woman of great courage. May your ongoing fight be free of pain and filled with love. Jayson Wolfe.*

When the signing was complete, Jayson put the pen in his pocket and pulled the guitar pick out of his teeth. He looked at it and handed it to Karen. "Give this to Jason. Tell him to wear it out."

She smiled and took it, closing her fingers around it as if he'd just given her a thousand dollars. She thanked him profusely, and they shared some small talk as the line moved on. When it was nearly Jayson's turn, he shook Karen's hand again and thanked her once more for sharing her story. She thanked him as well, and he moved to the ticket counter.

While going through security and waiting to board the plane, Jayson contemplated his encounter with Karen. He would never see her again, but she'd touched him with her kindness at a time when he'd needed it badly. He hoped he had touched her, as well. Once he was on the plane, Jayson's mood settled back into reality. Waiting for the passengers to board, he again became preoccupied with the rain drizzling down the window. He wondered if it was raining in Utah. Either way, it was raining in his heart, he thought, recalling a conversation about that he'd once had with Elizabeth. He wondered if it would be Will or Elizabeth there to meet him when he got off the plane. He wondered, as he did every so many minutes, if Macy was okay, cold, hungry, safe—alive. He wondered how he was ever going to get past the mess he'd made of his life. Overcome with a familiar sinking sensation, he got some water from the stewardess and took a couple of pills. He soon began to relax and was relieved when the flight got underway.

* * *

Elizabeth took care of an errand in downtown Salt Lake City that she'd been needing to do for a couple of weeks now, then she drove to the airport and parked the car. She arrived at the baggage claim area at exactly the time she knew Jayson's flight was supposed to land. She knew it would take him some time to traverse the long corridors and arrive at where she had to wait.

She felt impatient and antsy, glancing at her watch every two minutes, and watching the escalators closely. He'd promised her father he would be on that flight, but until she actually saw him, she would keep fearing that he'd regressed in the hours since they'd talked, and maybe he'd done the unthinkable after all. Maybe he'd told them he'd come just to patronize them, and he was even now seeking out some way of doing away with himself. Or maybe he already had.

Elizabeth caught her breath when she saw him at the top of the escalator, coming down. Even from this distance, she clearly recognized him. He wore the long, black coat she'd given him in high school, and he had on dark glasses even though he was inside on a cloudy day. He had a bag over one shoulder, and his hair looked a little rumpled—just the way he liked it. He had such a distinctive air about him that it was difficult to imagine the depths he'd descended to not so many hours ago. When he stepped off the escalator, she noticed he was wearing those old-fashioned, black lace-up shoes she loved so dearly. But she quickly moved her focus to his face. She saw him hesitate and scan the area until he looked directly at her. For a long moment they just stared at each other from a distance. She was wishing she could see his eyes when he took off his dark glasses, as if to see her better. They started toward each other in the same moment, and the world seemed to be going in slow motion as she opened her arms and allowed him to fill them. She couldn't hold back tears as she pondered how grateful she was to feel him in her embrace, alive, and breathing, and real. She felt him drop his bag and embrace her more tightly, as if they shared the same emotion without a word spoken between them. He finally drew back and looked at her tears with a furrowed brow.

"No need for this," he said, wiping them away.

"I'm just so grateful . . . that you're here . . . and you're all right."

"All right is relative," he said, picking up the bag. "But I'm grateful to be here as well."

She held his hand as they moved to the rotating luggage carousel. When the guitar case came over the edge, she said, "Oh, I recognize that. Don't leave home without it."

"Not for more than a few days, at least," he said and went to get it. He set it next to Elizabeth's feet and went to retrieve his other bag. She picked up the case, and he said, "I can get it."

"So can I," she said. "This way you can hold my hand."

She took his left hand into hers then looked down at it in surprise. There was something stiff and unnatural in the way he threaded his fingers between hers, as if it took conscious effort. He apparently noticed her attention to it when he said, "Yes, it's deformed."

"Does it still hurt?"

"Only if I try to do something that takes any effort—like opening a can or something."

Nothing was said as they walked to the car, except for Jayson commenting, "It's cold here."

"It's a beautiful fall day," she said. "Well, a little cloudy, but a nice day."

Jayson wasn't surprised to be loading his luggage into a Tahoe. It was different from the one she'd been driving in Phoenix, but obviously she liked this type of vehicle. Once she had driven beyond the airport and onto the freeway, Elizabeth said, "I hope you don't mind if I do a couple of errands before we go to the house."

"I don't mind," he said.

"Are you hungry? Dad's cooking dinner, but that's still a couple of hours away. If you're hungry, we can—"

"I'm fine," he said, looking out the window through his dark glasses.

"You okay?" she asked after they'd gone several miles with no conversation.

"I'm fine," he said again, but she wasn't convinced.

If only to fill the silence, she turned on the stereo, recalling now that she'd been listening to a *Gray Wolf* CD. She chuckled when Jayson's recorded voice filled the car—rather loudly. Then she gasped when Jayson pushed the eject button and tossed the CD into the backseat. She glared at him as a radio commercial took the place of the music. She turned off the radio and snapped, "What are you doing? I *love* that CD. What if you scratched it? I can listen to it if I want to!"

"Well, use headphones," he growled and turned back to the window. "I'll give you a new one."

"That's not the point," she said. "What gives you the right to toss my stuff around like that?"

"I'm sorry," he said, but he didn't seem to mean it. "I just . . . can't listen to it."

"Fine, but you didn't have to throw it."

"I'll give you a new one," he repeated and looked out the window.

Silence fell again, and Elizabeth was even more concerned now than she had been earlier. It wasn't like him to be so thoroughly irritable and sharp. She prayed that whatever was wrong, they could get past it—and soon. Having him under her roof could be a challenge if he was going to be in this kind of mood.

Jayson watched the scenery with little interest. He'd been to Utah before, but as with most places where he'd performed, he'd seen little but the inside of the concert hall. On the road, he'd been mostly sleeping, and in the city he'd been too famous to go out. Less than an hour from when they'd gotten into the car, he noticed an exit that said Highland, but she didn't take it. Then he remembered the errands. She took the exit for Pleasant Grove and drove a stretch of highway with islands down the center where trees grew. They went to a drive-through bank, dropped off some rented videos, then stopped at a copy center where she said, "You coming in or do you want to wait? I shouldn't be long."

"I'll wait," he said.

"You won't break anything while I'm gone, will you?"

"I promise," he said with subtle sarcasm.

He watched her go in with nothing but her purse and come out with stacks of paper that she set carefully in the backseat. It was getting dark as they parked next to an attorney's office where she took the papers inside and came out with a thick manila envelope.

"Okay, that's it," she said, putting the car in gear. And then silence fell again. "I must warn you," she added as she drove, feeling the need to counter the quiet.

"About what?" he asked, turning away from the window to peer at her through his dark glasses. She wished that she could see his eyes.

"My home has not been—nor will it ever be—on *Lifestyles of the Rich and Famous.*"

"What's that supposed to mean?" Jayson asked, sounding insulted.

"You don't need to get so defensive," she retorted.

"Well, I have to assume you're implying something," he insisted. "Forgive me if once having been *rich and famous,* I might sense some implication in such a statement."

"That's not what I meant."

"Then what exactly do you mean?" he asked.

"I mean . . . it's a nice home. It's beautiful and I'm grateful for it. I'm especially grateful that the life insurance paid off the mortgage. But it's a mess; plain and simple. Life has been . . . complicated. Cleaning and organization have not been high on my priority list, and there are no housekeepers or nannies in my life."

"I wouldn't expect there to be," he said, now sounding angry *and* insulted. "I would expect you to be leading a very normal life, doing your best to raise a family and cope with death, while I have been trying very hard to *learn* how to live a normal life and doing my best to accept that I have no family to raise. My life is a mess, Elizabeth. If your house is a mess, then I'll feel right at home." He turned back to the window and added with an edge to his voice, "You should know me well enough to know that I never led any kind of glamorous life. The public image had little to do with real life."

"I know that," she said in a gentle voice that Jayson found more soothing than he wanted to admit. She added lightly, "It's been a while since I had a rock star in my home."

"And you likely never will again," he said, meeting her momentary sharp glance. "My star status fell from the sky a long time ago. Former rock star is more accurate, although I am still rich," he finished more lightly.

In the same light tone she said, "I've had a brilliant genius musician in my home before, but not in this home."

"Do you know one?" he asked blandly.

"I do," she said proudly.

He again looked out the window. "Perhaps 'former' applies there as well."

"Never," she insisted. "That will always be a part of who and what you are."

Jayson wondered why such a statement made him angry. He wondered why he felt so strongly compelled to argue with her. But he didn't have the strength to pursue that impulse, so he let it drop. When the silence once again grew long, he said, "It's been a while since I've been to the home of the most magnificent woman in the world."

Elizabeth shot him an abrupt glance before she turned back to look at the road. She sensed his sincerity, even without being able to see his eyes. She wondered why she felt prone to tell him the very idea was ludicrous. She couldn't define the dark cloud hovering around her, but she knew she certainly was not—and didn't feel—magnificent. She drove the back roads in silence, hating the way darkness had settled in so early. She still hadn't adjusted to the recent switch from daylight saving time. And she wondered how she'd ever adjust to having Jayson Wolfe living under her roof for an undetermined length of time.

Jayson's thoughts wandered as he gazed absently out the window into the darkness. The vague sense of detachment from his surroundings felt familiar, as did the underlying fear that knotted his stomach. But he couldn't deny feeling some measure of comfort to be with Elizabeth. Her presence alone soothed something in him that he couldn't—or didn't want to—define. Seeing a vague glow in the night sky above the trees, he became preoccupied with what might be the cause. While he was considering the possibility of a ball field or a used-car lot, a gold statue atop some kind of tower appeared above the trees. A moment later, a magnificent, steepled structure rose in front of them. The building was completely lit up with a white glow that appeared almost heavenly. He caught his breath, then asked, "What is *that?*"

Elizabeth's heart quickened, and she wondered why his question would make her nervous. In a cool tone, she answered, "It's a temple."

"A *temple?*" he echoed as if he'd never heard the word before. "Seeing that we're in Utah, would that mean it's a *Mormon* temple?"

For a long moment Elizabeth's mind went back to conversations of the past. She knew Jayson's views of Mormonism were mostly related to a common gross misconception, and to the fact that his alcoholic father had been a Mormon. And now Jayson Wolfe had been abruptly transplanted into the middle of Mormondom. The sooner she told him where she stood, the better. She reminded herself of her convictions as she took a deep breath and said, "Yes, Jayson, it's a Mormon temple." She was aware of him craning his neck to look at the building as she drove past. She added firmly, "And I go there regularly."

His astonishment was evident even though she kept her eyes fixed on the road ahead. "I thought you couldn't go inside such places unless you're a Mormon."

"That's right," she said and briefly gave him a hard stare.

Even through the darkness she could see his bewilderment. "What are you saying?" he asked in a tone that implied he'd just been told she would die of some horrible disease.

Elizabeth looked straight ahead and cleared her throat. "I'm saying that I'm a Mormon; I have been for a few years."

"What are you saying?" he repeated, this time sounding angry. "You . . . *what?* You moved to Utah and had to conform to the crowd? Is that it? How could you embrace something that's not even Christian when—"

Elizabeth pulled abruptly to the side of the road and came to a screeching halt. The panicked noise that came out of Jayson's mouth made it evident he'd thought they were meeting imminent collision. When he realized they weren't, he turned toward her, his angry expression showing clearly in the glow of a nearby street-light. Wanting to look him in the eye, she pulled off his dark glasses and tossed them onto the dashboard. "Now that I have your attention," she said in the same tone he'd been using when she stopped the car, "let me make a few things perfectly clear. First, I have never in my life done *anything* to conform to the crowd. For you to assume that I would do so now is judgmental and ludi-crous. Second, this religion I have embraced is Christianity in its truest sense, and your saying otherwise only illustrates your igno-rance, along with your being judgmental. Third, if you don't think you can handle living in a Mormon home, I would be happy to get back on the freeway and take you to the airport."

Elizabeth watched his astonishment merge into something humble and apologetic as he muttered, "Forgive me . . . for being ignorant and judgmental."

Elizabeth looked down, feeling a bit embarrassed for her vehe-mence. "I forgive you," she said.

"May I ask why you never bothered to tell me that you'd made such a monumental change in your life? Years? You've been a Mormon for years and you didn't tell me?" In a lighter voice he added, "I told you when I became a rock star."

Elizabeth turned to face forward and put her hands on the steering wheel, but she didn't move the car. "I was happy for you when you became a rock star," she said in a serious tone that didn't match the lightness of his last comment. "I wasn't sure you'd be happy about my becoming a Mormon; although I must clarify, we don't generally call ourselves that. It's a nickname and not necessarily an accurate one. It's technically The Church of Jesus Christ of Latter-day Saints. To say that I am LDS is more accurate." She turned to look at him and added, "One would assume that a church named after Christ would be a *Christian* church."

"I'm sorry. I didn't know that," he said, and he seemed to mean it.

"There's a lot you don't know; a lot *I* didn't know. In reality, Mormonism is one of the most grossly misunderstood religions in the world."

"And apparently you've come to understand it," he said.

"Yes, I have," she said, but it sounded defensive.

"Are you happy about it?"

"Yes, I am."

"Then I'm happy for you," he said. A minute later he added, "Was Robert a Mormon? I'm sorry . . . LDS?"

"No," she stated. "He was very supportive . . . as he was with everything I did. But he had no interest in it. But that's how he was; content with life, no reason to change it."

"He was a good man," Jayson said.

"Yes," Elizabeth said, unable to keep the sadness from her voice, "he was a good man. He loved me, he respected me, he took good care of me. He was a good father. In fact, Robert was good at everything he did." She sighed. "Yes, he was a good man." She looked the other way and said, "He was good at everything but passionate over nothing. He had trouble understanding my passions—for music, for drama."

"For life," he said, and she turned to look at him.

She knew Jayson was well aware of the problems she'd had in her marriage, and the way those problems had been solved to some degree. Still, she didn't want to admit how deeply he seemed to understand her. She looked away and said, "He had trouble under-standing why I would commit myself to a religion that I had once spoken against. But then, religion of any kind had never been a part of his life. Still, he supported me without question. As you know, he was always content to stay at home and keep everything together while I went to plays and operas and concerts—and church. And he'd meet me with a smile and ask me if I had a good time." She laughed softly.

"You miss him."

"I miss him very much," she admitted.

"It was a good marriage, then," he said, "when all was said and done."

"Yes," she said in a voice that was almost dreamy, "it was a good marriage. You know it wasn't perfect. I had my frustrations; he had his. But I know many women who would have given their right arm to have *my* marriage problems. For women who have been abused and cheated on, having a good—but somewhat dispassionate— husband would have been a dream come true."

Suddenly uncomfortable, Elizabeth put the car into drive and moved back onto the road. "We should get home, I think," she said. "Dad will be terribly anxious to see you."

"As I am to see him," Jayson said. A couple of minutes later he added, "Why didn't you tell me?"

"That I joined the Church, you mean?"

"That's what I mean."

"You were struggling at the time. It didn't seem important, and then . . . one struggle led into another, and it just became such a natural part of my life that I hardly thought about it."

Jayson didn't say anything else. He couldn't explain why he felt deeply uneasy about this change in her life. Was she so uncomfortable or embarrassed over joining a new religion that she would completely overlook telling him?

As Elizabeth pulled into the driveway of her home, it felt vaguely familiar, if only from pictures he'd seen. They pulled into the garage, and he barely had his door open before Will appeared in the doorway to the house. Without a word, he wrapped Jayson in his fatherly embrace and they held to each other for a long moment. Then Will took Jayson's face into his hands. "I'm grateful to see you alive and well, son," he said.

"I'm grateful to be here," Jayson said.

Will helped carry Jayson's luggage into the house. Jayson noticed the home was beautifully decorated, as her previous home had been, and it had a cozy warmth to it that he'd expected. He noticed a little more clutter sitting about than on his previous visits to her home in Arizona, but he had trouble understanding what she'd meant when she said it was a mess. It looked pretty good to him.

He and Will followed Elizabeth down the stairs and into the first door on the left. As Will set down the bag he was carrying, she said, "I'm giving you Bradley's room. It's—"

"Oh, that's not necessary," Jayson said. "Surely there's a—"

"It's fine," she assured him. "We cleaned it out a long time ago. Turning his bedroom into a shrine would not have made me feel any closer to him. His belongings that had any sentimental value are at easy access, I can assure you. Actually, it will be nice to have somebody giving it some life. The closet and drawers are empty. Feel free to move in and make yourself at home. If you need something, you'll have to speak up and let one of us know." She motioned with her hand toward a door. "This room has its own bathroom, so you can have your space and privacy. And Dad's room is right there, if you need him." She pointed toward another door.

"Thank you," Jayson said, trying to be gracious and not let on to how tense and agitated he felt.

"I'll have supper ready in about ten minutes," Will said, putting a hand on his shoulder. "We'll see you upstairs."

"Thank you," he said again and watched them leave the room. With the door closed he hurried to find a couple of pills and take them, knowing he'd never get through the evening without them.

Elizabeth was urging the kids to the table when Jayson entered the dining room. Seeing him in good light without his dark glasses, she noticed that his eyes looked tired and strained. She introduced him to Addie, her youngest child that he'd never met, and he said to Trevin, "It's good to see you again." Trevin just gave a polite smile and went on in the same somber mood that had become almost constant of late.

After greeting the children, Jayson looked down into the face of a full-grown, rather fat yellow lab. The dog seemed to be sizing him up with friendly eyes. With light sarcasm, he said, "I think your dog wants to eat me." This got a chuckle out of everyone except Addie, who said firmly, "Mozie is a nice dog. He won't hurt you."

"Mozie?" Jayson echoed.

"His name is Mozart," Will said, and Jayson chuckled.

"Of course," he said and rubbed the dog's head. "Hello, Mozie."

"Don't feed him table scraps or I'll slap you silly," Elizabeth threatened. "We're finally getting him trained to know that he doesn't eat when we eat."

"I'll remember that," Jayson said and washed up at the kitchen sink before he sat down.

Seeing Elizabeth help her father set out a fine meal, Jayson felt he had to say, "You're going to have to let me pay rent, or earn my keep, or something."

Elizabeth tossed him a brief glare and said, "I can assure you if your presence here causes any burden, I will let you know. In the meantime, just try to be gracious."

"I'll do my best," he said, not feeling gracious at all.

Elizabeth noticed that as the meal began, Jayson seemed depressed and exhausted, and she felt deeply concerned for him. But by the time they were finished, he'd perked up considerably and was even joking with Will, almost like his old self. He insisted on helping with the dishes and seemed to have found a second wind.

When the kitchen was in order, Elizabeth sat to help Trevin with his homework while Will read Addie a story. Jayson wandered the house a bit and felt deeply comforted, but not surprised, to find the grand piano in the front room just off the entry hall. He was standing with his right hand on the piano and his left in his pocket when he looked up and saw a framed print that took his breath away.

"It's Jesus," Elizabeth said, startling him.

"I can see that," he said. "Although . . . I've never seen Him depicted quite that way before. He looks so . . . human."

"Recognizable as a man who could have walked the earth," she said. "Yet, there's something so God-like in the eyes."

Elizabeth watched Jayson take in the painting, and she wondered if it might motivate some productive conversation. But he turned to her and said with an edge of cynicism, "Why are His eyes blue? Everyone knows He's Jewish." · ⁓

"He was only half Jewish," Elizabeth said.

"The Bible clearly states his lineage," Jayson said. "He came from—"

"The Bible clearly states the lineage of Mary and Joseph; but Joseph was not His father."

She saw Jayson look confused, then his eyes widened with enlightenment. A defined intrigue filled his expression as he turned to look at the painting once more. "So, this is how Mormons perceive Him?"

"This is how one Mormon artist perceives Him. Perhaps if prophets had the ability to paint, we might have a depiction that we would know to be accurate."

"Prophets?" he asked using the same tone as when he'd said *temple* earlier. It was as if she were speaking a foreign language. "You mean like Moses and Abraham; men like that."

"And many, many others," she said.

"But that's ancient history," he said. Something else about what she'd said felt foreign to his beliefs, but it took him a moment to pinpoint it. He added with caution, "I don't claim to be well-versed on religion by any means, but . . . even when God spoke to prophets, wasn't it just like . . . a voice from the clouds, or a burning bush, or something?"

"Actually," she said, "there are many accounts in the scriptures of prophets talking face-to-face with the Lord." She met his eyes firmly and added, "Some of those accounts are far from ancient; quite recent, in truth."

Jayson heard a skeptical noise come out of his mouth before he even thought to hold it back. He wondered what kind of ridiculous concepts she'd been brainwashed into believing through this new religion of hers. But he didn't want to be impolite. He was a guest in her home; he needed to be gracious. Still, she would expect honesty from him, and he had to ask, "What are you saying, Elizabeth? That God is talking to people?"

"Certain people," she said. "Prophets."

"Prophets. What . . . now?"

"Yes," she said, and he laughed again. "If you're going to make fun of my beliefs, Jayson, then we'd do well not to talk about them at all."

"I'm sorry," he said. "I'm just . . . surprised. I mean . . . this is not like you. Religion just doesn't seem your . . . forté. And now you're not only talking religion, you're saying things that just seem way too outlandish."

"Do you think it's outlandish to believe that God would love His children on the earth today as much as He loved those who lived during biblical times?"

"Well . . . no."

"So, why would He send prophets then but not now?"

Jayson had to admit, "I can't answer that." But he kept his thoughts to himself that he simply didn't believe it could be possible. He didn't know why; that's just the way he felt.

Seeing a certain defiance in Jayson's eyes, Elizabeth said, "Maybe it would be better if we just didn't talk about religion."

"Maybe it would," he said, and she left the room.

CHAPTER 13

Jayson looked again at the painting hanging above the piano, unable to deny how it moved him. Instinctively he felt a deep belief that Jesus Christ was real; he'd been praying all his life, and he'd felt that power a number of times. But prophets? Temples? It seemed ludicrous. But most of all he hated the subtle rift between him and Elizabeth since she'd made her new religion known to him. He realized now that the last time they'd been together, in Denver, she had been a Mormon but had said nothing. And he wondered why. He'd felt comfortable with her then. Obviously it hadn't changed who and what she was. But still, it had changed something inside of her, and it left him feeling disoriented and out of sorts with her. He recalled now one of their conversations in Denver. Her words had left him confused and concerned at the time, and now they made perfect sense. *There have been some changes in my life that we haven't even talked about; things you're not aware of; things that could make a big difference in the long run. . . . I don't want to get into it right now. I promise I'll tell you everything when the time is right. It's nothing to be concerned about. I just . . . need some time to adjust.*

So that was it, he thought. She had made religion a part of her life, and it was one more reason for him to be excluded from it. Feeling a little sick over the thought, he went in search of Will, who was sitting in the basement in a spacious room that was like his little private den. It had a couch, a recliner, a television, lots of bookshelves, and a stereo. And it was decorated comfortably, scattered with pictures of his loved ones, even a few of Jayson.

"Wow, this is nice," Jayson said. "I take it you've settled in rather well here."

"Yes, I love it, actually," Will said as Jayson sat on the couch. "It's nice to be with Elizabeth and the kids. Beyond you, they're the only real family I've got."

"I don't know if I count," Jayson said.

"You most certainly do!" Will countered, almost sounding insulted.

Jayson smiled at him, then looked down. "So . . . what do you think of this religion thing that Elizabeth's become involved in?"

"Why is this coming up now?"

"I didn't know about it until today."

"You're joking."

"No," Jayson said. "She's never said a word until we drove past the temple today. Why would she keep something like that from me?"

"I don't know. But I'm sure she had her reasons."

"So, what do you think of it?"

"I think it's wonderful," Will said. "It's the best thing that ever happened to us."

"Us?"

"I was baptized a few months ago myself."

Jayson sucked in his breath, feeling suddenly left out in the cold. Beyond Drew, these people were the only family he had, and now they had eagerly embraced a religion that he knew very little about—and what he did know of it left him uneasy.

"Wow," Jayson said, then he changed the subject, figuring Elizabeth's suggestion might hold true with Will as well. Maybe it would be better if they just didn't talk about religion.

Following a brief visit, Jayson said good night and went upstairs, where he found Elizabeth in the kitchen. He told her good night, as well.

"Do you have everything you need?" she asked.

"I do, thank you," he said.

"It's good to have you here, Jayson. I feel a little less worried about you, knowing you're here with us."

"Well, it's nice to know somebody cares," he said, then went to his room and straight to bed. With the right amount of medication he slept deep and long. He woke up with a headache, took a couple of pills, and got in the shower. With hot water running over his face, he thought of the circumstances of his life, and an unexpected spurt of emotion rushed out of him. He leaned his head against the side of the shower and cried until he could manage to stuff the pain back where it belonged. He dried off and took a couple more pills before he got dressed and ventured through the house in search of life. He found it completely devoid of people, and no notes left in any obvious places. Standing in the kitchen, he turned toward the window and caught the view of the backyard. It was spacious and beautiful, with a lawn that sloped down into a wooded area. And kneeling in the middle of a large vegetable garden was Elizabeth. He went out the door onto a deck, down the wooden steps, and across the yard. Standing at the edge of the garden, he noticed her pulling carrots up out of the ground and shaking the mud off of them.

"What are you doing?" he asked, and she looked up at him.

"Oh, good morning. It's a soup day," she said matter-of-factly. "So, I'm digging up a few ingredients. Soon this will all be frozen."

Elizabeth leaned back on her heels and took in his appearance more fully. She was completely familiar with the ponytail and the earring; he'd worn them for as long as she'd known him. And she was well accustomed to his unique way of dressing. His clothes looked more suited to making a fashion statement than anything else, however tasteful they were. And just as yesterday, he was wearing dark glasses. She couldn't resist saying, "You look like a fish out of water."

"What do you mean?" he asked with a cynical edge.

"You look like a rock star standing in a vegetable garden."

He made a scoffing noise and scowled at her, but he didn't comment.

"It's cloudy, you know," she said. "They call those sunglasses because most people wear them in the sun."

"The light hurts my eyes," he said. "Cloudy or not."

"And why is that?"

"I have a headache," he said.

"Do you get headaches often?"

"Yes, actually," he said.

"And you never told me?"

"You never told me you were a Mormon," he said and pointed at her as he added, "Touché."

"Touché," she repeated and went back to her work.

"Where is everybody?" he asked.

"Dad had some errands. Trevin's in school. And Addie's at preschool. She only goes three mornings a week; this is one of them."

"I see," he said.

"Are you hungry?" she asked, coming to her feet. She brushed the dirt off her jeans and picked up the bucket that was full of vegetables.

"Not really."

"Well, you need to eat something."

"A piece of toast would be fine, and I'm certain I can get that myself by nosing around in the kitchen a little."

"You probably could," she said, walking back toward the house as he followed. She kicked off her shoes at the door since they were covered with mud. He just wiped his feet and went in, since his shoes were clean.

While Elizabeth washed vegetables at the sink, she told him where to find what he needed and let him make his own toast. He asked, "Do you have any coffee?"

"There's some instant stuff on the top shelf of that corner cupboard. I actually kept it with you in mind, hoping you might come to see us."

"What do you mean?" he asked, reaching for the coffee that was in an extremely inconvenient location.

"We don't drink it any more."

"What?"

"Coffee," she said.

"Why not?" he asked, astonished. He thought everybody drank coffee.

"It's against my religion," she said facetiously, but her eyes were serious.

He made that scoffing noise again, and Elizabeth stopped what she was doing and glared at him. "Tell me you're joking," he said.

"I'm quite serious," she said. "And just so you will know exactly where I stand on this and you can stop treating it like some kind of joke, I became a member of the Church because I know it's true. I know it beyond any doubt. I have not been buffaloed or coerced into anything. And I don't drink coffee because it's one of many things that falls under a guideline called the Word of Wisdom. It excludes caffeinated beverages, tobacco, alcohol, or any other harmful substances. Among other things, coffee is full of caffeine. It's addictive, it's a stimulant, and it's not good for you. It's as simple as that. You are welcome to drink coffee in my home. You are also expected to respect my wish *not* to drink coffee and not scoff at me because I don't."

"You sound awfully defensive," he said.

"And why wouldn't I when you act as if I've joined a monastery or something? This is exactly why I didn't tell you before now. I didn't want to share something important to me and have you treat it lightly."

"Is that the way you see me? Is that the way I am?"

"Only when it comes to Mormons," she said, looking out the window. She turned back to him and added, "Although, you've got a certain cynical edge about everything nowadays. Is it my new religion that has you in such a foul mood? Or is that just one more thing to be angry about?"

"What makes you think I'm angry?"

Elizabeth gave a scoffing laugh that was a fair imitation of his. "What makes you think I'm stupid? I know you, Jayson. And I know you're angry." Her voice raised enough to make it evident that she was angry, too. "You were angry enough to nearly kill yourself, Jayson, and I'm still having trouble coming to terms with that." She started to cry. "I don't understand. Help me understand why you would do that so I can stop fearing that you'll try it again."

Jayson sighed loudly and looked away. The reasons were complicated, and some of them he simply wasn't ready to talk about. But it wasn't difficult for him to admit his most prominent thought. "And why should I want to live when I am a failure at everything I have done in my life, everything that mattered to me at all?"

"Failure? Is that what you said? *Failure?*"

"That's right." He sounded insulted by her astonishment, as if she should agree completely.

"A failure? You? You've got to be kidding me."

"No, I'm not kidding, Elizabeth. Look at me. Look at my life. I failed as a husband, a father, a musician; I even failed my brother and . . ." his voice broke, "my mother."

Elizabeth made a noise of disbelief. "Where is this coming from, Jayson?"

"It's a fact, Elizabeth. Why is that so difficult to see? Do I have to spell it out for you?"

"I guess you do, because I *can't* see it."

He leaned forward, his countenance angry. "Fine," he said. "Let's start with my music. You know as much as anyone how music has been my heart and soul for as long as I can remember. It was all I ever wanted. Beyond the relationships in my life, it was everything to me. And I failed. I reached the top, and I fell from the sky like a comet."

"No, you blazed like a comet, Jayson."

"Past tense," he said. "I had it. I lost it. I was there, now I am not. Now I am nothing."

"Nothing? You don't look like nothing to me. You look like the same human being I knew twenty years ago. You're not a failure, Jayson. You're a blazing success. You did everything you set out to do. You empowered and inspired millions of people, just like you'd always wanted to. You made millions of dollars from your music, Jayson."

"I never did it for the money."

"No, you didn't. But the money is indicative of the impact you had. And unlike many musicians, your impact was for *good*. Those CDs are circulating all over the world; your music will continue to lift spirits and touch hearts for many years to come."

Jayson thought of the woman he'd spoken to in the airport, and he knew that was true. Still, he had to face reality. "But . . . for me it's all over now. It's who I am, and it's not there any more. So I don't know who I am."

"Are you trying to tell me your value as a human being is based on your ability to sell records and dazzle audiences around the world?" He didn't answer, and she went on. "You did what thousands of musicians never could do. I can understand why having that part of your career end the way it did would throw you off. But that's not who you are, Jayson. At heart you are a musician, not a performer. I mean . . . you are certainly gifted at performing. Your stage presence is incredible. But you were a great musician long before you ever got a record deal. You were a great musician in the front room of my home in Oregon. There are countless ways to find fulfillment and bless lives with your gift, Jayson. You still have so much life to live, so much to offer. The value of a gift is not measured in its ability to produce the dollar, or its popularity in a world that by its very nature is flaky and incongruous."

Jayson took a deep breath as if he could literally soothe his soul with her words. "Where do you come up with this stuff?" he asked, and she urged him into the front room where they sat together on the couch.

"I just say what I feel needs to be said."

"You do it well, I must admit. And you've given me something to think about, but . . ."

"But?"

"But . . . can you tell me how I'm supposed to cope with a failed marriage? If I had been any kind of a decent husband she never would have—"

"Whoa. Cut. Time out," she interrupted. "This is not the same man that I thought had come to terms with this a long time ago. I thought you were straight on the facts. Exactly *what* did you do to be less than a decent husband? Is there something you haven't told me? Were you getting drunk and beating her? Did you not provide well enough for her every whim? Were you belittling her? Talking down to her? Neglecting her?"

He sighed. "I was not a perfect husband. I wasn't there. I was on the road and—"

"Perfect? Who on the face of the earth is perfect? I know you well enough to know you're not perfect, but you're a good man, Jayson. And as far as being on the road . . . you called her twice a day. You flew home more than any other road musician ever would. You gave her every possible opportunity to be with you. She *cheated* on you, Jayson. Not because she was neglected or unloved, but just *because*. Just *because* she was bored, wanted attention. She admitted it, Jayson. She turned into a middle-aged groupie. She'd gotten everything she could get out of one rock star, so she moved on to another." He squeezed his eyes closed as if he couldn't bear the horror of what she'd just said. She softened her voice and put a hand on his arm. "You did nothing to warrant what she did to you, Jayse. Are you hearing me? Even *if* you had been neglectful or hurtful, any half-decent woman would go to her husband and say, 'We have a problem; we need to work it out.' Going to someone else's bed while you were on the road was inexcusable. And it does not in the remotest sense make you a failure."

Jayson couldn't find a comeback. He felt soothed and comforted by her words, instinctively knowing she was right, but perhaps just needing to hear it from someone else if only to know that it wasn't just his own rationalizations. Still, his mind went to the next issue. "I wasn't there for Macy. I should have paid closer attention. I should have listened to what she was trying to tell me."

"Oh, Jayson," she said gently, "I can't even imagine your heartache on that count." He squeezed his eyes closed again and tears leaked down his face. "But I know you well enough to know that you did the best you could. You're losing sight of something very important here, Jayson." He opened his eyes to look at her, his expression showing a glimmer of hope. "Macy, just like every other person who came to this world, came here with her free agency. As much as we'd like to, we cannot control our children's decisions. I could introduce you to a number of parents who are good, wonderful people, but they have children who have done it all: drugs, sex, drinking, even suicide. There isn't a parent on the planet who doesn't make mistakes, say things they regret. But you love her, Jayson. And she knew that. You were there for her a lot more than her mother was. You have every right to feel sorrow over her absence. Your fear on her behalf is normal and understandable. But you cannot blame yourself for her decisions. You didn't fail her, Jayson. She's just a fragile young woman struggling to under-stand a difficult world with too many voices coming at her in every direction. I think that when you see her again, she will tell you that you didn't fail her."

Jayson sobbed and hung his head, pressing a hand over his chest. "Oh, if I could just know that she's safe! Why doesn't she call me?"

Elizabeth put her arms around him and urged his face to her shoulder. "I don't know why, Jayson. We can only pray that she's safe and well and that she *will* call one day. And when she does, you will be able to let her know how much you love her." He sobbed again and held her tightly while he cried without restraint, eventually resting his head in her lap.

When he'd calmed down somewhat, she asked quietly, "Now, why don't you tell me how you failed Drew and your mother."

Jayson sighed. "Drew and I should be playing together. That's what he wanted. That's what Mom wanted. He always looked to me to keep it together, to know what to do. And I just . . . didn't know what to do. I couldn't come up with any answers. So . . . he went elsewhere. I can't blame him, and I'm glad he's got work, but . . . I feel like I let him down."

"Does Drew feel like you let him down?"

"I don't know; I never asked him."

"Well, maybe you should. Maybe it's good for the two of you to have some experiences apart. You're still brothers. Brothers are rarely as close as the two of you. Maybe you should be grateful for what you've shared with him instead of regretting what you can't share right now."

"Maybe," he said. "But maybe I'm so much in the habit of thinking negative thoughts that I don't know how to change them."

"Well, I guess we'll have to work on that. In the meantime, I'd like to know how on earth you could believe that you let your mother down. You were always her pride and joy. You took care of her. You met her every need as soon as you were capable. You were there for her. She died in your arms, Jayson. How could you have possibly done more than you did?"

"I don't know," he admitted. "I just feel like I let her down."

"I think the biggest problem is that you're depressed, and it's distorting your thoughts. Quite frankly, you're talking nonsense, my friend." She lowered her voice and pushed his hair back from his face. "You're a good man, Jayson."

He rolled from his side onto his back, keeping his head in her lap. Looking up at her, he said, "And I feel like I disappointed you, as well."

"Why?" she asked. "I've known you for more than twenty years, and I don't recall ever being embarrassed or ashamed of you or anything you've done."

"Until a couple of days ago," he said. She looked away and sighed loudly. She said nothing, and he added, "I nearly killed myself, Lady. Don't try to tell me that you're not disappointed in me."

"For that, yes. But I would say I'm more hurt . . . more afraid . . . than disappointed. I've never been suicidal, so I can't say I understand. But I'm not so naive or judgmental to think that your desire to do away with yourself was selfish or uncomplicated." She looked at him. "I just want to understand so that it never gets that bad again."

"I love you, Elizabeth," he said, reaching up a hand to touch her face. Not wanting her to mistakenly believe that he was implying anything romantic, he added quickly, "You're the best and truest friend a man could ever hope for."

"The feeling is mutual," she said with sincerity. "And I love you too."

But not enough, he added silently and went to the kitchen to make himself a cup of coffee.

The following morning Jayson was up before Trevin went off to school. He found Trevin dressed and ready to go, eating a bowl of cold cereal and looking depressed. Jayson talked to him for a couple of minutes but didn't get much response. Addie was wearing feet pajamas, her curly blonde hair a mess. She smiled at him when he talked to her, but she didn't say much. Mozie sidled up next to Jayson, begging for attention. Jayson gladly gave it to him and was rubbing the dog's head when Elizabeth came into the kitchen with wet hair—and it was curly. Since he'd seen her in Denver, he had only seen it straight, curled under slightly on the ends. After Trevin left for the bus stop, Jayson found Elizabeth in the biggest bathroom on the main floor, just off the master bedroom, straightening her hair with a blow-dryer.

"How long does it take you to do that every morning?" he shouted to be heard above the dryer, then he laughed when it became evident he'd startled her.

"You scared me to death," she growled, turning off the dryer. "And what difference does it make to you how long I take to do my hair?"

"I was just wondering," he said. "When it looks so good curly, why spend your time . . ." He stopped when she glared at him. "As I've told you before," he said instead, "you look beautiful no matter what."

A short while later he found Elizabeth in a little office at one side of the dining area, typing very quickly on the computer. "Wow," he said as he sat down and stretched out his legs, "I had no idea you were such a proficient typist."

"There's probably a lot about me you don't know."

"And vice versa," he said, knowing there were some things he hoped she never found out.

Jayson took in the decor of the room while he scratched Mozie behind the ears. There was a picture of the temple they'd driven past on their way into town, some family pictures in frames, and an older man in a suit. "Who's that?" he asked.

She barely glanced up, then kept typing. "That's the prophet."

"You mean . . . like currently? As in . . . he's still alive?"

"A prophet is much more effective that way."

Jayson didn't say what he was really thinking, that the idea of a living prophet was ridiculous. He simply said, "I never imagined a prophet looking like that."

"Well, he'd look pretty ridiculous if he dressed the way Moses did."

Jayson chuckled, then asked, "Is there something I can do to help while you're busy?"

"Yes," she said without looking at him, "take the dog for a walk. His leash is hanging in the garage."

"I think I could handle that," he said, even though he'd never actually owned a dog.

Jayson found the leash and easily hooked it onto Mozie's collar. When he realized how chilly it was outside, he concluded it wouldn't be a very long walk. He wasn't used to these Utah temperatures. With the sun shining, he soon adjusted to the chill, however, and they ended up walking three or four blocks and back again, although the neighborhood had curving streets and could by no means be measured in blocks. Three different times he saw people in their yards or getting into vehicles, and they all said something friendly. On the way back, just a few houses away, he was met by an elderly man who was putting something into his mailbox.

"Good morning, young man," he said.

"Good morning," Jayson replied.

"That dog looks familiar," he said, holding out a hand toward Mozie. The dog stopped walking and eagerly moved to the man in search of affection. "Well, hello, Mozie," the man said in a funny voice. He then looked up at Jayson and asked, "You must be staying with the Aragons. I usually see Will or Trevin walking old Mozie."

"I am, yes," he said, pleasantly surprised by the man's friendly demeanor. In all the years he'd lived in Los Angeles, he'd never once encountered friendly neighbors or gotten to know them at all. In fact, he'd never been on friendly terms with anyone in his neighborhood since he'd lived in Montana, and they'd lived there for years before anyone ever became friendly.

"Well, I'm Brother Bale," he said, extending a hand. Jayson assumed the *brother* part meant he was a member of the same church that Elizabeth and Will belonged to. "And who might you be?"

"Jayson," was all he said.

"It's a pleasure to meet you, Jayson."

"And you," Jayson said.

"Will you be staying long?"

"Perhaps," he said. "Will and Elizabeth are like my second family, and there's not much left of the first one. I might stay as long as they'll put up with me."

"Then I'll look forward to seeing you around," Brother Bale said, and Jayson walked on.

He had a similar encounter from Sister Fredericks who lived next door to Elizabeth, and he wondered if everyone around here was this friendly.

Inside the house, he let Elizabeth know he was back, then he took some pills and laid down. His headache was getting worse.

Over the next few days, Jayson observed Elizabeth's habits during the time he wasn't asleep or hiding in his room. He watched her doing laundry and cleaning, and she spent hours every day with her typing. She frequently went on errands, took the children back and forth to some lessons, and was often on the phone. Sometimes she was chatting, sometimes it sounded official. It rained off and on during the week, and she always used an umbrella—to keep her hair straight, no doubt.

He was also aware that Elizabeth made a visit to the temple. She left dressed up as if she were going to church, and she took a little suitcase with her. She was gone for more than three hours. When Jayson asked Will why he wasn't going too, he mentioned that there was a waiting period of a year following baptism before a member could attend the temple; he added that he was anxiously looking forward to that time. Jayson just listened politely and made no comment. The whole thing just felt weird to him.

Will stayed busy as well. He kept track of Addie while Elizabeth was working, and he did the majority of the cooking. He also did some accounting work from his own office in the basement. Jayson often asked if there was anything he could do to help, but they both insisted they were fine and he should just relax. He felt certain he was doing far too much relaxing, and he felt relatively useless beyond occasionally walking the dog—which brought more encounters from neighbors, including another visit with Brother Bale, who apparently spent a great deal of time in his yard.

Mozie took to following Jayson around, probably because he had more time to give the dog attention than anyone else did. Elizabeth mentioned once that the dog had been most attached to Bradley, which likely explained why Mozie sometimes slept on the floor near Jayson's bed—the bed where Bradley had once slept. But Jayson liked the dog; it seemed they understood each other. And if Mozie had a purpose in this household, maybe Jayson could, too. When he mentioned this to Elizabeth, he pointed out that they were both named after Mozart—Jayson's middle name being Amadeus—so they had a great deal in common.

"Mozie doesn't have the talent you have," Elizabeth said.

"At this point, we're probably pretty even," Jayson said, and Elizabeth looked astonished. "Don't be so surprised," he said. "It's all dried up inside of me. I don't think there's any gift left. No muse. No inspiration. Nothing."

"It will come back one day," she said, but Jayson didn't believe her.

Even though the weather was much cooler here than in Los Angeles, Jayson found he enjoyed sitting on the large deck that opened up from behind the living area on the main floor. Since the yard sloped downward, the deck was high above the back lawn, with a wooded area at the back of the yard—and above the trees, Jayson could see mountain peaks. He couldn't recall the mountains being so beautiful on his previous visits to Utah. But then, he'd not noticed much of anything beyond the fans. He discovered that the deck had two entrances, and the other came from Elizabeth's bedroom. Occasionally she sat there with him, although she was comfortable in a sweater and he was usually wrapped in a blanket.

"Cold?" she asked the first time she noticed him that way.

"Yes, actually. It's cold here."

"Not as cold as it's going to get," she said. "You grew up in Montana. Stop being such a baby."

"I've been living in LA for years. And don't call me a baby."

"I could sing it to you," she said, then broke into singing a song that he'd written.

Jayson met her eyes, hoping to find some humor. But he only saw the same subtly angry look he'd seen the majority of the time since he'd arrived in Utah. Was she angry with him? Or just angry? Both perhaps, but he didn't know how to address it.

As Jayson settled in, Elizabeth discreetly observed him, wondering what it was about his behavior that made her uneasy. He'd stayed in her home before, although it had been years ago. And she had stayed in his when his mother was dying. But he seemed different now. There were moments when he seemed almost like himself. At times he talked and laughed with her or her father, as if nothing in the world was wrong. He interacted some with the children, although Trevin didn't have much to say to him; however, he didn't have much to say to anybody. Her concern for Trevin was only further weighed down by her concern for Jayson. More often than not he was subtly irritable and easily provoked. He slept late in the morning, went to bed early in the evenings, and he took long naps. Sometimes he was shaky, almost despondent. And at other times he was full of energy. And he often wore those dark glasses, claiming that he had a headache and even the lights in the house hurt his eyes.

Five days after his arrival, all the evidence suddenly came together in her mind, and everything inside of her tightened into knots while she wondered how she could have been so stupid, so blind. She went that very minute to his room where she knew he was likely napping. She threw open the door without knocking and found him sitting on the edge of the bed, his head in his hands, as if he'd just barely come awake. He looked up at her, startled, just before she snarled, "All right. Where is it?"

"What are you talking about?" he countered.

"Where are you hiding it, Jayson? What is it? Cocaine? Heroin? What? How much of the time that you've been here have you been stoned? I may be slow but I'm not stupid." He stared at her, looking dumbfounded, and she shouted, "Where's the stuff, Jayson? You come clean with me or you can go back to LA and *rot!* I will not have hard drugs in my home!"

When Jayson had fully absorbed what he was being accused of, he came to his feet abruptly and stepped toward her. He saw fear in Elizabeth's eyes, and she took a step back. Was she afraid that his brain was completely fried and he might murder her under her own roof? "I thought you had grown beyond being prejudiced and judgmental, Mrs. Aragon. Maybe you should ask questions before you go jumping all over me when you have no idea what you're talking about."

"And how do I know you'll tell me the truth? I'm not naive enough to believe that doing drugs will make a person rational or honest."

"I've never lied to you, Elizabeth. I'm not going to start now. I have *never* touched the stuff you are accusing me of using. I saw more than most people how it destroyed lives. I lost a friend to an overdose, Elizabeth! I have never taken a drug that didn't come from a pharmacy. I have never even touched liquor. I am not now, nor have I ever been *stoned!* Unless I am asleep, I am fully aware of everything going on around me."

Elizabeth watched his eyes closely and had to believe he was telling her the truth. She took a deep breath and said more softly, "Then what's going on? Why all the . . . mood swings? All the sleeping? Why, Jayson? Give me a logical explanation and I'll believe you."

Jayson momentarily weighed his options. He wanted so desperately to fix this problem on his own, to not burden her with his stupidity. But he needed to be honest if he ever expected to maintain any level of trust between them. He sighed and looked down. He cleared his throat tensely. "I'm . . . taking some . . . prescription drugs. More than I should, but . . . I'm tapering off. But . . . they make me sleepy, and sometimes . . . irritable."

Elizabeth sighed loudly. "What are they for?" she asked.

Jayson chuckled tensely, with no trace of humor. "There's uh . . . one for . . . anxiety. A doctor put me on it after Macy left, and I . . . couldn't even function. I couldn't sleep. I couldn't cope. And it helped. And then . . ." He stuffed his hands into his pockets. "I . . . um . . . went on an antidepressant after Mom died. And there's some pain meds . . . for my hand."

Elizabeth said, "That surgery was months ago, Jayson. It can't be hurting enough to need prescription pain meds."

"No, but . . . after the surgery I started getting migraines. That's it, okay. It's easier for me to take something and sleep than to have a migraine. Simple as that."

Elizabeth still felt uneasy, but she reminded herself to be appropriate. "Okay," she said. "If you tell me that's the truth, I'll believe you. I'm sorry for jumping to conclusions."

"It's all right," he said. "I can understand your concerns. But I would never do that to you; I would never bring that kind of stuff into your home. I hope you believe me."

"I do, Jayson. I'm sorry."

He watched her leave the room and close the door before he sank back onto the bed and groaned. He'd told her the truth, but it wasn't the whole truth, and he knew it was only a matter of time before she figured it out. If he didn't get a handle on this soon, there would be the devil to pay with the only people left in the world who cared for him at all.

The following morning Jayson walked into the kitchen to find Will and the children sitting at the table, eating cereal and toast, all dressed up. Will barely said good morning before Elizabeth came into the kitchen, wearing a dress and some really great shoes. "Good morning," she said when she saw him.

"Where's everybody going?" he asked.

"It's Sunday, Jayse," she said. "We're going to church."

"Oh," he said and wondered how he could ask if he might go along. He didn't know if it was appropriate for non-Mormons to go to a Mormon meeting.

Will interrupted his thoughts by asking, "Would you like to come along, Jayson?"

"I'm sure he wouldn't," Elizabeth said, pouring herself a glass of orange juice.

"Why don't you let Jayson answer the question?" Will said.

Elizabeth looked at her father, seeming embarrassed, then she looked at Jayson. "Sorry," she said. "I'm jumping to conclusions again."

"I'd like to come," Jayson said, "unless that's a problem."

"Of course it's not," Will said.

Still feeling a little tense over Elizabeth's take on this, Jayson added lightly, "Maybe your daughter's embarrassed to be seen at church with me. After all, she says I look like a has-been rock star."

"I said you look like a rock star. Don't put words in my mouth."

"Okay, she said I look like a rock star. Maybe she's—"

"I can assure you I have never been—nor would I ever be—embarrassed to be seen with you; even at church. I only have one request."

"What's that?" he asked.

"Don't sit by me."

"Why not?" he asked, chuckling at her insistence.

"Because if you sit next to me, then everyone will automatically assume there is something romantic between us. You're like a brother to me. That's the truth, and that's all anybody ever needs to know. So, just make sure that my father or the kids or both are in between the two of us. That's all I ask."

"Fine," he said. "We wouldn't want anyone to think there's anything romantic between us." Elizabeth just scowled at him, and he added, "What should I wear?" He glanced at the white shirts and ties that Will and Trevin were wearing. "I don't think I've ever owned a white shirt, and I don't have a tie with me."

"That blue button-up shirt you had on a couple of days ago—that I just washed—will do fine," Elizabeth said. "I'm sure my father has an extra tie that would match it."

"I wore a tie to work every day," Will said. "I have quite a collection."

"Okay, but . . . give me something conservative. I don't want to embarrass your daughter."

While Jayson made himself a cup of coffee, he said to Elizabeth, "Is it okay to drink coffee before I go to a Mormon church meeting?"

"You can do anything you want, Jayson," she said, apparently not finding the humor that he'd intended in his comment.

"Is there anything I should know about before we go? I'm not going to be shocked by any rituals taking place or anything, am I?"

"Not likely," she said. "When they pass the bread and water for the sacrament, don't take it. The purpose is to renew baptismal covenants, and obviously that doesn't apply to you."

"Obviously," he said. "We're not going to meet any polygamists, are we?" The way she scowled at him when he said it made him wonder if they *would,* and he'd just put his foot in his mouth.

But she said, "Polygamy has not been practiced or endorsed by the Church for more than a century."

"Really?" he said, genuinely surprised. "So . . . those people you hear about on the news . . ."

"Have basically started their own church. Now who is jumping to conclusions?"

"Okay," he said, "but in my defense . . . plural marriage *is* a Mormon thing, right?"

"Plural marriage has been practiced with God's approval many times throughout history." He gave her a dubious glare, and she added, "Where do you think the twelve tribes of Israel came from, Jayson?" He didn't answer, and she stated, "Abraham had a son named Isaac, who had a son named Jacob, whose name was changed to Israel. And Israel had twelve sons—through four different wives who were all alive at the same time. It's in the Bible. You should read it sometime."

"Maybe I'll do that," he said and watched her walk away, amazed at how stupid she was making him feel with her sudden knowledge of religion. Where had he been while she'd been learning so much? Either grieving or touring Europe, he concluded. Or drugged.

Will had to help Jayson with his tie, since he'd not actually worn one in years. "Thanks, Dad," he said as Will straightened Jayson's shirt collar over the tie.

Will smiled, then glanced past Jayson's shoulder, as if to be assured that they were alone. He said softly, "You be patient with her, okay? There are some things she's struggling with that are a lot harder for her than she's letting on."

"Like what?" Jayson asked.

"Her grief is complicated, Jayson. You should know enough about grief to understand that."

"Yeah," Jayson said more humbly.

"And just between you and me, I think she's pretty ticked off with you."

"Why?" Jayson asked, startled by Will's forthright comment.

"That's complicated too, son. But you scared her senseless. She hasn't talked about it much, but she did say she could survive losing one man she loved, but not two. So be patient with her. Don't give up on her. She needs you, even though I think she's trying to convince herself that she doesn't."

Jayson nodded, overwhelmed with a deep regret over the hurt he'd brought into Elizabeth's life. However, he had to admit, "She's not the only one who's going to need some patience."

Elizabeth appeared, saying, "Okay, let's go. I hate getting there late."

Will drove the Tahoe to the church building, and since Elizabeth got into the backseat with the kids, Jayson got in front with Will. He drove about three minutes before he pulled into the parking lot of a large, red brick chapel with a beautiful white steeple rising up from the center. Walking toward the door, Will said to Jayson, "Now we actually have what they call a block meeting. So, after sacrament meeting, we all divide up and go to different classes. Elizabeth leads the music for the Primary, and I'll be going to—"

"What's that?" Jayson asked.

"The children's meeting," Will said.

"Do you think she'd be okay if I went with her . . . just to watch?"

Will smiled. "I don't know. Why don't you ask her? If not, you can come to the adult Sunday School class with me, and then to priesthood meeting." Jayson gave him an astonished look but didn't know how to form a question. Will seemed to understand when he said, "Every worthy man in the Church holds the priesthood, Jayson. I can see we're going to need to talk."

"Fine, we can talk, but don't try to convert me or anything."

"Would I do that?" Will asked, and they stepped inside.

Elizabeth took Jayson's dark glasses off of his face and put them in her purse. He scowled at her, and she muttered, "I think you'll live."

"Yes, Mother," he said with sarcasm.

Elizabeth was relieved when Will kept Jayson close to him and handled all the introductions with curious, friendly ward members. He kept a hand on Jayson's shoulder and told everyone who asked, "This is Jayson. He's practically a son to me; has been since he was in high school. He's staying with us for a while."

Jayson's first surprise was how normal everyone looked. He didn't know what he'd expected, but it wasn't this. He had to admit his mental images of Mormons had been somewhere in the category with the Amish. But that certainly didn't ring true with Will and Elizabeth now being members. They fit right in. Everyone looked relatively normal; they could get lost in a crowd. Or maybe not, he decided after looking more closely. These people were refreshingly well-groomed and lacked the tawdriness and pretentiousness he'd become accustomed to. In fact, he felt somewhat conspicuous with his ponytail and earring; he was reminded of his high school days when he'd always felt out of place, being the resident nonconformist. In the rock world he'd fit in more naturally, but he didn't necessarily think that was a good thing.

They sat on a pew near the rear of the chapel; he had Trevin and Will to his left, and Elizabeth to his right, with Addie between them. Once he was settled, he surveyed the chapel. It was beautiful, but he was surprised at how it had no pictures hanging in it whatsoever, no crosses or candles or any of the other things he might have associated with religion. It was simple and tasteful—and the benches were actually padded, something he'd never encountered in his youth.

Waiting for the meeting to begin, Jayson kept observing the people. He couldn't help noticing the teenage girls and thinking of Macy. As always, his heart ached for her. Recalling the way she had dressed and behaved, and the friends she'd hung out with, he looked at these young women—and the young men. They were clean and fresh, modestly dressed and well-groomed. While he held onto some measure of skepticism, he couldn't help being impressed with certain aspects of what he was seeing.

When a guy near his own age stood at the pulpit, wearing a basic suit and tie, Jayson leaned over Addie's head and whispered to Elizabeth, "Who is that?"

Elizabeth looked back at him and refused to start whispering back and forth. She pulled a notebook out of her bag and wrote, "That's the bishop."

Jayson read what she'd written and wondered why this guy wasn't wearing some weird robe or something. He kept the question to himself, but he reached across Addie to take the pen Elizabeth was holding so he could write, "You're beautiful when you're angry." He watched her read it, then smirked when she tossed him a disgusted glance.

When the organ began to play, Elizabeth handed him a hymn book. He looked at her questioningly, and she whispered, "You do know how to sing, don't you?"

"I used to," he said and honestly couldn't remember the last time he'd actually used his voice for music. It simply hadn't occurred to him that even without his hand, he could sing. He'd just always played and sung at the same time. He focused on the printed words and began to sing, *I believe in Christ; he is my King! With all my heart to him I'll sing; I'll raise my voice in praise and joy, In grand amens my tongue employ.* The song progressed while Jayson felt something settle into him that felt strangely unfamiliar. Something warm and hopeful. It was clinched for him when he sang the words, *I believe in Christ; he stands supreme! From him I'll gain my fondest dream; And while I strive through grief and pain, His voice is heard: "Ye shall obtain."*

Jayson couldn't fathom that this religion had any more truth or power than any other religion he'd been exposed to in his youth. But he did know that Jesus Christ was real, and that He lived. And for the first time in years, he felt the reality of that burning inside of him. He thought of the miracle that had saved his life not so many days ago, and he felt immeasurably grateful to be where he was in that moment. And then a thought occurred to him with a certain amount of force. *He could never get through it alone.* While he'd been telling himself that he could kick this prescription drug problem himself and avoid having Will and Elizabeth know the truth, he understood in that moment that he simply was not capable of doing it on his own, and he needed to have the courage to turn to these people who loved him and to be humble enough to ask for their help. The very idea made him sick to his stomach. He was so caught up in the thought that he was startled by the song ending, then Elizabeth leaned over and whispered, "We're not really Christians. We just sing songs like that to trick people into believing that we are."

Jayson just stared at her, not amused. He was surprised to feel Addie tugging on his arm. He leaned over, and she whispered in his ear, "Mommy's in a bad mood."

Jayson chuckled softly and whispered back. "Yes, she certainly is, but we love her anyway."

Addie nodded and maintained her hold on Jayson's arm.

Not many minutes later they were singing another song. When it ended, an elderly lady turned around and patted Jayson on the hand, saying softly, "You have a lovely voice, young man. You should be in the choir."

"You're very kind," Jayson whispered and returned her smile before she faced forward again.

CHAPTER 14

When the sacrament was passed, Jayson just handed the trays on to Elizabeth and kept his eyes turned downward. When that was over, he was expecting a sermon from the bishop, but instead, he announced some speakers and a musical number, then he sat back down. Jayson had been expecting something like the church experiences of his youth, with a pulpit-pounding minister who sounded frightening, speaking of a vengeful God. And now they were listening to a youth speaker, a boy no more than fourteen who talked about the need to have faith and accept the will of the Lord. While Jayson was marveling that such a concept would come out of a boy so young, the boy began to tell of how he'd been present when Bradley Aragon had drowned. He talked briefly but openly about how he knew beyond any doubt that it wasn't an accident, that Heavenly Father had taken him home when he was supposed to go. Jayson glanced toward Elizabeth, not surprised to see her crying with a tissue pressed over her nose. He reached a hand across Addie's lap and felt some relief when Elizabeth took it and squeezed tightly.

The next speaker was a woman who talked about the faith that someone named Joseph Smith had had when he'd gone into the woods to pray. She spoke of the experience as if it had changed the world, and Jayson had no idea who or what she was talking about. Jayson finally took Elizabeth's notebook and wrote, "Who is Joseph Smith?"

She looked stunned by the question and wrote something before she handed it back. He read, "I can't possibly answer that in a few sentences on a notebook."

That piqued Jayson's curiosity even further. The woman speaking then made the point that each individual person was entitled to personal revelation through the Holy Ghost, as to whether or not something was right. She said that we didn't have to just believe that what Joseph Smith had seen was true; we could know for ourselves beyond any doubt. She then bore testimony that she knew it was true and sat down.

A musical number began, and Elizabeth turned to look at Jayson. His brow was furrowed with deep concentration, or perhaps confusion. The music made it easier for her to whisper without causing any disturbance. She hoped she wasn't opening a can of worms when she leaned over Addie and whispered close to Jayson's ear, "Joseph Smith was the prophet who ushered in the restoration of the gospel in the nineteenth century. The full gospel gradually disappeared from the earth following Christ's death."

"A prophet?" Jayson whispered back skeptically. And she nodded. He thought about that a second, then asked, "And what did he see that this woman knows is true?"

Elizabeth looked into his eyes with an intensity that seemed to preamble what she was going to tell him. She put her lips to his ear and whispered, "He saw God the Father and His Son, Jesus Christ."

Jayson looked at her with such disbelief that Elizabeth feared he would stand up and leave. When he didn't, she picked up her scriptures and thumbed through them before she handed the book to him and pointed to a particular spot on the page. Jayson took it from her and read at the top of the page, *Joseph Smith—History. Extracts from the History of Joseph Smith, the Prophet.*

Jayson whispered to Elizabeth, "Do you believe he was a prophet? Do you believe he actually saw what he said he saw?"

Elizabeth whispered firmly, "No." And he expected her to offer some explanation of how she had trouble swallowing something so outlandish, but the Church had many good things to offer so she went along. Instead she added with conviction, "I don't believe it; I *know* it's true." Jayson turned to look into her eyes, startled to see her conviction echoed there.

The musical number ended, and Jayson turned to the book in his hands. In the absence of the music he couldn't help noticing how many children there were in the chapel and how noisy they were. His memories of church were of a deathly stillness, as if the kids had been scared out of their minds to make a peep in church.

Jayson didn't hear anything the last speaker said; he was reading the account of Joseph Smith. And while he wanted to believe that Elizabeth had not lost some portion of her mind, he simply couldn't fathom that a fourteen-year-old boy would have such an incredible vision. He had trouble believing that God would appear to *any* human in this day and age, but a fourteen-year-old boy? It was ridiculous. When he figured he'd read enough, he glanced through the thick book of scriptures in his hands. He realized it contained the King James version of the Bible, along with the Book of Mormon and a bunch of other stuff he'd never heard of.

When the speaker was finished, the bishop announced that the Primary children would be staying in the chapel for a short while to prepare for next week's big program. And then they would all be meeting together in the Primary room to practice their music, rather than separating for classes. Then the closing song began. Jayson continued looking through the book rather than sing.

When the meeting ended, Jayson handed the book back to Elizabeth, saying, "I'll respect your beliefs, but don't expect me to believe them."

He saw a flicker of hurt in her eyes, but he wasn't going to pretend he agreed with her just to keep peace between them. Before she said anything, he hurried to ask, "Can I go to Primary with you?"

She looked surprised but said, "I suppose."

Jayson turned to Will and said, "I think I'll stick with the lady."

"Oh, you'll enjoy the children," Will said. "I'll see you later, then."

"Just sit down and be discreet," Elizabeth said.

Jayson rested both arms along the back of the bench he was sitting on and watched with amused interest as Elizabeth and a number of other women—as well as a few men—attempted to organize a huge number of children into the seats behind the pulpit, and onto some extra chairs that were brought in. He counted more than eighty children. Trevin looked like one of the oldest, so he assumed eleven or twelve was the age at which they moved on to a group for teenagers. It was apparent from what the leaders were saying to the children that next Sunday they would be presenting a program in sacrament meeting. Jayson actually couldn't wait to see that. When the children were all finally in place, a lady told them to remember their seats and to come early next week and sit there. Then Elizabeth stood in front of them and told them they would go to the Primary room in a few minutes and go through all of their songs, but for now she just wanted them to do the first and last song of the program so they could see how it sounded in the chapel.

As the piano began, Jayson felt something stab at him. He noticed a young man seated there, playing rather well. And then the children broke into song with such beautiful intensity that he felt chilled from head to toe. And the lyrics caught his interest. *I am a child of God, and He has sent me here, has given me an earthly home with parents kind and dear. Lead me, guide me, walk beside me, help me find the way. Teach me all that I must do to live with Him someday.* They sang more verses, then Elizabeth praised them dramatically. She turned around and looked directly at him, asking, "Did it sound good?"

He gave her two thumbs up and she turned back to face the children. They then started another song; the verse was a little sketchy, as if they didn't know this one as well, but when they hit the chorus, the volume doubled, and the room was filled with their tender voices, singing, *We are children, holding hands around the world, like an army with a gospel flag unfurled. We are led by His light, and we love truth and right. We are building the kingdom of God.*

"Wow," Jayson said under his breath, then he watched with amusement the mass exodus to another room in the church building. He noticed that this room had pictures—some of men in suits, and a couple of Jesus with children.

The leaders attempted to get the children to sit in rows on the floor, youngest in the front. Adults were sitting on chairs around the perimeter of the room and he took a vacant seat next to a man in his early twenties, who extended a hand and said warmly, "Are you new in the ward or—"

"I'm just visiting," Jayson said. "I'm here with Will Greer and his daughter."

"Oh, they're great people," the man said. "I'm Brother Lackey. I teach the six-year-olds."

"Lucky you," Jayson said, and they shared a chuckle.

"You look awfully familiar. Could we have met before?"

"Not likely," Jayson said. "I've never been to Utah before. Well," he clarified in an effort to be honest, "I've been to Salt Lake on business a couple of times."

He realized that wasn't a good course when Brother Lackey asked, "What kind of business is that?"

Jayson was relieved when the children were quieted and they had a child read a scripture, another give a prayer, and another a little talk. Then the entire group of children stood to recite what they called the Primary theme. Jayson wondered what kind of brainwashing these people might be doing to their children, then he heard them all say with memorized zeal, "I am a child of God. I know Heavenly Father loves me, and I love him. I can pray to Heavenly Father any time, anywhere. I am trying to remember and follow Jesus Christ."

As the children sat back down, Jayson figured every child in the world could benefit from such beliefs. Elizabeth stood to lead the songs they needed to rehearse, and Brother Lackey whispered, "You look so familiar. It's really bugging me."

Jayson chuckled softly. There were moments when he really enjoyed this sort of thing. "If I told you the most likely reason for that, you might not believe me. Either that, or you might not want to sit next to me in church."

"What?" the man asked softly, with pleasant expectation in his face. Jayson just smiled, and Brother Lackey added, "I've seen you on TV. I swear I've seen you on TV."

Sizing up this guy's age, Jayson asked, "Did you ever watch the Grammy Awards?"

Brother Lackey looked straight at Jayson, and his eyes widened. "No way! I don't believe it. You're . . . you're . . ." He snapped his fingers quietly, then it came to him. "You're *Gray Wolf.*"

"I am," Jayson said. "Or at least I used to be."

"That's incredible. And you're here with Will Greer?"

"That's right."

"How long have you known him?"

"Since I was a kid, actually. He's like a father to me."

"I bet I have your CDs at home."

"Well, I hope they're not too dusty," Jayson whispered.

The children's song ended, and it was more difficult to exchange conversation without drawing attention to themselves. Jayson watched Elizabeth as she called attention to a couple of children who were visiting. She had them come to the front so the group could sing a welcome song. Then she looked right at him and said, "We also have a grownup visitor with us today. Brother Wolfe, we'd like you to come up here as well, so the children can welcome you officially."

Jayson scowled at her. Brother Lackey chuckled and nudged him as he reluctantly stood up and moved to the front of the room to stand beside Elizabeth and the other two visitors, who were much shorter.

"Now," Elizabeth said, "I know for a fact that Brother Wolfe really likes music a lot, so I want you to really impress him with your best singing voices."

"They already have," Jayson said and saw some beaming faces.

"You're going to love this," Elizabeth whispered to him before she began to lead the song.

When it was done, he whispered to Elizabeth, "I'm going to get even with you for this."

During the remainder of Primary, Jayson enjoyed listening to the different songs the children were singing. They sang about being kind to others, following the Savior, and other wonderful concepts. He had to slip out once to take a couple of pills at the drinking fountain, and as he did he recalled the thought that had come to him earlier. He couldn't overcome this alone. He needed help. The very thought tightened his stomach all over again.

On the way home from church, Will asked Jayson, "So how did you enjoy Primary?"

"It was great," Jayson said. When they arrived at the house he told them, "I'm afraid I've got one of those headaches. I hope you don't mind if I lie down for a while."

"No problem," Will said. Elizabeth said nothing.

Jayson slept quickly and was awakened by Will, saying, "Hey, Sunday dinner is nearly ready. You don't want to miss this."

"You've been cooking?" he asked, noting some pleasant aromas in the air.

"Oh, I help on Sunday, but Elizabeth does the cooking."

"I'll be there in a few minutes," Jayson said. "Thank you."

He went into the bathroom and splashed water on his face and took some pills, then he went to the dining room to see the table set with a beautiful meal. After Trevin said a blessing on the food, they enjoyed tender roast beef, mashed potatoes and gravy, cooked carrots, and homemade rolls that were still warm.

"This is incredible," Jayson said. "I don't think I've ever tasted anything so good in my life."

"You're flattering me," Elizabeth said.

"No," Jayson said, pointing his fork at her, "I'm telling you the truth. This is incredible."

"Thank you," she said. "I'm glad you like it."

When the meal was done, Jayson helped Will wash the dishes, then he went back to bed.

Elizabeth pulled her father aside and quietly expressed her concerns regarding Jayson's habits. She repeated their conversation about the drugs, and Will just said, "Give it some time; you'll know what to do."

That night before Elizabeth crawled into bed, she prayed fervently that she would be guided in helping Jayson, whatever the problem might be. In the middle of the night she woke up with a headache and opened the medicine chest in search of some Tylenol. Moving bottles around, she noticed a prescription with Robert's name on it and was surprised. She thought she'd gotten rid of all those. It was a generic painkiller he'd been given when he'd had some oral surgery done a month or so before his death. He'd only taken three or four of the original thirty pills. She set the bottle out on the counter to remind herself to dispose of the pills in the morning. She went back to bed and noticed the bottle there the next morning when she was brushing her teeth, but she'd gotten up late and had to hurry to get Trevin off to school. It was after lunch before she went back to that bathroom to put some clean towels away. She saw the bottle sitting there and took off the lid to dump the pills. She looked inside of it and asked herself if she was going crazy. Had she not seen this bottle nearly full in the middle of the night? And now there were only two pills left in the bottom. And then it hit her like a lightning bolt. She went downstairs to Jayson's room, knowing that he was in the kitchen with her father and Addie. She pulled open the dresser drawers and found some of them completely empty. She rummaged haphazardly through the ones that held his clothes and personal items, not surprised to see a prescription bottle, then another and another. She set them on top of the dresser and kept looking. Twelve, thirteen, fourteen. She lined the bottles up. Some were empty; most had at least a few pills in them. She looked at the labels. Different drugs. Different pharmacies. Different doctors. She felt sick to her stomach and started to cry. She opened the closet and checked the pockets of his clothes. She found two more bottles and some loose pills. She looked in his luggage in the bottom of the closet and found nine more bottles. She sobbed as she pulled them into her hands. She couldn't believe it. *She couldn't believe it!*

Jayson heard a strange sound as he approached the door to his room. He stepped in, and his heart nearly stopped when he saw Elizabeth kneeling on the floor by the open closet door, pill bottles in each hand—crying. He glanced at the dresser where the drawers were open and several bottles were lined up. He'd been busted. His first impulse was to get angry and tell her to mind her own business. But he knew he'd only be making a fool of himself. In his heart he knew he needed her help, and he couldn't go on pretending. On some level, this was what he'd been hoping for when he'd found the bottle of Hydrocodone on the bathroom counter this morning. He'd secretly wanted her to notice the pills missing, which would prevent him from mustering the courage to tell her the truth spontaneously. Maybe this was an answer to his prayers. But he had a feeling that the journey ahead of him was destined to be torturous. He took the first step on that journey when he forced a calm voice and asked, "What are you doing?"

Elizabeth turned to look at him and shot to her feet. "How many are there, Jayson?" she shouted. "How many different drugs?" He didn't answer, and she shouted louder. "How many different pharmacies? How many different doctors have you been seeing?" He said nothing, and she screamed, "You lied to me! You stole drugs from me! I want the truth—and I want it now!"

Jayson moved unsteadily to the edge of the bed and sat there, pushing his head into his hands. "I didn't lie to you," he said, his voice trembling. "I told you the truth. I just didn't tell you how many pills I was taking."

"Oh, I can't believe this," Elizabeth said, setting down the bottles in her hands with the others.

"I have trouble believing it myself," Jayson said, then Will appeared in the doorway, looking concerned.

"Why all the shouting?" he demanded.

"You tell him!" Elizabeth said to Jayson. "It's time you owned up."

"Yes, it is," Jayson said, his voice barely steady. Tears came to his eyes, and he could barely speak enough to say, "Just . . . give me a minute."

Will sat beside him on the bed and put a hand on his shoulder. While Jayson was trying to control his emotion, Will looked up at Elizabeth in question. She glanced toward the top of the dresser. Will's eyes followed, then widened in horror. But neither of them said anything. Elizabeth felt certain her father knew, just as she knew, that Jayson needed to admit to the problem himself.

"Talk to me, son," Will said gently.

"Uh . . . I, um . . ." He pushed his hands brutally through his hair and tugged at it, groaning. He swallowed carefully and tried again. "I . . ." He groaned again.

"Is it so hard to say?" Elizabeth asked.

"Yes!" he snapped and looked up at her. "Yes, it's hard to say, all right?" He shot to his feet and began to pace. "Maybe if I could have said it a long time ago, I could have told you over the phone and it wouldn't have gotten this bad. How can I say it when I have trouble even believing that it's come to this? How can I accept that . . ." His voice broke again. He looked at Elizabeth, then Will. "I . . . have a drug problem." He raised a trembling hand and wiped it over his face. "I have a serious drug problem."

Will said gently, "Then we need to do whatever it takes to solve the problem."

Jayson tried to chuckle but it came out as a sob. He hurried to say, "I thought I could beat it. I thought I could . . . have the discipline to just . . . stop. But I can't."

"You can't just stop taking stuff like this," Elizabeth said. "The withdrawal from some of these could kill you."

"How do you know that?" he growled.

"I catch an episode of *Oprah* once in a while. But it doesn't take a rocket scientist to figure that the combination of this many drugs has got to be close to lethal. How are you even alive?"

"There are only four different drugs there, Elizabeth. Some of them are different brand names for the same drug."

"And how did you get all of this?" she asked.

Jayson shook his head and sat back down where Will's arm went around his shoulders. "I don't think I should admit to that."

"Why not?" Elizabeth demanded.

"Because it wasn't necessarily legal."

"Oh, good heavens," Elizabeth muttered and moved toward the door.

"Where are you going?" Jayson demanded.

"I'm going to make some calls. I'm assuming you have enough money in the bank to pay for a decent rehab program."

Jayson just nodded and watched her walk away. Then he cried. He cried like he hadn't cried since he'd lost the use of his hand. And Will just gave him the shoulder to cry against.

Nearly two hours later, Jayson was all but asleep on his bed with Will sitting in a chair nearby. Elizabeth walked into the room and said, "Okay, here's the deal. Are you awake, Jayson? You need to hear this."

"I'm awake," he said but remained lying down. His head was killing him.

"God is smiling on us," she said, but she still sounded angry. "There is a relatively high-class rehabilitation center less than an hour from here. This place actually has specialists focused on prescription-drug addiction. And they have a couple of spaces open. We will be taking you there in the morning. You and your luggage will be searched for drugs of any kind, and you will not be popping another pill once you walk in the door, except for the medication you will be given under *one* doctor's supervision to help temper the withdrawal."

Jayson squeezed his eyes closed and groaned. "What is it, Jayse?" Will asked gently.

"Well . . . I've tried enough times to go off this stuff that . . . I have a pretty good idea what the withdrawal is going to be like. I doubt there's any medication they can give me to make it remotely bearable."

"They also said not to bring any hairspray, mouthwash, or—"

"Why not?" Jayson asked.

"Because they have alcohol in them."

"They think I'm going to drink hairspray?"

"Not you, necessarily. But apparently there are people in this place who will if they can get their hands on it."

Jayson groaned again. "People like my father, you mean. I could imagine him drinking hairspray if he couldn't get his hands on a bottle of booze."

"Which brings up a point," Elizabeth said and sat down. Jayson sat on the edge of the bed and looked at her. She sounded less angry now, almost compassionate. But he still couldn't look her in the eye.

"What point is that?" he asked when she hesitated.

"They asked if you had any history of alcoholism in your family."

"What difference does that make?" he asked, now feeling angry himself. Anything to do with his father made him angry.

"I was told that a tendency to develop substance addiction is often genetic." Jayson sat up straighter and felt his every nerve bristle. "I know you told me, Jayson, years ago, that your mother had heard this, and she had told you never to drink at all, because you were more likely to become an alcoholic because of your father. Apparently, it's the same with other substances. Another man might have been able to take the painkillers and not feel the effect that they gave you. Your body chemistry latched onto it—and quickly."

"So I have my father to thank for this."

"Maybe . . . partly. You still made a choice to keep taking pills." She sounded angry again. "You still made a choice not to tell anybody you had a problem. And you're going to have to come to terms with that. We will do everything we can; we will be there for you as much as they'll let us. But we can't help you get free of this, Jayson. These people can."

"And we'll mortgage the house to pay for it if we have to," Will added.

"Thanks," Jayson said. "But that won't be necessary. I really can afford it—whatever it may cost. That *is* why rock stars get paid so well, you know. So they can afford the rehab."

"Is that a joke or something?"

"It's supposed to be, but it's not very funny."

"No, it's not," Elizabeth said, and Jayson wondered what he would have ever done without them. If nothing else, he had evidence that God was mindful of him.

"Is there anything else I need to know before I sentence myself to this . . . prison?" Jayson asked.

"They said the fact that you're willing to get help is a huge step above most people they have to deal with; many of them are there on court orders."

"Oh, I'll give myself a pat on the back for that," Jayson said with sarcasm.

"Until you get through the initial detox process, we won't be able to see you," Elizabeth said, and he could almost believe she wasn't happy about that. "After that, we can have some visits at certain times, depending on what your counselor feels is best." Jayson nodded, then saw hesitance come into her eyes, as if there was something she didn't want to say.

"What?" he demanded.

"You can't take your cell phone."

"No!" he shouted and came to his feet, as if he could bolt out of the door and run away from facing this. Elizabeth stood to face him, taking his arms into her hands. "I can't do that."

"You have to be completely cut off from the world," she said. "It has to be that way."

"What about Macy? What if she calls me? I've kept that phone with me since the day she left. If she needs me, she'll call that number. I just . . . can't."

"It's okay, Jayson. I'll keep the phone with me. I'll keep it on. I'll keep it charged. If she calls, I'll take care of her. I promise."

Jayson looked into her eyes and realized that she meant it. He forced himself to relax. "Okay," he said. "If you promise."

Elizabeth nodded and left the room. Jayson wondered what he'd ever done to deserve being faced with this. He was grateful to know that Will and Elizabeth were behind him; otherwise, death seemed preferable.

Throughout the remainder of the day Jayson took the usual pills without feeling guilty. They knew he was taking them, if only to cope until he crossed the bridge into a drug-free world in the morning. He didn't have to worry about running out. He didn't have to wonder what he was going to do about this problem. But he felt scared out of his mind.

After supper, Elizabeth announced that it was time for family home evening, as she called it. Will explained that it was a Church program where Monday evenings were set aside for family lessons and activities. It was evident that Trevin had been in charge of doing some kind of lesson, but he'd forgotten and was feeling stupid over it. Will eased the tension by saying, "I'm certain we can think of something to do, and you can give a lesson next week." Jayson's heart ached on behalf of the boy. He was clearly struggling with the loss of his father and brother, but it was obvious that both Will and Elizabeth were baffled about how to help him beyond giving him the unconditional love that Jayson had seen them give abundantly during the time he'd been here.

"Hey, I have an idea," Will said to Trevin. "Why don't you and your mother and sister do that song for Jayson that you did in sacrament meeting a few weeks ago."

Trevin looked hesitant, but he gave in when Jayson said, "Oh, I would love to hear it."

Elizabeth sat at the piano and opened the songbook he'd seen her using to lead the music at Primary. Trevin left for a few minutes and returned with a violin and bow. He stood where he could read the music over his mother's shoulder. And Addie stood near the piano. Jayson was deeply touched as he recognized the melody on the violin that the children had sung in the chapel the previous day, while Elizabeth accompanied him on the piano. Following an excellent violin solo, Addie then sang two verses of "I Am a Child of God" with the piano, and the violin came back to join them on the last verse.

"That was incredible!" Jayson said when they were done.

Elizabeth hugged her children, saying, "I have incredibly talented kids."

"Brings back memories," Will said, and Jayson chuckled. "Although, this is somewhat different from 'Funeral for a Friend.'"

"I remember that song," Trevin said with the first enthusiasm Jayson had seen since his arrival. "I remember you playing that song on the piano when I was just a kid." He said it as if he were now an adult. "Can you play it again?"

Jayson sighed. "I wish I could, Trevin. But I hurt my hand a while back, and I can't play it."

Trevin looked disappointed, and Will asked Jayson, "So, it's still giving you grief?"

"It's all but useless," Jayson said.

"We'll have to work on that when you get out of the hospital," Elizabeth said.

Trevin asked, "Are you going to the hospital?"

Jayson was relieved when Elizabeth answered for him. "Yes, he is, honey. He hasn't been feeling well, so he's going to stay in a hospital that's going to help him get better. When he comes back, he'll be good as new. Then maybe we can do some therapy on that hand and he can play for us."

"I'll look forward to it," Jayson said.

Will then suggested they play a game together, so they moved to the dining room table where the five of them played Life. Addie won, but only because Jayson helped her cheat. Trevin came in second, but Jayson whispered to him that he was the *real* winner, which made the boy smile.

When the family meeting was officially over, Will offered to see that the children got ready for bed and did their homework. Jayson found himself alone with Elizabeth and wondered if Will had done that on purpose. Did he sense the tension between them that Jayson did? Again he wondered why he often felt that she was angry, while at moments she seemed glad to have him here. Attempting to break the silence he said, "It's wonderful the way you're teaching your children to play and sing."

"I haven't taught them myself; they do take lessons."

"It's still wonderful," he said. "Trevin does very well on the violin, and Addie has a beautiful voice—like her mother."

Elizabeth let out a sad sigh. "Bradley was gifted with the cello." Her eyes moved to a far corner of the room, and Jayson's followed to see a beautiful cello leaning there. "I haven't had the heart to put it away."

"It makes lovely decor," he said.

"So," she said, seeming to want to change the subject, "why is it that you've been here for days and you've not once touched the piano? And you brought your guitar, but it's still in the case. I thought the two of you were practically inseparable."

Since Elizabeth knew he had a drug problem, he didn't figure there was any point in avoiding the truth about everything else. He admitted with a heavy voice, "I haven't touched either one since the surgery, other than the one time I tried to do something with my right hand and it just didn't work."

He was surprised when she took his left hand into hers. "How bad is it?" she asked, and he slowly opened and closed his fingers, demonstrating their limited range of motion. "Where does it hurt?" she asked, rubbing the muscles of his hand. He flinched a couple of times, and it was easy for her to tell where without him saying anything. "Have you been doing the physical therapy?"

"Not lately," he said, and she gave him a sharp glare.

"Why not?"

"What's the point? The music is all dried up inside of me."

"Surely that's temporary," she said. "But either way, you need to do the exercises so you can regain the use of your hand. Whether you play music or not, you need your hand. Isn't it difficult to do a lot of things?"

"I manage," was all he said. He didn't want to admit to her what he could barely admit to himself, that he was using the pain and weakness in his hand as an excuse to hide from the music.

"Well, you need to do the therapy," she said, continuing to rub his hand. "You never know when your gift might return, and you'll wish you had your hand."

"It's a thing of the past, Elizabeth. It's over."

"I don't believe that," she said, but she sounded angry. Was she angry with him? Or angry because his career was over? "*Gray Wolf* was *your* brainchild, Jayson. It was a phenomenon."

"A short-lived phenomenon," he countered.

"That's just one piece of your life, Jayson. Surely the source of *Gray Wolf* is just dormant somewhere inside of you. Your gift is still in there somewhere, and it's incredible. Do you have any idea how amazing you are? Even in high school, I was so in awe of your talent."

"That's in the past," he said, and she just shook her head, seeming angry again. He appreciated her efforts, and the way she believed in him, but he wasn't certain he could ever believe in himself enough to bring his gift back to life.

It was quiet for a few minutes while she kept rubbing his hand, and he realized it actually felt good.

She finally said, "Who is going to walk Mozie while you're gone?"

"I don't know. Maybe they'd let me take Mozie with me. Then I'd have at least one friend."

Elizabeth smiled, but it was tense. "People will wonder where you are; they'll ask about you."

"Nobody even knows me . . . except for Brother Bale. And why should he care?"

"People met you at church, they've seen you out walking the dog. They've asked about you."

"And what did you tell them?"

"I told them you were like a brother to me. You don't want them thinking your living here is inappropriate, do you?"

"I don't care what anybody thinks. Especially people who gossip."

"Most of the people around here do not *gossip*. If they talk about others it is in the spirit of caring and concern. They'll wonder where you are. What do you want me to tell them?"

"I don't care what you tell them."

"So, you want me to tell them the truth?"

"I thought Mormons were *always* supposed to tell the truth," he said.

"Fine," she said, coming to her feet, "I'll tell them the truth." With that she hurried from the room. Jayson groaned and drove a fist into the couch, wondering if anything would ever be right between him and Elizabeth again.

After the children had gone to bed, Jayson found Will in the family room in the basement, where an entertainment center and some couches were located. Will looked over the top of the newspaper he was reading and said, "You okay?"

"Not really."

Will set the paper aside and motioned for Jayson to sit down. "Talk to me," Will said.

"I don't know what to say. I'm terrified. I feel like a fool."

"I can understand the fear," Will said. "As far as the other . . . well, life happens, kid. You know we love you no matter what."

"Yes, I know," Jayson said. "And I am eternally grateful for that, but . . ." He hesitated to admit to his most prevalent thought, but he had to talk to somebody about it. "I think your daughter is angry with me; disgusted."

Will sighed loudly. "I think Elizabeth is just angry. She was angry before you came."

"About what?"

"Well . . . as I see it, she has a great deal of faith. She understands that it was time for her husband and her son to be taken home. But the reality of having to live without them makes her angry. However, I will tell you . . . she has been *more* angry since . . ."

"Since I came here?" Jayson asked when he hesitated.

"More accurately, since she found out you nearly did away with yourself." Jayson groaned and hung his head. Will went on to say, "Maybe you should just talk to her. When it comes right down to it, I think she's just scared. She doesn't want to lose you, too."

"Or maybe it would be better if she did," Jayson said, and Will glared at him.

"We won't be having any of that kind of talk, young man. Elizabeth loves you."

"I know," Jayson said. *But not enough,* he thought.

"So, why don't you just stop assuming and playing games, and talk to her?"

"Maybe she'll bite my head off."

Will chuckled. "If I hear any yelling I'll come and rescue you." He motioned toward the stairs. "We'll be leaving early. It might be good to clear the air before you leave."

Jayson took a deep breath and forced himself to his feet. He knew Will was right, but he felt like he was going into a den of lions. He walked more slowly the closer he got to Elizabeth's room. Every other room was empty, and her door was closed, so he knew she had to be in there.

Elizabeth heard a knock at her bedroom door and felt certain it was her father. Jayson was usually asleep long before now, and her father was probably wanting to finish the conversation she'd walked out on twenty minutes earlier. He'd gently scolded her for not being more compassionate to Jayson's situation, and he'd told her that her anger was out of line. His tender lecture had triggered difficult memories of a time when she'd been angry with Jayson for something that had not been his fault. Then, just as now, she was terrified of losing him. But that was difficult to admit under the circumstances. She blew her nose and threw one more wadded tissue into the pile on the floor before she called, "Come in."

Jayson pushed open the door, startled to see her sitting on a small sofa, her head down, and several wadded tissues on the floor in front of her. "Am I the reason for all the tears?" he asked. She shot her head up, startled. She'd obviously not expected it to be him. She looked momentarily embarrassed, then resigned to the fact that she'd been caught crying and there was no point pretending now.

"Maybe," she said, looking away.

"Maybe? Either I am or I'm not. You can't give me a straight answer? I was under the impression that you had no trouble letting me know exactly what you think." She said nothing, and he added, "Come on, Elizabeth. For the most part I've felt like you've been angry with me ever since you picked me up at the airport. And you have good cause to be. You have a drug addict living in your home. Be angry, disgusted, whatever. But talk to me about it. I'd rather have you yell at me to my face than snarl and glare at me every time I turn around. So, I'm here. Let me have it."

"I *am* angry, Jayson." She sighed loudly and put her head into her hands. "But not for the reasons you might think." She looked up at him. "And believe it or not, I'm not disgusted. Disappointed, maybe. But not disgusted. I'm just . . . struggling to understand this. Why? Why did it come to this?" She started to cry again. "Could I have done something different to—"

"Oh, give me a break," he interrupted. "How could you remotely blame yourself for this? That's the stupidest thing I've ever heard."

"Well, it might sound stupid. I realize I live in a different state, but . . . I knew you were struggling. A hundred times I asked myself if I should go see you, spend some time, see how you were doing. And I always talked myself out of it; I was too busy, I didn't want to be too pushy, it was too complicated."

"Or uncomfortable?" he asked, and her eyes instantly met his. "When you know how I feel about you, it can't be easy living under the same roof with me and my distraught emotional state." He said the last with a touch of sarcasm, or perhaps self-recrimination.

"I've never let that stop me before," she said straightly.

"Well, maybe you just need to stop trying to come up with a reason why this is your fault, and just accept that it's mine. You were right, Elizabeth. I made a choice to take the pills. I made a choice to not ask for help or to tell you or your dad what was going on. At some level I recognized that I had a problem months ago. But I didn't tell anybody; I didn't ask for help. You and your dad have both offered dozens of times to let me come and stay. You've both asked me every few days if everything was okay, and I said it was."

"Yes, you did," Elizabeth said. "Why?"

"I just . . . didn't want to be a burden, I suppose. I didn't want you to know . . . what a fool I really am. Now there's no pretense. I'm a fool, and that's readily evident."

"It's more complicated than that, Jayson. I'm not assuming that you just decided to be a drug addict. I know you better than that. I guess what bothers me the most is . . ." she became emotional again, "wondering how bad . . . it must have been . . . for someone like you . . . to turn to this."

"I don't understand it myself, Lady. Maybe if I actually survive this place I'm going to, we should have this conversation again. Maybe they can help me understand . . . why."

Following a long moment of silence, Elizabeth said, "Jayson." He looked up. "You must forgive me . . . for my anger. I admit that I've been angry; I haven't been handling my emotions very well lately. I . . . uh . . . had kind of hit a new burst of grief the last few weeks. I've been . . . feeling sorry for myself, and feeling . . . very alone, even though . . . I look at your life and realize that I have no idea what alone really means." She sniffled and wiped her face with a fresh tissue. "Anyway, something kind of . . . snapped in me when . . . I called you in the middle of the night . . . and realized what was going on. But you have to understand, I was angry for the same reason that I would have snapped at one of my kids if they had run into the street, or . . ." she sobbed, " . . . or jumped into a river . . . without a life jacket."

Jayson watched her dissolve into tears and couldn't force himself to maintain the distance between them. He sat beside her and put his arms around her. She held to him and cried against his chest. When her tears finally became quiet, she spoke without letting go of him. "I couldn't bear to lose you, Jayson. Not to death, not to drugs. Losing someone you love to an accident or disease is horrible; you know that as well as I do. But how do you cope with losing someone you love when they made the *choice* to leave you?"

"You mean the way Debbie left me? And Macy?"

When he put it that way, Elizabeth was struck with a new grief on his behalf—and a new realization. "And me," she said.

He tightened his arms around her and murmured softly, "You're still here." But she heard the crack in his voice, felt the truth he wasn't saying. She wanted to spill her every thought on that count. She wanted to confess how deeply she had regretted that decision, and how her deepest fear was that much of the anguish of his life might have been prevented if she had made the choice to stay by his side, if they had just been together. But she couldn't open that can of worms now. When he had the drugs under control, when the dust had settled a bit, then perhaps they could talk all of that through and come to terms with it—once and for all.

"I will always be here," she said, tightening her arms around him.

Jayson closed his eyes and absorbed her nearness, wishing he could hold her close to him through the imminent purgatory that lay ahead. A thought occurred to him that he knew needed to be voiced. As difficult as it was for him to talk about, he didn't want any room for assumptions and misconceptions.

"Elizabeth," he said, "there's something I have to say. I hope you'll hear me out."

She sat up straight and looked at him. "Of course."

"As I mentioned, you know how I feel about you." She glanced down quickly, making it evident that this was difficult for her to talk about, as well. "I just want to be perfectly clear on where I stand. It would be ridiculous for me to pretend that I don't hope, at some level, that you and I could still have a chance together, that you might actually consider marrying me. But I'm not stupid enough to think that the possibility of that is very high."

"Why not?" she asked with enough surprise that he felt a little more hopeful. Still, the facts remained.

"Some of the things that were between us once no longer exist. My need to go out and make it big with my music is no longer relevant."

"What makes you think so?" she asked. "You can't possibly believe that your music career is permanently over."

"Yes, I do believe it, actually," he insisted, "and I'm not going to talk about music right now. I'm trying to tell you that while some things are no longer relevant, there are different gaps between us, and I'm well aware of those."

"Like what?" she asked more softly, but her tone implied that she was testing him to see if he had pegged the same problems she had.

"Religion, for one thing. I could never embrace your beliefs, Elizabeth. And it's evident you put a high priority on them. I could support you in them, but I could promise nothing more in that regard." He watched her head lower farther, as if to hide her expression from him. He felt compelled to add, "And I don't know if you can live with that."

"That's one thing," she said, still not looking at him.

"Beyond that there's only one obvious problem, in my opinion."

"And what is that?" she asked almost defiantly, lifting her head to look at him.

"I'd be a fool to believe that a woman like you would ever commit her life to a man who has a drug problem and suicidal tendencies."

Her eyes became defensive, then receded into hurt. She said with a firm voice, "That's only temporary."

Jayson gave a bitter chuckle. "I guess we'll see about that. Maybe I won't be able to kick it."

"You can kick it if you want to badly enough," she said, sounding angry again.

"Well, I hope so," he said. "But I still haven't made my point here, Lady. I want you to know that whatever may—or may not—evolve between us in the future is irrelevant to where I am, and where I'm going. I'm willing to go through this because I need to conquer it . . . for me. I admit that the love you and your father have given me makes a huge difference, but . . . I'm not doing it with the singular hope that you might one day change your mind and want to marry me. Truthfully, one of my biggest incentives is Macy. If she does come back, I need to be the best father I can possibly be. And I have to believe that she will come back. As for other aspects of my life, well . . . if I can beat this, then . . . I'll move on from there, knowing that, no matter what, you will always be my best friend."

"Yes, I will," she said, pressing a hand to the side of his face. She felt sorely tempted to kiss him, but after what he'd just said, she didn't want to promote more confusion or complication between them. Instead she took his face into her hands and pressed her brow to his, as if she could give him all her love and support by some kind of paranormal mind meld.

"I love you, Jayson," she muttered, unable to keep from crying again. "I wish I could go with you, stay with you."

"I wish you could, too," he admitted, "but . . ." he forced a chuckle, "I'm certain it won't be a pretty sight."

"I don't care," she said. "I would do it. I would hold your hand every minute if they'd let me. In a way it will be harder to be here and know what you're going through and not be able to even talk to you."

"I know your heart is with me," he said. "Somehow I'll make it through, as long as I know your heart is with me."

Jayson kept telling himself that, over and over, until he finally drifted to sleep that night. The following morning, he showered and was grateful to Will for helping him pack. His presence made it impossible to try to sneak pills in somewhere with the hope that they wouldn't be found. He left all the bottles sitting on the dresser and asked Will to get rid of the pills as soon as he returned from delivering Jayson to the facility.

"Aren't you taking your guitar?" Will asked, motioning toward the case sitting on the floor.

"Maybe I'll have you bring it later . . . if they'll let me have it." He looked at Will directly and said, "It's safer here. I don't want to do anything to hurt it."

Elizabeth drove and Jayson sat in the front passenger seat, while Will sat in the backseat with a book. They dropped Addie off at the home of one of her little preschool friends that she would be going to school with in a while, then they headed for the freeway. Little was said, but Elizabeth reached for Jayson's hand and held it tightly, well aware that he was trembling. But she just couldn't think about that too hard.

In the stillness, Elizabeth prayed, silently pleading with God to give Jayson strength and comfort—and hope. She knew his potential, and she knew that God knew it as well. For minutes she prayed the same phrases over and over, unable to do anything *but* express her reliance on a Supreme Being in the face of such a crisis. A human soul was at stake here; the future for Jayson hinged on the success or failure of this experience.

Elizabeth let out a breathy gasp before she consciously realized the abrupt warmth that had coursed through her. She took in the feeling more fully and relished the tingle of tears in her eyes that added verification that what she had just felt was real. She knew the feeling well, although it had rarely come with such force.

"What is it?" Jayson asked, and she was embarrassed to realize he'd noticed her reaction.

Not knowing how to explain, and certain he wouldn't be receptive to hearing it anyway, she simply turned to look at him and smiled, saying with perfect confidence, "I just really believe that everything is going to be okay."

Jayson noted her expression and the tears glowing in her eyes that seemed to contradict a perfectly serene countenance. For reasons he could never define, he felt inclined to believe her. Somehow he just *had* to believe that everything was going to be okay. He closed his eyes for a long moment and tried to imagine what it might be like on the other side of this horror. He wondered how it would feel to be free of these drugs—and the pain beneath them—and to once again hold his sweet daughter in his arms. He had to hold onto the hope that such a day would come. For now, hope was all he had.

About the Author

Anita Stansfield, the LDS market's number-one best-selling romance novelist, is a prolific and imaginative writer who wants her readers to know that she is "real." She and her husband, Vince—whom she calls "her hero"—have three boys and two girls: John, Jake, Anna, Steven, and Alyssa. She loves butterscotch chip cookies, long walks, and romantic movies. She loves to go out to eat, especially for seafood and steaks. Her favorite color is black. She loves lemonade and French fries with fry sauce. She loves her husband. She loves her kids. She loves her sisters, her brothers, her dad, and her friends. She loves her house and her neighborhood. And she loves Alpine, the little town she lives in. And—oh, yes—she loves to write stories.